Praise for *Deep Sleep*

"Techno-thrillers fans will delight in military vet Konkoly's obvious expertise when it comes to the authenticity and intensity of the numerous action sequences."

—*Publishers Weekly*

"A lively, roller-coaster thriller that moves like lightning."

—*Kirkus Reviews*

"Nobody's better at spy craft, action, and intrigue than Steven Konkoly. Thrilling entertainment from the first to the last written word."

—Robert Dugoni, *New York Times* and #1 Amazon bestselling author of *The Eighth Sister*

"Steven Konkoly has blown my mind! *Deep Sleep* is an intelligent, intense, and completely unpredictable high-concept spy thriller. I'm hooked!"

—T.R. Ragan, *New York Times* bestselling author of *Her Last Day*

"Fast paced, suspenseful, and wildly creative. A modern-day masterpiece of spy fiction."

—Andrew Watts, *USA Today* bestselling author of the Firewall Spies series

"A pulse-pounding conspiracy tale in the finest traditions of Vince Flynn and Nelson DeMille . . . *Deep Sleep* is a must-read roller coaster of a thriller."

—Jason Kasper, *USA Today* bestselling author of the Shadow Strike series

"Devin Gray is the hero we need in our corner. Relentless in pursuit of truth, vindication, and saving his homeland, he is the perfect protagonist for Konkoly's newest dive into the techno-thriller world. Again Konkoly proves his mastery of the genre, drawing from real-rowed events to create a plausible and frightening glimpse into what's happening underneath our feet and behind the walls of power."

—Tom Abrahams, Emmy Award–winning journalist and
author of *Sedition*

"Steven Konkoly delivers a conspiracy thriller unlike any other and proves he's at the top of his game. With a deft hand and an eye for plot intricacies, Konkoly will take you into a web of deceit that will shake you to your core and keep you turning until the very last page. The Lost Directorate has set a new bar in the world of thrillers, and Konkoly has taken his seat at the head of the table."

—Brian Shea, *Wall Street Journal* bestselling author of the Boston
Crime series and coauthor of the Rachel Hatch series

"A master of action-adventure, Steven Konkoly has done it again, weaving a tale of high-stakes espionage that's ripped from today's international headlines. Plan to stay up very late reading *Deep Sleep*, as he keeps the pages turning!"

—Joseph Reid, bestselling author of the Seth Walker series

"I love a great conspiracy thriller, and Steven Konkoly has conjured one that's utterly chilling with *Deep Sleep*. From the high-stakes setup to the explosive finale, there's barely time to take a breath. Crack this one open and buckle in for one hell of a ride."

—Joe Hart, *Wall Street Journal*
bestselling author of the Dominion Trilogy and *Or Else*

Previous Praise for Steven Konkoly

"Explosive action, a breakneck pace, and zippy dialogue."

—*Kirkus Reviews*

"Readers seeking a well-constructed action thriller need look no further."

—*Publishers Weekly*

"If you enjoy action thrillers that have both strong male and female characters, then this may be the series for you."

—*Mystery & Suspense Magazine*

"Exciting action scenes help propel this tale of murderous greed and corruption toward a satisfying conclusion. Readers will look forward to Decker and company's next adventure."

—*Publishers Weekly*

"Steven Konkoly's new Ryan Decker series is a triumph—an action-thriller master class in spy craft, tension, and suspense. An absolute must-read for fans of Tom Clancy, Vince Flynn, and Brad Thor."

—Blake Crouch, *New York Times* bestselling author

"*The Rescue* by Steven Konkoly has everything I love in a thriller—betrayal, murder, a badass investigator, and a man fueled by revenge."

—T.R. Ragan, *New York Times* bestselling author

"*The Rescue* grabs you like a bear trap and never lets go. No one writes action sequences any better than Steve Konkoly—he drops his heroes into impossible situations and leaves you no option but to keep your head down, follow where they lead, and hope you make it out alive."

—Matthew FitzSimmons, *Wall Street Journal* bestselling author

"Breakneck twists, political conspiracy, bristling action—*The Rescue* has it all! Steven Konkoly has created a dynamic and powerful character in Ryan Decker."

—Joe Hart, *Wall Street Journal* bestselling author

"If you are a fan of characters like Scot Harvath and Mitch Rapp, this new series is a must-read. Steven Konkoly delivers a refreshingly unique blend of action, espionage, and well-researched realism."

—Andrew Watts, *USA Today* bestselling author

"An excellent source for your daily dose of action, conspiracy, and intrigue."

—Tim Tigner, author of *Betrayal*

"Fans of Mark Greaney and Brad Taylor, take notice: *The Rescue* has kicked off a stunning new series that deserves a place on your reading list. Ryan Decker is a must-read character."

—Jason Kasper, author of *Greatest Enemy*

"*The Rescue* immediately drops the reader into a well-drawn world of betrayal, revenge, and redemption. Ryan Decker is a flawed, relatable hero, unstoppable in his quest for justice."

—Tom Abrahams, Emmy Award–winning journalist and author of *Sedition*

"From the very first page, *The Rescue* comes at you like the literary equivalent of a laser-guided missile. Impossible to put down, with explosive action, a great hero, and political intrigue. This one will grab you."

—Joseph Souza, award-winning author of *The Neighbor*

COMING
DAWN

ALSO BY STEVEN KONKOLY

DEVIN GRAY SERIES

Deep Sleep

RYAN DECKER SERIES

The Rescue
The Raid
The Mountain
Skystorm

THE FRACTURED STATE SERIES

Fractured State
Rogue State

THE PERSEID COLLAPSE SERIES

The Jakarta Pandemic
The Perseid Collapse
Event Horizon
Point of Crisis
Dispatches

THE BLACK FLAGGED SERIES

Alpha
Redux
Apex
Vektor
Omega

THE ZULU VIRUS CHRONICLES

Hot Zone
Kill Box
Fire Storm

COMING DAWN

STEVEN KONKOLY

THOMAS & MERCER

Published by Thomas & Mercer, Seattle

www.apub.com

Amazon, the Amazon logo, and Thomas & Mercer are trademarks of Amazon.com, Inc., or its affiliates.

ISBN-13: 9781542036627
ISBN-10: 1542036623

Cover design by Rex Bonomelli

Printed in the United States of America

To Kosia, Matthew, and Sophia—the heart and soul of my writing.

PART ONE

CHAPTER 1

His entire life's purpose came down to several lines of program code.

George McDonald strolled through the office suite, scanning the cubicles and outer offices for signs of life, hoping to find none. The team had been working late hours for the last three weeks, putting the final touches on a software update for the seeker-sensor that guided Lockram Industries' EPAC-3 (Enhanced Patriot Advanced Capability) missile to its target during the "moments to impact" phase of flight. Updates to their software always required the team's full attention and long hours because the terminal phase of a missile's flight determined a hit or miss. A success or failure.

They'd spent even longer on this latest update because the future of the company was potentially at stake. The recent catastrophic Iron Dome failure in Haifa had been tracked to faulty guidance-system software in a component designed and manufactured by Antheon, one of Lockram's key international and domestic defense systems competitors. Failure in Antheon's case had caused several hundred deaths in Haifa and triggered a momentary loss of confidence in US missile technology partnerships.

Governments spending billions of dollars on these systems wanted guarantees, placing Lockram's flagship missile export, the EPAC-3, in everyone's crosshairs. Hundreds of EPAC-3 missiles, loaded into dozens of integrated mobile launchers from Estonia to Greece, formed the backbone of Europe's antiballistic missile defense capability. Shortly after the Haifa tragedy, European Union member state defense ministers started to request assurances from Lockram, culminating in the demand for a series of successful live-intercept demonstrations.

Raising the stakes even higher, Lockram's missiles were the most replaceable component of the joint US-Italian-German air defense system. If the EPAC-3 failed to knock its targets out of the sky during the upcoming demonstrations, a foreign competitor would undoubtedly step in to fill the void—cutting off one of Lockram's most lucrative revenue streams.

McDonald's job as senior principal software engineer for the EPAC-3 seeker-sensor was to make sure nothing went wrong with the missile's tracking and guidance during live-intercept demonstrations scheduled at White Sands Missile Range a few weeks from now. His mission as a lifelong sleeper agent was to embed a string of code that would render the missile unable to engage targets flying at extremely low altitudes. The two tasks didn't conflict, since the tests at White Sands would be conducted against high-altitude, simulated ballistic missiles—the EPAC-3's primary air defense role.

The timing of CONTROL's order led him to believe that the Iron Dome failure had been purposefully engineered to trigger these missile tests and reignite confidence in the EPAC-3 system. It also gave him a convenient and compelling reason to push a software update to the missiles within a short time frame. Something big was afoot in eastern Europe, and the plan relied on a low-altitude-airspace penetration. Probably cruise missiles fired against key infrastructure and military targets. He'd never know. CONTROL gave orders, not explanations.

Whatever the Russians planned, the blame would eventually fall squarely in his lap as the senior engineer on the team. Not that he'd be around to face the music. McDonald would be long gone by the time Lockram and the Department of Defense concluded their investigations. After debriefing Moscow, he planned to spend his five-million-dollar repatriation bonus on a pleasant retirement in a cushy suburb of Niznhy Novgorod. An unexpectedly early but easy-to-swallow end to his service on behalf of Mother Russia.

CHAPTER 2

Karl Berg arranged to take the phone call away from Helen Gray's apartment, despite the oppressive ninety-three-degree temperature and light drizzle. It wasn't that he didn't trust the people back at the apartment. He trusted them implicitly. He did it out of respect and—most importantly—out of utmost concern for the retired FSB officer's safety.

Berg needed to speak freely with his old adversary turned friend, unhindered by the worry that he might repeat a word or phrase used by the Russian that could be tortured out of someone in the apartment, or even himself, to reveal his friend's identity. He understood the extreme unlikeliness of that scenario, but one could never be too careful in this business, particularly with the identity of a source like Kaparov.

And especially given that a Red Notice had been placed on his and Rich Farrington's names only days after the Baltimore shootout. Publicly, the FBI and Baltimore Police Department had attributed the multiple-location, high-casualty-count gun battle to a boiled-over turf struggle between two competing Russian Mafia factions. Internally, the truth would appear far more complicated.

Three of the dead Russians had established connections to Russian consulates, implying a state-sanctioned operation. The nexus between the Red Notice and the Russian-involved shootout would not go unnoticed. He scrolled through his Signal exchange with Audra Bauer a few days ago.

Bauer: Karl. Just got a call from Dana O'Reilly at the FBI. Russia and Kazakhstan filed Red Notices for you and Rich. She's looking into it on her end. I'll do the same. She's not worried about it. DOJ will most likely ignore the notice, unless the Russians or their puppet regime push the issue. No travel outside of the US for now. Hope you're not up to your old tricks! ;)

Berg: Old tricks die hard. Need to show you something. It's critical.

Bauer: Connected to Baltimore?

Berg: Who said anything about Baltimore?

Bauer: When and where to meet?

Berg: Within a few days. Need to sort a few things out. I'll get back to you with specifics. We didn't talk, in case anyone asks.

Bauer: Understood.

Berg: Look forward to catching up.

Bauer: Sounds like a real blast.

Berg: You have no idea. I'll be in touch.

Not finding any benches along the winding cobblestone walkways inside Green Mount Cemetery, Berg unslung a small backpack and took a seat on a concrete-and-stone retaining wall within sight of the entrance. Jared Hoffman had followed him here at a distance, just to be sure he hadn't been followed. The team had covered its tracks returning to Baltimore, but given the widespread penetration of the sleeper network, they weren't taking any chances. If Hoffman appeared inside the wrought iron gate at any point, Berg would know they'd been discovered.

He had to be careful with Kaparov. Berg's inside information into Russian security service operations had undoubtedly piqued the interest of the CIA and FBI at some point in the past. The Red Notice had the potential to reignite that curiosity.

A quick look at his watch indicated that Kaparov should call any minute now. They'd arranged three five-minute call windows to account for any unavoidable circumstance that might prevent either of them from talking. One now. One four hours from now. And one at midnight eastern standard time, which was eight in the morning in Moscow. If the two of them failed to make contact today, no further communication would be attempted—the assumption being that something had gone terribly wrong on one end.

He removed the satellite phone from his backpack and set it on the rain-drenched wall, wishing he had brought his umbrella. The drizzle turned out to be a little more than he'd bargained for. The phone rang, instantly distracting him from the weather. Berg answered the call, and they both negotiated the short passcode drill established years ago.

"I need to keep this short," said Kaparov. "I'm on the other side of Moscow, and I'd like to get home before the hoodlums take over the plaza in front of my apartment building."

It sounded like Kaparov had executed a surveillance-detection route prior to making this call. A promising sign that he'd uncovered sensitive information.

"Don't they know who they're messing with?" said Berg.

"Ha! Today's youth have no respect for anything," said Kaparov. "Especially us pensioners."

"It's not that much different over here," said Berg.

"Do they piss and shit on the tables and benches in your parks?" said Kaparov. "They're worse than the pigeons."

"I suppose not—but at least our pigeons sound the same. So there's that," said Berg.

Kaparov let out a hearty laugh. "I guarantee our pigeons are better behaved than yours."

"Always a competition with you Russians," said Berg.

"You Americans started it," said Kaparov.

"Very true," said Berg. "And you all very slyly convinced us that we won—while nothing could have been further from the truth."

"It certainly appears that way," said Kaparov. "Anyway. I think I found your man. General Grigory Kuznetzov."

A few seconds of silence passed, as if Kaparov expected him to recognize the name.

"The name doesn't ring a bell," said Berg.

"Tsk. Tsk. No wonder this whole mess slipped below the CIA's radar," said Kaparov. "Kuznetsov had risen to the second-highest position in the Fifth Directorate before he essentially vanished from sight. Care to guess when?"

"Around the same time Yuri Pichugin rose to prominence? Early two thousands?" said Berg.

"Bingo, as you Americans like to say—2003," said Kaparov.

The same year Helen Gray met with General Kozlov, who threw himself under a tram after passing her the names of five GRU sleepers.

"And you're sure he wasn't sidelined?" said Berg. "Or purged with the dozen or so high-ranking GRU officers that had suspicious accidents or suicides that year?"

"I'm told he still goes in and out of the Aquarium several times a week," said Kaparov. "Which is why I'm surprised you haven't heard of this guy. His departure from such a high position in the Fifth Directorate and subsequent failure to surface in an even higher position should have raised alarms. Top Fifth Directorate leadership positions are usually a stepping-stone to something more consequential."

"I haven't officially worked on Russia since the two of us faced off against each other toward the end of the Cold War," said Berg.

"We were so young back then—and extremely naive, given what I know today," said Kaparov. "It's hard to believe we're retired."

"Funny how I don't feel retired," said Berg.

"Trouble has a way of following you around," said Kaparov. "Which is why I probably should change my phone number."

"I'd still manage to track you down," said Berg. The pair had a quick laugh before getting back to business. "Are you sure Kuznetsov is still on active duty? He would have been a senior general back in 2003. We're looking at another twenty years on top of an already lengthy career."

"That's what I'm told," said Kaparov.

"Interesting," said Berg. "Any link between Kuznetzov and Yuri Pichugin?"

"None that my sources were willing to talk about," said Kaparov.

"Did you press the question?" said Berg.

"I nudged the question," said Kaparov. "And poured enough vodka to keep a target on my back."

"Fair enough," said Berg. "I'll ask some questions on my end. I'd be shocked if the CIA hadn't put the pieces together regarding Kuznetzov. He definitely fits the profile of an officer put in charge of a secret, highly compartmented division within the GRU. If he has ties to Pichugin, someone here will have noticed. That would be enough to justify grabbing him."

"Grabbing Kuznetzov? Good heavens," said Kaparov. "You're actually considering an operation on Russian soil?"

"Do you really want to know the answer to that question?" said Berg.

"Probably not," said Kaparov. "Just keep in mind that when I say Kuznetzov *goes in and out of headquarters*, I don't mean that he takes the Metro or one of those Uber things. He has serious security. Armored SUVs. That kind of thing. Not that a high-security situation has ever been a problem for your associates."

"True," said Berg. "And he'll undoubtedly be easier to access than Pichugin."

"Several magnitudes easier," said Kaparov. "But still difficult."

"We'll cross that bridge if it comes to that," said Berg. "Thank you again, Alexei. I owe you more than just a Caribbean vacation."

"All-inclusive Caribbean vacation," said Kaparov. "And not one of those knockoff places. I've been reading about Sandals. Adults only. No kids kicking sand in my face. That's where I want to go."

"Yes. Of course. Sandals," said Berg. "You've done your homework."

"Sounds heavenly," said Kaparov, a long pause ensuing before he continued. "I assume your team is going to need my help here in Moscow—if Kuznetzov is your man?"

"I have an idea that should keep you out of it," said Berg. "If that falls through, I may need some help."

"I'm not sure how much help a decrepit FSB retiree like me can offer," said Kaparov. "But I'll do what I can."

"I'll take whatever I can get," said Berg. "But you have to promise me something."

"I'm the one doing you the favor, and I have to promise you something?"

"Yes. If your help goes any deeper than playing tour guide, I insist on getting you out of there. For your own safety. At least for a while," said Berg. "We're not dealing with the incompetence of a government bureaucracy here. Pichugin's criminal enterprise is a well-oiled, well-paid, results-oriented machine. Anything overt, and they'll trace it back to you in no time."

"I'm a survivor," said Kaparov.

"I have a spare bedroom with a balcony, a deep-sea fishing boat, all the vodka you can drink, and I live where it's warm and mostly sunny all year," said Berg. "Consider it a prequel to your real vacation in the Caribbean."

"I don't even own a pair of shorts," said Kaparov.

"That's the best excuse you can come up with?" said Berg. "I'll buy you shorts and a matching shirt for every day of the week. And sandals. You'll fit right in with all of the other pasty-white old-timers. Say yes, or I'm not involving you."

"Maybe," said Kaparov.

"That's good enough for now," said Berg. "I'll be in touch as soon as I hear back from my sources."

"Stay safe, my friend," said Kaparov, and the call disconnected.

Berg stared at the phone for a few moments before turning his attention to the cemetery entrance. No sign of Hoffman, which meant no signs of trouble in the vicinity. He logged in to the Signal app on his satellite phone and composed a quick message for Audra Bauer.

Need you to investigate known or suspected links between GRU general Grigory Kuznetzov and oligarch Yuri Pichugin—before we meet up. Require answer ASAP regarding extent of link between the two—if any known to exist. Exercise extreme caution researching/acquiring information. Recommend directly accessing source material. Definitely do not run this by anyone below your pay grade. Will explain everything when we meet.

She wouldn't be able to access the message app until she left Langley, so he'd have to wait until at least tomorrow evening for an answer. That left him plenty of time to work on the more complicated side of his proposed Moscow intervention plan. Getting the Israelis involved would be a long shot, even after the Haifa tragedy, but they represented the most dependable and discreet option for getting his team into Russia undetected and supplying them with the necessary equipment.

If Berg couldn't secure the Mossad's backing of the mission, he'd not only have to lean far more heavily on Alexei than he'd like; he would have no choice but to work with an in-country criminal element to procure the illegal equipment the team needed. Probably the Chechens. He was persona non grata with the Solntsevskaya Bratva, the predominant Mafia organization in Russia. Berg might even have to go more obscure than the Chechens to stay off the wider criminal-underground radar, which meant greater risk.

He'd hard sell the Israelis and hope for the best. The Mossad owed him one, not that they played by those rules. Or any rules. The Mossad didn't mess around when it came to revenge. They'd want names up front, which Berg couldn't give them. Not until the Israelis had held up their end of the deal. They wouldn't hesitate to undermine the mission if an opportunity to take revenge suddenly materialized. That would be the challenge. The tightrope he'd be forced to walk the entire time. Still, the Israelis were his best bet. He scrolled through the contact list he'd uploaded to the satellite phone and paused on the name of a Mossad agent he'd struck a deal with in the past—then pressed "Send."

CHAPTER 3

Felix Orlov checked his phone: 6:55 p.m. Nearly an hour past the rental car agency's official closing time, but still an hour short of sunset. Given the choice, he would prefer to do this under the cover of darkness. Especially if the manager had parked in the front lot, visible from Route 31. Northbound traffic out of Nashville remained heavy, having barely lightened up since the late-afternoon rush. The last thing he needed was a witness to what was about to go down.

Pichugin had somehow managed to scare up a lead suggesting that a member of Devin Gray's crew had rented a vehicle here. With the strict privacy laws in the United States, Pichugin must have spent a small fortune acquiring this information. He'd expect a return on his investment, and Orlov intended to deliver one—no matter what. The Ozarks debacle had clearly dealt a significant blow to whatever scheme Pichugin had concocted over here.

The Russian crime lord had tripled the size of the team at Orlov's disposal—an unmistakable signal that he required immediate results. Unfortunately, he was still working with the somewhat-degraded remnants of his original team, having lost two of his primary direct-action operators in the forest to one of the machine guns he'd left in the helicopters. The new crew was in transit from Europe and South America, expected to assemble over the next few days in the DC area—where Pichugin hoped to find Devin Gray.

His earpiece chirped. "Lights are out. The manager is headed toward the front of the office."

"Move into position," said Orlov, before opening his car door.

He assumed the manager had parked behind the building with the rest of the employees, but had accounted for the possibility that she might have parked in the front lot by positioning Oleg and Ksenia across the street. If she headed for one of the dozen or so vehicles parked along the main drag, they'd race into the lot and hit her with a sob story about needing to rent several cars for a wedding or a funeral. Anything to get her back in the building or keep her around long enough for him to take over.

Orlov hustled across the patchy strip of grass separating the dollar store parking lot from the rental car agency and made his way to the green metal dumpster set against the back of the building. Lashev Pavlovich settled in next to him holding a small nylon duffel bag, his dour face betraying no emotion. The lanky sniper was out of his element here. The up-close-and-personal nature of this type of job was anathema to the man, but Orlov needed the extra set of hands. He had no idea how the manager would react, and they couldn't afford to botch this—even if the whole thing felt like a long shot.

"She's headed around back," said Oleg through his earpiece. "South side."

"Copy. Stay where you are for now," said Orlov. "I'll issue new instructions once we've figured out what we're dealing with."

"Got it."

They immediately took position on the north side of the dumpster, Lashev opening the duffel bag and placing it next to Orlov's feet. Orlov peeked slowly around the dumpster's edge; a slim middle-aged woman appeared at the corner of the building a few seconds later. She fast walked toward a line of several sedans parked in front of the weathered stockade fence along the back of the lot, clearly intent on spending as little time alone behind the building as possible without running. She held her fist tightly against her thigh, a few loose keys dangling below her hand.

Orlov backed up and crouched, retrieving a suppressed pistol from the duffel bag. His other option was a Taser, but something about her highly alert state told him the Taser would be a mistake.

"Don't get too close to her, unless you want a car key punched through one of your eyes," whispered Orlov.

"I'll only jump in to help if *you* lose an eye," said Lashev.

"Very reassuring," said Orlov, before taking another look.

The woman had already slid between two of the cars, the taillights flashing on the one to her right.

"Shit," he said, before bolting after her.

She'd already slipped into the driver's seat by the time he reached the back of the car, her hand stretching toward the open door to pull it shut. He steadied the pistol and drilled a single bullet through the door's window. She immediately retracted her hand and started the car. This one wasn't screwing around. Orlov dashed forward, jamming the business end of the long suppressor against her left temple before she could shift into reverse. He kept himself just out of her peripheral vision to make it difficult for her to employ any self-defense weapons.

"Hand off the gearshift," said Orlov. "Or they'll be cleaning your brains out of this car for a week before they can rent it again."

She released her grip on the shifter.

"Both hands on the wheel. I'm not fucking around here," said Orlov.

"There's no money inside," she said, taking the wheel with both hands. "Everything is done by credit card."

"This is something entirely different. I need to review your security camera footage during a specific time frame to determine whether a person of interest rented a vehicle or multiple vehicles from your office. They will undoubtedly have used fake credentials, so I must visually identify them," said Orlov. "Is that possible?"

"It depends," she said. "Which day are we talking about?"

"Three days ago," said Orlov. "Why?"

"Our security surveillance system can only store five days of camera footage," she said. "It automatically deletes anything older to make room for new recordings."

"Then we shouldn't have a problem," said Orlov.

"Is that it?"

"If I am able to confirm this person's identity in the footage, we can use the footage time stamp to pull license plates from a narrow range of rental agreements. If I can't visually ID them, I'll need the license plate information for every vehicle you rented that day," said Orlov. "I assume this won't be a problem?"

"No problem at all."

"How long will it take?"

"Not long. We typically rent around twenty to thirty vehicles a day. We can fast-forward the footage in between customers," she said. "Finding the corresponding rental in our system won't take more than a couple of minutes."

"That's music to my ears," said Orlov.

"What happens after that?" she said.

"You rearrange this glass to look like an attempted car theft, pick a different car to drive home, and forget that any of this happened."

She took a deep breath before responding.

"I have an out-of-work husband and two kids in high school. We barely make ends meet," she said. "This isn't fair to them."

"What's not fair to them?"

"You're going to kill me," she said.

"What's your name?" said Orlov.

"Deanne," she said. "Or just Dee."

Orlov crouched in the open doorway, keeping the pistol pressed against her head. The woman squeezed her eyes shut.

"Dee. I need you to look at me."

"I don't want to look at you," she said.

"Why?"

"Because I don't want you to have to kill me," she said.

"I think you've watched one too many American movies," said Orlov. "I'm not the least bit worried about you seeing my face. Because you're never going to tell anyone we met. I'm willing to bet the lives of two teenagers and a husband on that. Am I correct?"

She nodded almost imperceptibly. "Yes. I will never tell anyone about this."

"And as long as you don't say anything, nobody will ever figure out you helped me," said Orlov. "Understand?"

"Yes."

"Please look at me," said Orlov.

She took several moments to open her eyes. A few more to look in his direction. He removed the pistol from her head, but kept it pointed at her.

"I won't hurt you or your family—if you do as I say. Neither will any of my associates," said Orlov.

"I don't believe you," she said. "I think you're going to kill me after you get what you want."

"I said nobody will kill you . . . if you cooperate."

"You have to say that, or I'd have no reason to help," said Dee.

"I just threatened your family. That's your reason to help," said Orlov. "Unless you don't care about them."

"No. No," she said, in a panic. "I care about them very much. Please."

"Then you have a very important reason to help me," said Orlov. "Right?"

"And you're just going to trust me not to go to the police," she said.

Was he really having this conversation?

He grabbed her by the upper arm and yanked her through the open door.

"Get the fuck out of the car. Before I change my mind."

Twenty-three minutes later, Orlov drove out of the dollar store parking lot with the information he'd been sent to retrieve—and one less bullet in his pistol. He couldn't risk even the remotest chance that she would report the incident to the authorities. The two license plate numbers now in his possession represented the only chance of redemption in Yuri Pichugin's eyes.

CHAPTER 4

Devin turned onto his side after the first speed bump, not wanting to directly absorb another sharp rise and fall with his spine. He guessed that they'd just entered MINERVA's parking garage, the first half of this morning's long journey in the trunk of a car almost complete. He had no one to blame but himself—the whole thing having been his idea from the start. Devin had put a lot of thought into this trip, starting with a simple question.

How do you secretly meet someone who is being followed? Easy problem to solve. Assuming your contact has countersurveillance experience, you have them execute a lengthy, well-planned surveillance-detection route. A nearly fail-proof method, and in the highly unlikely event that it doesn't shake pursuers, you just call off the meeting. Nothing lost. Nothing gained. Under normal circumstances. But there was nothing normal about the meeting Devin had requested with Brendan Shea, his boss at MINERVA, a Beltway-connected boutique countersurveillance-counterespionage firm.

He needed enough time to walk Shea through his mother's work, the events of the past week, and their inescapable nexus to DEVTEK—one of MINERVA's key clients. DEVTEK, a cutting-edge Silicon Valley–based software and operating system development company, with significant contracting ties to several US Department of Defense and Intelligence Community agencies, had hired MINERVA to get to the bottom of a sustained cyber campaign to penetrate their server network.

The DEVTEK connection raised the stakes in this situation, changing everything. If the Russians discovered or even somewhat suspected that Devin had brought the link to MINERVA's attention, they'd abandon their plan to exploit DEVTEK, slamming the door on a never-to-be-repeated opportunity for Devin and his team.

The DEVTEK connection represented a potentially exploitable weakness in the sleeper network. An extraordinarily rare chance to covertly watch one of the sleepers in action and gain some insight into Yuri Pichugin's endgame.

So the real question was, *How do you covertly meet that same someone without your contact making it obvious that they've purposefully ditched surveillance?* A much harder problem to solve. But not impossible. Intelligence agents and their spy assets have done business in the open for as long as espionage has existed, but those interactions were usually very brief. Brush passes to hand over microfilm or a USB drive. Signals of future intent left along regular routes. Dead drops at prearranged, nearly-impossible-to-covertly-watch locations.

Devin had spent the better part of a decade trailing foreign espionage agents and their suspected contacts, attacking the challenge from every angle imaginable. From mind-numbingly boring electronic surveillance staged out of a nearby apartment to complexly orchestrated nail-biters conducted over miles of urban terrain—and everything in between. At one time or another, he'd fallen prey to every countersurveillance trick in the book—real-life, humbling experiences he'd used to sharpen his skills to a razor's edge.

He understood the hunter in this game, his twelve years at the FBI a study in his own limitations and strengths as a surveillance specialist—which was why he knew he'd have to meet Brendan Shea at the office. Devin had no choice but to assume that Pichugin's people would be all over MINERVA's operational leadership team outside of the headquarters building.

MINERVA kept a very low public profile, but they were a well-known commodity inside the various alphabet agencies within the Beltway. A reasonably well-placed sleeper agent in one of those agencies could access the necessary information to target the right MINERVA employees. Assuming the Russians had been watching his boss's movements for the past week or two, a fair assumption given the circumstances, even the smallest deviations from Shea's normal routine might raise a red flag.

The bottom line? He had to meet Shea at MINERVA, which presented a few challenges since Devin couldn't drive in on his own. If the Russians were keeping an eye on Shea, they were most certainly watching the pedestrian and vehicle entrances to MINERVA. The solution was simple. They'd smuggle Devin in and out of headquarters, hiding him in a vehicle that the Russians wouldn't suspect.

A less-than-elegant but agreeable plan—until Brendan Shea's "smuggler" pulled up to the remote rendezvous point in a compact sedan. The possibility of riding in a trunk space smaller than a coffin simply hadn't occurred to Devin. He'd just assumed they'd smuggle him into MINERVA in the back of a tinted-windowed SUV or van. One of several dozen parked at headquarters in the underground garage.

Teams went in and out of the garage at all hours of the day. Diverting one to pick him up on the way back from an overnight stakeout wouldn't have drawn any undue attention outside of MINERVA. But Shea wasn't taking any chances inside MINERVA, either. He'd dispatched someone Devin had never met before to smuggle him inside the garage, maintaining the lowest possible profile for the visit—which he both appreciated and understood.

MINERVA still hadn't decided how to proceed in light of the news surrounding his mother. Both the optics of keeping him as an employee and firing him for no real reason looked terrible. Devin guessed they'd give it a few more weeks and offer him a juicy separation package, the medium- to long-term damage to their reputation far outweighing the financial hit from a one-time, high-six-figure nondisclosure agreement sealed payout.

He'd dangled just enough in front of his boss to get in the door one last time. At least Shea had taken the meeting. Or so Devin hoped. He'd placed all his faith in the hands of the balaclava-clad man who'd patted him down for weapons and surveillance gear before stuffing him into the trunk of his car. For all Devin knew, Shea had connected the dots in the news—opting to turn him over to the feds instead. Instinct said Shea's loyalty to MINERVA's clients trumped wherever the dots may have led him. Devin hoped his gut hadn't led him astray on this one.

The car eased to a stop after a slow but sharp turn, giving him the impression that they'd just pulled into a parking space. When the engine cut off, he knew the moment of truth was a few seconds away. A car door opened and slammed, followed by a brief muffled discussion between two men—shedding no light on Devin's impending fate. A longer-than-expected pause ensued before the trunk lock double-clicked. Devin squinted into the thin line of fluorescent light that pierced the trunk's absolute darkness. When the trunk rose the rest of the way, he covered his eyes with a forearm, the light contrast piercing his eyelids.

"Sorry about the trunk routine," said a familiar voice—Brendan Shea. "Whenever you're ready, I'll help you out. Take your time."

Before he could respond, Shea broke the ice. A good sign overall.

"First time riding in a trunk?"

"First time since college," said Devin, blindly reaching upward.

A warm, strong grip yanked him out of the trunk, letting go only after he'd stood firmly on the parking garage's concrete deck for several seconds. Devin opened his eyes halfway, taking in Shea's silhouette, the man's face quickly coming into focus. Everything about him oozed neutrality. His folded arms. His serious expression. Brendan Shea would not be a pushover. Far from it. Devin had his work cut out for him. He grabbed his briefcase before shutting the trunk.

"Thanks for agreeing to meet with me. I know it was an unortho-dox request, given my situation," said Devin, his eyes darting around to locate the man who had smuggled him into MINERVA's parking garage.

"He's gone for now," said Shea. "Someone we use from time to time to run discreet errands."

He didn't want to know any more about these errands. The guy's thick neck, viselike grip, and dead eyes suggested that Devin wasn't the first and wouldn't be the last person to be stuffed in that trunk—alive or dead.

"I have a room set up for us," said Shea, before walking swiftly away.

Devin followed Shea past the elevator to a featureless door painted to match the dark-gray concrete parking garage walls. A well-camou-flaged rectangular slab with barely visible hinges. A quick glance around the parking level confirmed that no cameras covered this particular area of the garage.

"I never noticed that before," said Devin.

"Most employees don't know it exists," said Shea, holding a black keycard against the part of the door where you'd normally expect to find a handle. "Some of our clients require discretion that goes beyond nondisclosure agreements."

He could interpret that in one of two ways. Either the client demanded the extra precaution, or MINERVA wanted to minimize exposure to the client. Devin knew his situation fell into the latter cat-egory. The door crept several inches outward soundlessly. Shea opened it the rest of the way and stepped inside, triggering a set of soft overhead lights. Devin followed him out of the harsh, utilitarian world of the parking garage into a luxuriously appointed, fully equipped conference room. He never heard the door shut behind him.

"This is impressive. I feel like I stepped through a magic portal," said Devin.

Shea nodded at the refreshment center. "Coffee before we get started?"

As much as he'd like a coffee—his journey to get here having started long before dawn—Devin wanted to get this over with.

"I'm good for now," he said, placing his briefcase on the table.

"All right. Let's get to it," said Shea, taking a seat.

Devin opened the briefcase and handed him a folder labeled DEVTEK. "I've outlined everything relevant to what we've discovered regarding the DEVTEK connection in that file," he said. "Including photographs."

"Who's we, specifically?" said Shea.

"Myself and a small group of ex-CIA black ops types," said Devin. "That's all I can say right now."

"And how did you connect with this group?" said Shea. "Did they seek you out, or the other way around?"

"Neither. My mother put this together. She'd worked with one of them at the CIA. Said she trusted him implicitly," said Devin. "I understand that her endorsement doesn't exactly carry much weight at the moment."

"As long as you understand my position," said Shea, opening the file.

"Maybe I'll grab that coffee while you take a look," said Devin.

Two Nespressos later, Shea closed the folder. His face still unreadable.

"Jolene Rudd connects the DEVTEK operation with the reported organized crime shootout a few weeks ago."

"She connects the DEVTEK operation to the attack on my life—and the Russians," said Devin. "Which in turn links all of the above to my mother's work."

"Her conspiracy theory," said Shea. "And I think you're getting ahead of yourself. I stated precisely what this file corroborates, given what has been reported publicly. A territory dispute between two rival eastern European Mafia crews got out of hand. What else do you have?"

"Plenty. But none of it corroborates with publicly reported information," said Devin. "Am I wasting my time with the rest of this? Or your time?"

"I'm just trying to remain as objective as possible, keeping the best interests of the firm's client front and center," said Shea. "Let's dig deeper into what this means for DEVTEK."

Here was where he'd either lose Shea completely or haul him onto the boat—the hook set deep. Devin took the laptop out of the briefcase and opened it in front of Shea before navigating to the slide presentation he'd spent most of the previous night and day assembling. The slide deck covered everything the team had unearthed, starting at Helen's apartment and culminating with the raid deep in the Ozarks.

"Before we go there, I need to very briefly explain what my mother discovered, and what I now firmly believe got her killed and framed—"

"Devin. I need to keep this focused—"

"Brendan. You have to hear me out," said Devin. "If my team is right, DEVTEK *is* one of the main focuses of the Russian operation. It has to be."

Shea pushed his chair back a few feet, a slightly exasperated look on his face. "Fine. Hit me with it, but I'm gonna hit back if I smell bullshit."

"I'd expect nothing less," said Devin. "Fifteen minutes is all I ask for."

A little over an hour after he'd first started clicking through the slides, Shea asked him to stop. The former Special Forces officer turned FBI special agent turned elite private surveillance specialist stared at a frozen still from the helicopter raid video montage created by Berg's electronics team, rubbing his chin and slowly shaking his head.

"That gun battle wasn't staged?" said Shea. "Or creatively edited from something else somehow?"

"I was there. We barely made it out alive," said Devin.

"Senator Filmore and his entire family died in a private-jet crash somewhere over southeast Montana a few days ago," said Shea. "They were headed back to Billings for a fundraiser. All of their bodies were positively identified, including the two pilots. DNA matches. Dental. The feds don't mess around when a US senator dies of unnatural causes."

Devin shrugged. "You're looking at Emma and Thomas Filmore. The images are crisp. I can only speculate about how they got the bodies from that camp to the aircraft."

"This is insane," said Shea.

"Which part?"

"All of it. The video. The whole story," said Shea. "It's so far-fetched I'm having a hard time believing it. At the same time, my gut is telling me this all makes perfect sense. Maybe I don't want to believe it."

"I didn't want to believe it, either. Even though it completely exonerated my mother," said Devin. "A big part of me kept hoping we'd find a fatal flaw in her theory. That it would become obvious that the whole thing was a figment of her imagination, and that she'd just pushed the wrong Russian mobsters a little too far. The ramifications of her being right were mind-blowing, and not in a good way."

"I think I understand what you mean," said Shea. "I still don't know what to make of this."

"Exactly. A massive Russian sleeper network deeply embedded in nearly every level of state and federal government? Our military? Our intelligence agencies? Infrastructure? This may sound bizarre, but I would have gladly let go of any hope of vindicating my mother for this to be some kind of entirely fabricated by-product of a mental illness. But it isn't. She was right."

The stoic facade Shea had maintained for most of their meeting had softened just enough to suggest Devin had made enough of an impression to reel him on board. The next few moments would determine whether he had recruited a potent ally in the fight or been played by Shea.

If his boss walked away from the table with the DEVTEK theory and cut ties to Devin, the DEVTEK angle would be lost forever—but they'd be no worse off than they were before he'd climbed into that trunk. If he agreed to join forces, or at the very least enter into a limited cooperation agreement, they stood a strong chance of bringing this fight close to Pichugin, where the Russian would find himself in an unfamiliar position. On the defensive.

Shea leaned back in his seat. "I need to see the whole enchilada before I take this any further."

"By 'whole enchilada,' I assume you mean my mother's apartment and all of the information she collected?"

"For starters. I also want access to all of the unedited video from the camp raid. I should be able to tell whether you're pulling my leg or not by looking at the footage from the various gun cameras," said Shea. "And I will need to speak with each member of your team. If I don't smell a rat at that point, we should be good to go."

"Unlimited access, basically," said Devin.

"Solely related to your mother's work and the events that have transpired with the team since her death," said Shea. "Before I stick my neck out at MINERVA on any level regarding what you've shown me, I need to be one hundred and ten percent on this."

"I completely understand," said Devin. "How does ten a.m. tomorrow sound? I'll pick you up at a prearranged location of your choice, and we'll execute an SDR before approaching the apartment?"

"I'm going to need a few days to do my own research into your story. Check into stuff I can discreetly corroborate," said Shea.

Devin removed a folder from one of the briefcase's file pockets.

"I figured you would want to independently verify what you could, so I put together a list of the events and names referenced. The attack at the town house in southeast Baltimore. The two sleepers we caught in a tryst in Indianapolis. Everything related to the Ozarks operation. Just be extremely careful with whoever you approach. I listed the vetting criteria that seem to apply to most sleepers, but it's impossible to know for sure."

"How do you know I'm not a sleeper? From what I gathered earlier, sounds like I fit the criteria," said Shea.

"The most obvious reason is that you would have undermined the DEVTEK sting. No way that honeytrap operation would have gone down if you were part of the conspiracy. By that same logic, we're fairly certain MINERVA hasn't been compromised, since this was a relatively high-profile operation within the firm," said Devin.

"Fair enough," said Shea.

"And just to be sure, an associate of ours had a word with your parents and grandparents up in Boston the other day. They also spent some time nosing around your old neighborhood in Southie," said Devin. "If the Sheas are a family of sleeper agents, we may as well start learning Russian, because the US is finished."

"Pops told me someone had been by," said Shea. "I figured it had something to do with our meeting."

"We can't be too careful, and neither can you. I can't stress that enough."

"Understood. I'll send you a meetup location the night before I'm ready. Ten a.m. pickup the next day," said Shea. "We'll use the same encrypted app to communicate."

Devin closed the computer and started to pack up the briefcase.

"I appreciate you trusting me with this. Especially under the circumstances," said Shea. "MINERVA isn't likely to keep you on board for very long. I wish I had a say in the matter, but I'm not as important around here as I like to think I am."

Devin laughed for a few moments, breathing some levity into Shea's olive branch.

"I knew that coming in. I figured even if you walked away without taking another meeting, the Russians' plans at DEVTEK would be permanently thwarted. Not as good as driving a stake through the heart of the whole conspiracy, but at least it'd be something."

Shea nodded. "We'll take things one step at a time, like we have today, and if everything checks out, I'll bring this to DEVTEK. There's no guarantee they'll be up for another sting operation after the last one, but who knows. Maybe you'll get a chance to put a few more of them in the hospital."

"I've put several of them in the ground since we last met," said Devin, closing the briefcase. "You'll have to come up with something better than that."

Shea grinned. "I'll be in touch."

CHAPTER 5

One and a half miles straight as an arrow down a meticulously groomed, tree- and shrub-lined gravel road. And they still had another quarter mile to go, according to the written directions Karl Berg had scribbled back at the apartment. Nothing about the estate had been provided digitally or conveyed over an electronic device, and they'd been told to leave their phones at Devin's mother's apartment. Berg had gone so far as to watch Devin and Marnie Young place their phones in Helen's safe immediately prior to departing.

Whoever owned this place was important, and Berg wasn't taking any chances. Judging by the size of the estate, Devin could guess why. A private tract of land this vast, so close to the Beltway, meant generational, Founding Fathers–level wealth—and the influence that came with it. He had no idea how Berg and Farrington were connected to someone who owned a property like this, but he was grateful.

After the Ozarks raid, they could no longer risk gathering the entire team in the apartment. Twelve strangers filing in and out of a three-family housing unit were bound to attract an unhealthy amount of attention from the neighbors. He'd been concerned enough about the team assembling in the immediate aftermath of the Airbnb massacre. Now? A call to 911 could get them all killed.

Without any concrete leads from the Ozarks, the Russians would turn their attention back to the greater DC-Baltimore area, and direct all their resources—sanctioned and unsanctioned—toward finding Devin and his new colleagues. At this point, they could only guess how far those resources could take the Russians. It all depended on how deeply the sleeper network had infiltrated the alphabet agencies. The one thing everyone agreed on was that their time in Baltimore had a rapidly approaching expiration date.

A well-placed agent or two with access to any of the National Security Agency's unpublicized threat-assessment and tracking tools could shift the balance of this cat-and-mouse chase squarely in favor of the Russians. And they had every reason to assume that the NSA had been compromised on some consequential level.

His mother's process for pinpointing sleepers had its limits outside of publicly identifiable figures, which shielded her from a solid ninety-nine percent of alphabet agency employees. She'd been able to find the two counterintelligence officers at the CIA only because she had direct access to their names while she was still working at Langley.

They had to assume that the Russians had put their sleepers at the NSA and FBI to good use, which meant the team had to maintain the minimal essential footprint at his mother's apartment. Devin, Marnie, Berg, and Farrington would scour Helen Gray's files and strategize, while the tech specialists worked on digitally archiving the main body of her work. A painstaking but critical task that would cut their ties to the apartment and allow them to go dark on their own terms.

The rest of the crew had settled into a motel a few minutes away, where they could serve as a quick reaction force in the unlikely event that the Russians found his mother's apartment before the team moved on. Only Emily Miralles moved between the two locations or made trips for necessary supplies. As the newest member of Farrington's crew, she was the least known and presumably least-recognizable member of the entire entourage. Overall, hardly an ideal arrangement. The sooner they got out of the North Baltimore neighborhood, the better.

The trees lining the road began to thin, revealing the outline of a massive structure to their right, which came into full view a few moments later when they emptied onto a long, curved drive. Devin's first impression was that the owner's generational wealth had very likely been built on the backs of slave labor.

"Wow. I feel like I just stepped back in time," said Marnie. "Where exactly are we, again?"

"On the set of *Gone with the Wind*, apparently," said Devin.

"We're less than ten minutes from the Beltway."

"We're in Northern Virginia," said Devin. "Didn't your parents take you to any of the historic plantations when you were little?"

"Uh. No."

"Neither did mine," said Devin.

He slowed the car to take it all in. If he had to describe the property in a few words or less, "sweeping estate" would be his choice. Nothing but manicured grass holding up century-old trees.

"Look back the way we came," said Marnie.

The line of trees bordering the road extended beyond sight. An interesting feature added within the last decade or two, judging by the size of the maples and poplars. Diminutive compared to the trees rising from the endless lawn. New ownership? Or new purpose? Or both?

"Interesting. Not part of the original design," said Devin. "Very utilitarian."

"Kind of makes you wonder exactly what this place is designed for," she said.

"My guess is it's no longer a residence," said Devin. "Maybe this will be our new Bat Cave."

"Beats sleeping on the floor at your mother's apartment."

"Anything beats that."

He eased his foot off the brake and picked up some speed, searching ahead for the left turn that would take them around the back of the eight-column, Greek-revival-style mansion. After they made the turn, the drive wound in a long arch through the towering oaks before slowly descending a gentle hill and depositing them on a sprawling, empty cobblestone parking pad. Karl Berg stood in front of an open garage door bay, motioning for them to drive inside. Devin drove past Berg and pulled into the ten-bay garage, which contained the team's four additional vehicles, including the electronically tricked-out Suburban.

"Ready?"

"Do I have a choice?" Marnie said.

"Not really," said Devin, getting out of the sedan. He joined Berg outside on the parking pad. "Is it fair to assume that this is not available to the general public through Airbnb or Vrbo?"

"A very fair assumption. It belongs to a friend of a friend . . . of a friend," said Berg. "Who would not be keen on us being here."

"The feeling is mutual," said Marnie. "It's kind of creepy. On the outside."

"Yeah. It's a little too antebellum for my taste as well. At least on the outside," said Berg. "But it's safe from prying eyes, which is why I called in this favor. And the isolation makes it ideal for detecting any surveillance that may have been eluding us. Graves and Gupta have drones up scanning the main road leading to the gate. Nothing followed any of us here. Beats running a two- to three-hour SDR."

"We still did one," said Devin.

"Of course you did," said Berg.

"What about hostile drones?" said Devin, scanning the darkening sky. "If I were following us, I would be using a relay of longer-range, higher-speed drones. The Albatross that we used in the Ozarks would be a good choice. Not fast enough for highway pursuit, but no problem tracking a vehicle along these country roads."

Berg pointed to a white, two-story carriage house in the distance. "It's hard to tell from here, but there's a small radar on top of the roof."

Devin squinted at the structure, barely making out the round white radar dome. It was too small to be of any practical use as a conventional air-tracking radar. The range would be too limited.

"A dedicated drone-detection radar?" said Devin.

"Three-dimensional, three-hundred-and-sixty-degree coverage. Apparently, it can differentiate between drones and birds, and even classify the type of drone," said Berg. "Gupta is still drooling over it."

"That doesn't surprise me," said Devin.

"Range?" said Marnie.

"Four to five kilometers based on the size of the drone," said Berg. "The smaller the shorter the range."

"The owners must really value their privacy," said Marnie.

"That may be an understatement," said Berg. "Every inch of this estate is monitored by a sophisticated array of motion detectors, thermal imaging, day-and-night-vision-capable cameras, directional microphones. Nothing moves on this estate without tripping some kind of sensor."

"Who's monitoring the sensors?" said Devin.

"The system is essentially automated, all pushed right to the device or devices of your choice, if you don't have a dedicated team to staff the security operations center," said Berg.

"My guess is that most of these friends of friends of friends have their own staff," said Devin, "in addition to a platoon of guards to roam the property?"

"I wouldn't know, but I'd say that's a good guess," said Berg.

"What do we have?" said Marnie.

"We have Graves and Gupta with their laptops," said Berg.

Marnie shrugged. "Combined with Farrington's field operatives, we're probably on par with these friends of friends."

"Probably better off," said Devin.

"Shall we?" said Berg, nodding at a portico set into a corner of the mansion.

"How long do we have access to this place?" said Devin, before heading toward the most elaborate back door he'd ever seen.

"I told my friend we'd be out of here by daybreak tomorrow," said Berg.

"That soon?" said Devin. "You could have saved that favor from your friend and put us in a few connecting rooms in Ocean City. The place is packed this time of year. Easy to hide."

"I'll file that away for later," said Berg. "For the moment, I wanted a place where we could focus on a plan to move forward. Relax a little without looking over our shoulders."

Devin glanced back at the carriage house with the radar. "Doesn't feel so relaxed."

"You know what I mean," said Berg. "Anyway. There have been a few developments. This is probably the last time you'll see Farrington and a big slice of his team."

"Can't say I'll miss them," said Marnie.

"Neither will I, to be completely honest. They're an ugly means to an end," said Berg. "But they're all we have. And they always get the job done, even if things tend to get a little messy."

"A little?" said Marnie.

They paused at the steps to the double doors, Berg turning to Marnie. "It's a messy business. There's no way around it. And the higher the stakes, the messier it gets."

"Messier than the past few weeks?" she said.

Berg didn't answer right away, a pained look slowly taking over his face.

"I'd be shocked if we've seen the worst of it," said Berg. "We're back to taking desperate measures. Like I said. There have been a few developments over the past several hours. We'll go over them inside."

He shared a look with Marnie, who shook her head in disbelief.

"She can't wait," said Devin, motioning for the door. "After you."

CHAPTER 6

Marnie followed Berg through the mansion's unexpectedly modern interior. The wide hallways and expansive open spaces gave off a vibe somewhere between boutique hotel and Scandinavian retreat. Warm and comfortable, with an air of practicality. Luxuriously utilitarian? Luxe IKEA? If there was a word for the decorating style, she didn't know it. All she knew was that it couldn't have differed more starkly from the Old World exterior, the juxtaposition making it even creepier.

"What exactly is this place?" she said.

"Feels like a hotel. Almost," said Devin, who looked the way she felt—apprehensive.

Berg talked over his shoulder as he navigated the seemingly endless trek. "From what little I know about this place, I suppose one could classify it as a hotel of sorts," he said. "A very exclusive hotel."

"Barely used, by the look of it," said Marnie.

"Maybe they change the furniture in between uses," said Devin.

Berg snickered at the joke. "At this level of wealth and privilege, nothing would surprise me, though I think the more plausible reason for its pristine condition is the restricted membership list. I suspect this place doesn't get utilized very often."

They emerged from a marble-floored hallway into a cavernous, lobby-like room with a wide travertine stone fireplace on the interior wall and expansive floor-to-ceiling windows overlooking the estate's lush rolling landscape on the other side.

"What level of clientele are we talking about?" said Devin.

"I'm obviously not at liberty to say," said Berg, before pointing toward a closed door set into the wall next to them. "The team is waiting inside the secure conference room. I'll just be a minute."

Marnie ambled toward the conference room with Devin, while Berg made a beeline across the room to a door that had been left a few inches ajar. She turned and positioned herself in front of Devin as the door opened for Berg.

"Don't look behind you," said Marnie. "Act like we're talking."

"Did you see we're going to get rain this weekend?" said Devin in a low, conversational tone. "Might have to cancel my plans to take down the Russians. Kind of bummed about that. What have you been up to lately?"

"Nothing much. Just flying helicopters over Russian sleeper camps," said Marnie, shifting a few inches to the right to bring the doorway into view. "The usual stuff."

A serious-looking woman in a dark suit appeared momentarily, stepping aside to let Berg inside. When she backed out of the way, Marnie caught a glimpse of a stylishly dressed middle-age woman seated on a dark-leather couch. The peek lasted less than a second before the executive officer shut the door abruptly. Long enough for her to identify the friend who had granted Berg access to this private, lifestyles-of-the-rich-and-famous enclave: Senator Margaret Steele.

The living definition of generational wealth, from what Marnie understood, who had made it her own personal mission to put that wealth to work for the underdog after losing her daughter and husband to a rather nasty tragedy.

"See anything you shouldn't have?" said Devin, glancing over his shoulder at the closed door.

"I saw one of the most prominent—and wealthy—members of Congress," said Marnie.

"Here?" said Devin.

"No. Last year at the Capitol."

"Funny," said Devin. "I guess it makes sense. Berg did briefly mention something about a benefactor underwriting Farrington's team for this whole thing. A benefactor with a vested interest in national security. A woman."

"Senator Margaret Steele," said Marnie.

"You actually saw Senator Steele?"

"No. I just made all of this up," said Marnie, rolling her eyes.

"Sorry. Sorry," said Devin. "I didn't mean it that way. I'm just surprised Berg is so well connected. He doesn't strike me as a friend of the establishment."

"From what I've read, the senator has spent the past several years ruffling the establishment's feathers," said Marnie. "Maybe that's how their paths crossed."

Devin nodded. "However it happened, I feel somewhat better knowing she's on our side, even if money can't entirely solve our problem."

"It certainly can't hurt," said Marnie, before nodding at the conference room door. "We better get inside before Berg figures out that we've identified a member of the super-secret mansion club."

Devin opened the door to a surprisingly loud and boisterous group, the room's obvious soundproofing having flawlessly prevented any noise from escaping.

Marnie had worked in and around a variety of sensitive compartmented information facilities during her dozen or so years in the Marine Corps. Most SCIFs were just crude structures built to physically separate and protect classified documents from unauthorized access. A metal CONEX box placed next to a mobile headquarters. One way in. One way out. Guarded twenty-four seven.

On a few occasions, while attending classified briefings at a major permanent military installation, she'd seen far more sophisticated versions. Designed specifically for the larger-scale discussion and dissemination of classified information, they were constructed to prevent physical breaches, acoustic eavesdropping or electronic snooping from adjacent rooms, or hostile surveillance located outside the building.

Before stepping inside, she predicted that the space would be windowless—her instincts proving to be correct upon crossing the door's threshold. The exterior-facing wall featured an exhibition of framed black-and-white landscape photographs, instead of acoustically exploitable glass. The conference room had undoubtedly been designed to the highest SCIF standards money could buy. A smart investment when you considered the kinds of schemes and deals struck at this level of wealth and power.

The team immediately quieted, all heads turning in their direction. She immediately noted a new face, in addition to Farrington's conspicuous absence. Aside from that, the entire original crew was present.

Devin zeroed in on the stout man with gray hair standing in the far corner next to Alex Filatov. "Who's he?"

Jared Hoffman stepped away from the well-appointed coffee-and-snack bar on the other side of the conference room. "Nick Jones. Formerly Nikolai Mazurov," he said. "A legacy member of the team. He was recruited and trained by General Sanderson before any of us were even a gleam in the general's eye."

"I lived undercover in Moscow for nearly a decade, starting in the late nineties," said Nick, having somehow overheard their conversation from a distance. "A sleeper agent in the truest sense of the word. I executed one mission before I was brought back. A seemingly minor—"

"But important mission," said Farrington, who had entered the room behind them unnoticed.

"More important than any of you will ever know or could possibly guess," said Berg, who stood next to Farrington.

She'd heard the team toss Sanderson's name around enough to know that Farrington's team was either a spin-off from or successor to a covert-operations program started years ago by the general. Nick's statement suggested that the original program could be close to thirty years old, assuming Nick had spent more than a few years training for his role as a Moscow-based sleeper. Some of Sanderson's operatives had been at this since Marnie was in elementary school. Who were these people?

"What exactly does that mean?" said Devin, reading her mind.

"Some secrets go with you to the grave," said Berg, closing the door.

"All the two of you need to know is that Nick is fully vetted," said Farrington. "He'll join us in Russia."

"We're headed to Russia?" said Marnie.

"Just a few of us," said Farrington.

"Isn't that a little risky with a Red Notice to your name?" said Devin.

"Extremely risky, but we're working on a relatively foolproof way of getting into Russia without attracting any attention," said Farrington. "Shall we get this show on the road, so to speak?"

Nick and Alex took their seats at the far end of the table, while Berg shuffled his way toward Anish Gupta and Tim Graves.

"Please. We have a lot to cover," said Berg. "G and G, how are we looking?"

Gupta answered without looking up from his laptop. "We good."

Graves gave his colleague a disapproving look and shook his head before expanding on the report.

"Nothing followed Devin and Marnie by road or air—from what we can tell. And all estate sensors are quiet," said Graves. "Our plan is to land both drones in about thirty minutes and swap out their batteries. We can launch one or both drones within a moment's notice if something trips any of the sensors."

"In other words," said Gupta, "we good."

Graves rolled his eyes and went back to scanning his laptop screen.

Berg started the moment everyone had found a seat. "There's no sugarcoating this. Our already tight timeline has been drastically compressed," he said. "The attack on the camp in the Ozarks, combined with our detour to Indianapolis, triggered a more extensive cleanup than we initially predicted. On top of completely erasing the Senator Filmore angle, most of the sleepers on Helen's wall have gone dark. Sudden vacations. Unexplained work absences. Regularly active social media accounts with no activity for close to a week. My guess is they're in Moscow, or some other safe haven."

"You said *most*," said Devin. "Not everyone has disappeared?"

"My contact at the CIA tells me that the two suspected sleepers embedded in counterintelligence haven't gone anywhere," said Berg. "And from what we can tell, about a half dozen of the sleepers on your mother's wall appear to have remained in place."

"Interesting," said Marnie. "Why would they stick around?"

"We'll get to that in vivid detail later tonight," said Berg. "First things first. Rich and a few others are headed to Moscow."

"We heard," said Devin.

Berg nodded. "My CIA contact did some digging into General Grigory Kuznetzov—"

"I don't remember us talking about him previously," said Marnie. "But I'm not the best at remembering names."

"We haven't discussed him. I was given his name by a separate contact," said Berg.

"At the CIA?" said Marnie.

"At the nunya institute," said Berg.

"Where?" said Marnie.

"The nunya business institute," said Devin, chuckling along with a few of the operatives.

"Funny." Marnie shook her head.

"Anyway. General Kuznetzov should have retired from the GRU close to a decade ago, but he's still on active duty or plays some kind of very active role at the GRU. He's been seen coming and going from their headquarters during the week," said Berg. "That's how my contact managed to identify him. He's a bit of an anomaly. Kuznetzov was on a career fast track at the GRU when he essentially vanished from sight—around the same time Pichugin rose to prominence."

"So this whole thing could still be a GRU operation?" said Devin. "Kuznetzov directs the various sleeper networks' activities on behalf of Pichugin, who uses them to further his own goals—and ultimately those of Putin. Everybody wins. It's a clever arrangement. Nobody the wiser outside of their small conspiracy circle."

"My contact at the CIA told me something that has me thinking that this is no longer in GRU hands, like we suspected," said Berg. "Kuznetzov splits his time between two locations. Half of the week at GRU headquarters, and the rest of the week at a secure compound about fifteen miles west of Moscow. CIA sources haven't been able to penetrate the compound to any degree. It's vast, isolated, and heavily guarded."

"Guarded by who?" said Marnie.

"Unmarked, heavily armed guards," said Berg.

"Mercenaries," said Devin.

"Most assuredly," said Berg. "And the land is privately owned."

"Let me guess. Pichugin?" said Devin.

"No."

"Putin," said Marnie.

"Suleymon Durov," said Berg. "But yes—basically Putin. Durov is one of a dozen or so oligarchs who lend their name to Putin's land and estates so the Russian president can avoid the kind of negative public attention that might stem from an elected official owning dozens of billion-dollar estates around Russia."

"They're running the show from this compound," said Devin.

"The main show at least," said Berg. "I suspect Kuznetzov still runs a sideshow or two out of GRU headquarters."

"Like the team that ambushed you and Ms. Young after leaving the Airbnb town house," said Rich. "A quarter of them had verifiable Russian consulate ties."

"Where does the network of retirement-aged sleepers fit into this?" said Marnie.

"That's a good question," said Berg. "The Rudds and the other members of their crew appeared out of thin air a few years after the Soviet Union fell. Nearly two decades after the earliest suspected first-generation sleepers started showing up. Same with Jonathan Hayes, Ray Dillard, and Hailey Barna—the people Devin put in the hospital."

Devin had been part of the MINERVA surveillance team hired by DEVTEK to investigate a possible case of attempted corporate espionage. MINERVA had arranged a sting at a swanky DC hotel, which quickly morphed from a straightforward honeypot operation set up by the sleepers into a blatant kidnapping. To survive and protect the DEVTEK employee used as bait, Devin had been forced to severely injure the young woman who took the bait, along with two men who tried to kill him while he was escorting the employee to safety.

"And Jolene Rudd murdered them," said Devin.

"She murdered the two men taken by ambulance to Howard University Hospital. We haven't identified the late-middle-age gentleman who put a pillow over Hailey Barna's face at George Washington University Hospital," said Berg. "Either way, they're all connected. I just don't know how, exactly."

"We have a theory," said Graves.

"The floor is yours," said Berg.

"We suspect the team that hit the Airbnb town house was specifically deployed to the US to support the original sleeper network. Same with the three snuffed out in their hospital beds," said Graves.

"That's one hell of a claim," said Berg.

"Given what Devin's mother found?" said Marnie.

"Good point," said Berg.

"I know it sounds far-fetched. I mean—two separate sleeper networks dedicated to the same mission? I wouldn't have considered one

43

sleeper network on this scale a possibility just three weeks ago, but here we are."

"None of us would have—or did, frankly," said Berg. "Until presented with overwhelming evidence. And even then, it was hard to believe."

"Exactly. And this second network shares a similarity with the first generation of sleepers. They appeared out of nowhere," said Graves.

"Isn't that the definition of a sleeper agent?" said Rich.

"Told you he'd say that," said Gupta.

Graves fought off a frown, which caused her to stifle a laugh. Marnie had come to appreciate the levity that G and G's constant bickering pumped into the group's unwavering dire mood. It brought back memories of her years with the Marines, where well-timed, sarcastic fits of black humor eased even the darkest moments.

"Why wouldn't he say that? That's what anyone would say," said Graves. "We've been over this."

She pressed her lips tight, trying not to crack a smile. Devin looked to be in the same situation.

"Just pointing it out," said Gupta.

"Just trying to annoy me," said Graves. "Anyway. Here's the big difference—and why I think they were sent here for the very specific purpose of supporting the network Helen Gray uncovered. None of them held jobs. That sounds very unusual for a sleeper agent. Right?"

"Yes. Traditionally, they would try to blend into the community in every possible way," said Berg. "Are you sure they never worked?"

"We can't find a shred of evidence suggesting that any of them have ever been employed. Attended a trade school or college. Or done much of anything other than just live in the homes that also magically appeared with them. The home deeds we could access digitally all told the same story. The sleepers owned their homes outright. Deeds and titles transferred upon their arrival, from what we can tell."

"That can't be the norm," said Devin.

Berg looked disturbed by the revelation. More than usual. "It isn't."

"And I bet if we could access their bank accounts, we'd find very regular transfers of money over the years from a shell company," said Graves.

"It's not unusual for sleepers to show up with seed money and receive semiregular sums of money to pay for rent while they establish themselves, but full home ownership from the start?" said Berg. "I've never heard of that before."

"Without the need to make money or any societal obligations, they'd be free and clear to execute orders at a moment's notice. A dedicated—and always available—support network," said Graves.

"I think you're on to something," said Farrington. "Pichugin and Kuznetzov would need a separate network to do any dirty work required to pave the way for the primary sleeper network's success. That's essentially what Devin witnessed with the DEVTEK sting," said Farrington. "I bet Kuznetzov runs this second wave of sleepers from GRU headquarters, which is why he splits his time between the two locations."

"Right under the GRU's nose," said Marnie.

"Putin's nose," said Berg. "Nothing on that scale happens in Russia without Putin's approval."

"But why two locations?" said Devin. "Why not consolidate them at the compound outside of Moscow?"

"If I had to guess, I'd say they didn't want a repeat of when Kuznetzov took control of the original sleeper network and moved it to the compound," said Berg. "It obviously didn't go unnoticed—and the cleanup was messy. They killed at least a dozen high-ranking GRU officers in the process. Things are corrupt in Moscow, but there's always a limit. Kind of."

Devin nodded at Rich. "Then I guess the big question is, What's the plan for your team in Moscow? Grab Kuznetzov? Try to breach the secure compound? Both?"

Rich rubbed his week-old, dark-gray beard. "You might be overestimating our capabilities. I'm not ruling out either option, but our goal is to identify something in between. Something the four of us can pull off without committing to a suicide mission."

"Yeah. I'd like to steer clear of suicide missions at this point in my career," said Jared.

"Ditto," said Alex. "I just shifted most of my 401(k) assets into a low-risk bond portfolio."

Everyone but Marnie and Devin laughed at Alex's joke. Marnie looked to Rich, who shrugged.

"We don't offer a 401(k), in case you're considering a stint as one of our pilots," he said.

"I figured as much," said Marnie, finally chuckling. "I'm still weighing my options. Kind of leaning away from the offer without retirement benefits."

"Probably a wise move," said Rich, grinning. "Back to Devin's original question. We're going to tail Kuznetzov and look for an opportunity that doesn't guarantee our deaths. That said, there's no guarantee of anything on a mission like this. Working illegally in Russia presents an outsize risk."

"That's an understatement," said Nick.

"I can't even begin to conceive of how you'll get to Moscow undetected, let alone run an intensive surveillance operation against a top GRU general without painting a target on your back," said Devin.

"Seriously. How is this even in the realm of possibilities?" said Marnie. "And I ask that fully aware that the Russians are doing the exact same thing here. It just has to be exponentially more difficult over there. Right?"

"It is. Which is why I called in the few remaining favors I hadn't used prior to retirement," said Berg, shifting uncomfortably in his seat. "The Israelis will get our team to Moscow. They also agreed to facilitate the acquisition of weapons and any specialized surveillance gear."

"They must have owed you one hell of a favor," said Devin.

Berg winced before sharing a tense look with Rich. "The favor got me an audience. Your mother's research, everything we've uncovered to this point, and whatever we discover along the way is payable in full after we shut down the US side of the sleeper conspiracy. The Israelis obviously have a vested interest in getting to the bottom of the Iron Dome sabotage in Haifa. The conversation got heated, and they wanted names—now. I promised them everything once we get our own house in order. All or nothing."

"The Israelis won't leave you alone in Moscow. Not after Haifa," said Devin, looking at Rich. "The moment your surveillance target is revealed—all bets are off."

"I would expect nothing less from our Mossad friends," said Berg. "Which is why I agreed to pass along the digitized version of your mother's research upon the successful infiltration of Rich's team into Moscow as a down payment, and made it perfectly clear that the rest of the deal was off if they interfered or intervened in any way with our operation."

"Obviously, you didn't mention Kuznetzov or Pichugin," said Devin.

"I didn't. But it won't take them long to determine that Kuznetzov is our primary target," said Berg.

"About five minutes," said Rich.

"Exactly," said Berg. "And the connection to Pichugin won't be far behind. I assured the Israelis that it was in their best interest to let us get to the bottom of the conspiracy before they exacted revenge—which they are entitled to after what happened in Haifa."

Jared shook his head. "They'll be all over us in Moscow, and they'll flip this deal on its head in the blink of an eye if it benefits them."

"Yes. They will. As would we," said Rich. "Unfortunately, the Israelis are our only option. There's simply no other way to get into Russia without going to extremely risky lengths. We hold up our end of the bargain and hope they do the same. That's all we can do. The deal Karl struck is fair, and our interests are well aligned—for now."

"Don't worry about Rich's crew. They've pulled off some real miracles in the past—under far worse conditions," said Berg.

Rich shook his head and smirked. "Don't jinx us."

"No jinx intended," said Berg, before turning his attention to Devin. "So. Where do we stand with Mr. Shea, your contact at MINERVA?"

"I got a text from him a few hours ago," said Devin. "He'd like to take the next step and examine my mother's research. I could arrange to bring him to the apartment as early as tomorrow afternoon—after taking all of the necessary security precautions."

"I'd like the option of assembling my team in your mother's apartment tomorrow—to finalize the Moscow details with Graves and Gupta," said Rich. "Until Shea commits, I'd like to keep contact with my team to a minimum."

"I can bring him the day after. Unless you think you'll need more time," said Devin.

"I don't want to delay striking a deal with Shea any longer than necessary," said Berg.

"I agree," said Rich. "We'll clear out by close of business tomorrow. How long do you think it'll take for the Israelis to get their shit together?"

"It's already together," said Berg. "As soon as you wrap things up at the apartment tomorrow, they'll send instructions."

"They're not messing around, are they?" said Rich.

"No. They're not," said Berg. "Devin. How quickly do you think Shea can put the DEVTEK sting into play?"

"Assuming Shea agrees to move forward with our proposal," said Devin. "Frankly, this is probably going to be the slowest-moving part of our plan. He'll have to clear it with someone above him at MINERVA. Then he'll have to pitch it to DEVTEK. Best-case scenario is one week. Two weeks is more realistic."

"Feels like an eternity with all of Helen's sleepers vanishing," said Berg. "The Russians are getting close to some kind of endgame. They wouldn't wipe their roster clean if they didn't have all or most of the pieces already in place."

"Maybe it's time to drag the CIA a little deeper into this," said Rich. "Add a few more heads to the hydra—before Pichugin manages to cut a few off."

Marnie didn't like the sound of that at all, but she understood Rich's strategy, and why it was so important. The conspiracy uncovered by Helen Gray represented a threat to national security, on a previously unimagined scale that could permanently tip the balance of power between the West and Russia in Putin's favor. Bringing the CIA on board, while admittedly a risky proposition, could light a second fuse—in case Pichugin snuffed out the first.

"I'll see if my contact's willing to take a trip out to Helen's apartment," said Berg.

"We'll have the entire collection digitally archived in about four days," said Graves. "You can bring the apartment to your contact at that point."

"I don't know if we have that kind of time," said Berg. "She isn't a shot caller at the CIA anymore."

"How far along are you in the archive process?" said Devin.

"About halfway," said Graves.

"We can give what we have, along with the same gun camera and drone footage that I showed Shea," said Devin. "That should be more than enough for her to make an initial judgment. Maybe even enough to take to a trusted colleague."

"I'll give her a call," said Berg, grudgingly. "What else—before we start brainstorming?"

Marnie and Devin spoke simultaneously with nearly identical questions, the same thought weighing heavily on their minds. Who would replace the veteran members of the team headed to Russia? Rich took the question.

"Elena and Gilly will be here tomorrow," said Rich, the team mumbling their approval. "That gives us two more top-tier operators."

"What about the other two?" said Berg.

The team instantly quieted, their entire focus on Rich's answer.

"Still haven't heard from them," said Rich.

"If you don't hear from them before you leave tomorrow, assume they're not interested and pick two others," said Berg.

"Who are we talking about?" said Marnie.

"It's a long story," said Rich.

"And not worth telling if they don't show," said Berg.

"You're the one who brought it up," said Marnie, a little annoyed at being dismissed.

"True. Sorry," said Berg. "The two operatives in question are legends in the business. Bringing them on board is a long shot. I don't want to waste what little time we have together talking about them."

"Fair enough," said Marnie. "Will four more operatives be sufficient?"

Devin shook his head. "In terms of the capability to conduct separate, simultaneous operations, if the opportunity and need arises. That's going to require a bigger crew."

"He's right," said Scott. "The ability to move in two directions at once could spell the difference between the success or failure of this entire venture. We can split Graves and Gupta, but that only leaves us with four shooters per team. It's not enough."

"Three per team," said Emily, turning toward Marnie. "Devin and Marnie can hold their own, but they don't have the same training. No offense."

"None taken. I couldn't agree more," said Devin.

"No argument from me," said Marnie. "I fly helicopters."

"I'll see what I can do," said Rich. "We had seven shooters going into the Ozarks. I can't muster that kind of manpower without dipping into the merc pool—and I really don't want to have to rely on contractors."

"It'll be my problem," said Scott, appearing to answer one of Marnie's most burning questions—*Who would be in charge with Rich overseas?*

"Actually, it'll be Devin's problem," said Rich. "He'll be in charge. His mother started this. He should finish it."

If Scott or any of the operatives didn't agree with Rich's statement, they didn't show it. Half nodded. Half didn't react. Marnie couldn't read them at all—like always. The team's discipline had been impressive from the beginning. True professionals on every level, including Anish Gupta. She glanced at Devin, who had cocked his head and raised an eyebrow.

"It would have been nice if we had discussed this earlier," said Devin.

"We made the decision moments before this meeting," said Rich.

"This is your show," said Berg. "Helen put this in your hands."

"And yours," said Devin. "She sent both of us to that restaurant."

"From what I remember, Helen was always a very pragmatic CIA officer," said Berg. "I wasn't brought into this to call the shots. Helen put us together so I could make the right phone calls. And I might know a thing or two about analyzing and unraveling conspiracies."

Devin swallowed hard. "All right. Scott runs the tactical side. Karl runs intel and planning. G and G owns surveillance. And I'll command by negation."

Rich chuckled. "Off to a good start."

"Told you," said Berg.

Command by negation was a decentralized military leadership concept that granted decision-making autonomy to individual commanders, freeing up the overall commander of the larger force to focus on the bigger picture. Individual commanders report their intentions, and unless otherwise directed, they execute them.

In this far-less-complicated and far-more-compact situation, Devin had essentially told them he would only interfere under the most extreme circumstances. In other words, no real change to how the team had previously operated. It was a savvy way to take the reins without yanking them. And a shrewd way for Rich to hand them over without ruffling any feathers on the team.

Marnie had paid close attention to the team's dynamic over the past two weeks. Discipline and cooperation appeared unconditional, but every organization or team had a hierarchy, which inevitably led to power dynamics when leadership changed. The moment she heard that Rich would be headed to Russia, she started doing the math.

Rich was the undisputed leader of the team. Below him, you had a few long-standing members. The core group—Alex, Jared, Melendez, and the recently deceased Mike—all knew each other from "back in the day." She'd thought they represented the earliest iteration of the program until Nikolai introduced himself a few minutes ago. He clearly dated all of them by close to a decade, including Rich, but given his physical state and general demeanor, they'd dragged Nick out of a very cushy retirement. Seniority alone didn't equal leadership status in this strange realm of covert operatives. The calculation was far more complicated.

Case in point: Scott had jumped in to assume command, by her calculation, skipping the line. From what Marnie had gathered, he'd joined the team a number of years after the core four had proved their mettle. A combat-tested, former Navy SEAL lieutenant commander who blended seamlessly into Sanderson's project. In other words, a proven leader. She couldn't say the same about the rest of the core group, based on what she'd overheard and observed.

Melendez and Jared were the team's snipers. Lethal to a fault at any range, but exceptionally skillful at dealing long-range death. Neither of them were seemingly interested in any other role. That left Alex. The absolute last person you wanted to engage in a gunfight at less-extreme ranges. A very useful tool in ninety-five percent of combat scenarios, but not a leader.

Much of this had become a moot point a few minutes ago. Jared and Alex were headed to Russia, which took them out of the calculation. Scott was the most logical choice, but team undercurrents could never be underestimated. Marnie had to give Rich credit. Passing command to Devin instantly quelled the possibility, however unlikely, of building resentment among team members.

She just hoped that Scott had paid close attention to Rich over the years to fill just one of his shoes. The team's margin for error moving forward would be nearly nonexistent. It would take all of them working together flawlessly to pull off whatever complex stunt Berg had in mind. Which brought her to the million-dollar question, which she flippantly presented to Devin.

"So. What's the plan?" said Marnie. "How do all of the heads of the hydra work together?"

Devin shrugged. "Karl?"

"I should have an answer for you by tomorrow morning," said Berg. "We have a long night ahead of us."

CHAPTER 7

Felix Orlov scanned the faces of the pedestrians on both sides of Cathedral Street, the task rapidly underscoring the relative futility of his undertaking. Lady Luck, as the Americans say, would have to be on his side for him to pick out any of his targets from a moving vehicle. And that might be an understatement.

A quarter of the faces escaped him entirely. They either turned away from his SUV when he passed, or he missed them while looking in another direction. He caught a glimpse or partial view of another quarter, but not enough to make an identification, or even determine whether the subject required a closer look.

The remaining faces were still a blur, so he focused on the men, cutting the number of possible targets in half. He screened for physique next, eliminating anyone who looked even moderately overweight. An easier task in the summer heat than winter temperatures, thanks to fewer layers of clothing. Even after instantly eliminating three-quarters of the sidewalk traffic, the process left him struggling.

Screening on the move was neither efficient nor effective. The process required a driver and a spotter, leaving him with only six vehicles to cover a ridiculously large geographic area. A densely populated urban square mile. Everything within reasonable walking distance of East Chase Street, from Central Street to the east and Howard Street to the west. A few hundred streets and several thousand residences. A laughable job, really, which was why he'd already sent his employer a request to triple his current team of twelve.

With three dozen operatives, he could shift to a slightly better strategy. A loose framework of strategically located, one-person stakeouts focused on intersections, high-pedestrian-traffic streets, and busy takeout establishments. Still nowhere remotely close to perfect, but the best he could manage short of deploying a battalion of mercenaries to comb through a city square mile. Not without another surveillance miracle, like the one placed in his lap early yesterday.

Pichugin's people had somehow managed to track two of Richard Farrington's associates from the entrance of a parking garage in South Baltimore to separate drop-off points along East Chase Street—where they promptly vanished again. Roughly a twelve-minute Uber ride for each of them. Add that to the fifteen minutes or so Farrington's people spent on camera at the Nashville car rental agency, and you had the entire sum of time Orlov had been able to "see" his target since the Ozarks. Barely more than a half hour over a nine-day time frame.

The only reason he had even the vaguest sense of their location was entirely thanks to some serious investigative magic. Tracking a credit card hit on a possible alias to a rental car agency was one thing. Locating the two rental vehicles represented an entirely different level of surveillance voodoo, especially since it was assumed that Farrington's crew would disable any agency- or car maker–installed GPS tracking technology. On top of that, the vehicles had been found deep inside a parking garage, where satellite tracking wasn't even possible. He had no idea how Pichugin had found the two SUVs—and didn't want to know. Orlov already had enough problems sleeping at night.

Not wanting to spit in luck's face, he had placed two extremely well-hidden cellular trackers on each vehicle. Motion activated, the trackers would immediately transmit to a brief cellular signal receiver located in a nearby parked car—and go silent. A minute after the initial transmission, the receiver unit in the parked car would trigger a cellular call to Orlov's phone, warning him that one of the target vehicles had been moved. He could ping the tracker at will once the SUVs exited the parking garage, leaving him with two options.

He could position his operatives at a safe distance for a discreet surveillance run, with the hope they might lead him to Helen Gray's apartment, or he could guide his team in for an immediate intercept. Since he highly doubted Farrington's people would go near the apartment with one of those vehicles, the parking garage scenario realistically offered him a single choice—to intercept the vehicle and try to capture one of Farrington's operatives alive. A costly proposition based on the deep dive he'd taken into the intelligence dossiers Pichugin had finally released.

Based on what he'd read in the files—painfully reinforced by what he'd experienced firsthand in the Ozarks—Richard Farrington's team was the real deal. A carefully selected and highly experienced team that had trained together extensively for years. Entirely dedicated to each other. Superior on every level to any mercenary crew he could assemble, and unlike anything he'd gone up against previously.

Luckily, the parking garage gambit was the least likely to pay off. Without another gift from Pichugin's uncannily resourceful surveillance network, Orlov's best chance of success lay right here—on the sidewalks of North Baltimore. All he needed was one positive ID. A single match to one of Farrington's known or highly probable associates. Fourteen faces, including Gray's and Young's.

If his people spotted any of them on the streets, Orlov would have to proceed swiftly but cautiously. Smartly without overthinking. A delicate balance between hesitation that could kill the opportunity and impatience that could kill his entire team. The moment would have to be right, because he wouldn't get another chance. Not with this group. They'd go dark for good this time. A group like this didn't make the same mistake twice.

He'd already decided on a few ground rules to simplify the decision-making process. Devin Gray and Marnie Young would be abducted immediately. He felt highly confident in his ability to break either of them alone. If they surfaced together, even better. Neither of them would have a personal reason to protect the apartment—only each other. And Orlov would test that theory with all the pain and brutality he could inflict upon them. One of them would crack.

Karl Berg and Farrington's team was a different story. On top of the lethal price he'd pay to grab one of them, the chance of breaking them in the time frame required was zero. Nobody could withstand torture forever, but he wouldn't have that kind of time. The clock would start ticking the moment he sprang the trap. He'd be working with minutes, not hours. Certainly not the days he'd likely need.

No. A street sighting would turn into a complicated, high-stakes surveillance exercise. Something his team had little to no experience executing. They were more of a blunt-force instrument, brought in to solve problems when all other options had been exhausted. Or in Pichugin's case, when the client reached untouchable status and no longer had to play games.

All the more reason Orlov needed more operatives sooner than later. If he made a positive ID right now, the odds of successfully finding Helen Gray's apartment and neutralizing his targets hovered right around zero. He didn't have the numbers to pull it off, which made this a complete waste of time.

"Up there. Pull over," said Orlov, pointing toward a stretch of open curb space ahead of them.

Lashev Pavlovich straightened in his seat and tightened his grip on the wheel. "You see something?"

"No. I'm just hungry," said Orlov. "I hope you like Mediterranean food."

They'd just passed a restaurant with Greek lettering.

"I could go for a falafel sandwich," said Lashev, pulling off the road. "A drink or two wouldn't hurt, either."

"We'll grab some liquor for the team on the way back to the hotel," said Orlov.

Lashev checked his watch. "I was thinking now."

"I was thinking right after lunch," said Orlov. "I'm pulling us off the street until at least half of our reinforcements arrive. We'll put our heads together, before we have a few drinks, and come up with a better search strategy."

"When can we expect the other teams?" said Lashev.

"They start trickling in tonight," said Orlov. "We should have a second full team at our disposal by nightfall tomorrow. I've tasked Dmitry Garin with getting them equipped and organized. I believe you know him. He lands tonight with a few others. The third team won't be assembled for another forty-eight hours."

"Garin's solid," said Lashev. "I've worked with him on several occasions before you started paying more."

"Apparently I pay more than whoever used to pay Garin," said Orlov, the two of them briefly laughing.

"It's hard to find deeper pockets than Pichugin's," said Lashev. "Who's taking the third team? Oleg?"

"Oleg and I work better side by side," said Orlov. "We go way back. I have Fedir Severny running the third team."

"I've heard of him," said Lashev, before putting the car in park.

"That's it?" said Orlov.

"You know the old adage," said Lashev.

"If there's nothing good to say?"

Lashev shrugged before getting out of the SUV and slamming the door. Shit. The last thing Orlov needed under these circumstances was bad blood on the team. He met Lashev on the curb, blocking him from the sidewalk.

"We're not going to have a problem, are we?" said Orlov.

"Not if you keep him as far away from me as possible," said Lashev.

"I really can't guarantee—"

Lashev glanced around furtively, like he was checking for witnesses. Orlov tensed, ready to draw the pistol concealed in a holster pressed against the small of his back. Lashev shook his head.

"Take it easy, Orlov," he said, putting his hands out in front of him. "Just keep him off my back. He likes to push people's buttons, and we have a history. I can keep it professional, but I have my limits. Severny doesn't have that kind of filter."

"I'll let Oleg know there's an issue, so we can both keep an eye on it," said Orlov. "What happened between the two of you?"

"That's between me and Severny."

"Just make sure it doesn't come between you and the mission," said Orlov. "I don't want to spend the rest of my life sleeping with one eye open because of a personal squabble."

"Then keep him under control," said Lashev. "Or cancel his contract."

"I can't cancel his contract," said Orlov. "I lured him off another job, along with his team."

Lashev shook his head. "A whole team of Severny devotees? Have you worked with him before?"

"I've never needed this many people for a job before," said Orlov.

"You didn't answer my question."

"No. I've never worked with him before," said Orlov. "I heard he was a hothead and avoided him. But beggars can't be choosers when it comes to appeasing Pichugin."

"You have to keep him on a very tight leash, Orlov," said Lashev. "Fedir's a wild card under the best of circumstances. He's good at his job, but he can leave a wide path of destruction in his wake. And he'll sacrifice anyone to get the job done. I know that from personal experience."

Orlov wondered if he'd made a mistake bringing Severny into the fold. The last thing he needed on this mission was a loose cannon.

The situation would be explosive enough, given the circumstances. Farrington's people wouldn't go down without a serious fight, which meant his window of opportunity to pull off a clean sweep—neutralize targets and sanitize their operations center—would be tight. Everything leading up to the initial breach would have to be timed and executed perfectly. There would be no room for distractions or unauthorized deviations from the plan. If feasible, he'd hold Severny in reserve.

"I appreciate the warning," said Orlov, patting Lashev's shoulder. "Let's get that falafel, and a few drinks."

CHAPTER 8

Rich heaved an oversize travel backpack onto his shoulders and approached him with an open hand. Devin glanced at his hand for a few moments before accepting the handshake.

"Still not sure about me?" said Rich.

"Karl trusts you," said Devin, eager to escape Rich's viselike grip. "I mostly trust Karl. Which means I more or less trust you. That's as good as it gets."

"Fair enough. Though you might want to rethink your assessment of Karl," said Rich, glancing over Devin's shoulder.

"I heard that," said Berg.

"You were supposed to," said Rich, releasing the handshake.

Karl joined the two of them, a rare smile on his weathered face.

"I'm jealous."

Rich shrugged. "Jealous of what?"

"You get to see Russia again. I always wanted to go back," said Berg.

"I'm sure your Israeli friends could rustle up another set of papers if you wanted to see Moscow again," said Rich. "There's always room in the surveillance van for a keen eye."

"Hmm. Yeah. Still a hard pass for me. If I'm going to throw my life away, I'd prefer to do it here in the United States. Not that I think anything will go wrong for you in Russia," said Berg.

"Careful, Devin. Don't let Karl's gushing optimism paint too pretty a picture of the situation," said Rich.

Devin stifled a laugh. "I'll be sure to take that under advisement."

"Hey. I learned long ago to assume the worst and consider that the best-case scenario," said Berg. "It tends to keep me and the people I work with alive. Emphasis on *me* and *alive*."

"Speaking of people we've worked with," said Rich. "I heard from our two friends. They're interested."

"Really?" said Berg, skeptically.

"I begged," said Rich. "I never beg."

"And just like that—they agreed?"

"They didn't agree to anything," said Rich. "But they got back to me. First time in close to six years."

"You gave them my satellite number?" said Berg.

"That and the necessary information to send messages through our encrypted app," said Rich. "Maybe they'll bite on this one."

"I'm not counting on it," said Berg.

"I know we really can't afford to turn down the help," said Devin, "but they sound a little high maintenance. If they walk through these doors, I need to know that they won't bail on us. They have to be one hundred percent in—or out."

"If they say yes, they won't quit on you," said Rich, before lowering his voice. "Trust me. They're worth the up-front games, and whatever quirks they bring to the table. They work as a couple, equally capable of blunt-force direct-action work or soft-touch espionage jobs. They've pulled off some serious coups in the past. The kind of stuff most of my team can only dream about."

"And Karl can handle them?" said Devin.

He sensed some hesitation from Karl regarding their possible arrival.

"Nobody can entirely handle or control them," said Rich. "But they won't undermine your mission. Karl knows how to pull the levers that need to be pulled."

"They're like a fire-and-forget missile," said Karl. "You identify the target, set a few nonnegotiable parameters, and let them worry about the rest. Ideal for something like . . . hunting down and grabbing any of the sleepers that decided to stick around instead of taking the free flight back to Moscow."

"It's almost like the script was written specifically for them," said Rich.

"They sound delightful. I'll let you deal with them if they show up," said Devin. "Any news on the additional backup? You mentioned dipping into a mercenary pool?"

"I did," said Rich. "I probably should have worded it differently. We're talking about more of a closed, extremely well-vetted mercenary loop. Mercenaries we've hired before. The inbound crew has worked together extensively, and they bring a ton of useful skills to the table. We have a former Delta NCO, Marine sniper, Army Special Forces, and a Legionnaire commando. They jumped at the opportunity."

"And the pay," said Berg.

"Always the pay," said Rich. "But they cleared their schedule after I gave them a taste of the bigger picture. And they're connected to the patron that's underwriting most of this. She doesn't do business with scoundrels, and they don't want to lose her business. You don't have to worry about them."

"I'm feeling better about this," said Devin.

"You should," said Rich. "And if you can convince Shea to donate a few elite surveillance specialists from MINERVA, the deck will be stacked firmly in your favor."

"After a few hours in this room, we should be able to convince him to loan us half of the firm," said Berg.

"I'd settle for a sting operation at their Silicon Valley headquarters," said Devin.

"Whatever you do, don't tell Shea that on the ride over," said Berg.

Rich laughed. "Devin knows what he's doing."

"You better hope so," said Devin. "You're the one that put me in charge."

"I'm not worried," said Rich. "Between whatever you can pull off here and anything I manage to scrounge up in Moscow, we should be able to take this show prime time. Either hand it off to an organization with the resources and the will to burn the sleeper network to the ground—or do it ourselves."

"The *will* to act being the key term here," said Berg. "We'll have to weigh our options very carefully when the time comes to make a decision. Plenty of organizations with the resources. Not sure how many will have the will to do what needs to be done to fumigate the entire nest of sleepers. The government's first instinct will be to cover their ass. The scope of this security breach is a stunning embarrassment for our intelligence communities, and there's no way to fully zap the problem without creating a stir that is guaranteed to go public. They'll think long and hard about ways to make this go away without the public embarrassment. I don't see how. Backroom talks with the Russians will only result in the illusion of a successful fumigation. Putin would never give up his most strategically placed sleeper assets. He might recall a significant number of sleepers if provided a sizable incentive, but he'll keep his trump cards in place. The US will pay a steep price to inadequately neutralize a dire threat."

"Did you ever consider bottling up some of that overflowing optimism and selling it?" said Rich.

"Don't you have a private jet chartered by Mossad to catch?"

"Something like that," said Rich, readjusting his backpack. "See you on the other side of this thing."

"Watch yourself over there," said Berg. "If anything feels unusually off to you, at any time, pull the plug, run an exhaustive SDR, and get in touch with my contact immediately. He's made arrangements to hide you long enough for us to put together an extraction. The Israelis may or may not help, depending on the level of scrutiny you've attracted. Getting you inside Russia when nobody is looking is one thing. Getting you out when everybody is watching is another."

"Thank you. That's quite unexpected, and not at all necessary. Your contact has risked enough for us over the years," said Rich.

"He insisted," said Karl. "Retirement doesn't suit him very well. I know the feeling."

"You're preaching to the choir, my friend," said Rich, turning toward the open door behind him.

He stopped just outside of the apartment and poked his head back inside, scanning the room behind them before speaking.

"You and Ms. Young. I see a bright future. Don't screw it up," he whispered, and disappeared.

Devin glanced over his shoulder, relieved to find the kitchen empty. He didn't think she'd be bothered by Rich's comment, but it was impossible to say. They'd kept their connection as low profile as possible, but it was impossible to keep a secret when the entire team had pretty much spent most of the past two weeks either crammed into this apartment, stuffed into SUVs, or split between a few motel rooms.

And it wasn't like their relationship was serious. Something had bubbled up between them. More than a rekindled friendship. Definitely outside of the friend zone. Beyond that, neither of them really knew what to call it or how to describe it—and they weren't in a hurry. They had agreed to sideline "this thing" until the storm his mother unleashed had passed. He looked at Berg, who shrugged.

"I agree with his assessment, but two lifelong bachelors-slash-work-aholics are the last people you should turn to for relationship advice."

"I'll take it with a grain of salt then," said Devin.

"Or ignore it entirely—for now," said Berg. "We have a long way to go before any of our lives return to anything resembling normal."

"First things first," said Devin.

PART TWO

CHAPTER 9

It shouldn't be long now. Based on new information provided by Pichugin, Orlov had confidently narrowed his search block to a third of its previous area. The same credit card used by one of Farrington's associates at the rental car agency in Nashville had been swiped at Sonny's Trattoria—just two blocks from the Mediterranean restaurant where he'd eaten lunch with Lashev. On the very same day. His targets were close, and it was only a matter of time before one of them crossed paths with his network of spotters.

While it remained entirely possible that whoever used the credit card had driven clear across town to dine or pick up food at Sonny's, he strongly suspected they hadn't ranged too far from home. *Home* in this case being the apartment Pichugin so desperately wanted him to sanitize. After documenting any files found on-site—if practical. Orlov didn't see that happening, given the stiff resistance Farrington's people would undoubtedly offer upon his arrival at the target location.

They'd be lucky to neutralize the opposition before the police arrived. Even destroying the documents would be a tall order, most likely requiring them to torch the apartment and run, in order to avoid a messy encounter with law enforcement. Photographing files and extracting any computer gear? Not without punching a bloody hole through the police response, which would be swift and sizable—likely including FBI agents.

The unprecedented multilocation shootout between Farrington's and Pichugin's people on the southeast side of Baltimore had spawned a joint local-federal task force. His boss didn't seem to care one way or the other, but Orlov generally understood the enhanced capabilities a federal response team typically brought to the table. Better training and weapons. Nothing his people couldn't handle, but something to strongly consider. The main question being, How many operatives could he afford to lose to pull off a full mission sweep?

The most tempting and basic answer was *everyone but himself.* But it was never that simple. Sacrificing the team would put him out of business. Pichugin paid well. This contract represented the most lucrative opportunity he'd been handed in his career. But it wasn't retirement money. Far from it. Full payment would keep him afloat for a few years. Five years at most, if he stretched it. Not worth the everlasting professional damage he'd suffer throwing his team away to accomplish every item on his boss's wish list.

Then again, what did he care if he could permanently secure Pichugin's generous patronage by running the board on this one? Ultimately, money was all that mattered to most of the mercenaries on the market, including himself, and Pichugin had plenty to spread around. Everyone in the business understood this, which guaranteed that Orlov's well of potential operatives would never go dry. As long as he remained on his boss's good side. That was the big catch.

If he ever fell out of favor with Pichugin, his days as a mercenary team leader were over. He'd have to settle for security-detail work at the lowest oligarch tier, or heaven forbid, join a mercenary crew as a rank-and-file member. Just the thought of either demotion made his skin crawl. Unless a non-self-destructive opportunity to document the apartment's files presented itself, he'd stick with the primary objectives. Neutralize and sanitize—at any cost.

That said, Orlov had a plan to buy them some additional time. When the time came to strike Devin Gray's hideout, he'd initiate a sweeping, violent diversion on the opposite side of the city, with the hopes of drawing the bulk of the city's elite police response as far away from North Baltimore as possible.

Of course, the general success of the mission hinged on his ability to locate the target apartment, which first required him to spot a member of Devin Gray's capable entourage on the streets of North Baltimore. The shrinking of the search area, concurrent with the expansion of his resources, gave him hope. On top of that, Pichugin had sent him an unexpected resource—surveillance drones—and an experienced team to operate them. He was about to meet with the drone operators, along with Oleg Yefremoz, who would directly oversee them.

Orlov opened the SUV door and stepped onto the trash-littered sidewalk.

"Good luck," said Lashev, nodding from the driver's seat.

He shut the door without acknowledging the comment. Orlov wasn't in the mood for any of Lashev's bullshit right now. Nothing about this meeting would be pleasant. Oleg had barely spoken a word when Orlov passed along the new assignment. The seasoned mercenary had swallowed his pride and accepted the order without question. But holding your tongue over the phone was one thing. Keeping cool in person was another. He made his way to a basic but lively coffee shop a few storefronts down and stepped inside. Oleg got up from a booth in the back, leaving his two new friends. He met Orlov halfway, the two of them stopping out of earshot of the booth.

"So?" said Orlov.

"Sounds like they know what they're doing," said Oleg. "Pichugin isn't fucking around."

"Apparently not," said Orlov, before grasping Oleg's shoulder. "Sorry about this. I know it's not what you—"

"It's fine," said Oleg. "I understand the logic. You need a babysitter."

"*They* need a babysitter," said Orlov. "I see the merit in having aerial surveillance at our disposal. Especially in the city. I just can't have them rethinking their contract when we start killing people. Hiring them was a last-minute decision by Pichugin, which forces me to sideline my best operative to ensure that the idea doesn't backfire."

"Where did he find them?" said Oleg.

"Advertisement on the dark web."

Oleg grunted.

"I know," said Orlov. "All we can do is make the best of it. Pichugin understands this and stressed the disposable aspect of the situation, which is why I need you sitting on these guys. Hopefully, it won't come to that, but if there's any serious doubts—"

"Got it," said Oleg. "I assume we'll implement a strict compartmentalization of operational information and orders?"

"As strict as possible. All communication with the team will flow through you, so you can filter accordingly. The less they know about us and the overall mission, the better," said Orlov. "My plan is to station you and the drone team on the highest rooftop feasible, within the search area, so the team can maintain line-of-sight control of the drone."

"How long will we be up there?" said Oleg.

"As long as it takes," said Orlov.

"I meant how long each day?"

"Twenty-four hours," said Orlov.

"This keeps getting better," said Oleg. "What about resupply?"

"The resupply situation will depend on where you're located. If we can rent a space with easy rooftop access, problem solved. You can stock up and wait in comfort," said Orlov. "If we're forced to improvise, plan on taking enough food and water for several days."

"By improvise, you mean scale the side of a building and squat on the roof," said Oleg.

"Something like that. So it might not be a bad idea to buy a few low-profile tents to shelter from the rain."

"And the sun," muttered Oleg.

"Better than kicking the door in at the target apartment. Not everyone will walk away from that one," said Orlov. "Count your blessings. Dead men don't collect payment."

Oleg shrugged. "I guess. Want to meet your drone team?"

Orlov glanced over Oleg's shoulder, making eye contact with the two thirtysomething, scruffy-on-purpose-looking guys seated in the booth. One with sandy blond hair and beard. The other dark brown.

"A couple quick words."

He followed the mercenary to the back of the coffee shop and slid into the booth next to him. The blond drone guy offered a handshake across the table. Orlov stared at the extended hand until the man awkwardly withdrew it.

"I'm Josh. This is—"

"No names and no questions about anything other than the drone job you're being paid to do," he said, before nodding at Oleg. "You do exactly what my associate here tells you to do. Nothing more. Nothing less. I apologize if this comes across as rude, but the years have taught me that the less interaction between contractors, the better—for everyone. Keep it to business. Okay?"

"Sure," grumbled the man who had tried to introduce himself.

His partner shrugged, trying to suppress an irked face. "Works for me."

"Good. We're on the same page," said Orlov. "What kind of drone capability do you bring to the table? My employer didn't provide details. Like me, he's a man of few words."

"Two RQ-11 Raven Bs with multiple battery packs and rapid-recharge capability for continuous aerial coverage. Electro-optical and infrared sensor gives you day and night surveillance. Whisper enabled for quieter runs over the target. We can mark and automatically track multiple targets."

"At night?" said Orlov, testing them.

"You've done your homework," said the blond operator, relaxing a little. "We had some custom software added to the ground control unit's operating system, which gives us a limited ability to automatically track targets at night. The catch is that the track can be easily broken. If the target mixes with a crowd or vanishes behind an obstacle for more than a few seconds, we have to manually reacquire. It hasn't been a problem for us."

"That's good to hear," said Orlov. "This will be an on-demand mission, since we obviously can't have your drone flying around the city for hours at a time. I'll need the drone airborne at a moment's notice to track a positive or probable ID."

"Not a problem. We can launch the drone in the time it takes one of us to flip two switches and throw it into the air."

Orlov suddenly clapped his hands together, startling the drone guys.

"Then we're set. Do what my guy here says, and you're looking at an easy payday."

"I like the sound of that," said the dark-haired guy, drawing a quick, reproachful look from his colleague.

He slid out of the sticky booth. "They're all yours."

"Sure you don't want to stick around for a cup of coffee?" said Oleg.

"Very sure," said Orlov. "I need to work on your base of operations."

"Hopefully I won't need to visit a sporting goods store anytime soon," said Oleg, picking up one of the menus on the table.

"If I can't figure something out by this afternoon, stock up on sunscreen."

CHAPTER 10

Marnie grabbed one of the camping chairs stacked just inside "the vault" and entered the front of the apartment. She unfolded the chair and set it at the kitchen table across from Devin and Scott Daly, who barely looked up from the laptop in front of them.

"Coffee or anything while I'm up?" she said, and they both shook their heads.

She stepped into the kitchen. "Rico?"

"I'd love one of those Nespressos. Thank you for offering," he said, emphasizing the *thank you*.

"If you wanted a coffee, all you had to do was ask," said Scott.

"What? I didn't say anything," said Melendez, before winking at Marnie.

"Uh-huh," said Scott.

Melendez sat against the wall next to the leftmost front window, a suppressed M4 rifle in his lap. Everyone except Berg, Gupta, and Graves took a four-hour shift by the windows. Instead, they watched the extensive network of camera feeds covering the street, serving as the apartment's early warning system. If they detected a threat, whoever had "window duty" would be the first line of defense, engaging targets on the street to buy the rest of the team time to respond.

From what she gathered, the response would be brutally lethal. Explosives formed the backbone of their defense, augmented by expert shooters—from inside the apartment and out. A second team waited a few minutes away, stationed in a Motel 6 just north of the Route

40 bypass. Four seasoned operators ready to pounce at a moment's notice—the motley crew of mercenaries Farrington had miraculously arranged at the last minute. They'd take Pichugin's force by surprise, hitting them from multiple directions on the street.

That was the plan, at least. The big question was whether they'd show up in time. Depending on what Pichugin threw at them, three to five minutes might not be fast enough, especially if the Russians managed to penetrate the building before reinforcements arrived. Once inside, Pichugin's assassins would have hardened cover from an external attack, allowing them to focus most of their energy on breaching Helen's apartment—which brought up a critical question.

How the hell would they escape from the apartment if Pichugin's people controlled the ground floor? She still hadn't pried a clear answer out of Scott regarding his plan to evacuate the apartment if they could no longer defend it. Starting out on the third floor didn't leave them with a lot of solid options. Or any, from what Marnie could tell. Blazing a hole through a small army of Russian mercenaries didn't sound like a good solution. But it appeared to be the only way they could get out of here once surrounded, unless she had missed something. A conversation for another time—hopefully soon.

She placed one of the paper cups under the Nespresso's dispenser and paused.

"Espresso or a cappuccino?" she said.

"Whatever Scott will allow," said Melendez.

Scott grinned and shook his head. "See what I put up with? Cappuccino."

Marnie pressed the right combination of buttons and approached the table, putting a hand on Devin's shoulder. He placed his hand over hers.

"Looks like a long drive ahead of you," she said. "Is that Rehoboth Beach?"

"Broadkill Beach, Delaware. Just a little north of Rehoboth," said Devin. "Three hours for me. Two hours—maybe longer with traffic—for Shea."

"Six-hour round trip," she said. "That's a long morning."

"That's what I said," said Scott.

"We have to assume Pichugin has upped his game and thrown more resources into finding us. If it were me, I'd watch the comings and goings of MINERVA as closely as possible. With our families hidden away, MINERVA is their only obvious link to this group. That said, Pichugin can't watch everyone, and Shea will very likely pull the same kind of trick he used to bring me to MINERVA. Unless Pichugin has a source inside MINERVA, which doesn't appear to be the case, it'll look like Shea arrived early for work, like usual, and put in another long day."

"If Pichugin's people somehow start to suspect that he's up to something, they might grab him," said Marnie. "Like you said, they don't have many leads to work with at this point—and they have to be getting desperate. We have to assume that Pichugin can identify the bigger players at MINERVA."

"She has a good point," said Scott. "If they pick up Shea, we should expect visitors sooner than later."

"It's always a possibility, but Shea is one of a dozen operational team leaders," said Devin. "Based on what we've run up against in the past, it doesn't appear they have the resources to closely surveil even a fraction of that many targets. And they can't afford to take a stab in the dark. One miss and MINERVA goes on red alert. I feel comfortable saying that the risk of Pichugin grabbing Shea is close to zero."

"But not zero," said Marnie.

"True. It'll never be zero," said Devin. "For any of us—at any time. Not with the stakes this high for them."

"Which is why I'm sending Gilly to tail you by about five minutes. Consider it an insurance policy. If you detect anything during your SDR, give him a call," said Scott, handing Devin a note card with a number on it. "He'll break off and head back once you've made contact with Shea."

"Just make sure he doesn't follow me off Route 1," said Devin. "I wouldn't be surprised if Shea positions pickets on the back roads leading to the meetup location. We don't want to spook him."

"I'll keep him on Route 1," said Scott.

"Are you sure I can't keep you company on the ride out?" said Marnie. "You could drop me off on Route 1 near your destination, and I'll hitch a ride back with Gilly."

"It would be nice to have the company," said Devin. "But—"

"I don't recommend it," said Berg, appearing in the doorway to the vault.

"Which is what I was about to say," said Devin. "It's risky enough for one of us to be out and about. Two at the same time—together—is just inviting trouble."

"You're probably right," said Marnie.

The Nespresso machine beeped, indicating the drink was ready. She left the table for a moment to deliver the steaming hot cup of coffee to Melendez, who took a cautious sip.

"Thank you," he said, raising the cup in a toast. "This hits the spot."

"My pleasure," she said, peeking through the nearest window.

Berg made his way over to the coffee maker as she returned to the kitchen.

"We're going to need more Nespresso capsules," he said.

"I can swing by a Target or something with Shea," said Devin. "I had planned on running at least one countersurveillance stop on the way back."

Berg checked his watch. "You better get rolling, if we're going to give Shea enough time to look through Helen's files and ask questions. A six-hour round trip puts you back here around noon. To Marnie's point, on the outside chance Pichugin's people are watching Shea's comings and goings, we don't want to give them any reason to single him out.

He needs to be driving out of MINERVA's parking garage no later than seven tonight."

Devin got up from the table and grabbed the small dark-blue mini-backpack next to his chair.

"Got everything?" said Marnie.

"Sat phone. Burner cell. A few preloaded credit cards. Cash. Binoculars. Pistol. Spare mags. Snack bars. Water bottle. Quick change of clothes. Ball cap. Insurance policy," said Devin, placing Scott's note card in the front zip pocket. "Hopefully I won't need anything beyond the sat phone and some cash for breakfast."

"Let's hope," said Marnie. "Walk you out?"

"I wouldn't have it any other way," said Devin, turning for the door. "This might be the last time you see me."

She couldn't tell if he was mocking her or just making a joke in general about the potential threat they all faced. Her face must have betrayed the confusion.

"I didn't mean that to sound patronizing or flippant," said Devin.

"That's not how I took it," she said.

"Good," he said, looking genuinely relieved. "Walk me all the way to my car? That way we both get nabbed."

She shook her head.

"Jesus. I'm really digging a hole here," said Devin. "Jokes were never my strong suit."

"I think it has more to do with you being flustered," said Berg.

Devin turned a few shades redder, while appearing to struggle with what she assumed was a retort that would only make things worse for him. She grabbed his hand and pulled him toward the front door.

"I think we'll survive a few blocks on the mean streets of Baltimore," said Marnie.

CHAPTER 11

Felix Orlov interrupted Ksenia's sighting report when she started to drift away from the facts. He had no interest in her theories at this point. Theories didn't find targets. Relevant data did. Information that narrowed his search was the only currency he would accept right now.

"Just send me the digital file," he said.

"You should already have it," she said.

Orlov checked his laptop, immediately finding the file she'd uploaded to the secure digital drop box. He opened the file and examined the images she'd chosen to send him. At first glance, the woman captured on camera didn't bear the striking resemblance to Marnie Young that Ksenia had conveyed. Running shoes. Gray sweatpants. Oversize blue T-shirt. Orioles ball cap. It took him several seconds of sifting through the multiple images to see why she had drawn Ksenia's attention.

Blonde hair in a ponytail sticking out of the back of the ball cap. Young was blonde. But that was only part of why Ksenia had flagged her. A small part. The Marine Corps emblem on the left front thigh of her sweatpants had sealed the deal.

"I see what you mean," said Orlov.

Then again, one pair of Marine Corps sweatpants in an area housing a few hundred thousand people wasn't a sure thing. Neither was the blonde hair. He'd assumed from the beginning that all his targets had changed their outward appearances. A quick do-it-yourself haircut and hair coloring was one of the easiest and most effective ways to throw off a search.

Under normal circumstances, he would divert only a portion of his surveillance resources to prosecute the lead, while maintaining his team's presence throughout the entire search area—but there was nothing normal about the current operation. With his future in the mercenary business at stake, not to mention his life, Orlov didn't see any other choice but to take a calculated gamble and focus on the new lead.

He'd move the search grid north to Preston Street and east to Charles, cutting his current search grid in half. Ten square city blocks, give or take. A slightly more reasonable task, given what he had to work with. Twenty-four operatives. Sixteen of them parked at strategically selected locations—coffee shops, major intersections, popular take-out restaurants—and five roving vehicles equipped with dual-sided video cameras. Ksenia's digital footage had been taken from one of those cameras.

He'd implemented the camera tactic after previously assessing the futility of trying to live-spot their targets on the move. His operatives could only process a fraction of the street scene moving by them at the minimum speeds required to blend into traffic. The camera caught everything. Problem solved. But they still had to review the captured video of two simultaneous camera feeds, which unearthed another hitch in the system.

Ksenia and the rest of the reviewers alternated watching five-minute stretches of video from each of the two cameras at seventy-five percent speed so they didn't miss anything. Five minutes instantly turned into six and a half minutes. Rewatching potential target hits added a few more minutes to the process. Per camera feed. Every five minutes of dual feed taken by each car took a minimum of twenty minutes to review.

Ksenia had already fallen close to an hour and a half behind this morning, when she first identified a possible match to Marnie Young.

The lead was more than just stale by the time he saw the images; it had dried up and blown away in the wind. Marnie Young, or whoever they had captured on video, could be anywhere inside a hundred-mile radius of Baltimore right now—but his gut told him she was close. Within easy walking distance of where she had been spotted. Lashev craned his head over to take a look at the screen.

"You think it's Young?" said Lashev.

"Watch the road," said Orlov, zooming the image.

He opened the target-identification file on his laptop and selected Marnie Young, comparing her most-recent photos to the digital images sent by Ksenia. None of them jumped out and screamed "match," nor did any of them eliminate the possibility. The Marine Corps sweatpants bumped up the probability, but why the hell would she be out walking at 6:30 in the morning? A quick look at Google Maps told him she had been headed north when photographed, away from any nearby coffee shops or breakfast joints.

It didn't make a lot of sense. Why expose yourself to possible detection for no reason? Then again, from their perspective, a quick stroll through an obscure neighborhood probably didn't register as dangerous, especially if you had no reason to suspect or assume that your hunters had so rapidly and drastically narrowed their search area. And given the recent nearby credit card hit, it didn't appear that his targets considered a quick trip to grab takeout to be risky.

Without a doubt, they would be taking precautions. He didn't expect to find them all gathered in front of a window at a packed restaurant or taking in an evening baseball game, but without knowing how far the net had tightened around them over the past several days, it was fair to assume they'd continue to venture outside, where his people would be watching for them.

Once they were spotted, Orlov now intended to exclusively use the drones to track his targets directly to Helen Gray's apartment. He strongly suspected the apartment was close. A big assumption, but why else would his quarry have stuck around? After the messy shootout on the other side of the city, any black ops team worth their salt would have put as much distance between themselves and Baltimore as possible.

Instead, they'd effectively returned to the scene of the crime a little more than a week later. Hardly enough time for things to cool off. This told Orlov they didn't have a choice in the matter. That they had something more important to protect than themselves. The big secret Pichugin wanted erased. Gray's apartment.

"Kind of looks like her," said Lashev, after stealing another glance.

"I'd say there's a sixty-five percent chance," said Orlov.

"Sounds like a scientific calculation."

"Hardly," said Orlov. "Find us the nearest coffee shop. I need an espresso and a table. We need to revamp our entire surveillance plan. With the search area cut in half, we'll have to be extremely careful not to tip our hand."

CHAPTER 12

Devin pulled into the Amtrak parking lot next to Baltimore Penn Station and lowered his window to take a ticket. He'd picked the lot over street parking based on the same factor that had influenced his every decision this morning. Counterintelligence value—compliments of Shea.

"Ready?" he said, reaching for the half-exposed ticket in the machine next to his window.

Brendan Shea flipped his sun visor down and opened the mirror, making a few quick adjustments to the disguise he'd donned before they'd reached the outskirts of Baltimore. A surprisingly realistic, unkempt brownish-gray beard held in place by elastic bands hidden by a well-worn, faded green John Deere hat. These final touches had completed the outfit he'd worn to the beach meetup. Oversize, threadbare jeans, a ripped black AC/DC T-shirt, and an olive drab Vietnam-era Army jacket. The perfect camouflage for melting into North Baltimore's omnipresent panhandling crowd. Shea wasn't taking any chances.

Devin had initially assumed that the ruse was purely a self-preservation measure in the unlikely event things went south on them in the city. An incorrect notion quickly corrected by Shea, who'd told him upon first donning the disguise that the primary reason for altering his identity was to keep him from being connected to Devin, which ultimately protected MINERVA's client—DEVTEK.

It all made sense, even before Shea had begun to explain. If Devin's recent work on his mother's conspiracy couldn't be linked to

MINERVA, Shea could still act on DEVTEK's behalf. Shea could slip away, if things went sidewise, and warn his client of the potential danger lurking in the form of a sleeper agent inside or outside of the company. He had to admire the guy's dedication to the firm.

Shea flipped the visor back into place and opened the car door. "How long should we give it?"

"The route felt clean, but you know, right?" said Devin, taking the ticket.

"Right."

"I'll pass you at the first street corner west of here—in fifteen minutes. That should be more than enough time to shake out any surveillance that followed us here. They won't be able to resist taking a closer look."

"See you in fifteen," said Shea, slipping out of the car with a half-stuffed, light-brown canvas backpack.

By the time Devin turned into the first row to start his search for an open parking space, Shea had taken a seat against the wrought iron fence along the sidewalk next to the lot's entrance—backpack in his lap. Only a trained professional, closely observing his car through binoculars, would have noticed the slick transition, which was why Devin had sped up a few blocks back and turned into the parking lot without warning. Shea would have melted into the streetscape long before a tail could have moved into position to watch the car. Just another drifter taking up sidewalk real estate—same as the dozen or more they had passed since getting off the interstate.

Devin coasted the parking lot for a few minutes before settling on a spot one row from the rear of the lot. He backed into the space, Penn Station's formidable concrete facade looming in the rearview and side mirrors. Devin passed the next ten minutes scanning the streets with a pair of compact binoculars. Nothing grabbed his attention. The flow of cars along adjacent streets remained steady. No slow movers. No lingering pedestrians. Nobody peeking around the corners of buildings.

Every parked car in sight appeared empty. Five vehicles had entered the parking lot in the fifteen minutes he waited, their luggage-dragging passengers wasting no time vacating the area.

From a professional standpoint, he felt good about their situation. He'd taken every countersurveillance precaution possible this morning. Unfortunately, every trip outside his mother's apartment posed a risk. They had no intelligence regarding Pichugin's efforts to find them, and no true idea if they had cleanly escaped the Ozarks.

They were effectively blind when it came to the Russians, forced to operate under the assumption that the billionaire oligarch had significant US intelligence and law enforcement sleeper assets at his disposal. An assumption that kept them mostly confined to the apartment and underscored the urgent need to catalog Helen's findings and put Baltimore behind them. One thing was certain. The longer they stayed in one place, the shorter their odds of being discovered by the Russians. Time would never be on their side.

Devin donned an unbranded, olive drab ball cap and a pair of throwaway sunglasses before getting out of the car. A crude but surprisingly effective disguise. He used to carry at least three different hats, a fake mustache or two, and a variety of eyewear while tailing known or suspected espionage officers during his FBI years.

Street countersurveillance training concentrated on the quickest and easiest ways to identify a tail—almost all of them focused on the head and face. A sizable, well-trained surveillance team would frequently rotate multiple operatives in and out of the surveillance effort, always wearing a different disguise, to minimize the chance of detection. The same tactic was regularly and simultaneously employed by their targets, who would duck in and out of stores or restaurants, emerging moments or minutes later looking different. A perpetual game of hide-and-seek in plain sight.

For the next several blocks, Devin and Shea would assume the role of *target*, taking all the necessary street-level precautions to ensure an undetected arrival at his mother's apartment. He made his way to the back of the parking lot and scaled the wobbly chain-link fence that separated the lot from Penn Station's northernmost tracks. After carefully lowering himself onto the narrow, flat patch of scrub and dirt just beyond the fence, he took a moment to test the ground beneath him.

One wrong step and he'd slide down a steep embankment to the outermost track, undoubtedly drawing the concentrated attention of every passenger on the platform. Then he'd have to figure out a way to get back onto the streets—which looked like it would involve crossing several tracks while dodging a few slow-moving trains, climbing one of the platforms, and exiting through Penn Station—without getting arrested. Devin kept one hand on the fence as he slowly plodded through the bushes toward the end of the chain-link fence.

He pushed through a dense row of bushes just past the fence and joined the light pedestrian traffic headed north on Charles Street. A few people nearby gave him a funny look when he emerged from nowhere, but quickly went back to minding their own business. Shea was waiting for him half a block away at the corner of Charles and Greenway. Less than a minute later, Devin passed him headed north, the two of them ignoring each other. They had already worked out their approach to the apartment.

Devin stopped in front of a tapas restaurant a block up the street and pretended to check out the menu, scanning the sidewalk behind him with his peripheral vision. Empty. Shea had already crossed the street, staying about a half block behind. A few cars passed, keeping their speed and clearing the area. The mostly quiet streets made it nearly impossible to conduct covert, ground-level surveillance. No crowds to blend into. No way to inconspicuously double-park. Basically, no way to follow Devin or Shea without being detected. He didn't see any need to drag this out any further.

He turned north and continued to Lafayette Avenue, where he turned east. His mother's apartment sat about two and a half blocks away, down this road. Devin stayed on Lafayette until he reached Calvert Street, where he took a short detour through a community garden to reach an alleyway that wound its way to the apartment. He paused for a minute just inside the alley to listen and observe.

Nothing but the staccato chirping of birds, humming of air conditioners, and distant thrum of traffic on North Avenue. Even Shea was nowhere to be seen—by design. According to their prearranged plan, Shea would have continued north on Charles until McCallister, the first street past Lafayette, where he'd take a right and walk parallel to his mother's street. He'd approach the alleyway from the east, opposite of Devin. Overkill in the grand scheme of things, but the stakes were too high to skimp on countersurveillance tricks.

Devin reached the narrow, one-vehicle gravel driveway behind his mother's apartment a few minutes later. Marnie immediately opened the door at the top of a crumbling concrete stoop. She wore an olive drab, low-profile plate carrier over a black T-shirt, blue jeans, and a pair of dark-brown combat-style boots. The Scorpion EVO 3 submachine gun from his mother's gun vault hung from a single-point sling attached to the plate carrier. She scanned the alleyway for a few seconds before stepping onto the stoop.

"Anyone follow me?" he said.

"Not that G and G could tell," she said. "They saw Shea continue up Charles Street. Nobody followed him, either."

Graves and Gupta had installed two cameras on the street in front of his mother's apartment, one facing in each direction. A second pair of cameras watched the east and west alley approaches. A fully charged quadcopter drone sat flip-of-a-switch-ready on the rooftop to investigate the streets outside of camera view—if something suspicious drew their attention.

"Good. He should be here shortly," said Devin, taking a seat on the steps. "I'll wait around so he sees a familiar face."

"I'll keep you company," said Marnie, settling in next to him. "How was the trip?"

"Long and boring," he said, wanting to add *without you*. "Shea's not much of a talker."

"I imagine we won't be able to shut him up after he gets a close-up look at your mother's work," said Marnie.

"I don't know. He's still pretty skeptical about the whole thing," said Devin. "His default mode is to protect MINERVA and the firm's clients. He's put up quite a shield."

"I don't blame him. Biting off on your mother's conspiracy puts the firm's reputation and his own career on the line," said Marnie. "The more cynical at first, the better. When he's finally had a chance to fully digest what your mother spent the past decade assembling, the stronger he'll feel about throwing MINERVA's support behind us."

"Behind helping DEVTEK," said Devin.

"Same thing," she said. "Ultimately."

"The safest and surest thing for him to do would be to take this information back to MINERVA and forget about us. Figure out a way to insulate DEVTEK from the sleeper network and let someone else fight the rest of the war," said Devin. "That's what I'd do."

"But that's not what you did," said Marnie, squeezing his hand. "You could have left him in Berg's very capable hands and walked away, but you didn't."

"I couldn't exactly let my mother's—"

"That's only part of it. No doubt an important part for you, but this is so much bigger," she said. "Like you. Like me. Like Berg and his team of mercenaries. Shea won't be able to turn his back on this any more than the rest of us."

He interlaced his fingers between hers and put his head on her shoulder. "I hope you're right. We're going to need all the help we can get to drive a stake through the heart of this thing."

The radio clipped to Marnie's vest squawked. *"Shea just entered the alley off Barclay."*

He let go of her hand so she could answer the radio.

"Copy that. We're standing by to receive him," she said, before patting Devin on the shoulder. "I guess we're about to find out if Shea's the real deal or if he's just using us."

"I guess we are," said Devin.

CHAPTER 13

Felix Orlov listened closely to the back-and-forth chatter over the radio. Two of the mobile teams had been arguing about a homeless guy for the past minute, jamming the satellite radio net. He waited for a brief pause in the bickering to jump into the conversation.

"This is Orlov. Everyone shut the fuck up!" he said, before letting go of the button.

There was no point in trying to talk on the net if the two teams were still trying to get the last word in. When the radio remained quiet for a few seconds, he continued: "Are we looking at a possible target sighting?"

"That's what we're debating," said Maxim, Dmitry Garin's second-in-command.

Orlov and Garin had agreed to put him in charge of coordinating mobile surveillance, which basically consisted of ten low-budget rental cars rotating through the search area. The goal was to cover every street a few times per hour, without any one vehicle driving down the same street more than once every two-hour rotation. At the end of each rotation, the drivers switched vehicles and changed their personal appearances with rudimentary disguises. Far easier said than done, particularly with this motley crew.

"You're clogging up a vital coordination net," said Orlov. "Hash out your disagreements on one of our undesignated channels, or contact me on the priority channel if it's that important. Are we clear?"

"Clear," said Maxim.

"Understood," said Iskra Lavrov.

"Good," said Orlov. "Now what's the big deal with this vagrant?"

"The guy just vanished," said Maxim.

"And?" said Orlov.

"He was walking south on Guilford Avenue, between McCallister and Lafayette, when we passed him. I sent Iskra to take a look. She was less than a minute away. The guy was gone by the time she cruised up Guilford."

Iskra responded before Orlov could press the transmit button.

"We saw him headed north on Charles Street about ten minutes earlier," she said. "He didn't raise any alarms. Just some bum out for a walk."

"Then he just disappears?" said Maxim.

"Maybe he lives nearby," said Iskra.

"Wait. You said he was homeless," said Orlov. "What made the two of you originally assume he was homeless?"

"When I said *he lives nearby*," she said, "I meant that he probably camps out somewhere in that area. There's a community garden up there. A park. Not to mention a massive cemetery."

"But he looks homeless?" said Orlov.

"Yeah," answered Maxim. "I'd guess he was some kind of down-and-out veteran. Army jacket. Beat-up backpack. Worn-as-shit hat. Walked with a limp. No way he's renting an apartment anywhere around here. Some of the streets are a bit run down, but overall, it's on the up and up. And most of the homeless people seem to congregate where there's foot traffic. The streets up there are dead during the day."

"What kind of hat?" said Dmitry Garin.

Garin hadn't said a word over the radio since his team joined the effort. The squat, stoic mercenary made him nervous. A man of few words. Orlov had a hard time reading him.

"Green in the front. Light colored in the back," said Iskra.

"John Deere?" said Garin.

"I'm not familiar with the term," she said.

"The front was solid green and the back was a light mesh fabric? Yes?" said Garin.

"I think so," she said. "Do you want me to check the video feed?"

"Do it fast. Both of you. Just send me the best-quality still image you can isolate in the next thirty seconds," said Garin. "Orlov?"

"Yes?" said Orlov, his curiosity piqued.

"I'm pretty sure I saw this guy sitting in front of the Amtrak parking lot entrance on Greenway Avenue about thirty minutes ago," said Garin.

"So?"

"I grabbed a coffee at a café right across the street from that parking lot, and he wasn't there when I arrived," said Garin. "But he was there when I left."

Orlov did the math. The timing of the team's sightings several blocks north of the train station suggested that the guy hadn't stayed in front of the parking lot very long.

"You said he was sitting?" said Orlov. "Did he have a cardboard sign? Was he begging?"

"No sign. No cup for spare change. He just sat there, cross-legged, with a backpack in his lap," said Garin. "I didn't think anything of it at the time, but in light of the odd timing—my gut says to look for this guy. Just to be sure."

The circumstances surrounding this random "homeless" guy's exceedingly short stay indeed sounded strange, but why would Gray or any of Berg's people be milling around the area, dressed as hobos? What would be the purpose? And why hadn't any of the seasoned mercenaries involved in the conversation brought up these obvious questions? Fuck it. None of that mattered.

"Just send me all the video feed you have on this guy. I'll check it out," said Orlov. "And get everyone out of that neighborhood until further notice. Just in case there's more to this than a homeless guy ducking into an alleyway to take a piss."

A long pause ensued, suggesting that his last sentence may have rankled them.

"I just drove back down Guilford," said Maxim. "Nobody pissing in any of the alleys. He's gone."

"What the fuck?" said Iskra.

That was an understatement. Breaking surveillance protocol was tantamount to disobeying an order. He'd contact Garin to discuss Maxim's future on the team the moment he finished analyzing the homeless-guy video feeds.

"Send me the full video of each recorded encounter with this homeless guy," said Orlov. "And stay the fuck away from that neighborhood! Out."

His satellite phone buzzed a moment later, Garin hoping to smooth things over for Maxim. Orlov had done his homework. The two of them had worked together for close to a decade, building a very solid reputation as reliable mercenaries.

"One more fuckup like that, and he's gone. Period," said Orlov the moment he answered the call.

"Understood," said Garin. "I'll make sure he appreciates the second chance."

"Make it crystal clear. I don't care about the radio shit show between him and Iskra, but violating surveillance protocol is a different story."

"I agree," said Garin. "He let Iskra get under his skin."

"She has a way of doing that," said Orlov, his attention suddenly diverted to his laptop. "Hey. I'll call you back. I just got the video downloads."

"No need to call me back," said Garin. "I just wanted to let you know I'll square away Maxim."

"Okay. Good. I'll be in touch shortly," said Orlov.

"Want me to find us a nice coffee shop so you can spread out and focus?" said Lashev.

"Nice try," said Orlov, clicking on the encrypted app they used to send messages and share data.

They had been parked on the rooftop level of the West Oliver Parking Garage since sunrise, the sedan's air conditioner barely keeping up with the relentless midday summer sun. He was just as eager for a change of scenery as Lashev, but strategically, it didn't make sense to risk giving up this parking spot. Without leaving the car, they had a sweeping view of the Greenmount West neighborhood. The rooftops, at least. Better than sitting in a parking space along one of the streets all day, and about a thousand percent less conspicuous.

"The homeless-guy caper, huh?" said Lashev, nodding at his computer.

Orlov shrugged. "It's the most excitement we've had since we got to Baltimore."

"That's true," said Lashev.

"I'll get someone to bring us some coffee and lunch in a minute," said Orlov.

"You read my mind."

"Five references to food in less than an hour is kind of a dead give-away," said Orlov.

"I want to try some seafood," said Lashev.

"You're not stinking the car up with fish."

"I was thinking crab cakes. They're supposedly a big deal in Baltimore," said Lashev.

"Not in this neighborhood. And I don't need you trying new foods while we're stuck in this car," said Orlov. "Pizza. It's the same everywhere, and it won't mess with your stomach."

"It's not the same everywhere. The pizza here is crap," said Lashev.

"But we all agree it won't give you the shits, right?"

Lashev shook his head and laughed. "No argument there."

"I'm glad we can agree on something," said Orlov, the first of the images filling his laptop screen. "I'll order enough pizza for lunch and—hold on."

Interesting. He sifted through several still images, noting three things. First. The man indeed wore a John Deere hat. This established with reasonable certainty that the man Garin saw seated in front of the Amtrak parking lot was the same man wandering the neighborhoods north of the station. Second. His beard didn't look quite right for a homeless person. It was long and scraggly, but the color appeared a little too dark and uniform. No gray or sun-bleached streaks running through it.

A small detail in the grand scheme of things, but worth noting—particularly considering his third observation. The guy looked extremely alert. He could see it in the eyes. Not every homeless person was a glassy-eyed burnout nursing a cheap bottle of booze hidden in a crumpled brown bag, but there was something different about this guy. He studied each image closely, noticing more details supporting his suspicion.

The man's hands, the visible parts of his face, and the back of his neck appeared clean. Too clean for someone living on the streets. Same with the guy's clothing. Everything appeared well worn—threadbare in the knees and elbows, as one would expect, but nothing looked even remotely grimy or scuffed. In other words, the whole ensemble came across as a disguise. A damn good one on the surface, but not one that would survive excessive scrutiny by a man with his career and life on the line. He needed to find this guy.

It was entirely conceivable that they were all wrong, and he lived in the neighborhood. Rented a room on the cheap or shared a room with a few other down-on-their-luck types. Even Iskra's theory could be possible. The guy lived in a well-concealed tent or makeshift shelter somewhere nearby. Any of these ideas could explain the cleaner-than-expected condition of his clothing.

And maybe this was all just part of the guy's daily routine. He wandered around all morning until it got too hot to stay outside, and Garin had just happened to see him taking a short break on the sidewalk in front of the Amtrak parking lot before he headed back home. It sure made a lot more sense than thinking that one of Berg's people or Devin Gray had decided to dress like a bum and surveil the streets. He *really* needed to find this guy.

"Lunch might have to wait," said Orlov.

"How long?" said Lashev.

"I don't know! Why don't you go grab us a few sandwiches or something."

"From where?"

"Just figure it out," said Orlov. "I'll take anything but tuna salad. Same for you. I don't want to smell that shit in here."

"Okay. Okay," said Lashev, opening the door. "What kind of chips do you want?"

"I don't give a fuck! Just get out of here!" said Orlov.

Lashev slammed the door and stormed off, gesturing wildly to the light-blue sky. Orlov had already dialed Oleg by the time he disappeared in the stairwell.

"Sounds like you have your hands full," said Oleg.

"It's only going to get worse," said Orlov. "What do you think about this homeless guy?"

"Knowing far less than you or the teams on the ground, because I'm stuck up on a blistering-hot roof with no access to the street feeds, I'd say something's off."

Oleg and the two American drone operators had settled on an elementary school, about a half mile southwest of the search area, for their base of operations. Ideally, he would have liked them closer, but the Americans had pointed out that the school would be mostly empty during the summer, minimizing their chance of discovery, and the flat, expansive rooftop would allow them to recover the drones.

In other words, ordering a drone launch no longer represented the near-certain loss of the drone. The Americans had only two. Now Orlov could use them a little more liberally instead of reserving them for critical situations. He still had to be wary of the city's airspace restrictions. The operation of any type of drone within city limits was highly restricted, and any sustained drone operations were very likely to draw law enforcement attention. The last thing he needed.

What he had in mind right now was a short-duration flight to scope out the neighborhood in question, and hopefully shed some light on this homeless guy's whereabouts. A long shot for sure, but at the very least it would give the drone team a chance to shake off the cobwebs. Orlov guessed they didn't have extensive experience operating fixed-wing drones in heavily congested urban environments. Their website featured pictures of drones flying over open prairies and moderately forested terrain. They talked a good game. Time to make them walk the walk.

"Maybe. Maybe not. Impossible to say without more information," said Orlov.

"You want to use the drones to find the guy?"

"Am I that transparent?"

"Yes. But not in this case," said Oleg. "I had the same thought and prepped one of the drones for immediate launch. No harm in taking a quick look. If we find him, mystery solved. If not, we keep an eye out for him. He'll show up again if he's just a local. If he doesn't reappear by tomorrow at the latest, we'll know where to focus our search—and we'll have the aerial imagery to make it easier. I don't see a downside."

"Neither do I," said Orlov. "Launch the drone and patch the feed through to me."

"I'll have a link ready for you to access as soon as the drone is airborne and transmitting," said Oleg. "Make sure to use the high-speed antenna the Americans provided. They said the feed would be choppy without it."

"Yes. I'll, uhhh . . . I'll get it set up immediately," said Orlov, wishing he hadn't sent Lashev away so hastily.

Lashev had taken one look at the box with the antenna and said something like "no problem."

"The kit has two cords. One is the power cord, which comes with a cigarette lighter adapter. The other plugs into the ethernet port on your computer. I assume you know how to identify the ethernet port?"

"I have no fucking clue what an ethernet port is, but I'm sure I can figure it out," said Orlov.

"Yes. Easy enough," said Oleg. "Once the power and the ethernet cord are connected, all you have to do is click the link in the message I send you, and the system should do the rest."

Voices erupted in the background. Urgent-sounding voices.

"Okay. I'm being told that you have to download an application from the internet to interface with the antenna," said Oleg.

"Oleg. I'm losing my patience."

"I understand. Hold on."

Several seconds passed before Oleg returned. "No worries at all. I will send you a link to the application. Just click the link and approve the installation."

"And that's it?"

"Well. Not exactly. You'll have to restart your computer," said Oleg.

"Of course. Why wouldn't I?" said Orlov. "Put me on speakerphone."

"You're on speakerphone," said Oleg, his voice now sounding slightly distant.

"Ten minutes."

A long pause ensued. "Ten minutes?"

"If I'm not watching the drone feed in ten minutes, I'm driving over there to have a chat with our American friends," said Orlov.

The background voices sounded more urgent this time.

"They assure me it will work," said Oleg.

"Is one of them willing to stake their life on it?"

Complete silence in the background.

"Which one?" said Oleg.

"I won't know until I get there," said Orlov. "Whoever gives off the wrong vibe."

"I'm going to hand you off to one of the Americans, who says he can walk you through this in five minutes."

"Put him on."

Seven and a half minutes later, the drone feed was up and running.

CHAPTER 14

Marnie shut the alley door and engaged the dead bolt. She was about to slide the floor-mounted barricade plate into place when a heavily armed Emily Miralles appeared at the bottom of the ground-floor staircase. She slid past Devin and Shea without acknowledging them. All business. All the time.

"I'll take care of that," said Miralles.

"I think I can slide a piece of metal into place," said Marnie.

"I have no doubt you can, but it's my responsibility," she said. "Protocol."

Marnie handed the book-size reinforced metal plate to Emily without saying a word, and joined Devin at the stairs. Shea looked up and down the hall a few times, appearing to assess their security. Devin immediately took his cue.

"We added the floor plates recently."

Shea shrugged. "That buys you thirty seconds at most."

"Structural security on the ground level is designed to momentarily delay and stack inbound threats," he said. "We have a command-detonated Claymore hidden on the western side of the carport—aimed at the back door. The wire runs up the back of the apartment, behind the downspout."

"You guys don't fuck around," said Shea. "Stack and kill. What about the front?"

Devin pointed at the fifth stair. "We removed the riser and did a little carpentry work to fit a Claymore behind it. It's angled slightly downward to keep the collateral damage on the street to a minimum."

Shea backed up to the door and studied the staircase. "Tidy. I don't see a wire."

Devin nodded at Miralles, who was headed back up the hallway from the alley door.

"He approves of your work," said Devin.

"Great. I'll add that to my résumé," said Miralles, brushing past them and heading up the stairs.

She stopped halfway up the first flight. "I drilled a hole on the side of the tread to run the wire under the decorative stringer with putty."

"Nice touch," said Shea.

"Yep," said Miralles, before disappearing up the stairs.

"And that's the most in-depth conversation anyone's had with her since she arrived," said Marnie.

Shea chuckled. "Are they all like that?"

Marnie turned to Devin. "You didn't warn him?"

"Warn me about what?" said Shea.

"It's an interesting crew," said Devin. "Let's leave it at that."

"That's one way of putting it," mumbled Marnie.

Shea glanced at her before giving Devin a skeptical look.

"They grow on you," said Devin. "And they're good at what they do. The best from what I can tell."

"Based on my research into the events of the past few weeks—the Ozarks, the shootout in Fells Point, Indianapolis—I don't doubt it," said Shea.

"Given MINERVA's extensive reach, I assume you were able to dig a lot deeper into the fallout of each incident?" said Devin.

"Once I finish the due-diligence portion of my visit, I'd be happy to fill in any blanks, to the extent that I don't implicate any of our sources," said Shea.

"That would be helpful and very appreciated," said Devin. "We were hoping to draw enough attention to the Ozarks camp to get state law enforcement or a federal agency to take a look."

Shea raised an eyebrow. "I hate to be the bearer of bad news, but nobody's getting a look at the camp. The entire incident was contained. All authorities, local to federal, were barred access."

"By who?" said Marnie.

"The property owners—presumably," said Shea. "Local authorities never received a specific call for help from anyone on the property or any of the adjacent properties. Just reports of gunfire and an explosion called in from dozens of locations around the lake. The fire department was interested, but someone met them, and the police, at the property line, and assured them everything was under control. And that it was none of their business."

"I don't see how a helicopter crash is none of their business," said Marnie. "The explosion must have lit an entire acre of forest on fire."

"A Taney County Sheriff's Department helicopter confirmed that all of the major fires had either been extinguished or contained by three in the morning," said Shea. "No mention of helicopter-crash wreckage in any official reports that I could access."

"What about the helicopter I landed at the Diamond City Marina?" said Marnie.

"Locals reported hearing a helicopter close by, but none was found," said Shea.

Devin laughed. "We got so caught up in getting out of there alive, we overlooked the obvious. One call to the sheriff's department could have given them all the reason they needed to search the property."

"And a few wire snips on the helicopter could have turned it into a marina tourist attraction the next morning," said Marnie.

Shea shrugged. "If it's any consolation, I believe that everything you told me about the Ozarks is real. I just need to lay my eyes on the source of the information that set everything in motion."

"Then we're wasting time," said Devin. "Everything's on the third floor."

"What about the first and second floors?" said Shea.

"The apartments are empty for now," said Devin. "I sent the occupants away at the start of all of this. They've been well compensated—and sufficiently warned."

Shea examined the fifth step's riser, locating the wire under the stringer.

"I hope they have insurance."

"The building is insured, and the tenants are well covered," said Devin. "My mother made sure of that. She apparently knew all too well the risks involved. Had one hell of a life-insurance policy, too. I think she pretty much expected everything to end this way."

Shea dropped his stoic routine for a moment. "I can't imagine how tough this has been for you."

"Honestly. The past few weeks have been easy compared to the fifteen years I spent thinking my mother had left us to chase a delusion," said Devin. "But thank you."

Marnie touched his arm with the back of her hand for a moment. She wanted to say that she'd always be there for him, but now wasn't the time. Not until this whole mess was well past them. She had his back, and he had hers—and that was enough for now.

"Well. Let's take a look at what your mother's been working on for those fifteen years," said Shea.

Marnie followed them up the stairs to the third-floor landing, where Berg awaited them with a dour face.

"I think we might have a problem," he said abruptly without introducing himself.

CHAPTER 15

Devin went with a very abbreviated introduction. Berg hadn't looked this nervous since the moments preceding the Airbnb massacre in Fells Point.

"Karl, this is Brendan. Brendan. Karl," said Devin. "What's going on?"

Berg quickly shook Shea's hand. "Let's get to the bunker. I'll explain on the way."

"That bad?" said Devin, ushering Shea into the front room of the apartment.

"Probably nothing," said Berg, urging them toward the kitchen.

"Doesn't sound like *nothing*," said Shea.

Melendez stood next to the window, his suppressed rifle held in a low-ready position. His eyes scanned the street below. A stark contrast from this morning, when he'd lounged in the adjacent folding chair—coffee in hand—making jokes. Miralles stood just inside the front doorway, loading rifle magazines into the pouches on the plate-carrier vest she'd somehow donned in the short time it had taken them to walk up the stairs.

"Doesn't look like *nothing*, either," said Devin.

"Marnie. Would you mind sticking close to Emily? She might require some help momentarily," said Berg.

"Sure," said Marnie, shifting her submachine gun into a more accessible position before joining Miralles.

"What the fuck is going on, Karl?" said Devin. "And don't say *nothing*."

"We're not sure," said Karl.

Scott Daly emerged from the bunker a few seconds later, wearing body armor. He cradled a suppressed, short-barreled HK416 in one arm and carried an oversize duffel bag in the other. He nodded at Shea on his way to deliver "the bag" to Miralles. Devin knew that the bag contained explosives. A few Claymore mines. Grenades. Remotely detonatable blocks of C-4. Something had spooked the team into a full defensive posture.

"I'll be right back," said Daly as he passed Devin.

"This looks a whole lot like something," muttered Devin.

They slipped into the bunker moments after Daly cleared the doorway, Berg heading straight for Graves and Gupta at the desk in the middle of the room. Devin stayed with Shea, who stopped in his tracks a few feet into the room.

"Holy shit," said Shea—his eyes fixed on the "conspiracy wall."

"Yeah. Digital pictures don't do it any justice," said Devin.

"They really don't," said Shea, before turning his head to take in the bookshelves filled with binders. "Incredible. This is thousands of hours of work."

"Tens of thousands, when you consider the travel necessary to build each dossier," said Devin.

"Devin," said Berg, standing behind Graves and Gupta at the team's makeshift command-and-control center. "I need your attention here for now."

"Sorry," said Devin, before heading over. "What are we looking at? Why the red alert?"

Graves answered: "We had a double hit on the same vehicle, confirmed by both of our east-facing cameras. The first instance occurred while our guest was on Guilford, between McAllister and Lafayette. A gray hatchback driving north to south."

"I remember the vehicle," said Shea. "I didn't get a look at the passengers because it approached me from behind."

"The second time occurred about three and a half minutes later. South to north. Same two passengers, and they were most definitely paying close attention to Lafayette Avenue and our alley. White guys."

"Any unusual chatter?" said Devin. "Satcom bursts?"

"Nothing that stands out," said Gupta. "But this is a tough intercept environment for line-of-sight communications."

"Right," said Devin, turning to Shea. "Any chance anyone saw you go down the alley?"

"If someone were hiding in a parked car or an apartment a few blocks in either direction on Guilford, I can't say with certainty that I would have detected them," said Shea. "But Guilford and any street within view of the alleyway entrance was empty of vehicle traffic when I made my move."

"And nothing passed by the alley in either direction before Shea entered the apartment," said Graves.

"Can you bring up some imagery of the passengers?" said Devin. "Zoom in as tight as possible without going blurry."

The first image filled one of the screens in front of them. Devin immediately placed his finger on the screen.

"Never mind the faces," he said. "What's that in the back seat?"

"Shit," said Berg the moment the image shifted and zoomed in a little farther.

"Dashcams mounted to the rear-side windows," said Devin.

"One on each side," said Shea. "From the look of it."

"A surveillance team going in for a second look," said Berg.

"Nearly four minutes later?" said Devin.

"Maybe they were trying not to be too obvious," said Gupta.

Devin glanced at Shea, who shook his head. He was thinking the same thing.

"I have a different theory," said Devin. "How many vehicles passed the alleyway in between the first pass and the second?"

"I got this. What's the time stamp?" said Gupta.

"One thirty-two," said Graves.

Gupta typed away at his keyboard, quickly navigating the surveillance-software interface. The east-facing alley feed appeared on the screen in front of him a few moments later, the gray hatchback frozen in place. He fast-forwarded through the next three minutes and thirty-four seconds in about ten seconds, until the hatchback appeared again.

"I counted four vehicles," said Berg.

Everyone concurred.

"Not a ton of traffic. This should be easy," said Devin. "Go back and take a screenshot of each vehicle. Then run the same drill on the Lafayette feed, facing Chase Street. Start five minutes before I turn onto Lafayette and go about five minutes after Shea appears on Chase," said Devin.

"Look for a match," said Berg.

"Exactly," said Devin.

A few minutes later, they had a hit. A red, midsize four-door sedan driven by a blonde woman. Dashcams mounted on the rear-side windows. The red car passed the alley entrance on Guilford Avenue about twenty seconds after Shea had disappeared into Helen Gray's apartment building. Less than a minute after the hatchback made its first pass.

"My guess is someone decided to take a second look at you and got very suspicious when you vanished into thin air within a minute," said Devin.

"If we're dealing with professionals, my disguise won't hold up under close video inspection," said Shea.

"Yeah," said Devin. "I think it's fair to say that the neighborhood is about to get a little crowded."

"We were really careful," said Shea. "I don't see how they could have tracked us on any level."

Devin thought about it for a moment.

"I agree. They must have somehow narrowed their search area considerably over the past week," said Devin.

"I think it's fair to assume they've just narrowed it even further," said Berg. "Possibly down to a few blocks. If that's the case, we need to decide right away whether to stay or go."

"We need to go—like right away," said Devin. "It's only a matter of time before they identify me on one of those dashcam feeds. Then we'll have a small army camped out in the neighborhood. Scott?"

Daly appeared in the doorway to the kitchen a moment later. "Building security is set, and I've put the quick reaction force on immediate alert."

"Bring the QRF to their one-minute standby positions," said Devin. "We're slipping out of here while we still can. Pichugin's people are sniffing around the neighborhood. I may have underestimated his sleeper network's access to highly classified domestic-surveillance programs."

"How do you want to exfiltrate?" said Daly.

"We have to assume they're watching the neighborhood from a distance," said Devin. "We could probably get away with one pickup at the front door with one of the SUVs. Simulate an Uber trip. Driver could get out and load some of our bags into the back. That gets two, maybe three, of us out. The rest go out the back. I think one vehicle pickup in the alley is feasible, if the car sticks to the alleys to get here. Pack as many in as possible and stay out of sight. Whoever's left gets to walk out. We space those departures by a few minutes and head north. QRF scoops you up once you've cleared the neighborhood."

"Maybe we space this out a little further," said Berg. "It's not like the Russians will be kicking in doors and searching apartments."

"If they find the cameras on Lafayette or in the alley, they'll be able to narrow their search down to a few apartments," said Graves.

"And given what's at stake for Pichugin, that's as good as a death sentence for anyone who stays behind," said Devin.

"Agreed," said Berg.

"I think the Uber trick is too risky," said Graves. "If they're watching closely enough, even from a distance, that could draw undue attention to this address."

"We could use the drone to better assess the situation," said Gupta. "I can fly it just above the rooftops and discreetly scan the streets. Maybe find a hole in their coverage. If they're not directly watching the alley and McAllister Street, it might make more sense for all of us to walk through the alleyway. Emerge on McAllister for a convoy-style pickup."

"That's a solid idea. Let's get the drone up," said Devin.

"We can use the drone reconnaissance time to prep for departure," said Berg.

"I'll get the QRF moving," said Daly, grabbing the phone clipped to his vest.

"Four vehicles," said Devin. "And make sure they take everything with them. We won't be coming back anytime soon."

Daly nodded at Devin, already on his way out of the bunker with the phone to his ear.

"What can I do?" said Shea.

"I could use some help watching the street-camera feeds while I fly the drone," said Gupta. "Graves needs to prep our portable electronics gear for quick removal."

"Sounds easy enough," said Shea.

Graves got up from his seat. "I can give you a quick tour of the system and our comms setup."

"I'm a quick learner," said Shea, settling in next to Gupta.

"Sorry about this, Brendan," said Devin. "We haven't had a single whiff of the Russians since we returned to Baltimore."

"Must be my lucky day," said Shea.

"You're probably thinking that we faked all of this so we can whisk you out of here before you get a chance to dig through the files and conduct your interviews," said Berg.

"I'd be lying if I said the thought hadn't crossed my mind," said Shea. "But I'll have plenty of time to chat with the team later—and Devin said most of the files have been archived. I mostly wanted to lay eyes on this room. Make sure it wasn't some kind of CGI deep-fake bullshit."

"Unfortunately, it's very real," said Berg. "Before we scoot out of here, you need to conduct a random spot check of Helen's files to verify that they're real. We can't afford any lingering doubts."

"I plan on grabbing three at random on my way out," said Shea. "To compare them with the archived versions."

"That works," said Devin, before turning to Berg. "You're in charge of carrying the backpack with our sensitive files. Do you have room for a few more?"

"I'll make room," said Berg.

"What's in the sensitive files?" said Shea.

"Anything Devin's mother gathered on the two sleepers that have not been recalled by Pichugin," said Berg. "We removed their profiles from the wall and moved things around to fill in the blank spaces left behind. Any cross references found in separate files have also been removed. If the Russians ever find this place, we'd like to keep those two in our back pocket."

"Smart," said Shea, before Graves commandeered his attention.

Devin scanned the bunker, looking for any intelligence material they may have missed—finding nothing. Any paper notes taken during meetings were triple shredded after being digitized. After returning to Baltimore from the Ozarks, the team had kept the apartment sanitized of sensitive information and ready to abandon at a moment's notice.

The only thing left to grab was the backpack filled with the remaining cash and Visa gift cards from his mother's original stash. They'd gone through about half of the hundred thousand dollars she'd left in the safe—split evenly between the cards and cash. He swung one of the bookcases on its hidden hinges, noting a few additional items of interest in the safe.

"I have two ballistic vests, two pistols, a short-barreled AR-15—and plenty of ammunition," said Devin. "Anyone interested?"

"I'll take the rifle and one of the vests," said Shea.

"Sold. We like to keep our guests happy," said Devin. "Karl. Can I interest you in a pistol?"

"I'm good," said Berg. "If it comes down to me using a pistol, we're pretty much done for."

Devin tossed one of the vests at Berg instead, catching him off guard and nearly knocking him over. "Just in case."

Berg straightened up and grunted. "If you insist."

"I do."

Devin donned the backpack and tucked one of the pistols, along with a few spare magazines, into his pants, before delivering the rifle and last vest to Shea.

"How's the drone looking?" said Devin, leaning over Gupta's shoulder.

"Ready to go," said Gupta.

"Then what are you waiting for?" said Devin.

"Permission from Dad," said Graves. "Go ahead and launch, Son."

Everyone laughed except for Gupta, who just shook his head and flipped a switch on the drone flight controller in front of him. Moments later, the multicamera video feed on Gupta's ultrawide computer monitor lifted away from the apartment rooftop.

CHAPTER 16

Orlov sat on the scorching hood of his car and tracked the drone, one hand shielding his eyes from the overhead sun. The other holding a satellite phone against his sweat-soaked face. He didn't like what he heard. Even with it flying at nearly twice the FAA-permitted maximum drone altitude, he could still hear it over the ambient urban background noise. What might sound like a very distant Weedwacker to most would be instantly identifiable to a seasoned mercenary or surveillance professional.

Thankfully, the Raven was compact and fast, which made it difficult to spot from the ground—and apparently the roof of a parking garage. Every time he diverted his attention to the live aerial footage streamed to his laptop, it took him several seconds to find the drone again. He glanced at the computer screen, noting the time. Coming up on six minutes of flight time. They were pushing their luck at this point.

"Anything at all?" said Orlov into the phone.

"Nothing. Which is still something," said Oleg.

"I'm not in the mood for your cryptic messages," said Orlov. "It's hot and I'm fucking hungry."

"Sounds familiar," said Oleg. "Anyway. There's no homeless population in that neighborhood. The guy must have entered one of the apartments—which seems odd to me."

"Yes. Very odd. They're close by. I can feel it," said Orlov. "It's only a matter of time."

"But not right now," said Oleg. "The drone team is getting a little antsy. They want to bring the drone back and wait a few hours before putting it up again. They say we need to be cautious during the day. People will call the police if they see a drone overhead."

"That's the last thing we need," said Orlov. "Have them recover the drone. I'm going to make a call to see if our patron can work some of his behind-the-scenes magic to examine real estate records. Anything that might help us narrow things down."

When Oleg didn't answer right away, he checked the phone to see if the call had been disconnected. Orlov did the hanging up when talking with the team. Not the other way around. The phone indicated that the call was still in progress.

"Oleg? Hello?" he said, not getting a response. "Oleg! Are you still there?"

"Yes. Yes. I'm here. Sorry about that. The Americans found something," said Oleg. "Take a look at the live feed. They found a quadcopter drone moving low and slow over the buildings. It either just launched or it's been there the whole time, and they just noticed it. One of them is reviewing all of the camera feed we've collected since the drone took station over the neighborhood."

"I see it," said Orlov.

The drone crept along the northern edge of a row of rooftops overlooking East Lafayette Avenue, near Calvert Street. Not only were his targets close, but they were also nervous. Something had spooked them enough to take a clandestine look around the neighborhood. That something being Maxim's extra pass on Guilford Avenue. Devin Gray and Karl Berg's people were good at this. But why incur the seemingly unnecessary risk of putting a disguised surveillance asset onto the streets?

Something about their use of that tactic bothered him. Did they somehow discover that he'd narrowed his search down to this close to them? Was the wandering homeless guy a ruse to draw Orlov into an ambush, like the one they sprang at the town house on the other side of Baltimore? Would they really try the same trick twice, knowing that he'd most certainly been warned about it?

Unfortunately, he didn't have the luxury of sitting on this long enough to adequately assess that possibility. Orlov couldn't risk even the slightest chance that Gray and his friends might try to slip away before he pounced. He was unlikely to get another shot at this.

"Even if they find the point of origin on the recorded feed, they keep the Raven up until the quadcopter finishes whatever it's doing," said Orlov. "I need to be one hundred percent about the target location."

"I'll make sure they understand that your request is nonnegotiable," said Oleg.

"Very nonnegotiable," said Orlov. "They'll get reimbursed for the loss."

"Understood. Hold on. I need a minute or so to talk to them."

"Call me back when you've found something," said Orlov, disconnecting the call and dialing Lashev's phone.

"I'm glad you called," said Lashev. "The only place within walking distance is a Mexican—"

"Get your ass back here now," said Orlov. "We found them."

"Okay. I'm heading back," said Lashev. "Do you want a cold drink or something? I can grab—"

"Lashev. If you're not back here in three minutes, I'm designating you as our next target. Are we clear?"

"Yes. See you in a few—"

Orlov ended the call and slid off the hood. He couldn't think straight with the sun blaring down on him. He got in the front passenger seat and turned the air-conditioning to the highest setting before directing all available air vents toward his face. The cold air steadily revived him to the point where he felt somewhat normal again. Now for the fun part.

He noted the quadcopter's location on the live drone feed before switching to Google Maps and navigating to East Lafayette Avenue. Orlov activated Google's satellite-imagery option and centered the map on the stretch of road between Guilford Avenue and Calvert Street. Helen Gray's apartment sat somewhere on this two- to three-square-block grid of streets and alleys. Time to start moving the pieces into place. He took a minute or so to study the neighborhood's ins and outs before settling on a general plan that could be modified on the go.

They'd breach both the front and back of the apartment building simultaneously, while blocking vehicle access to the street in front of the target. The teams barricading each end of the street would keep the police at bay with grenades and automatic gunfire. The use of military-grade firearms and explosives would guarantee a robust SWAT response, but they'd be long gone before the Baltimore Police Department could throw that at them in any meaningful way. Orlov's phone buzzed, displaying Oleg's number.

"That was fast," said Orlov.

"They found the drone's original launch point: 2852 East Lafayette Avenue. North side of the street. The alley behind the apartment connects with a wooded park to the west and Guilford to the east, right about where Maxim saw our homeless guy. I bet he ducked down the alley shortly after Maxim passed by. Iskra couldn't have missed him by more than a few seconds."

Orlov's prefrontal cortex went into overdrive, throwing several options at him in rapid, almost instantaneous succession. Decision time—but not without more information.

"How long has their drone been in the air?"

"About five minutes. Our drone guys say it looks like they've been scanning the streets for surveillance."

"They know we're on to them," said Orlov. "They'll bolt as soon as they assess that the streets are clear."

"That doesn't leave us with much time," said Oleg.

"No. It doesn't," said Orlov. "Let the drone guys know I want continuous coverage before, during, and after we hit the apartment. I don't want any of our targets slipping away."

"That's what I figured," said Oleg. "I told them to assume the drone was a loss. They'll keep it up as long as needed."

Orlov whispered. "Can the drone team hear my voice right now?"

"Not at all."

"Keep a close eye on them when the shooting starts," said Orlov. "We can't afford any last-minute ethical dilemmas—if you know what I mean."

"I do."

Oleg's clipped, generic responses indicated that he must be standing close to the drone team. He'd discussed the issue in private with Oleg earlier, deciding it was better to keep them in the dark regarding the final stages of the operation. They came across as a little green, but they weren't naive—and they certainly couldn't claim to be innocent. You didn't advertise sophisticated surveillance services on the dark web unless you were willing to get dirty. The question was *how dirty*. They agreed it was better not to ask up front. There was no telling how long it might take to find another drone team.

"I trust your judgment. No need to call should a problem arise," said Orlov.

"Understood."

"I'm going to move the teams into the staging area south of the target neighborhood. We'll move out when the quadcopter returns to 2852 East Lafayette Avenue. Hit them while they're preparing to leave."

CHAPTER 17

Devin watched the drone feed over Gupta's shoulder. So far so good. No obvious signs of street-based surveillance and the more worrisome radio frequencies were mostly quiet. The rooftop antenna picked up a few satellite bursts, indicating push-to-talk satellite-phone communications, but nothing persistent or patterned.

The Russians were playing it safe. Hoping they hadn't tipped their hand. Keeping quiet and maintaining a safe distance—until they could figure out a way to specifically identify his mother's apartment. His mother had covered her tracks well, but if Pichugin's sleeper network could narrow their search down to the Greenmount West neighborhood in little more than a week's time, Devin guessed it wouldn't be too long before they had a street address.

He took a long look around the room, at his mother's magnum opus, before ordering the final departure preparations.

"Scott. I'm thinking half of us out the front. The other half out the back. At the same time. Just pull the Band-Aid off and be done with it. Ripley and Enzo will pick up Karl, Graves, Rico, and Miralles on Lafayette. Garza and Max grab the rest of us in the alley."

Daly nodded. "It splits up our shooters pretty evenly. I'll have Miralles retrieve the Claymore hidden in the steps on the way down. I'll grab the one in back when we head out the door."

"The thought of riding around in a car with a recently armed anti-personnel mine kind of scares the shit out of me," said Berg.

"We're not leaving any of the Claymores behind. The crate we *acquired* several years ago is running low," said Daly.

"How old are these things?" said Berg.

"We picked them up from a Central American source," said Daly. "So they were probably part of a military aid shipment given to the Contras to fight the Sandinistas."

"You're telling me the Claymore mines are roughly forty years old," said Berg.

"I never really thought of it that way," said Daly. "Maybe we shouldn't throw them around like we do."

Shea stifled a laugh, which rippled through the rest of the team.

"Now you're just messing with me," said Berg.

"Karl, why don't you ride with Rico," said Devin. "At most, he'll be carrying a grenade or two."

"Funny," said Berg.

Devin patted Gupta's shoulder. "How are we looking?"

"The streets are clear as far as I can tell. Nothing unusual on thermal imaging. No running cars. No recently parked vehicles. Nobody lingering on the stoops or hanging around the street corners."

"Nobody with eyes directly on the apartment," said Devin.

"Correct. But indirectly? It's impossible to be certain," said Gupta. "But I'm not picking up any unusual line-of-sight frequency transmissions. If they had a camera in a tree or a car close enough to keep an eye on the apartment, it would transmit continuously . . . and I'd like to think we would have picked that up. The bottom line? We're intimately familiar with the background radio frequency signature of the neighborhood—and nothing has changed."

"I concur," said Graves. "Anish has this locked down."

"That's good enough for me," said Devin. "Let's put the drone in an overwatch hover at four hundred feet and transfer the feed to one of the laptops."

"Do you want me to bring the controller?" said Gupta. "We could recover it a few blocks away."

"The fewer distractions on the way out, the better," said Devin.

"I'll program it to land on the roof when its battery runs low," said Gupta.

"Perfect," said Devin. "Brendan. Now would be a good time to grab those random files."

"I grabbed them while you were in the other room," said Shea.

"Then that's it," said Devin. "Once the drone is up, and you've transferred the feed, we're out of here."

CHAPTER 18

Orlov's phone buzzed in his lap. Showtime. The entire mercenary contingent had consolidated into a single double-parked convoy facing north on Barclay. Seven vehicles, each carrying three operatives. He'd hoped to have a quick word in person with Garin and Iskra, the two team leaders, before commencing the assault on the apartment, but he couldn't afford the delay. He'd have to relay the small but important change to the assault plan over the satellite-phone net.

Orlov expected Iskra to meet with the most resistance in front of the apartment. Several windows faced Lafayette Avenue, giving the defenders ample positions to rain gunfire down on her highly exposed team. The alleyway approach offered Garin's team significantly more cover, and presented fewer windows. Instead of a simultaneous arrival, he wanted Garin's team to arrive thirty seconds earlier—to distract the apartment's defenders. Thirty seconds should give Garin enough time to reach the back door and set breaching charges. Iskra would start her run down the street the moment he detonated the charges.

He answered the call as Lashev pulled them even with the convoy's lead vehicle, simultaneously motioning for Garin to head out.

"We're on the move," said Orlov.

"We have a problem."

He grabbed the push-to-talk satellite phone in the cup holder, ready to call off the attack.

"How big of a problem?" said Orlov.

"They parked the quadcopter in a stationary hover about four hundred feet above the apartment," said Oleg. "They basically have a bird's-eye view of Lafayette Avenue and every adjacent street. If the team operating the quadcopter installed a motion-tracking countersurveillance application, our drone guys said that they'll spot our convoy two blocks out."

Orlov let the scenarios play out in his head over the course of the next several seconds, coming to the same conclusion each time. If Devin Gray's team of extraordinarily lethal friends spotted the convoy two blocks out, the plan would fail. If he called off the attack and tried to tail them, there was no guarantee he could pull it off. Gray was a countersurveillance expert. Berg was ex-CIA. And Farrington's people seemed capable of anything. He had no good choices. All because of a damn quadcopter parked four hundred feet above the apartment. Parked stationary. As in easy target.

"Oleg?"

"Yes?"

"Tell our drone team to hit the quadcopter with the Raven," said Orlov. "Knock it out of the sky. They can do that, right?"

A long pause ensued.

"Oleg?"

"Hold on. They're discussing it."

"There's nothing to discuss!" said Orlov. "They've already written off the drone."

"It's not that. They're not sure they can hit it using the front camera feed," said Oleg. "They've never done anything like this before. Almost everything is automated with the drone."

"I could shoot it down with my rifle," said Lashev. "Just get me close enough."

"How close?"

Lashev rubbed his chin—appearing to run the calculation.

"Anywhere inside of one thousand feet away from the apartment," said Lashev. "At that height, the range to the drone won't be much farther."

Orlov gave Lashev's proposal some serious thought. A single vehicle wouldn't draw too much attention. He could approach Lafayette Avenue with Lashev in the back seat and drop the sniper off somewhere just out of sight of the drone, then continue down the street. They might not even notice that he stopped. Or he could park the car and Lashev could fire from the back seat. The only problem was time. His targets could walk out at any moment. Orlov needed to hit the apartment immediately.

"They figured it out!" yelled Oleg. "It has something to do with the tracking software. They can designate—"

"I don't give a shit about the details. Just have them do it! Right now!" said Orlov. "And initiate the diversion."

"Copy that," said Oleg. "I just sent the signal to the explosives."

They'd planted half-pound plastic explosive devices in the bathrooms of three touristy bars in the Fells Point waterfront area, set to detonate thirty seconds apart.

"What about the Raven?" said Orlov.

"They're doing it!" said Oleg. "The Raven just made a sharp turn and is dropping altitude."

"How long until impact?" said Orlov.

"Hold on," said Oleg, before passing the question along. "Thirty-three seconds. They've pushed the drone to its maximum speed."

"This better work," said Orlov.

"They've assured me it will," said Oleg.

"Make sure they get the second Raven up. I want continuous coverage," said Orlov.

"One of them just launched it," said Oleg. "They're sending it straight to the neighborhood. I'm being told there will be a short gap in coverage. Fifteen to thirty seconds."

"A fucking eternity in this business," he muttered, before switching to the push-to-talk satellite phone.

"All teams. This is Orlov. Pull over immediately. We have a thirty-second delay, and a slight change to the assault plan. Pay close attention. I only have time to explain it once."

CHAPTER 19

Marnie Young crouched next to the back door, the stock of the Scorpion pressed into her shoulder. Brendan Shea stood on the other side of the door, his rifle held tight. Devin settled in next to her, followed closely by Gupta, who held an open laptop with two hands, never taking his eyes off the drone feed.

They had decided to treat this like a hostile breakout instead of a mad scramble to evacuate. The drone feed and the street cameras told them the coast was clear, but all of that could change in an instant. Daly wanted them alert and covering the various threat sectors from the moment they stepped out of the apartment, until Devin and Shea declared they were free and clear of any surveillance.

Daly joined them a moment later, struggling under the weight of an overstuffed black duffel bag. What Miralles liked to call the "frag bag."

"Berg insisted," said Daly. "How does it look out there?"

Gupta put his back against the wall and slid into a sitting position, balancing the laptop on his knees. He spent the next several seconds studying the screen, zooming in and out a few times, before raising one of his hands. Devin pulled him to his feet.

"My eyes and all of the software we installed say the coast is clear," said Gupta.

Daly nodded before triggering the radio attached to his ballistic vest. "We're clear for pickup."

"You good?" said Devin, putting a hand on Marnie's shoulder.

"I'm good," she said, tightening her grip on the Scorpion. "Just going over the exfiltration in my head."

He got the hint and moved on. She was in no mood for small talk.

"Brendan? Having more fun than you expected?" said Devin.

"I'm still not one hundred percent convinced this is real," said Shea, the sober look on his face indicating otherwise.

"Pickup is about thirty seconds out," said Daly.

"Still clear," said Gupta.

"Perfect," said Devin.

"It'll take me about fifteen seconds to disarm and collect the Claymore," said Daly. "Everyone but Anish needs to remain outside of their vehicles, covering their assigned sectors."

"Got it," said Marnie.

"Yep," replied Shea.

"What the fuck?" said Gupta.

Here we go. Gupta had the worst sense of timing when it came to humor.

"Stay outside of the car if you want," said Daly. "Doesn't matter to—"

"No. It's the drone feed. Something's wrong," said Gupta.

Daly grabbed the screen. "Did we lose the connection somehow?"

"Not that I can—"

"The drone is spinning and falling fast," said Marnie. "Something hit it—hard."

A quick look at the screen told Marnie the whole story. A helicopter pilot's worst nightmare—and a scenario they trained extensively to survive.

"A bird?" said Devin.

"Possible. But unlikely," said Gupta. "Scott. You might want to slow things down, just in case we have a bigger problem."

Daly contacted the QRF drivers. "Pickup postponed. Stay close and keep a low profile. We may have to shoot our way out of here."

"Shit," said Devin. "Could they be that close?"

"Marnie?" said Shea. "No shit. Is this real?"

She nervously laughed. "Very."

"Son of a mother," he said—then yanked the AR-15's charging handle back and chambered a round.

They were all on the same page now. The loss of their drone coverage wasn't a coincidental accident. Melendez yelled down the hallway from the front of the building, a nearby car alarm suddenly blaring in the background.

"Something just dropped out of the sky and landed on the car right across the street! Did we just lose our drone?"

"Our drone is still—" started Gupta, the feed going dead moments later. "Now it's down."

A second, more distant car alarm wailed, immediately followed by Melendez. "I think something else just hit the street to the east! What's happening? What are we doing?"

"Anish. Can you still access the street cameras?" said Devin.

"With a click of the mouse," said Gupta, pressing the touch pad.

When Lafayette Avenue appeared on his screen, their "bigger problem" came into stark focus. A drone had indeed hit the car directly across the street from Helen Gray's apartment building, but it wasn't their quadcopter.

"That's a Raven," said Gupta.

"They've been watching us the whole time," said Daly.

"Upstairs. Now," said Devin. "And get that Claymore back in place on the stairs. Get all of the explosives back in place. We're about to have visitors."

Daly took off, barking orders down the hallway.

"I'll cover the back door until Miralles is finished," said Marnie.

Devin looked like he was about to disagree—but nodded instead.

"Cover the door from a position deeper in the hallway," said Devin. "In case they shoot up the back of the apartment before they breach."

"Care for some company?" said Shea.

"I got it," said Marnie. "It shouldn't take long to rig the Claymore."

"I'll tell Miralles to yell for you when she's done," said Devin, and the two of them took off.

The apartment went dead quiet while she waited, the rest of the team having cleared the stairway.

"You still there?" said Marnie.

"Almost done," said Miralles. "I had to do a little rewiring work and run it back through the tread. I cut it too close to the hole on the way out. Didn't expect we'd be back so soon."

"None of us did," said Marnie.

Someone yelled down the stairs, but she didn't catch what they said. It sounded like Shea, and judging by the urgency in his voice, she assumed their time on the ground floor had just expired.

"Three vehicles just turned off Guilford into the alley. The front is still clear," said Miralles. "Give me ten more seconds here."

"Take your time," she said.

Pebbles crackled over the low rumble of a car engine beyond the back door. She had to remind herself to breathe.

"They're right behind the apartment," said Marnie.

"You can pull back," said Miralles. "I'm almost done."

She crouched low and braced her arm against the wall, aiming at a point a few feet to the right of the door—toward the center of the carport. With the Scorpion steadied, she slowly backed up along the wall.

"Just tell me when you're done," said Marnie.

More yelling down the stairs. This time she heard Shea clearly.

"Get out of there now! We're blowing the Claymore!"

Jesus. She'd forgotten that the Claymore defending the back door faced the inside. She turned and ran, not wanting to be in the hallway when several hundred BB-size steel balls shredded the back of the apartment. The moment Marnie reached the foot of the stairs, Miralles grabbed her vest with both hands and swung her out of the hallway, pinning her against the first-floor apartment door.

"Clear!" screamed Miralles. "We're clear!"

A single thunderous clap shook the building's bones, the hallway instantly snapping and crackling like a dozen kids jumping up and down on Bubble Wrap. One of the front door's side windows cracked, and a tiny hole appeared in the center of the glass spiderweb. Several steel balls rattled and rolled around the worn hardwood foyer. Miralles released her grip and went back to work on the stairway wiring.

"Go. I got this," said Miralles. "Just a few more seconds."

Tires screeched somewhere down Lafayette Avenue. Multiple vehicles.

"Go!"

Marnie bolted up the stairs, taking them two at a time. Halfway up, Miralles started her climb—yelling as her boots pounded the stairs.

"The staircase is ready! I'm clear!"

Rapid, sustained gunfire erupted from the third floor, a combination of sharp cracks and ear-piercing blasts. Two shooters blasting away at whatever the Russians had driven down the street. A heavy, metal crunch echoed through the stairway, followed almost immediately by a second, less-substantial-sounding crash and screeching tires. Then a peculiar silence, punctuated only by the sound of her own footsteps.

Marnie hit the third-floor landing in a sprint and burst into the room to find Melendez and Daly changing magazines, their rifles pointed west down Lafayette through separate windows. Marnie's first instinct was to help them out by providing covering fire while they reloaded, but Melendez waved her away the moment she turned in their direction.

"Get to the bunker," said Melendez. "We'll be right there. We're just buying some time."

Both window casings splintered simultaneously, and the two operatives dropped to the hardwood floor as shards of glass and wood fell on them. Bullets bit into the wall a few feet to Marnie's left, indicating that the barrage of gunfire had come from the east. She started for the window to lay down some suppressing fire in the new direction, but a pair of strong hands yanked her back and swung her toward the kitchen. Marnie quickly regained her balance and spun around, but Miralles's body blocked her.

"Are you out of your mind? Every gunsight out there is aimed at those two windows," said Miralles, before crouching. "And get the fuck down."

Bullet holes steadily punctured the walls on both sides of the apartment in a chest-to-head-height pattern, as Daly and Melendez crawled away from the windows. She'd been a fraction of a second away from getting herself killed.

"Fuck," said Marnie, taking a knee. "That was stupid."

Miralles nodded before moving out of her way.

"Yep. Now shake it off and get in the bunker," she said. "And do exactly what we say, when we say it. That's the only way any of us get out of this alive. In case you haven't noticed, we're sort of trapped in a third-floor apartment."

"I did notice."

"There's a way out," said Daly, crawling toward the apartment's front door. "We just need to buy some time."

"How much time?" said Marnie.

"Enough to figure out how to escape using the rooftops," said Daly.

"Good thing I didn't ditch my disguise," said Shea.

Shit. All this time and none of them had put any real thought into the most obvious scenario. How to get out of the apartment if they can't use the stairs.

CHAPTER 20

Lashev skidded the car to a halt in the middle of the intersection as the rest of the cars in the convoy turned west on Lafayette Avenue and barreled toward the target apartment. Sustained, rapid gunfire exploded from the apartment's third-story windows before Orlov got his door open, the convoy's lead vehicle careening left and slamming into a parked car.

The driver of the second sedan slammed on the brakes, clipping the back of Iskra's vehicle before screeching to a stop in the middle of the street. Bullets thumped into its hood and roof, and shattered its windows, with only the back-seat occupant escaping to take cover behind a parked SUV. The third sedan in the convoy braked and swerved right, slipping through a gap in the parked vehicles and jumping the curb.

The car stopped a few feet short of T-boning the adjacent apartment building's redbrick facade, its three operatives immediately hitting the sidewalk and dashing to covered positions behind the nearest apartment stoops.

He had another complete disaster on his hands.

Both prongs of his attack had been stopped cold, their team leaders presumably dead. Only four out of nine mercenaries had survived the ambush on Lafayette Avenue, from what he could tell, and he still hadn't heard from anyone on Garin's team. Depending on how they'd approached the back of the apartment, the explosion could have wiped out the entire team.

Orlov triggered his radio as he hopped out of the car.

"West block. West block. Suppress those windows."

He dashed around the trunk to the driver's side, where Lashev had already started to remove their small arsenal from the back seat. He handed Orlov a short-barreled M4 assault rifle and four thirty-round magazines before reaching back inside the car for his sniper rifle. Automatic fire started to rattle from the western intersection, chipping away at the brick and windows on the third floor of Helen Gray's apartment.

"Set up behind the hood and watch the windows," said Orlov, stuffing three of the rifle magazines into his pockets. "I'm moving in with whatever we have left."

"I think we should cut our losses and get the fuck out of here," said Lashev. "The police will be here any minute."

"I bought us some time," said Orlov, loading the rifle with the remaining magazine. "This ends here."

Lashev cradled his Dragunov SVU, a compact version of the quintessential Soviet-era sniper rifle, before grabbing the small duffel bag containing grenades and ammunition.

"More money for all of us," said the sniper. "Right?"

"Exactly," said Orlov. "But only if I survive. Don't forget that."

"Yeah. And the money's only good if I'm alive or out of prison to spend it," said Lashev. "Understood?"

"Message received," said Orlov, before taking off.

He kept to the sidewalk, moving from one apartment stoop to the next until he linked up with the remnants of Iskra's team, who had taken advantage of the lull in hostile gunfire to regroup and direct fire at the apartment.

"Keep those windows suppressed," said Orlov. "We're going to consolidate and hit the front door."

The mercenaries barely nodded, their entire focus on preventing another volley of lethal fire from the apartment. They were in shock, having just watched more than half of their team get unexpectedly slaughtered in a matter of moments. Orlov understood that his time to rally the remnants of his broken team was limited.

Once the initial shock wore off, reality would set in. Reality in their case being that very few of them would survive the next several minutes, and those who survived would be unlikely to escape the police—including himself. With that cheerful thought in mind, Orlov got to work.

"West block team leader. Send two down Lafayette toward the target. We're going to breach the front door and finish the mission," said Orlov. "Keep one in place at the intersection and hold the police at bay. It is imperative that the police do not approach the target apartment. Any and all force is authorized. Understood?"

"Copy that," said the team leader. "Sending Matvey and Sasha."

That gave him seven going in the front door. A few going through the back, or at least watching the back, might make all the difference.

"Back door. This is Orlov. Is anyone still mission capable?"

"This is Maxim. Garin is dead. I have three mission capable, including myself. Those fuckers set off a Claymore mine or something right before we breached the back door."

Shit. Orlov really wished Maxim hadn't said that. The last thing he needed right now was for the rest of the team to be thinking about the limb-sheering effects of a Claymore mine.

"Copy that," said Orlov. "Take positions in the alley to keep our targets from escaping down the fire escape or any of the rear windows. I'll let you know if we need you for the assault."

"We're looking for some payback, so don't be shy," said Maxim.

"Good to know," said Orlov. "Oleg. Are you seeing anything?"

"No target movement," said Oleg. "The police scanners are going crazy, but no police units inbound. Yet."

"The drone team?" said Orlov.

"I don't foresee a problem."

"Good," he said. "Pass any relevant tactical information over this net."

The second Raven had started transmitting imagery about thirty seconds before Garin's team turned down the alley behind Helen Gray's apartment. Nothing Orlov observed in that half minute suggested that both of his teams were headed directly into an ambush. He'd simply been outplayed up to this point. Lured into a vulnerable position designed to reduce his numbers. But now what?

Gray and his friends couldn't possibly remain in the apartment. Not if they wanted to continue the war they had started against Pichugin. Once the police swooped in, they'd have to shoot or sweet-talk their way out of a federal holding cell. And no amount of on-the-spot clarification or negotiating was going to explain away the dead and mangled bodies left behind by the detonation of an antipersonnel mine.

That alone would bring at least three federal agencies to bear on Gray and his friends. And that was just the beginning. God knows what investigators would find in Helen Gray's apartment. They'd be lucky if they saw the outside of a US federal detention center in the next six months, and if they did, it would probably be through the seams of a black hood during a Learjet transfer to a CIA black site.

Time was on neither of their sides, but Orlov had one significant advantage. Two, actually. First, he held the streets—their only escape route. There would be no helicopter miracle this time around. Second, he had no problem killing cops. His people could hold this position on the streets until Gray couldn't possibly evade whatever police response Orlov brought down on the neighborhood. It was Gray's move now—which would seal his targets' fates.

Orlov glanced over his shoulder at the intersection, confirming that Lashev was behind the scope of his rifle, ready to cover their approach. Time to put a little pressure on Gray and his friends. Let them know that they were running out of options.

"Kostya. Karina. Breach the front door," said Orlov. "Everyone else move forward, but stay tight against the buildings. Intersection blocks, watch those windows."

The two mercenaries broke cover and raced toward the apartment. When they reached the front stoop, one of them aimed their rifle into the building, while the other climbed the stairs and placed a small explosive charge on the door and pulled the pin on the attached igniter. They quickly scattered, stacking up against the face of the apartment—several feet from the entrance. A sharp detonation blasted the door off its frame. The two mercenaries mounted the stairs and disappeared inside the building.

"First-floor hallway and staircase clear," reported one of the operatives.

"Matvey. Sasha. Reinforce the breach team. Do not proceed to the second floor," said Orlov. "Just secure and hold your position."

The two operatives sent from the west intersection emerged from their covered position behind one of the apartment stoops and sprinted toward the target. The first one hopped the wrought iron handrail and landed on Helen Gray's porch. The second took the stairs and followed him inside. Orlov rose and nodded at the two operatives crouched behind a parked SUV.

"Let's move up."

Before any of them started forward, an explosive maelstrom of thick wooden splinters, glass, and mangled body parts blasted the street in front of the apartment, shattering nearby vehicle windows and setting off dozens of car alarms. Orlov sank a little lower behind the porch stoop and watched the debris settle over the cars, street, and sidewalks.

He doubted anyone had survived that blast, but it was always possible. The Claymore directed most of its explosive energy and all its lethal payload in a sixty-degree arc facing to the front of the mine, which is why the business side of the mine was literally labeled FRONT TOWARD ENEMY. To avoid any confusion by the user. If any of his operatives had been standing to the side or behind the Claymore, they'd feel like a car had hit them, but they'd be alive—and possibly useful.

"Kostya. Karina. Matvey. Sasha. Report your status," he said, getting no response.

He tried one more time, with the same result. Orlov got the attention of the two remaining operatives.

"Igor. Head back to the intersection and help Lashev control the police response," he said.

The stocky Russian nodded and took off, keeping as close to the buildings as possible on the short trip to reach Lashev behind the sedan.

"Darya. I need you at the other intersection to help Erik."

"Do you want me to use the alley?" she said.

"I don't care how you get there," said Orlov.

"Then cover me," she said. "I'll use the sidewalk and make a quick assessment of the damage on my way by the target."

"Suit yourself," said Orlov, lifting his rifle and bracing it against the edge of the concrete stoop. "Erik. This is Orlov. I'm sending Darya over to keep you company."

"Copy that."

Orlov kept a close eye on her through his rifle's magnified sight, his finger taking some of the slack off the trigger—just in case. He couldn't afford to lose another operative. Darya paused several feet before she reached the jagged hole that used to be the front entrance to Helen Gray's apartment. She took a few more steps before crouching and scooting against the neighboring apartment. Something was wrong. He took the rest of the slack off the trigger.

A figure jumped to the sidewalk in front of her. Orlov pressed the trigger twice in rapid succession, his bullets striking the person center mass and knocking them backward into the porch stoop. A third bullet, presumably fired by Erik, snapped the figure's head forward and splattered Darya with gore.

"Cease fire! Fuck!" said Darya. "You just shot Karina."

Orlov studied his target through the sight and confirmed Darya's statement. Karina's blonde hair was no longer hidden now that Erik had blasted the ball cap off her head.

"Forget the damage assessment," said Orlov. "Just get over to the intersection."

Once Darya was clear of the target apartment entrance, Orlov took a seat on the sidewalk and leaned his back against the side of the stoop. He needed to gather his thoughts and figure out if he was still looking at a salvageable situation.

He briefly considered calling Pichugin's front man and explaining the dilemma, but just as quickly dismissed the idea. This was the end of the line for him if he didn't succeed. There was no going back.

It was time to call Gray's bluff. He'd give the order to seal off the neighborhood and wait for Gray to make the next move. He still had eight mercenaries in the fight and an eye in the sky. Enough to fend off the police and keep his targets trapped in the building until Gray hit the point of no return and had to decide whether to stay in the apartment and go to prison or take his chances against the Russians.

His satellite phone rang. He dug it out of a cargo pocket and checked the screen. Interesting. Orlov accepted the call.

"What the fuck is going on, Orlov?" said Fedir Severny, the third team leader. "I thought I heard a few distant explosions—then I turned on my police scanner."

"Fedir."

"Automatic gunfire and multiple explosions reported on East Lafayette Avenue," said Severny.

"Fedir! I need you to be listening and not talking! Are you listening?"

"Yes."

"How many of your people are ready to work right now—at double the pay?" said Orlov.

"As in double the contracted amount?"

"As in I need them at 2852 East Lafayette Avenue in under five minutes," said Orlov.

"There's five of us at the staging house," said Severny. "We'll gear up and head out immediately. I can be there in four minutes."

"Just grab weapons and ammunition," said Orlov.

"Three minutes."

"Better," said Orlov. "Approach the address from the east. I'll meet you at the intersection of Lafayette and Guilford. You might have to dodge the police on your way in. Shoot your way through if that's what it takes to get to me."

"Wait a minute. What am I walking into here?" said Severny. "How bad is this?"

Fedir wasn't impulsive or suicidal, and Orlov needed him to be both right now. He'd need more convincing. With fifteen of the original twenty-four mercenaries dead, Orlov had enough unclaimed contract shares to up the ante. Twenty years in this business had taught him that greed often bypassed a person's innate sense of self-preservation—and nobody was entirely immune to temptation.

"Make it triple for each of you," said Orlov. "Better yet. Ten extra shares that you can distribute however you like to whoever survives."

"That bad, huh?"

"It's worse."

When a long pause ensued, Orlov knew Fedir had taken the bait.

"Count us in," said Severny. "I have some debts I need to pay off."

CHAPTER 21

The Claymore's one-and-a-half-pound explosive charge shook the floor beneath Devin's feet, its detonation sounding like a sudden clap of thunder after a lightning strike just down the street. Car alarms and shattering glass competed with the ringing in his ears. Devin thought about Henrietta Silver and her family—their homes on the first and second floors turned into a war zone. Helen's promise of homeownership complicated by two high-explosive blasts and the inevitable law enforcement response. But still theirs to keep when the dust settled, with plenty of money to rebuild. An odd thought to cross his mind at this crucial moment.

Farrington's crew slipped into the bunker, Daly nodding at him.

"The apartment door is secure. We rigged a smoke grenade to detonate in the kitchen if they breach the door. That should slow them down significantly if they persist. Baltimore SWAT will have this entire neighborhood surrounded by the time they get through the bunker door. We can rig another inside the bunker. Really fuck them over if they somehow get inside."

"Do it," said Devin, turning to face the folding ladder leading into the attic space above them.

His mother had clearly planned for the possibility of being trapped in the third-floor apartment. The ladder led directly to a plywood platform in the shallow attic, which sat underneath a hinged, watertight door that opened to the roof. Once on the roof, you could traverse the entire block of apartments, from Guilford Avenue to Calvert Street, accessing any of the few dozen fire escapes leading down to the alley.

Under normal circumstances, this could work, but there was nothing remotely normal about the group plotting their next move against them.

"What if they have another drone up? They won't waste their time trying to breach the apartment if they spot us moving along the rooftops. They'll gravitate toward wherever we try to reach the street."

"Nothing we can do about that," said Daly, grabbing a black backpack lying on the floor next to the bunker door. "But we can make it as difficult as possible for them on the ground. I have ten military-grade smoke grenades in this backpack. Modified M8s. The kind we used in the teams. They burn thicker and last longer. If we place them strategically on the street and in the alley, they'll be blind."

"So will we," said Devin.

"Even odds," said Daly, shrugging.

"Once we reach the ground," said Marnie. "Until then, we're climbing down on top of them."

"The smoke should obscure everything," said Daly. "And we'll have Rico watching over us."

"His IR sight is at the motel," said Devin. "He'll be just as blind as they are."

"We don't have any other choice," said Daly. "And the clock is ticking."

Devin turned to Gupta, who, with his laptop, had taken his former seat at the desk in the middle of the room.

"What are you seeing out there?"

"One of them is headed back to the Guilford intersection," said Gupta. "And the other is . . . headed for the front door."

"Seriously?" said Miralles. "That's gutsy."

"She's moving cautiously," said Gupta.

"Want me to reach out and touch her before we close up the bunker?" said Melendez.

Gupta shook his head. "They have a sniper set up on the hood of the sedan parked in the intersection. Bullpup design. PSO-style scope. Probably a Dragunov SVU."

"Those are pretty rare," said Daly.

"Says something about the user," said Melendez. "We definitely need to stay out of his line of sight."

"Smoke grenades," said Daly, offering the backpack to Devin.

Devin snatched the backpack out of his hand. "What do I do?"

"Throw one as close to the Guilford intersection as possible," said Daly. "Spread the rest between the alley and street between here and Calvert. I'll direct the QRF drivers to rally near the intersection of McAllister and Calvert, at the northwest corner of the community garden."

A series of gunshots echoed through the room, causing all of them to crouch, except Miralles, who calmly walked to the bunker door and pulled it shut. The door's locking mechanisms clicked and whirred for a few seconds before going silent.

"What the hell was that?" said Devin, moving behind Gupta to look at the laptop screen.

"Looks like they shot one of their own people," said Gupta.

"The one checking out the apartment?" said Daly.

"No. I think someone survived the Claymore blast," said Gupta. "They must have wandered onto the sidewalk at the wrong time."

"They're jumpy," said Melendez. "The smoke will mess with them even more."

Devin looked to Shea. "What do you think?"

"I think we do whatever your friends say," said Shea. "Sooner than later. I'd rather not spend the night in jail."

"Only a night?" said Berg.

"MINERVA's in-house legal team is top notch," said Shea. "And given the DEVTEK operations I'm going to propose, I'm sure they'll spare no expense springing me as quickly as possible."

"So you're on board with the DEVTEK angle?" said Devin.

"Only if you get me out of here alive," said Shea.

"Then we better get this show on the road," said Devin, starting for the attic ladder.

CHAPTER 22

Felix Orlov took a knee next to Lashev and checked his watch. Severny's crew should be here any minute. With five additional bodies to throw at the problem, plus a drone overhead, Orlov felt confident that he could salvage the contract. *Salvage* being the operative term. There was simply no conceivable way he could satisfy every condition in the original contract right now. Nobody could.

The combination of Gray's, Berg's, and Farrington's unique skill sets had neutralized even the most aggressive measures Orlov had brought to bear on the situation. In retrospect, the only way Orlov could have fulfilled the contract under the current circumstances would have been to detonate SUVs packed with high explosives both in front and back of the apartment building—bringing the entire unit down with his targets in it. He'd be sure to keep that in mind if Pichugin gave him another chance. For now, he'd focus on three key objectives.

Kill Devin Gray.

Kill Karl Berg.

Destroy "certain materials" in the apartment.

If he nailed at least two out of the three revised objectives, Pichugin should keep him on the job. Who else could he hire at this point?

Certain materials. What the fuck did that mean? His few attempts to gain some clarity regarding these materials had resulted in hard-core stonewalling. "You'll know when you see it" had been the best guidance provided by Pichugin's front man. Bullshit in the grand scheme of things. His phone buzzed. Oleg.

"Must be important if you don't want to use the radio net," said Orlov.

"Important enough. First things first. Gray and company are on the roof headed west," said Oleg.

"What? How the fuck?" said Orlov.

"A well-camouflaged hatch toward the back of the apartment," said Oleg. "We didn't detect any sign of it earlier. They're moving fast. Half of them have already hopped over to the next apartment roof. It's a clear shot to Calvert Street for them, but I suspect they'll try one of the alley fire escapes on the way."

"Understood. What else?"

"We're seeing some suspicious vehicle movement," said Oleg. "Hard to pinpoint, but three vehicles are converging on the intersection northwest of the neighborhood. Calvert and McAllister. If I had to guess, I'd say this is their extraction point. The vehicles started moving around the same time that they emerged on the roof. They were less than a quarter mile away."

"Shit. There's more to this than meets the eye," said Orlov. "What about the police?"

"Their response has been delayed. The few units to respond are keeping their distance. The closest unit reported its position around Saint Paul and Charles Street. I think this is on purpose," said Oleg. "Looks and sounds like they'll keep their distance until their SWAT units arrive."

"Good. That'll buy us the time we need."

"To do what?" said Oleg. "We're talking twenty minutes, at most, before the Baltimore Police Department deploys three to four dozen SWAT officers against you."

"I'm going to burn Helen Gray's apartment to the ground," said Orlov. "And take as many of our targets down as possible before we have to leave. Does that sound acceptable to you?"

"Sorry. I didn't mean—"

"No offense taken," said Orlov. "Just keep the information flowing. By the way, your good friend Fedir Severny is on the way. He's headed directly for the Guilford intersection. That's why I'm feeling a little more confident about our situation."

"How many is he bringing to the fight?"

"Five. Including himself," said Orlov. "Straight from the staging area."

"Severny is exactly what we need right now," said Oleg. "This might work out."

"I'm surprised to hear you say that," said Orlov.

"Just because I don't like the guy doesn't mean he isn't right for the job," said Oleg. "He's a bit of a loose cannon, which could work in your favor."

"I'm banking on it," said Orlov. "How is the drone team doing?"

"Nervous," said Oleg. "But only because they've already written off the second drone. I think this job has wiped their inventory clean."

"Make sure they understand that if they keep up the good work, they'll never have to worry about work again," said Orlov. "Our patron will keep them busy."

"I hope the same applies to us," said Oleg.

"We'll know in a few minutes," said Orlov. "Use the radio net from this point forward. Lashev is second-in-command on the scene—if anything should go unexpectedly wrong."

"Big plans?"

"Let's just say I've decided to take a slightly more proactive role in what's about to unfold."

"Glad I'm sitting on my ass a mile away," said Oleg.

"See? I wasn't kidding when I said you'd be better off with the drone team," said Orlov.

"I guess I owe you," said Oleg. "If we ever collect on this contract."

"Yes. That's the key. Isn't it? Living to collect payment," said Orlov. "I'm heading out. See you on the other side of this."

"Or not."

Or not was right. Oleg had meant no disrespect. He was simply speaking the hard truth.

"Lashev. Shift your attention to the rooftops," said Orlov. "They're topside now. Headed west."

"Yep," said the sniper, lowering himself by a few inches to angle the rifle upward.

"I'm going to join Maxim in the alley," he said. "When Severny arrives, have him send two my way and two into the target building to try and breach the third-floor apartment. There's a duffel bag filled with explosives and a few different types of incendiary grenades in the trunk. Tell them to put it to good use."

Lashev glanced nervously toward the trunk. "Jesus. Now you tell me."

"Keep one of them here to watch your back," said Orlov. "The police are already starting to form a perimeter. They'll keep their distance for now, but my guess is that they'll start probing us sooner than later in order to give their SWAT teams some intelligence."

"Got it," said Lashev, his eye never leaving the scope. "I can relocate to the alley and try my luck there—or climb the closest fire escape and scope the entire rooftop. I don't anticipate Gray and his crew rappelling down onto Lafayette Avenue. My job is essentially done here."

Orlov considered Lashev's offer and decided to shift his strategy.

"Keep two of Severny's people here and tell them to hold the intersection," said Orlov. "Send Fedir and the other two into the apartment with the duffel bag. Then join me in the alley. That's where we'll earn our pay today."

"A triple share?" said Lashev.

He turned to the sniper, who remained focused on the rifle scope's sight picture.

"Yeah. A triple fucking share," said Orlov. "But not a word about it to anyone else. Agreed?"

"Hold on," whispered Lashev, intensely peering through his scope.

Orlov raised his rifle and scoped the roofline, moments before a small object arched skyward, headed in their direction. Lashev fired twice before ducking below the hood. Orlov remained upright, shaking his head. The metallic object hit the street and skidded toward the intersection, exploding in a billow of white chemical smoke twenty feet away. A second smoke grenade sailed over the roofline, landing amid the two machine-gunned cars halfway down Lafayette Avenue.

"They really thought of everything, didn't they?" muttered Orlov, before turning to Lashev. "Change of plans. I'll deal with Severny when he arrives. Make your way to the top of the nearest fire escape, but keep yourself concealed from our targets for now. I'll be in touch over the tactical net shortly with further instructions."

Lashev lifted his rifle off the hood and slipped behind Orlov in a crouch. "I'll let you know when I'm in position."

"Watch yourself," said Orlov. "They never seem to run out of surprises."

"It appears that way, doesn't it?" said Lashev, before taking off.

"It certainly does," mumbled Orlov, watching a nearly impenetrable wall of light-gray-and-white smoke fill the street.

He covered the target apartment windows and the roofline until Lashev reached the safety of the apartment block. Tires screeched somewhere in the near distance, and he spun with his rifle to scan the streets—just in case the police had decided to probe the area. A black SUV raced into view to the north, turning on Guilford from McCallister. Reinforcements had arrived. He waved them down for a few seconds before contacting Oleg with the satellite phone he used for off-net discussions.

"Miss me already?" answered Oleg.

"I have an idea that's going to require your close coordination," said Orlov.

"That's what I'm here for," said Oleg.

Severny's SUV skidded to a stop several feet behind him, its doors flying open and disgorging five operatives.

"Fedir just arrived," said Orlov. "I need to speak with him. I'll call you back when I'm on the road. I'm taking his car. This is about to get ugly."

"Uglier than it already is?" said Oleg.

"Way uglier."

CHAPTER 23

Devin pulled the pin on the cylindrical smoke grenade and got a running start before throwing it in a high arc toward the eastern intersection—careful not to expose himself. He'd taken a quick look in that direction a few seconds ago, the sniper shifting his aim the moment his head appeared above the roofline. Anyone showing their face at this point would likely take a bullet between the eyes. Two gunshots snapped overhead the moment he released the grenade, reinforcing his point.

Marnie ducked instinctively before handing him a second grenade. "I don't think we should waste too many more on Lafayette Avenue. We're going to need all of the concealment we can get in the alley and the community garden."

"I agree. The next two after this go to block the western intersection," said Devin. "Then we start on the alley. We're hoping to attract a few of them to Lafayette before we show our hand."

"It's pretty obvious we aren't going to climb down the front of the apartments," said Marnie.

"They don't know that," said Devin.

He pivoted to his left, pulled the pin on the grenade, and tossed it in a direction about halfway between the intersection and the front of his mother's apartment. By his calculation, that was right about where Melendez and Daly had stopped the convoy. When he turned around, Marnie held two grenades.

"Get started on the alley," she said, underhanding him two grenades in rapid succession. "I'll take care of the western intersection."

Devin snagged the first grenade out of the air but missed the second, which clattered to the roof several feet behind him. Marnie had already taken off for the western end of the rooftops.

"Keep your head below the roofline!" said Devin.

"I got it!" she said, hopping the concrete divider between apartment rooftops.

Devin hunted down the loose grenade, which had rolled to the front of the apartment's roof. He got down on all fours and crawled along the superheated tar paper rooftop until he could grab it, careful to keep his head out of the sniper's line of fire. With the two grenades in hand, he backed up until it was safe to stand. Gunfire erupted from somewhere on Lafayette Avenue, in Marnie's direction. He spun to find her crouched low near the edge of the roof two apartments down. A second volley of gunfire exploded the bricks next to her.

She backed up several feet and pulled the pin out of the grenade in her hand, then overhanded it in the direction of the intersection. Marnie then repositioned herself closer to the center of the rooftop, where she'd be safe from any gunfire, and started jogging directly toward the western end of the row of apartments.

The rest of the team, along with Brendan Shea, had congregated toward the back of the third apartment from Calvert Street, where they'd wait for the smoke screen to thicken and the sharpshooters to take their positions before attempting to climb down to the alley. They'd use two separate but adjacent fire escapes to expedite the evacuation, with a shooter posted on each of the exposed sides. The four military-grade smoke grenades would effectively drop visibility to nearly zero for a minute or so. Hopefully long enough to get the bulk of the team down, because once the smoke thinned, the shooting would start.

At that point, they faced a half-block trek through the overgrown community garden to reach the QRF vehicles. Daly had guessed this would be a difficult slog under fire, which was why he wanted Devin to save at least one of the smoke grenades for the garden. Devin wasn't looking forward to that part of their escape. Nobody was, but they'd decided it was too risky to bring the cars any closer. Lafayette Avenue was obviously out of the question, and one side of the tight alley was blocked by the Russians' vehicles and an unknown number of pissed-off mercenaries. That left a single approach, with one way in and one way out. Not exactly a smart move in this game.

Devin made his way toward the back of his mother's apartment, passing the watertight hatch she'd built into the roof. Not only had she thought to install an escape route, but she'd also built it to lock from the outside, making it close to impossible for anyone to follow her out. Two well-greased, heavy-gauge steel bars slid through rings welded to the frame and hatch to hold it firmly in place. In a low crouch, he cautiously approached the roof's edge until he'd reached a point about five feet back from the wood-and-brick parapet. Daly caught his attention and motioned for him to start throwing the grenades.

He pulled the pin and tossed one into the alley directly behind his mother's carport, drawing gunfire when the grenade sailed clear of the roof. Devin hopped the rooftop divider and overhanded his second grenade into the alley behind the building adjacent to his mother's. Marnie joined him moments later with the duffel bag, the two of them deploying one grenade each in rapid succession before they reached the team at the fire escapes.

"Put one in the alley about twenty yards to the west. In case the crew at the intersection gets curious. Gilly and Elena are making their way through the garden, but they won't have a direct line of sight to anyone that appears in the alley off Calvert Street," said Daly. "And I don't want to involve the QRF vehicles. They're our only hope of getting out of here before the police seal off the area."

"I'll take care of it," said Marnie, grabbing one of the grenades from the bag and heading out.

"That leaves one for the garden," said Devin, offering it to Daly.

"I trust your judgment. Or hers," said Daly, nodding toward Marnie, who chucked the grenade high above Miralles's head.

Gupta elbowed Daly. "I can't see shit on any of the camera feeds. I'd say this is as good a time as any."

Daly took a quick look at Gupta's laptop screen. Complete white-out on all six of the feeds watching over the alley and Lafayette Avenue.

"Looks good to me," said Devin.

"Agreed," said Daly, before turning to the rest of the group. "Okay. This is it. Miralles and Melendez will provide cover fire from the roof-top. Devin and I will go first. Give us about fifteen seconds to test the waters out there before you start to climb down. Once we reach the ground, we'll shift our attention to the most pressing threat and cover you while you make the climb. Whatever you do, don't stop on the way down. We need to pull this off as quickly as possible. They'll be shooting at us, but they won't be able to see us. The less time you spend on the fire escape, the better. Everyone good?"

Gupta closed his laptop and stuffed it in his backpack just as Marnie rejoined the group.

"What did I miss?" she said, kneeling next to him.

"We're about to head out," said Devin. "You and Brendan cover us for about fifteen seconds, then lead everyone else down."

"Easy enough, I guess," she said, shifting the Scorpion into a ready-to-fire position.

"Glad you're optimistic about this," he said, winking.

A thin grin broke across her grave, determined face. "I'm trying."

"Let's go," said Daly.

Devin nudged his pistol a little deeper into his waistband and followed Daly to the alley-side edge of the rooftop. Two thin ladders extended a few feet above the roof, each of them anchored to the parapet and leading directly to a narrow metal platform even with the second-floor alley windows. A drop-down ladder attached to the front of each platform would get them to the carports below.

When they reached the ground, they'd be momentarily separated by the stockade fence separating the two carports. The plan was for Devin to join Daly in the eastern carport and mount whatever defense was necessary until they could get more shooters to the ground. Keeping as low as possible, Devin gripped one of the side rails, his heart pumping hard enough that he could feel the blood coursing through his hand.

"Ready when you are," said Devin.

"Up and over, then."

They rose simultaneously and grabbed the ladder's side rails, ready to step onto the parapet and turn one hundred and eighty degrees around for the climb down the first ladder. Devin had set one boot on the parapet when automatic gunfire exploded from the alley to the east. Daly pitched sideways and knocked him flat on his stomach as a hail of bullets snapped overhead.

He turned his head, a quick look at Daly confirming the worst. A bullet had entered Daly's right temple, leaving a dime-size red hole. Devin couldn't see the other side of his head, but judging by the pool of blood spreading across the coarse rooftop underneath it, he didn't need to. Daly was gone.

Devin rolled on his side to check on the rest of the group. Everyone had dropped to their hands and knees except for Melendez and Miralles, who fired repeated short bursts over the parapet, into the thick smoke. Graves rose to a crouch and pushed through the group to reach Daly. He'd grabbed the back of the dead operative's vest and turned him over when his head snapped backward—a pink mist exploding from the back of the tech's head. *That didn't come from the alley. Neither shot came from the alley.*

"Get down! Rico. Miralles. Get the fuck down!" said Devin.

Melendez hesitated for a moment before dropping below the parapet. A single, heavier-caliber bullet clanked off the ladder rail a few feet beyond the space his head had occupied just a fraction of a moment ago.

Devin did the geometry in his head. "Sniper to the east! On our rooftop!"

The gunfire from the alley slackened, replaced by sporadic semiautomatic fire. The bullets smacked into the parapet, spraying pieces of brick and wood over the group. Judging by the high number of snaps and cracks overhead, most of the bullets missed. The Russians couldn't see the roofline. The gunfire was meant to pin them in place for the sniper.

He grabbed Daly's rifle and took a few thirty-round magazines from the operative's blood soaked vest, stuffing them in his pants pockets and waistband. Next, he removed the encrypted radio from its vest pouch, disconnecting the headset wire. Now for the headset. The thought of taking it off Daly's destroyed head made him nauseous. He paused for a few moments and looked away. Gupta started to crawl toward Graves's crumpled form.

"Anish," said Devin, shaking his head. "I'm sorry. He's gone. You don't want to see it."

"I need to empty his backpack and dig through his pockets for any sensitive information," said Gupta, tears streaming down his face. "I'll get the headset."

Devin nodded before looking over the rest of their group. They were at a breaking point. He could read it on their faces. Fear. But mostly anger and frustration at the prospect of having been beaten. Melendez looked to be one bad impulse away from getting a bullet between the eyes, his body tensed—ready to rise.

"Don't do it, Rico," said Devin. "Their sniper has the drop on us. Save it for later, and make it count."

Melendez glanced over his shoulder at Daly and Graves, muttering something under his breath.

"Marnie," said Devin. "Toss the last grenade toward my mother's apartment. We need to obscure the sniper's line of sight."

Marnie immediately dug through the duffel bag next to her and removed the grenade. She twisted onto her back and pulled the pin, cocking her arm to throw it.

"Stop! Don't throw it!" said Devin. "Not yet! They're watching us from the sky. That's the only way they could have known we were gathering here, and that we were about to climb down. Melendez scanned the rooftop for hostiles and came up empty."

"The rooftop was clear. Same with the one across the street," said Melendez.

"They're taking their cues from a second drone. Even if we blind the sniper, the drone operator will let them know we're making our move. The shooters in the alley were close enough to put steel on target, and the sniper has probably zeroed in on the ladders."

"That would be my primary point of focus at the moment," said Melendez.

"We need to drop the grenade right here and blind all of them," said Devin.

Shea shook his head. "If they're using another Raven, they'll have thermal-imaging capability. See right through the smoke."

"Fuck. He's right," said Devin.

"So. We need to get off this roof without using the ladders or standing up, basically," said Berg.

"Sounds about right," said Devin.

"I don't see how that's going to happen," said Marnie.

"Neither do I," said Berg. "Jail isn't sounding so bad anymore."

"Then this was all for nothing," said Devin.

"Just being realistic, Devin," said Berg. "I say we give everything we have to Shea. MINERVA's lawyers will spring him by tomorrow."

"The police or feds will keep everything but the clothes on his back," said Devin.

"Can we transmit what we have via Wi-Fi?" said Marnie, turning to Gupta.

Anish lay next to Graves, transferring the contents of his friend's backpack into his own. He glanced in Devin's direction, a blank look on his face, and shook his head.

"I could get some of it out," he said. "But we're talking a shit ton of data. No guarantees. If we had like an hour up here, we could get it all out."

They didn't have that kind of time. Police scanner activity suggested that the response would be delayed due to a suspiciously timed series of explosions in Baltimore's Inner Harbor, but it wouldn't be enough.

"We don't have an hour," said Devin. "Baltimore PD has been delayed, but they'll have a helicopter overhead in ten minutes. SWAT officers all over us within twenty to thirty minutes, tops."

"Then I guess we have to take our chances with the fire escape," said Berg. "Like Devin said—we've come too far to throw this away. The Russians have something big planned, which will be long finished by the time we get the band back together."

"We can't use the fire escape," said Marnie. "Not enough of us will reach the ground to repel whatever they throw at us from the alley."

"Back to square one," said Devin.

"I have an idea," said Miralles. "But it's going to be messy."

"How messy?" said Devin.

"C-4 messy."

"Can't be any messier than what we already have on our hands," said Devin.

Miralles grinned. "You haven't heard my idea."

CHAPTER 24

Marnie dropped from the attic onto a smoldering pile of splintered wood and drywall chunks. She stood there for a moment, taking in what looked to be a young child's bedroom through a thick haze of smoke and drywall dust. Stuffed animals strewn across the charred carpet. A four-post bed leaning on two broken feet, only one of its posts intact. Purple walls peppered with fragments. A shredded dresser with a shattered full-length mirror, a few pieces of glass barely hanging on to the frame. Thank god nobody was home when they blew a hole through the roof and ceiling.

"Keep moving," said Melendez, grabbing her arm and directing her toward the open bedroom door.

She made her way out of the bedroom into a dust-choked hallway, where Devin stepped out of a dark doorway to stop her.

"Miralles is about to set off the next breaching charge," said Devin.

"We're lucky we didn't kill anyone with the last one," said Marnie. "Did you see the room?"

"I did," said Devin. "Miralles peeked out of the front window. The adjacent stoop is directly below where she's going to blow the hole. She's convinced she's about to punch a hole through to the third-floor landing or staircase."

"Let's hope so," said Marnie.

Berg bumped into her, nearly knocking her over. Devin kept her upright until she'd regained her footing.

"Sorry," said Berg. "I can't keep my eyes open for more than two seconds with all this shit in the air. What's our status here?"

"Ears-and-mouth drill!" yelled Miralles, suddenly appearing at the end of the short hallway. "Fire in the hole!"

Marnie covered her ears and turned, opening her mouth to equalize the pressure on her lungs. The loudest explosion Marnie had ever experienced tore through them a few moments later. Berg dropped to his knees and shook his head. He hadn't taken any of the precautions to minimize the pressure damage from the close-proximity C-4 detonation. Likely, he'd be fine. Just some temporary hearing loss and shortness of breath.

"That's our status!" she said.

Berg shook his head. "Great. Thanks for the update!"

"Anytime," said Marnie, before following Devin down the hallway.

When they got to the front of the apartment, they found Miralles peering through a jagged three-foot-wide hole near the bottom of the wall, next to a singed and smoking, light-blue velvet recliner.

"The good news is we didn't kill anyone," she said.

"What's the bad news?"

Miralles shook her head. "Nothing but good news. We broke through to the third-floor landing."

"Nice job," said Devin, before triggering his radio. "How are we looking back there, Rico? Emily punched a nice hole in the wall."

Marnie didn't hear the response because Farrington had redistributed their limited supply of radios when the reinforcements had arrived. Only Farrington's people, minus Karl Berg, fielded a radio. Tactically, the decision made sense. The shooters needed to closely coordinate their efforts. Practically, it frustrated the shit out of her. One-sided conversations didn't work, especially when life-and-death decisions relied on a full grasp of the situation.

"Copy. Make sure the fire's out. It'll take us a minute to get everyone through," said Devin. "QRF. We're no more than two minutes from breakout."

"What did they say?" she said.

"What?" he said, his attention clearly torn between her simple question and the hole in the wall.

"Devin. Four of us don't have radios. We're entirely dependent on you to pass us information. Particularly the two of us who are expected to defend the group," she said, referring to herself and Shea. "We don't need a word-by-word replay, but we need something."

Devin nodded, a pained, almost ashamed look on his face. Maybe she'd gone too far. He'd shouldered full responsibility for their escape the instant Daly died—and hadn't skipped a beat.

"Sorry. I just—" she started.

"You're right," said Devin, squeezing her shoulder. "QRF is standing by for exfiltration. Let's get everyone down to the ground floor. We still have the fight of our lives in front of us."

CHAPTER 25

"Pull over for a moment," said Orlov, grabbing the driver's arm. "Oleg. Say that again. I don't think I heard you right."

"They vanished!" said Oleg. "They set off a smoke grenade on the roof, right in the middle of their group. Twenty seconds later, they were gone!"

"All teams just reported an explosion. Did you see an explosion?" said Orlov.

"No. I can't see anything through the smoke, except for their thermal signatures," said Oleg. "And those just fucking disappeared."

A second concussive boom reached the car, vibrating the rearview mirror. "I just heard another explosion."

"Nothing but smoke on the regular drone feed. The whole neighborhood is obscured," said Oleg. "I do have a small heat signature now on the thermal camera. Possibly a small fire. Did they blow themselves up?"

Orlov was trying to listen to the radio-net chatter on his push-to-talk phone and Oleg on another, the task proving to be pointless now that Oleg had nothing of substance to report.

"Oleg. Can you see anything at all right now?" said Orlov.

"No. No live bodies. Maybe a fire? Something bright is flickering down there, but it almost looks like it's partially obscured," said Oleg. "I'm having the drone team alter the drone's current course, so I can— wait. I think I just saw someone down there. Now the fire's out. Fuck. They blew a hole in the roof and jumped down!"

Orlov processed Oleg's unexpected statement, instantly validating it. Of course they blew a hole in the roof. Just like the concealed door to Helen Gray's roof was their only escape from her apartment, a makeshift hole was their only way off the roof and back onto the street without facing a guaranteed firing squad. The only question now was whether they'd exit the front or back door of the new apartment. Or both.

But he couldn't cover both. Not with the smoke obscuring everything. He had Severny and another operative on Lafayette Avenue, approaching Helen Gray's place, but he needed them to focus on destroying "certain materials," whatever that meant, or the whole damn building if they ran into trouble breaching the apartment. They were all running out of time.

"How does the smoke look on Lafayette?" said Orlov.

"Thinning out a little, but still a mess."

"What about the alley?"

"Thick. And it's not clearing," said Oleg. "The drone team said the wind is dead still out there."

"Anything going on with the vehicles parked at the corner of McAllister and Calvert?"

"No movement at all," said Oleg. "They're still sitting in their cars."

Interesting. Given the setback Gray's crew suffered on the rooftop, he'd expected some movement. Apparently, the plan remained the same, which made things easier for Orlov. He'd center his efforts on the alley, leaving a small insurance policy out front.

"What about the police?" said Orlov. "How much time do we have?"

"Still not much activity in your area," said Oleg. "They've formed a loose perimeter with the few responding units, but that's about it. The diversion in Fells Point drew most of Baltimore's finest to the harbor."

"Perfect," said Orlov. "Pack up the drone team and get out of there. There's nothing more for you to do at this point. This'll all be over in a matter of minutes."

"I can pick up any stragglers," said Oleg. "I'm just a few minutes away. I can slip through a gap in police coverage to the south. A few of the alleys are still clear."

"No. Make sure the drone team gets away clean, then head directly to the staging house," said Orlov. "Pack up everything and wait for my call."

"What if you don't call?"

"If I don't call you within fifteen minutes, get the fuck out of Baltimore," said Orlov. "The show is over."

"Good luck," said Oleg.

"Not much of that going around apparently," said Orlov, disconnecting the call.

He dropped the phone in one of the center-console cup holders and switched to the push-to-talk satellite radio.

"All units. This is Orlov. The targets have blown a hole in the rooftop and are making their way to the street level. I strongly suspect they'll stick to their same plan and try to escape through the community garden. Their backup vehicles are still parked at the northwest corner of the park, on McAllister and Calvert," said Orlov. "Maxim. Stay in place and stay quiet. They know you're there, but I'm going to flush them in your direction. They won't have a choice."

"Copy that," said Maxim.

"West block," said Orlov. "I'm going to drive down McAllister and take out their backup crew. When the shooting starts, drive to the Calvert Street end of the alley and set up covered positions aiming east. The smoke should be thin enough down there for you to pick out targets. Wait for them to get as close as possible before opening fire. They'll either hop the wall into the garden to escape your fire or head in the opposite direction, where Maxim will be waiting."

"We'll be ready," said Erik.

"Lashev. There's no more business for you on the roof," said Orlov. "Head back to Lafayette and find some cover where you can watch the street, just in case they send a few out the front door. If you run into something you shouldn't handle by yourself—emphasis on *shouldn't*— give Fedir and Andrei a call over the net."

"Already on my way down."

"Fedir and Andrei. Did you copy that?" said Orlov.

"Yes. Yes. But maybe we should just go with the explosives. Bring the whole apartment down," said Severny. "I can't exactly rush breaching the apartment. I need time to sweep for traps. Time I'm guessing we don't have at this point."

Severny was right. They were already looking at having to shoot their way past the police to get away. Every minute added to their stay reduced their odds of escaping from the area. But demolishing the apartment might not satisfy Pichugin's requirement to destroy "certain materials." His front man had been adamant about that aspect of the contract.

"Set the explosives," said Orlov. "But I really need you to get into that apartment and destroy any materials left behind before you bring the entire building down. You can't exactly set a pile of bricks and rubble on fire."

"No. But we could climb the fire escape and place a series of incendiary grenades on the roof from front to back. Shouldn't take those more than seconds to burn through the roof and ceiling of the apartment," said Severny.

"They'll burn all the way to the ground floor," said Orlov. "But it'll still take too long to set the place on fire."

"As soon as the incendiaries burn holes through the roof, we'll drop white phosphorous grenades right behind them—directly into the third-floor apartment," said Severny.

Orlov felt a pang of jealousy. The idea was brilliant. The white phosphorous grenades would explode inside Helen Gray's apartment, each scattering hundreds of burning particles in every direction. The third floor would be consumed in flames by the time they climbed back down the fire escape.

"We may not need to use the explosives," said Orlov.

"Now that I think about it," said Severny. "Probably not. But we'll plant them anyway. Just to be sure."

Severny was starting to grow on him.

"If time permits," said Orlov. "Be ready to abandon the explosives if we run out of time."

"Understood," said Severny.

Orlov motioned for the driver to get moving again. It was time to set the final trap in motion and turn the page on the messiest contract he'd ever taken.

"All units. We're on the move again. Turning onto McAllister in a few seconds."

CHAPTER 26

Garza glanced nervously between the MP7 submachine gun in the passenger seat and the rapidly thinning smoke to his south on Calvert Street. Another minute and he'd be staring at the vague outline of a car carrying two killers, who may or may not know that he worked for the other team. Radio chatter suggested sophisticated aerial surveillance. Sophisticated enough to have made him and the rest of the QRF team? That was the question. When the smoke cleared, something had to give.

Formerly Delta Force, recently a stakeholder in a successful private investigation firm—currently wondering what the fuck he'd gotten himself into—Garza had no intention of today being his "last watch." Two factors had landed him in this seat. Three really. Number three being a bourbon-fueled plea by number two to lend a hand. Number two being Ripley, former Navy SEAL and longtime mercenary collaborator, back when Garza did this kind of work. Number one had been Senator Margaret Steele.

Her endorsement of whatever the hell was going on here, confirmed by a trusted acquaintance, had been what had pushed him over the edge.

"QRF. Change of plans. Send one car down Calvert to block the west entrance to the alley. Engage hostiles at the intersection of Calvert and Lafayette," said the new voice barking orders over the net.

"On the way," said Garza, shifting his sedan into drive.

"Gilly and Elena. Head down the sidewalk—"

Long bursts of automatic gunfire erupted on McAllister Street, distracting him from the rest of the transmission. He had no idea who was shooting who and didn't intend to find out. He'd been given his orders. Garza hit the gas, intending to close the short distance in a few seconds. Someone yelled "QRF is under attack!" over the net, but that was Ripley's problem now, and he had plenty of firepower to deal with it.

Halfway to the alley, a car burst out of the smoke screen obscuring the Calvert and Lafayette intersection. He jammed on the brakes and grabbed the MP7 with both hands, lifting its barrel above the dashboard before his car screeched to a stop. Garza's first three bursts created a soccer ball–size opaque obstruction in his own windshield.

"Fuck me," he said, before leaning as far over the center console as possible to reacquire his target.

Immediately noting that his first bursts had neatly perforated the glass directly in front of the driver, he centered the MP7's red-dot sight on the front passenger. Three rapid trigger pulls sent at least a dozen of the submachine gun's uniquely powerful four-point-six-by-thirty-millimeter bullets through both windshields, obscuring his view again.

Gunfire still raged just to the north of him. Garza slipped out of the driver's-side door while reloading to assess his accuracy. The enemy sedan coasted past the alley, drifting slowly to the right, until it scraped along a parked car and came to a stop, its windshield riddled with holes and splotched bright red.

He stayed low and pivoted, just as a black SUV entered the McAllister intersection. Its occupants unloaded on Ripley's vehicle, parked directly in front of them. Garza snapped off several shots focused on the driver before he was forced back inside his car by frighteningly accurate gunfire. He crawled across the front seats and opened the passenger door as bullets shattered the windows and punctured the backrests just inches above him.

Dropping to the street, he inched left until he had a clear line of sight to the SUV. He got off a long burst at the rear driver's-side passenger before he was driven back by a near miss that skipped off the pavement a few inches from his left arm. Garza scrambled around the front of the sedan, putting the engine block between himself and whatever gunfire might be coming his way. He needed a few seconds to think.

He'd spotted Ripley when he was on the pavement. His friend had pulled the same trick, climbing over the front seats to escape the torrent of gunfire aimed at his vehicle. Ripley had been crouched behind the front of his car, snapping off shots. If the Russians rushed him, he was a dead man.

"Rip. Sending some rounds your way," said Garza.

"Appreciate it," said Ripley.

Garza quickly leaned beyond the bumper and sighted in on the shooter pounding Ripley's car with automatic rifle fire. The man spotted him just as Garza pressed the trigger, the short burst punching through his face. The SUV's tires screeched a few seconds later, the vehicle racing north. Both Ripley and Garza fired controlled bursts at the SUV as it sped away, their efforts going unrewarded when the vehicle executed a controlled turn off Calvert Street, vanishing from their lines of sight.

"QRF. We're hearing a lot of gunfire. What's your status?" said the new guy. "Is the alley entrance clear?"

"We got wiped out is what happened!" said Ripley. "Ambushed by an SUV packed with shooters. How did that slip through the radar?"

"Did Elena or Gilly make it?" said the voice. "Are they headed for the extraction point?"

"Dude. Whoever this is," said Ripley. "We got hammered. I don't see anybody moving in QRF Three or Four. I think I see one of your people lying on the sidewalk next to QRF Three. Nobody is headed to the extraction point."

"Copy."

Jesus, Ripley. Get ahold of yourself.

"This is Garza. QRF One. The Calvert Street alley entrance is clear. Lafayette intersection targets have been neutralized," said Garza. "We can cover the extraction point, but we don't have much to work with in the way of vehicles. Mine is drivable if we knock the windshield out. Rip's looks out of commission."

"I've got two flat tires," said Ripley. "I don't know about QRF Three and Four."

"How many seats do we need?" said Garza.

"We have seven. Daly and Graves are dead. This is Devin Gray."

Shit. The bodies were stacking up on this one.

"Rip. Check out QRF Three and Four. Look for survivors and a working vehicle. If none of those cars work, we can use the hostile vehicle from the Lafayette intersection," said Garza. "One way or the other we'll get two drivable vehicles to the extraction point."

"Copy that," said Rip.

"And grab all of their radios," said Garza.

"Anything else?"

"Weapons and ammunition—since you asked."

"Don't push it," said Rip.

"Good thinking. We're heading out in a few seconds," said Devin. "I expect heavy gunfire from the east. The smoke is still pretty thick, so it won't be accurate, but it'll slow us down."

"We'll have the vehicles ready by the time you reach Calvert Street," said Garza. "We won't get past the police in these. Just saying."

"We'll figure that out later," said Devin. "First things first."

CHAPTER 27

Devin followed Melendez and Miralles out the back and down the short stoop into the acrid smoke, which had dispersed significantly more than they'd initially assessed. He could clearly see the ends of the stockade fences flanking the carport and easily distinguish objects on the other side of the alley. Secretly accessing the adjacent apartment may have saved their lives. A Russian firing squad likely awaited them one apartment over.

Their rifles pointed east, toward the threat, and the three of them took positions to cover the rest of the group's passage to the next apartment's carport. The plan was to move from carport to carport until they reached the end of the alley, where the cars would pick them up along the Calvert Street side of the last apartment—out of the Russians' line of fire.

He glanced over his shoulder. The smoke was even thinner toward the west end of the alley, which would complicate the final moments of their withdrawal, but also render the Russians' job nearly impossible once they escaped the alley. Any Russians who tried to follow them onto Calvert Street would be slaughtered.

The trick was getting everyone out of the alley safely, and peering into the smoke to their immediate east, he wasn't sure how they'd pull that off. Somewhere in that mess, at least five shooters waited for his group to make the first move. Time to find out what they were up against.

Devin lay flat on the uneven concrete near the end of the fence and triggered his radio. "Stand by to move. Single file and fast. Go."

Shea burst through the open doorway and headed for Devin, followed by Berg and Gupta. Marnie had just hit the ground when gunfire exploded from the east, bullets zipping overhead and stitching through the fences on the eastern side of the carport. Devin pressed the trigger repeatedly, shifting his rifle's aimpoint slowly back and forth at shin height, hoping to catch someone in the face or leg.

Marnie hopped over him, her submachine gun rattling a few seconds later.

"Go! We're clear!" she said.

Devin scrambled around the fence and immediately moved to the same spot on the other side of the new carport, lying flat in the coarse gravel next to a weed-infested, chest-high cinder block wall. The carports were bordered by a hodgepodge of barriers reflecting the owner's level of give-a-shit, some of them rusted chain-link fences. Fortunately, they had solid cover until they reached the end of the alley.

Marnie stayed crouched at the corner of the stockade fence, firing the Scorpion until it ran out of ammunition. She took off for the small group huddled behind the dilapidated concrete stoop next to the building. Bullets popped through the fence in front of and behind her as she ran. Devin held his breath until she finally reached the stairs.

Miralles bolted around the fence and dropped to the ground before firing a long series of two-round volleys. Devin joined in, spraying the alley until his rifle's bolt carrier locked back. Melendez still hadn't appeared by the time he finished changing magazines.

"Where's Rico?" he said over the radio net.

"Went back into the house," she said.

"What?"

"He's going to double back into the other apartment and hit them from behind. This carport-hopping plan isn't going to work with the smoke thinning," said Miralles.

Devin glanced over his shoulder. They were right. There was no conceivable way to get to the end of the alley without taking casualties.

"Agreed. What does he need from us?"

"We need to draw the Russians into this carport," said Miralles. "Which means we need to get everyone up and over this cinder block wall, not around it, and then over the wall on the other side. Not around it. The alley is too dangerous."

"Got it," said Devin, before dashing for the group hunkered down behind the porch stoop.

Marnie made some room, a tight fit behind the crumbling stairs, her Scorpion pointed at the bullet-splintered fence several feet away. Shea lay flat, behind the bottom step, his rifle pointed in Miralles's direction. Berg huddled against the apartment, next to Gupta, who looked entirely detached from the situation.

"Where the fuck is Rico?" said Berg.

"Don't ask," said Devin. "We need to get up and over this wall, and the next—immediately. Marnie and I will give everyone a boost, and we'll help each other over. Don't stop once you're over the wall."

"I don't get it," said Marnie. "What happened to the plan?"

"No time to explain," said Devin. "Let's go."

He took off and crouched next to the wall, interlacing his fingers. Marnie mimicked him a few feet away. Berg arrived first, placing a foot in Devin's locked hands before grabbing the top of the wall. Devin shot his legs upward and lifted with his arms, heaving Berg high and far enough that he tilted forward when he landed on the top of the wall and simply toppled onto the other side. Gupta was next, stepping into Marnie's hands. She propelled him to the top of the wall, where he managed to balance himself long enough for a controlled drop into the adjacent carport. Within the span of several seconds, everyone was over, headed for the next wall.

CHAPTER 28

Rico Melendez crouched motionless next to the scorched hole Emily had blown in the walls, listening carefully for any indication that the Russians had seen him reenter the apartment. The gunfire echoing through the hallways intensified, suggesting that the Russians had moved into the carport behind the adjacent apartment. A door slammed shut a few moments later, the gunfire now marginally muted. They didn't have time to search, so they'd shut the back door as a basic precaution.

He made his way to the stairwell, cautiously descending to the ground floor. The layout was different. The stairs led to a small foyer, indicating that the ground-floor occupants had expanded into the space occupied by a hallway in the other building. With the gun battle raging, Melendez front kicked the door three consecutive times until the doorknob, dead bolt, and slide-chain lock failed, and the door swung open.

Remaining still for several seconds, he listened for signs of activity. Nothing. And there was no way any of the Russians had heard anything over the gunfire. He arrived at the back door and peeked outside. A man lay on his back in the middle of the alley, legs kicking while a female mercenary pushed a blood-soaked compress down on his neck. A few moments later, she threw the compress to the ground next to him and took off, firing as she disappeared beyond the stockade fence. He triggered his radio.

"Em. Rico. I'm in position. Any idea what I'm up against?"

"I'd say four or five. It's hard to tell," said Miralles. "We're ready."

"Count to twenty and stop shooting," said Melendez. "Heading out."

"Good luck."

Melendez threw the dead bolt and slowly opened the door inward. The carport and alley behind the apartment stood empty, except for the mortally wounded mercenary, whose legs barely twitched now. He slinked along the worn stockade fence, keeping low. An occasional bullet popped through the planks a few feet over his head. He peered around the end post and scanned for targets, finding only one in the adjacent carport. The woman who had been tending to the mercenary bleeding out behind him. She fired a few bursts from her rifle before crouching to reload.

He sighted in on her, placing the green, illuminated tip of the ACOG's reticle just under her nose. A single trigger press slammed her head against the fence, the suppressed shot seemingly going unnoticed in the chaos. Melendez slipped around the fence and approached the dead mercenary. He propped her against the fence and used her as a shield, bullets cracking inches past his face and punching through the wood around him. A few seconds later, the volume of gunfire in the alley noticeably dropped.

Time for payback.

Melendez crept around the end of the fence and assessed the situation. Two Russians spread out along the cinder block wall, and behind the back of a parked car on the other side of the alley crouched another—who had just noticed him. He tilted his rifle and used the side-angle-mounted, short-range red-dot sight, firing twice before shifting his aim to the others. There was no need to check his work on the first target. The man had dropped like his legs had been kicked out from under him.

The rest was too easy. Too merciful. He shifted from one Russian to the next along the cinder block wall, firing twice at each of their heads. It was over in a few seconds. He spun and scanned the alley behind him, looking for any signs of a possible threat. Several apartments down,

Melendez saw the outline of a car, mostly obscured by lingering smoke, and guessed it was the first of the three cars that had delivered the initial wave of Russians.

"This is Rico. I have five Russians down. I think that's all they had left in the alley."

"Copy," said Devin. "We're moving toward the extraction point."

"You might want to hold up," said Melendez. "The Russians that tried to breach the back of your mother's apartment left three vehicles in the alley. Remember? The Claymore was directed at the apartment. We might have three undamaged, way-less-suspicious cars in our possession. It's worth checking out," said Melendez.

"Okay. Clear the alley up to my mother's apartment," said Devin. "We'll start moving in your direction."

Melendez was surprised Devin didn't put up an argument. Then again, he was in charge of the tactical side of things now that Daly was gone. Had Devin made the shift in his head that quickly? Melendez hadn't given it a thought until now.

"Copy," said Melendez, still not sure what to think of Devin Gray.

He moved quietly toward the cars, scanning both sides of the alley as he walked. From what he could tell from here, the cars were still running. One carport away from the first vehicle, a rapid series of metal clangs drew his attention upward and to the right, to the fire escape leading down from the rooftop of Helen Gray's building. Slightly obscured by the lingering smoke, a figure with a rifle slung over his back climbed down in a hurry with his back turned to the alley.

Melendez had stopped and raised his rifle when the man yelled something in Russian halfway down the ladder, indicating he wasn't alone. Melendez slid up to the fence next to Helen Gray's carport and took a quick look at the back of the apartment. No sign of anyone outside. The guy shouted again, and this time someone responded from deep inside the building. The apartment's smoke detectors started shrieking a moment later. *Perfect cover.*

Melendez unsheathed the compact knife attached to his vest and rushed toward the bottom of the ladder, intercepting the Russian the moment his feet hit the ground. He covered the man's mouth and yanked his head backward, repeatedly stabbing him in the front of his neck until he went completely slack. After lowering the mercenary's body, Melendez sheathed the bloodied knife, listening for any unusual activity inside the apartment. Satisfied that his deed had gone unnoticed, he clicked his radio transmitter in a prearranged pattern.

Two short clicks followed by two long with a short break before repeating the pattern. After the second series of clicks, he got a response.

"Holding in place. Advise when clear," said Devin.

He shouldered his rifle and entered the Claymore-blasted apartment, careful to avoid any loose debris on the white-drywall-dust-covered floor. A head poked around the mangled staircase corner, barking a seemingly annoyed question over the earsplitting smoke detector alarm. Melendez reflexively fired twice, both bullets striking him in the face and splattering the jagged, splintered front doorway with dark-red gore.

Continuing down the hallway, he arrived at the foot of the demolished staircase to discover that the man had fallen on top of a duffel bag. Melendez pulled the bag clear, finding enough Semtex plastic explosive blocks and electric detonators to bring the whole building down. A whiff of something caustic caught his attention. Almost garlicky. Shit. That was why the other guy was on the roof. They must have somehow dropped a white phosphorus grenade into Helen Gray's apartment. The Russians weren't fucking around. Time to get as far away from here as possible until they could regroup and figure out how to hit them back. He activated his radio.

"The alley is clear. Keys are in the vehicles."

CHAPTER 29

Lashev heard two suppressed gunshots and assumed they came from Helen Gray's apartment. Everything had gone deathly quiet in the alley a few minutes ago, and nobody was responding to his radio calls. Not even Orlov, who may not have survived the plan he'd set in motion.

The gunfire at the start of Orlov's rolling ambush sounded promising but died off a little too quickly. A solid half minute of automatic fire followed by several sporadic bursts and screeching tires. Then nothing until the alley gun battle. Now nothing again, except for the two suppressed gunshots. Since none of the Russians carried suppressed weapons, it was fair to assume that the entire team in the alley and apartment had been slaughtered. Lashev was on his own.

He sighted in on what was left of the front entrance of the target apartment and waited for someone to stick their head out. No such luck. Nothing moved on Lafayette Avenue. Even the smoke had mostly dissipated, leaving the carnage plain to see. He tried the radio again.

"Any unit. This is Lashev," he said. "I need a pickup at the intersection of Guilford and Lafayette."

Nothing.

"Pickup at the intersection of Guilford and Lafayette. Is anybody out there?"

Static.

"Fuck this."

He stood up just as the three cars that Garin's team had driven into the alley raced across Lafayette Avenue, headed south on Calvert.

Definitely no survivors, or they would have answered his radio calls. He dropped back down just before the last car slowed, gunfire erupting from its rear passenger window. Bullets stitched the air just above his head, a few chipping the concrete.

He pressed himself flat against the sidewalk and gave it a few more seconds before peeking around one of the steps. The cars were gone. Someone on their team speaks Russian. They'd heard his call for help over the radio and knew where to look for him. He looked over his shoulder and considered the car he had driven here with Orlov, dismissing the idea just as quickly.

The chances of running into a police roadblock were too high, and he couldn't shoot his way out of it by himself. His only viable option at this point was to put a little distance between himself and this mess, mainly using the alleys, and break into a garage or apartment. He'd hide out until things cooled off a little and the police loosened their grip on the area. A few hours at most.

Once the cops finally moved in and surveyed the scene, they'd quickly assess that whoever had survived this battle was long gone and shrink the police cordon to the area immediately surrounding the crime scene. Lashev would be well outside of the police line when he hit the streets to link up with whoever had survived the disaster that had just unfolded. Oleg, for sure, and the members of Severny's team who had yet to arrive.

Or maybe he'd skip that part altogether and book a quick flight to Mexico City. Buy a car with cash and drive to a lesser-known resort town on the ocean. The fallout from this spectacular failure threatened to swallow everyone involved. Hiding out for a while until he determined which way the winds would blow sounded like a better strategy than standing under a tree with the other survivors when the inevitable thunderstorm rolled in.

CHAPTER 30

Orlov walked briskly through a public-school parking lot just off North Avenue, looking for an opportunity to hijack or steal a car. He'd ditched his bullet-riddled mess as soon as he turned off Calvert Street, knowing full well he wouldn't get more than a block in it. Police cars and SUVs had finally screeched into position at every intersection in sight on North Avenue as he crossed the busy street in front of the school. It was only a matter of time before they found the gun-battle-scarred SUV with one of Severny's people dead in the back seat, and when they did—his minutes were numbered.

Nothing about his physical appearance screamed that he might have been involved in the shootout that had just taken place a few blocks south. He hadn't suffered any injuries, and he'd used a packet of baby wipes that he'd found in the glove compartment to wipe the driver's blood and brains off his face and neck. Would he pass a close look at his blood-speckled pants and shirt? Probably not. Which was why he needed to get out of the area fast. The satellite radio in his pants pocket crackled.

"Any unit. This is Lashev. I need a pickup at the intersection of Guilford and Lafayette."

A few seconds later.

"Pickup at the intersection of Guilford and Lafayette. Is anybody out there?"

Nobody was coming for him. The lack of radio chatter told the story. Everybody was either dead or on the run. He considered responding, just to give Lashev some hope, but thought better of it. Karl Berg was probably listening to one of the radios right now, waiting to put his Russian-language skills to good use. Orlov dropped the radio on the parking lot pavement and stomped on it for several seconds. For all he knew, Gray and his people could use one of the other radios to ping his location.

He wasn't having any luck finding the right car. Orlov needed something significantly older and relatively valueless. In other words, a vehicle that cost less to replace than to equip with an alarm. The last thing he needed right now was to set off a car alarm. He kept walking, still not seeing anything that might work.

They must pay teachers more than he'd been led to believe by Russian television broadcasts. This looked like a luxury car lot. He wasn't surprised, since pretty much everything he saw on Russian TV today, ironically, made America look and sound like the shittiest parts of the Soviet Union back in the eighties.

Orlov had almost reached the end of the parking lot when his personal satellite phone rang. Pichugin's front man already? But there was nobody to rat on him. Everyone was either dead or running for their lives. He pulled the phone out of his pocket and checked the number.

Not everyone.

"Oleg. I didn't realize you were back from vacation," said Orlov.

If Oleg mentioned a specific country in his response, Orlov would know that he was under duress. He couldn't imagine any way the Americans had caught up with him and forced him to make this call, but he couldn't take any chances. For all he knew, Pichugin had a shadow team watching his every move and had surprised Oleg at the staging house. The presence of Pichugin's enforcers would motivate Oleg to give him a call.

"And miss all the fun in Baltimore?" said Oleg.

Not a country. Oleg didn't have a proverbial or literal gun to his head. "Where are you?"

"At the staging house," said Oleg.

"And the drone team? Did that go right at least?"

"They're here, too."

"What?" said Orlov, about to go off on Oleg.

"No worries. They're dead," said Oleg. "I tried my best to convince them that they'd be compensated for the drones, and that the rest of the contract would be honored, but they insisted on receiving some of the money immediately. I told them that this wasn't exactly the best time for this kind of distraction, because we had a bit of a situation on our hands. They followed me to the staging house instead of driving away—so now we won't get the deposit back for the house rental."

Orlov chuckled. He wanted to laugh out loud, but he couldn't bring himself to do it, considering the circumstances.

"I didn't like them anyway," said Orlov. "So. Here's the situation. I'm on foot, just outside of the police cordon north of the target area. I'm probably safe for a few more minutes, but once they find the SUV, all bets are off. I need an immediate pickup."

"Just you?"

"Just me. Lashev might be the only other survivor, but he's on his own until he can get clear of the area."

"What's the pickup location?"

"Pick me up on the north side of whatever school lies between Calvert and Guilford," said Orlov.

"Hold on, I'm punching it in my cell phone," said Oleg. "Okay. Looks like the Dallas F. Nicholas Sr. Elementary School. Jesus. You didn't make it very far away, did you? Are you sure the area is secure?"

"If you quit asking questions and start driving, it won't be a problem," said Orlov.

"Be there in less than two minutes," said Oleg.

"Yep," he said, and ended the call.

Orlov hopped up on the brick wall at the end of the school parking lot and hung his feet over the sidewalk, listening to the growing chorus of sirens a few blocks behind him on North Avenue.

CHAPTER 31

"Slow down," said Devin, before glancing over his shoulder at Gupta, who typed frantically on his laptop in the back seat.

Marnie eased off the accelerator, the car dropping from an already painfully slow speed to a brutal fifteen miles per hour, buying them several seconds of time.

"Where to, Anish?" he said. "We're running out of room. Calvert Street crosses the Penn Station tracks just a few blocks ahead. The police will have something set up on the other side of that overpass."

"The antenna situation sucks. This portable rooftop unit is barely getting what I need. It's just going to take a little more time," said Gupta.

"No problem," said Devin. "Do what you need to do. Just get us off the streets until you have a handle on this."

"Take a left here on Federal and look for an alley or some street parking."

Marnie turned the sedan, careful not to squeal the tires.

"There's an alley right before that brick building with the graffiti," said Devin, pointing to the left side of the street.

"I see it," said Marnie, before guiding the car through an impossibly tight backstreet.

His radio chattered.

"What are we doing?" said Melendez.

"Buying Anish some time," said Devin.

They emerged in a fully occupied, angled parking lot, which didn't seem affiliated with either of the buildings that flanked it.

"Stop here," said Devin, before turning his attention back to Gupta. "Is there anything we can do to help? What if we took the antenna off the roof and climbed up one of these fire escapes?"

"No. It has nothing to do with that. You can pick up police radio transmissions anywhere in the city. I just need time," said Gupta. "Baltimore PD encrypts their police traffic, which requires every transmission to negotiate with each radio's encryption key, resulting in a very specific, very brief back-and-forth radio frequency signature when the radio traffic is passed. Once I nail down more of this signature, we just need to start moving again, and I can fix nearby units' positions. It's taking time because Baltimore PD has taken some serious steps to prevent criminals from intercepting or spoofing their communications."

"How long?" said Devin.

"I really don't know," said Gupta. "This isn't like the movies, where I have a status bar counting down the time."

"Is the nine-one-one system ready to go?"

Gupta checked the laptop on the seat next to him. Graves's laptop.

"Yep. I just need to figure out where they have a gap in coverage."

The system in question had been designed by Gupta to divert police resources by simultaneously flooding 911 calls. A tackle box resting in the footwell behind Marnie contained fifteen cell phones, each of them hardwired to some kind of circuit board that fed into Graves's laptop through a wired connection.

Once they identified a weak spot in the police cordon, Gupta could divert those units to an entirely fabricated, nearby crisis by typing in a street location and a few variations of the crime in progress. The system would dial 911 through all fifteen phones and report the crime using a digital voice-mimicking program, each call sounding different enough to fool anyone monitoring all of them at once—hopefully.

"We're good here," said Devin, surreptitiously squeezing Marnie's hand. "For a few minutes, at least."

She raised an eyebrow, likely acknowledging the reality of their situation. If a police car pulled up on either side of this tight alleyway, they were screwed. Their entire escape plan depended on not drawing law enforcement attention prior to making their final move out of the police perimeter.

They'd all agreed from the start that engaging law enforcement with lethal or disabling force was off the table, and given what had just gone down at his mother's apartment, any run-in was likely to get ugly, fast. Better to avoid them altogether. The entire city's police department had to be on edge right now. This was the second small battle to take place in Baltimore within the past few weeks.

"Got it!" said Gupta. "And you were right about the overpasses. They're massed on the other side of the Penn Station tracks. North is not an option, either. North Avenue is saturated with cops. Same with Greenmount Avenue to the east, along the cemetery."

"What about the west?" said Devin.

"The west is basically a wedge that squeezes you over the tracks or onto North Avenue," said Gupta. "They pretty much have this entire area locked down, waiting for SWAT."

"Any ideas?"

Gupta squinted, his eyes darting back and forth across the screen for a few seconds before nodding.

"The southwest corner of Green Mount Cemetery," said Gupta. "The tracks go into Union Tunnel right at the corner, so there's no overpass. It's just city streets, and Baltimore PD has set the southern limit of its perimeter on Oliver Street, right at the entrance to the cemetery. If we can shift them north a few streets, we could slip south of them on Oliver and melt away into North Baltimore."

"Sounds like a plan," said Devin, before passing along the same information to the other two cars.

Marnie took a right out of the parking lot a minute later and snaked their convoy southeast through the alleys and backstreets to the intersection of Brentwood and Oliver, where she stopped them several feet short of exposing the car to the police at the Greenmount and Oliver intersection to their left. Choosing Brentwood had been a stroke of genius on her part, since it was a one-way street, headed south. If the police fell for their trick, they wouldn't turn up the street off Oliver.

"Work your magic," said Devin.

Gupta picked up the second laptop and typed away for a half minute before looking up at Devin and nodding. "The calls are going out. I basically said two guys with rifles just passed a mini-mart a few blocks north of here, headed toward a bunch of kids in a park."

Several sets of tires screeched nearby, two police SUVs racing past a few seconds later. They'd taken the bait. Bad guys with guns threatening kids had done the trick.

"How are we looking on the map?" said Devin.

"Completely clear," said Gupta. "Every unit at the block has pressed north. I have a few units moving into the general area, but my guess is they'll probably join the fun."

Devin triggered his radio. "Anish cleared the way. Follow us out."

Ten minutes later, they were headed north on Interstate 95, Gupta's computer wizardry indicating that they hadn't drawn any police vehicles with them.

CHAPTER 32

Devin Gray and the team formed a loose circle behind their vehicles, which they'd parked in a Family Dollar parking lot less than a mile northeast of the Baltimore city limit.

"We're about ten minutes from Interstate 695," said Devin. "Brendan. What are you thinking? North or south on 695?"

"First things first," said Anish. "When are you going to take off your disguise? It's kind of disturbing."

Shea adjusted his beard. "I'll take it off when I'm one hundred percent convinced that I'm not under drone surveillance."

"Or in a few weeks," said Berg. "Whichever comes first."

"Seriously," said Shea. "To answer your question, I say we head north and make our way to Frederick, Maryland. Frederick is roughly equidistant between DC and Baltimore. I'm going to call in a high-priority emergency at MINERVA. The highest priority I'm authorized to initiate without explaining myself right now. We'll get you set up with three clean vehicles; then I'll head back to the office. I intend to brief the board of directors first thing tomorrow morning. We need to get this DEVTEK sting rolling immediately. If the Russians are desperate enough to shoot up a city block and demolish a three-story apartment building to deep-six your mother's work, they must be very close to their endgame. Sending discreet assassins is one thing. This is something entirely different."

"I agree," said Berg. "They're on the cusp of something big."

"Any chance the board of directors will cut us completely out of this?" said Devin.

"Yeah. There's always a chance that'll come up," said Shea. "But my presentation will demonstrate the value of going beyond just circling the wagons around DEVTEK. Specifically, the value of playing a key role in taking down what looks to be the greatest threat to national security ever discovered. I'm thinking that will appeal to the board."

"I bet it will," said Berg. "I wish I could make the same pitch to the CIA and have the same impact."

"I can't imagine they wouldn't be all over this," said Shea.

"They haven't for close to ten years," said Devin. "Which is why we're in this situation."

"He's right," said Berg. "Nobody, including me, took Devin's mother seriously then—I don't expect they would take it seriously now."

"Even with all of this evidence?" said Shea. "And your team's testimony?"

"Underneath its slick sheen, the CIA is just another bureaucracy," said Berg. "You could drop this in the director's lap, and it would be a month before he passed it off to the FBI. I have a contact at the CIA that might be able to get some off-the-books support. That's the best we can hope for."

"And the team in Russia?" said Shea. "I'm still a little foggy about their mission."

"They're in place, where they need to be," said Berg. "If MINERVA commits to a partnership with us on the DEVTEK angle, we'll fully brief you on the Russia mission."

"I'll need something to satisfy the board."

"Tell them we're surveilling one of the masterminds behind the sleeper network."

"That should do it," said Shea.

"I should hope so," said Berg.

"What are we thinking after Frederick?" said Devin.

"We need to get my Suburban," said Gupta. "Unless you want to drop me somewhere up ahead. I can Uber back, grab my ride, and meet you in Frederick."

"Back to Baltimore?" said Berg. "I don't think that's a good idea."

"It's in the Symphony Center Parking Garage, less than a minute walk from one of the light-rail stations," said Gupta. "I just need to get to any rail station in the city."

"I don't think using anything connected to a credit card is a good idea. Even if it's issued under a fake name or to a dummy corporation," said Devin. "I don't know how they found us, but I guarantee it's connected to our financial transactions. From this point forward, we use cash or one of the prepaid cards from my mother's vault."

"So you're saying Uber isn't an option," said Gupta.

"Take a cab and use cash," said Devin. "We have plenty to go around."

"A cab? Yuck," said Gupta.

"Just deal with it," said Melendez.

"I still don't like it," said Berg. "I think we need to let Baltimore simmer down for a few days."

"I'll keep him company," said Miralles. "And out of trouble."

"Yay for me," said Gupta. "I get to spend a few hours alone with Miss Personality."

"Back to my original question," said Devin. "Where do we go after Frederick?"

"I know a place," said Melendez. "Karl's been there. Once . . . I believe?"

"That place?" said Berg. "Is it even habitable?"

"Rich takes a trip out there now and then. For old times' sake," said Melendez. "He says it's still standing."

"There's a big difference between still standing and habitable," said Berg.

"What are we talking about here?" said Marnie.

"Somewhere entirely off the grid a few hours west of DC," said Melendez.

"Off the grid—as in no running water or electricity," said Berg. "Unless someone has been maintaining the generators."

"It isn't a resort. There's no day spa. It's a secure location in the middle of nowhere, but it's close enough to the DC area for us to make day trips, or host trusted guests," said Melendez.

"Sounds perfect for now," said Devin. "We could use some time off from looking over our shoulders. Does anyone other than Karl have a problem with this idea?"

"I'm fine with it," said Berg. "But we should pick up a few portable generators along the way. And some camping gear in case the critters have taken over."

PART THREE

CHAPTER 33

Yuri Pichugin had balked against seeing Kuznetzov at the Ostozhenka Street residence, one of his few remaining sanctuaries that hadn't been invaded by the overstuffed general. He'd relented only because Kuznetzov had said it was absolutely critical—and despite the man's many flaws, he had never been prone to hyperbole. Whatever he needed to pass along clearly couldn't wait.

He paid top dollar to hire the best cyber and communications security experts in the business to shield his every spoken word and digital transaction from outside interception, but given what he knew about the zero-day technology exploits he'd purchased recently and the "zero-days" his sleepers still actively pursued, nothing was truly safe in the new digital age.

And with the stakes of OPERATION BLACKOUT increasing by the day, he'd decided to fully adopt Vladimir Putin's approach until the operation had concluded. Nothing written. Nothing typed. Nothing spoken in the presence of a phone or electronic device. Everything passed in person, subject to the strictest anti-technology protocols. It was the only way to ensure that his messages couldn't be intercepted, and if for some reason an information breach occurred, he'd know exactly who was responsible.

At least the visit would be quick. There would be no hospitality this time around. No vodka, caviar, and finger sandwiches. Not even a glass of water. Pichugin was in a hurry to get back to Saint Petersburg. Despite his extreme wealth, ruthless reputation, and highest-level connections, Moscow had a dark undercurrent that left him feeling uneasy. He spent as little time as possible here. His current trip was a necessity to ensure the full and unhesitant cooperation of the Russian Western Military District's senior chain of command in his upcoming operation.

He'd spent the evening dining and drinking with a select group of Army generals and colonels, all willing participants in BLACKOUT. They were no strangers to the murky military situations, many of them having ordered or led units into the Donbass region to execute questionable missions.

But BLACKOUT would be unlike anything they'd previously supported. Pichugin had flown in to assure them that their reward would reflect the magnitude and importance of their loyal participation, giving them a taste of the opulent life that awaited them, capped off by an exceedingly rare appearance by Putin himself. The visit had been calculated to make a lasting impression.

If there had been any doubt in anyone's mind last night about their involvement in Pichugin's plan, Putin's ten-minute meet and greet had erased all of it. The president's visit should have solidified at least three things for all of them. One. The operation had been sanctioned by Russia's highest authority, meaning Putin personally benefited from it. Two. Not only would they become wealthy beyond their wildest dreams, but they'd also have name recognition in Russia's most exclusive power circle. Three. If they fucked this up in any way, the same power cabal would crush them underfoot and twist, leaving nothing more than a smear on the pavement. They were still bugs until the mission succeeded.

Speaking of insects, he signaled for the mercenary guarding the door to admit Grigory Kuznetzov. Time to get this over with—and out of Moscow. He met the general halfway across the dimly lit mahogany office and ushered him to two leather club chairs arranged around an empty marble-topped drink table. The general glanced around as he took his seat, clearly disappointed that Pichugin hadn't broken out any refreshments.

"What was so urgent?" said Pichugin.

"How did the dinner go?" said Kuznetzov.

He imagined the general was a little miffed at having been excluded, but Putin had made it a condition of his appearance that Kuznetzov not be there. No explanation was given, and none was needed. Putin couldn't stand him, either. Like Pichugin, he acknowledged Grigory's indispensable role in taking FIREBIRD to the next level and spearheading OPERATION BLACKOUT, but they didn't click on any level. At all.

The difference being that Pichugin had no choice but to interact with Kuznetzov. Often. Which had left him scrambling to fabricate a reason the general hadn't been invited to tonight's dinner. If Kuznetzov suspected that Putin actively disliked him, the general might have second thoughts about the aftermath of BLACKOUT.

Putin didn't have to like you to do business with you or give you a life-changing nod, but people he disliked didn't tend to outlive their practical usefulness to him. And once BLACKOUT had concluded, Kuznetzov's usefulness as a retirement-age GRU general would be hard to define. He'd told Kuznetzov that Putin didn't want any tangible link between the GRU's involvement and his own. Pichugin had no idea if he bought it.

"Wined and dined," said Pichugin. "Each of them sent to luxury suites with an obscene amount of cash and a digital tablet featuring a wide menu of taboos. It went well."

"I imagine Putin's appearance made an impression?"

"Long lasting," he said. "What brings you here at close to midnight? I have a plane to catch."

"Don't you own the plane?"

"You know what I mean."

"We've had another setback," said Kuznetzov.

"You're starting to sound like a broken record. Now what?"

"Orlov found Helen Gray's apartment," said the general. "It was in a North Baltimore neighborhood. They were able to use the digital hits generated by FIREBIRD to narrow the search enough to actually spot one of them on the street, going into the apartment."

"Grigory. I'm trying really hard right now to imagine how this could have possibly turned into a setback," said Pichugin. "Orlov had twenty-four mercenaries and a military-grade drone team to work with."

Kuznetzov sighed. "The good news is that Orlov managed to burn down Helen Gray's apartment, along with everything inside."

"Were Devin Gray, Karl Berg, Richard Farrington, and the rest of the entourage inside when it burned down?"

"No. That's the bad news," said Kuznetzov. "And the fact that only three members of Orlov's entire mercenary group survived the attack," said the general. "That's twenty-six lost in total, including five members of Fedir Severny's team. Apparently, they were nearby, and Orlov summoned them to the scene."

"Severny's gone?" said Pichugin. "I kind of liked his methods."

"Me too. He was well on his way to replacing Orlov," said Kuznetzov.

"How destroyed was the apartment?" said Pichugin. "US federal agencies will be sifting through this wreckage."

"They used white phosphorus grenades. Orlov's idea."

"Okay. He hasn't completely lost his touch."

"The building burned to the ground within a matter of minutes, along with most of the block," said the general. "But we obviously have to assume Gray and Berg made some kind of copies or record of Helen Gray's work."

"Obviously," said Pichugin. "So we're basically back to square one."

"Yes and no. Gray's crew took a number of casualties. Six, from what Orlov reported. Unfortunately, none of them are on our high-priority list."

"Exactly how did this go so badly for Orlov?" said Pichugin.

"I spoke with Yefremoz—"

"He's been Orlov's right-hand man for a number of years," said Pichugin.

"I understand that, but Oleg watched this unfold from a different perspective. He was with the drone team, passing along information as it unfolded," said Kuznetzov.

"Go on."

"He said that they lost five to gunfire and six to an explosion in the initial approach. All within seconds of each other," said the general. "Then four more in a second explosion about a minute later. Claymore mines, from what they could tell."

"Sounds like this Farrington guy's work. I wonder if he's for hire," said Pichugin.

"I'd make him an offer if I could," said Kuznetzov. "His people are exceptionally well trained."

"If we don't kill him by the time this business is concluded, we could always pursue that avenue," said Pichugin. "I'd be happy to set him up for life, just to keep him out of my hair!"

"Probably not a bad idea."

"Of course it isn't," said Pichugin. "So. Severny's people made zero difference?"

"Farrington's crew tossed ten military-grade smoke grenades onto the streets and alleys surrounding the apartment block. Lashev managed to snipe two of them on the roof. Orlov used some of Severny's people and killed four more before he was driven away by gunfire. After that, it was a close-quarters shootout in the smoke between whoever remained. Farrington's people came out on top, and promptly disappeared."

"They're good at disappearing—and killing," said Pichugin. "But the real question is, How good are they at selling Helen Gray's story? Because we must assume they've archived her research by this point, and that her work was extensive. She clearly couldn't sell it to anyone, which is why she went after Wilson. But this crew is savvy, sophisticated, smart, and not to be underestimated."

"We found them once. We'll find them again," said Kuznetzov.

"It doesn't do any good to find them if we can't kill them!" said Pichugin.

"We can fire Orlov and start over. Double or even triple the number of mercenaries available for the job. Give this whole thing a reboot."

"Not after today," said Pichugin. "Not after the FBI determines that twenty-six of the heavily armed corpses found at the latest shootout in Baltimore belong to Russian nationals or citizens of our former Baltic states. Add that to the fiasco a few weeks ago involving more Russians, including a few with diplomatic ties, and I have a feeling the US Department of Homeland Security will be screening heavily for Russians fitting a certain profile. No. Orlov stays. He's already in-country, and he knows more about Farrington's capabilities, patterns, and tricks than anyone else at this point. He's paid dearly for that knowledge. Starting over with a new team leader would just guarantee another disaster."

The general nodded. "He also has the rest of Severny's team, and we can bring in some of our established Latin American and South American assets. The Americans won't be screening for them."

"Their primary job will be to disrupt Gray and Berg's next move," said Pichugin.

"They're going to be twice as hard to find this time around."

"Agreed. We need to think about our critical vulnerabilities and how they might be attacked or exploited, because I guarantee Gray and his friends will emerge from this latest attack more focused and determined on bringing us down than ever before. We have to assume they'll make some kind of progress, which is where Orlov will come into play, but this time the situation will be reversed. Orlov will be the spider waiting for Gray to step onto the web."

"I don't see how Gray can interfere with OPERATION BLACKOUT," said Kuznetzov. "It's too far removed from Helen Gray's work."

"Really? Have you put your eyes directly on her research?"

"Obviously not, but nobody was kidnapped from the Ozarks camp," said the general. "And Gray's team never set foot inside the administrative section. Her work uncovered what was obvious—"

"I wouldn't call it obvious," said Pichugin.

"Of course. Credit given where credit is due. She surprised us all, with a little help from the traitor, General Kozlov," said Kuznetzov. "But let's face it, once you knew exactly what to look for, anyone with a good mind for conspiracy and enough time on their hands could identify the public-facing sleepers. I'm sure she suspected there were more, and probably suggested it in her work, but without some kind of sweeping, federally mandated look into every US citizen holding a security clearance for their jobs—it's statistically impossible for Devin Gray and his admittedly resourceful friends to unravel the threads needed to stop OPERATION BLACKOUT."

"On their own, I agree that it's impossible," said Pichugin. "But my guess is they'll give the CIA another shot. Berg burned a lot of bridges while he was with the CIA, but he may still have some friends there willing to listen, and possibly take some kind of action."

"Even with the CIA involved, they can't stop BLACKOUT," said Kuznetzov. "Could they get the FBI involved and eventually shut down what remains of FIREBIRD in the US after BLACKOUT? Sure. But we agreed that FIREBIRD wouldn't last forever. It was always a means to an end. An end yet to be identified when it fell into our lap. Now we know the endgame."

Kuznetzov was right, as much as he hated to admit it. BLACKOUT would wreak havoc on European and US relations, while at the same time delivering Russia a long-coveted prize. The rest of Europe would fall in line shortly afterward. Most importantly, his influence and wealth post-BLACKOUT would expand with few limits. With that thought in mind, he decided they couldn't risk even the outside chance that Gray and his friends could build enough momentum to thwart his plan.

"Grigory. I need you to accompany Colonel Petrushev and General Taskin on their flight back tomorrow. Spend some time with Taskin in Pskov, then head to Ostrov with Petrushev to the First Helicopter Assault Brigade. Make it clear that the entire operation must be ready to launch no later than three weeks from today. Preferably two."

Kuznetzov stiffened. If he'd been holding the drink he so desperately looked like he wanted—he would have crushed it in his hand or dropped it.

"But, Yuri, we're still missing a critical component of the operation. We could be weeks or even months away from acquiring it."

"We don't have that long. Not with Gray and his friends working against us," said Pichugin. "Two weeks."

"Three weeks is pushing it," said Kuznetzov. "Two is just—I don't see that happening."

"What's the fucking problem here? They're just the taxi service. They fly in. They drop off my mercenaries. They fly out."

"That's not the issue. I'm sure they can accelerate the mission-training schedule," said Kuznetzov. "But what if the last piece hasn't fallen into place by then?"

"You'll make it fall into place," said Kuznetzov. "Even if you have to fly to California to oversee the job yourself."

"Two weeks. Fuck. I'll need to visit Staraya Russa, too," said Kuznetzov.

"Bring Colonel Petrushev with you. He needs to spend some time with the regiment. I'll let them know you're coming."

CHAPTER 34

Karl Berg leaned forward in his seat and peered through the trees ahead. He could have sworn he'd seen a light, but that wasn't possible unless they'd taken a wrong turn at some point, or someone had decided to squat in one of the buildings.

"Did you see a light?"

Melendez nodded and slowed the SUV. "Maybe one of those barn lights?"

"I don't remember one of those the last time I was here," said Berg. "But it was close to a decade ago, and I wasn't exactly paying attention."

"I came out here with Rich a few years ago, and I don't remember a barn light," he said, stopping the vehicle.

"Everything okay?" said Devin over Berg's radio.

"Have them hold up here," said Melendez. "We'll range ahead and check it out."

Berg activated his radio. "We spotted some kind of light up ahead, which both of us agree probably shouldn't be there."

"Probably?" said Devin.

"It's been a while since either of us has been here. Hold here while we take a look."

Garza chimed in over the net. "Need some backup?"

Melendez shook his head. "This isn't the Russians. They wouldn't advertise their presence. I'm guessing it might be poachers or some local teenagers."

"Rico says we'll be fine," said Berg.

"Suit yourself," said Garza.

"You sure we couldn't use some backup?" said Berg.

"I don't plan on spending more than a few seconds deciding whether to stay or go," said Melendez.

Berg opened the glove compartment and removed the Glock he'd taken from one of the dead Russians. They'd taken a few moments to loot the mercenaries' equipment, weapons, and ammunition before stealing their cars.

"Now you consider yourself a tactical asset?" said Melendez, his tone clearly lighthearted.

"Oh. This is purely for self-defense," said Berg. "I didn't mean to threaten your job."

Melendez laughed. "I'm glad we cleared the air on that. I was starting to get worried."

"Let's get this over with," said Berg.

Melendez eased the SUV slowly down the winding dirt road toward the light, until they caught a glimpse of the farm through a break in the trees. The main house looked to be occupied, its front windows lit behind curtains and the expansive farmer's porch warmly illuminated by light spilling out of its open front door.

"Did Rich sell the place?" said Berg. "I mean, if he did, you'd think that might be something he would have mentioned when we told him we were headed here."

"He didn't sell the place," said Melendez. "You want to keep going? If someone moved in, they've probably uncovered some of the goodies we keep stashed here. We could be in for an explosive greeting."

"I can't imagine someone just moved in—but what the hell else could this be?" said Berg.

"Meth heads?" said Melendez. "Clearly someone who doesn't give a shit about property rights. You sure you don't want to approach this differently? We can head back to the main road, and I'll recon this place with Ripley and Garza later tonight. Assess what we're dealing with."

"They already saw our headlights," said Berg. "If someone turned this into a drug lab, they'll be on high alert all night. Let's just take a quick look. Say we're lost if anyone comes out to greet us. If it turns out to be a sketchy crew, we can decide whether to evict them late at night or leave this place alone."

"It's your call," said Melendez. "But if I see a gun, I'm getting us straight the fuck out of there."

"Fair enough," said Berg.

Neither of them said another word until their SUV broke out of the dense forest and the farmhouse came into clear focus. Melendez jammed on the brakes before they'd traveled more than a few car lengths into the open. Two figures sat on rocking chairs next to the front door, both giving the SUV a quick wave. Neither of them got up, which was kind of a relief. Berg wasn't exactly sure what to think of their reaction to a strange car driving out of the forest at night.

"I'm about to pull the plug on this," said Melendez, putting the SUV in reverse.

Berg started to laugh.

"What?"

"They beat us here," said Berg.

"Who beat us?"

Daniel and Jessica Petrovich, or whoever they called themselves today, stood up and saluted them with tallboy beer cans.

"Well, look at that," said Melendez, smiling. "Never in a million years."

"A billion," said Berg, not at all exaggerating. He'd never expected to see either of them again.

Melendez drove to the front of the house and turned the SUV to face the barn before killing the engine. Berg opened the glove box to return the Glock, hesitating for a moment. His history with these two was complicated. One far more than the other. He dropped the pistol inside and shut it. There was no forgiving what he'd done to Jessica.

Not entirely. But they'd managed to work with each other in the past without too much friction. He triggered his radio.

"It's all good. Someone we trust warmed the place up for us," said Berg. "Meet us at the front porch. You'll see what I mean."

"Copy that," said Devin. "We're on the move."

Melendez chuckled. "Don't oversell them. They're not exactly the warm-and-fuzzy types."

"Not around me. That's for sure," said Berg.

Melendez hopped out of the SUV and headed for the porch steps. Berg waited in the front seat while Melendez greeted his longtime friends. The three of them had forged an unusually tight bond years ago working for General Sanderson. Daniel had spent close to a year training Melendez as a sniper, and Jessica had whipped him into shape with her knife-fighting and hand-to-hand combat classes. They'd fought together and lost friends together. They were still close, even after all these years apart.

When the hugs ended and another beer was pulled out of the cooler on the porch, Jessica hopped down the stairs and approached Berg's window.

"Really?" said Jessica. "You're just gonna sit in there and sulk?"

He turned to face her, still barely able to look her in the eyes.

"I didn't want to crash the reunion," he said.

"Karl," she said, opening his door. "It's time to bury the past. I've long ago forgiven you for whatever you think you did to me."

"I haven't forgiven myself," said Berg, looking away.

"Look. I'm not going to get all psychological here and try to convince you that my life would have been a train wreck even if you hadn't recruited me. You know, because I was abused as a child by immigrant parents and would have continued to circle some existentially assigned drain for the rest of my life. I spoke fluent Serbian. I have a high IQ. I'm a quick learner. And I'm a natural survivor. I was a good match for the program. That's it. You did your job. It didn't exactly work out so well for me at the time. If anyone should be apologizing, it's me."

"You?" said Berg. "Now you're fucking with me."

"Get out of the car and grab a beer," said Jessica. "From what I understand, you could use one."

"Or five," he said.

"There's plenty," she said.

Karl Berg stepped out of the car and faced Jessica Petrovich for the first time in over ten years. She'd aged exactly as he'd expected. Not at all—somehow. Same with Daniel, who nodded at him from the porch. The two of them seemed frozen in time. She probably thought the same thing about him, and maybe they were. Nearly a decade later, they were right back where they started. Staring down the barrel of another loaded conspiracy—from this godforsaken farm in the middle of nowhere.

Jessica stepped in and gave him a hug he didn't deserve as the other two SUVs pulled out of the forest.

"See. That wasn't so hard," she said.

"I suppose not," said Berg, still nowhere close to letting go of the regret he'd held on to for so long.

"Heads up!" said Daniel, drawing Berg's attention to the porch just in time to catch an ice-cold beer. "Is Anish with you?"

"No. He's about an hour behind," said Berg. "He had to go back to Baltimore to pick up his tricked-out Suburban."

"How's he doing?" said Daniel, leaning on the porch rail.

"Not good," said Berg. "It happened so quick. Graves was there one second. Gone the next."

"That's how it usually happens," said Daniel, raising his beer. "To Scott and Tim."

"To Scott and Tim," said Berg, taking a long drink from his can.

Daniel nodded at the approaching vehicles.

"What are we looking at here?" said Daniel. "Rich said they were pretty green, but he seemed impressed."

"When did you talk to Rich?"

"Right after we landed in DC and saw that someone had started a small war in Baltimore," said Daniel.

"It felt like war. That's for sure," said Berg. "Did he say anything about Moscow?"

"No. They were in the middle of a surveillance," said Daniel. "He just told us to come straight here and fire up the generators, which thankfully started on the first try. We would have diverted to the Marriott if they hadn't."

"I'm still considering it," said Jessica. "The place could use a deep cleaning."

"And a fumigation," said Berg, "if I remember correctly."

"That too," she said. "But it'll do. Like it always did."

"Right. And to answer your question about our crew," said Berg, turning toward the two inbound SUVs. "Let's just say that I can't tell you how happy I am to see you. We're going to need all the help we can get."

CHAPTER 35

Devin still didn't know what to think about the property. He wasn't put off or disturbed by the fact that the mercenaries Berg had hired for the job maintained a secret training facility in the Allegheny Mountains— he simply couldn't entirely reconcile having discovered two diametrically opposed facilities within a span of two weeks. Places like this didn't exist in "reality."

Both the sleeper training camp in the Ozarks and "the farm," not to be confused with the CIA's training facility, were the kind of places that existed only in fiction novels or movies. But just like his brief foray into the Ozarks sleeper camp, here he sat, next to Marnie, in a modern conference room hidden inside a seemingly dilapidated cowshed attached to the farmhouse by a long, sketchy breezeway.

The entire property looked worn down and abandoned, but appearances here were very deceiving. Even more so than the Ozarks facility. To the outside observer, every structure on the property looked borderline condemned or completely neglected. But on the inside, despite a thick layer of dust and a few critter infestations, the place was a frozen-in-time, entirely functional storage depot and operations center.

The satellite communications equipment, computer networking gear, and digital media outfitting were a little antiquated, but Farrington's people had been well ahead of their time the last time they'd upgraded. It had taken them half the night, and a few replacements from "the vault," to get everything working again, but all the electronics functioned at an acceptable level by the time they had finished.

Reestablishing the facility's basic living functions had required the most time. Nearly ten hours of nonstop work once the digital suite was up and running. Chasing out critters. Figuring out the water system. Connecting the propane tanks to run the limited air-conditioning, water heater, and stove. Precisely the kind of work you would say "fuck this" to within the first hour, unless you were desperate—which pretty much defined their entire situation.

The only thing keeping his eyes open at this point was the combination of the unblemished, stainless steel La Marzocco Strada espresso machine installed in the kitchen and a fifty-pound stash of "Munoz's Best" discovered in the airtight pantry. He had no idea who Munoz was, but his coffee was excellent, and the machine was worth the time spent mastering its complexities.

Marnie lightly elbowed him. "Wake up. We're about to go live."

Apparently, the coffee hadn't kept his eyes open.

"Yep. Thank you," he whispered, barely managing to focus his attention on the home theater–size screen in front of him.

Richard Farrington's face appeared, taking up the whole wall.

"Rich. You might want to back up from the camera or hold the phone a little farther away," said Anish. "We can count your nose hairs right now."

"Ha fucking ha, Anish," said Farrington. "You know goddamn well I'm jammed into a studio apartment with the whole team. A Moscow studio, basically meaning there's a curtain separating the shitter from the rest of the room."

"Well. If it's any consolation, I'll be sleeping in a dusty, stale bunk room that smells like raccoon piss," said Anish. "Or I'm told I can have the squirrel suite in the main house."

Farrington grinned. "Small consolation. But I'll take it. How's everyone doing overall?"

"We're holding up under the circumstances," said Devin, being as blunt as possible.

"We've been awake most of the night getting this place operational," said Berg. "And yesterday was especially rough."

"Rich. Good to see you again," said Daniel Petrovich, obviously changing the subject. "So. What do you have for us?"

"Always getting down to brass tacks," said Farrington.

"I get the sense that we don't have a lot of time for small talk right now," said Daniel. "And your feed looks like shit—so spit it out. We're all getting dizzy here."

Farrington laughed. "Can I assume that you're familiar with our mission in Moscow?"

"I just brought them up to speed," said Berg.

"Perfect. I won't waste time with the setup," said Farrington. "General Kuznetzov presumably met with Yuri Pichugin in Moscow at 11:08 p.m. local time. The meeting was clearly a spontaneous event triggered by the Baltimore attack. Kuznetzov had been asleep at his flat prior to racing across the city. This is only the second full day we've watched him, but our local intelligence indicates that he religiously goes to bed between nine and ten every evening, which he did earlier that night."

"Did you see Pichugin?" said Devin.

"No. We never saw Pichugin at the address, but Ostozhenka Street is basically oligarch central here in Moscow, and a small fleet of SUVs left the building's parking garage around 11:30 p.m. and proceeded directly to a private-jet terminal at Sheremetyevo Airport. We feel confident it was Pichugin. Unfortunately, we couldn't follow closely enough to ID him boarding a plane."

"I suppose this confirms what we strongly suspected. That Kuznetzov is Pichugin's direct intermediary in *all* matters related to the sleeper network," said Berg. "Not just running the network itself."

"Did Kuznetzov accompany him to the airport?" said Marnie.

"Kuznetzov returned to the secure compound on the western outskirts of Moscow, where he remained until around noon," said Farrington.

"Sounds like he didn't get any sleep, either," said Berg.

"Probably not," said Farrington. "And I don't anticipate much sleep in his immediate future. The Baltimore raid set something in motion. Kuznetzov's convoy picked up two serious-looking guys at the Ritz-Carlton around one in the afternoon. He actually got out to greet both of them as they emerged from the hotel and escorted them to his armored SUV."

"Any idea who they are?" said Berg.

"No idea. If I had to guess, I'd say they were senior field-grade military officers. That or very recently ex-military. Probably Army. Late thirties to early forties. Tightly faded haircuts. Physically fit. A certain bearing. You can spot it a mile away if you know what to look for."

"Maybe Kuznetzov's trying to recruit them for Pichugin's Wegner Group," said Berg. "My guess is that field-grade officers are hard to come by in the private-military contractor world."

"They are, but here's where it gets interesting. Kuznetzov's convoy drove them directly to the same private section of Sheremetyevo Airport presumably used by Pichugin the night before, but this time we had courtside seats. After Pichugin's convoy departed last night, we positioned Alex in the forest flanking the hangar and tarmac area with a few days of water and Russian MREs. He took pictures of Kuznetzov boarding a Hawker 4000 with the two mystery men. I think this is all fairly significant, and very possibly related to Pichugin's bigger plans for whatever's left of the sleeper network in the US."

"It's very significant, given the role Kuznetzov plays in Pichugin's organization. The general runs the sleeper network. He's been intimately involved in every detail from the beginning. And the Ritz-Carlton? Doesn't sound like they were there on any kind of official military-subsidized business. It's fair to assume there's a substantial link between

Pichugin's plans for the sleeper network and the two men. We need to identify them immediately. Maybe an obvious pattern will emerge."

"Karl. Can your friend at the CIA help us out with that?" said Farrington.

"Bauer hasn't retired yet?" said Jessica.

"Two years, or so she says," said Berg. "She's working in an oversight position right now."

"Oversight?" said Daniel.

"Oversight of some pretty important stuff. That's all I'll say. If these colonels are on file with the CIA or DIA, she'll be able to help us. I'll send the photos to her immediately," said Berg.

"Has she contacted you since the attack yesterday?" said Farrington. "I can't imagine that went unnoticed at Langley."

"We traded messages and agreed to postpone our meeting until things have settled," said Berg.

"Things may never settle," said Devin.

"He makes a good point," said Farrington.

"That's not what I meant," said Berg. "We agreed to postpone until I know more about *how* or even *if* MINERVA and DEVTEK intend to collaborate with us. If there's minimal to no collaboration, then our options are limited. We'll essentially be out of the active conspiracy-busting business, unless Rich and his crew can identify an opportunity."

"Raiding or electronically snooping on the secure compound isn't a viable option," said Rich. "It's guarded by at least an infantry company–size group of mercenaries, on constant patrol and manning fixed hard points. My guess is that it's protected by the latest and greatest in security and surveillance technology. Anti-drone. Thermal imaging. Motion detection. Pressure pads. Sound detection. Communications encrypted with something we haven't seen yet. You name it."

"What about grabbing Kuznetzov or someone that works under him?" said Berg. "I'm not even going to ask about Pichugin."

"Kuznetzov travels with more security than Pichugin," said Farrington. "We'd need some serious backup and support to pull off something like that."

"Maybe the two officers will present an opportunity. Once we ID them," said Devin. "But if that turns out to be a dead end, how do we take this any further?"

"I see three options, and none of them are great, or even good," said Berg. "Turn everything over to the FBI, the CIA, or the media. The media might not be a terrible option anymore. I know I discouraged taking this prime time the last time we discussed it, but things have changed enough since then to possibly consider it. But none of these options are quick fused.

"The FBI will take months. They'll take a fine-tooth comb to Helen Gray's work before launching their own investigation. The media will take months. They'll want to vet as much of Helen's findings as possible, which will prove problematic. And the CIA? Once we hand it off, we'll likely never hear anything about it again. Not the most satisfying move, but of the three, I think handing everything off to the CIA is the best option. I do believe Langley would immediately get to work figuring out Pichugin's bigger plan."

"Then we wait to hear back from Brendan Shea and Audra Bauer," said Devin. "Hopefully one of those avenues keeps us in the game."

CHAPTER 36

Karl Berg's satellite phone rang, drawing all eyes off their lunches and in his direction. He'd sent the photographs of the Russian Army officers to Audra Bauer as soon as they'd finished the call with Farrington. The screen displayed a number starting with 8816. An Iridium satellite phone prefix. Could be anyone, but he had a feeling it was Bauer. And if Bauer had switched to a satellite phone to call him, she must have big news.

"You gonna answer that?" said Melendez, twirling spaghetti with his fork against a spoon.

"You gonna quit pretending you're at a fancy restaurant? It's Ragu and pasta. I know because I made it," said Berg, holding up a finger to quiet everyone down before accepting the call.

"Karl Berg," he said.

"These pictures are real? They haven't been doctored?" said Bauer. "And they were taken this morning?"

"And hello to you, too," said Berg. "I'm not messing with you. Jared Hoffman and Alex Filatov, two of Farrington's associates—"

"I know who they are. I know who they all are," said Bauer. "The older ones, at least."

"Hoffman and Filatov snapped these between one and two in the afternoon, Moscow time, in front of the Ritz-Carlton and at a private-jet terminal in the southwest corner of Sheremetyevo International."

"We need to meet. I need to see everything else," said Bauer. "This is an odd combination of people to be gathered in Moscow. A dangerous combination, particularly since they departed on a private jet together."

"Who are we looking at?"

"General Taskin of the Seventy-Sixth Guards Air Assault Division and Colonel Petrushev of the recently formed First Helicopter Assault Brigade. Both based around Pskov, near the southeastern border of Estonia. Petrushev is subordinate to Taskin. Most of Petrushev's brigade is based in Ostrov, about twenty or so miles south of Pskov," said Bauer. "We keep a close eye on these units via signals intelligence intercepts, frequent satellite imagery, and local contact reports, because between the two of them, they command several thousand Russian soldiers, their gear, equipment, and vehicles—all located a few hours' helicopter ride from any of the Baltic state capitals. It's something that keeps the region's analysts awake at night."

"Who was it?" said Devin.

Berg put a hand over the phone.

"Two Russian Army officers. An air assault division commander and helicopter assault brigade commanders," he told the group at the table before returning to the call. "Sorry about that. I'd put you on speakerphone, but the call would fall apart within seconds. Everyone is very eager to take next steps here. Speaking of next steps, do you think Farrington should divert a team to start poking around these bases?"

"I think a look around is warranted. Never know what they'll find," said Bauer. "I'll check with the head of the Russian-Baltics analyst team and see if they've picked up on anything noteworthy around Pskov recently. Who knows. We might get lucky again."

"Be discreet, Audra," said Berg.

"It would help if you told me who to avoid," said Bauer.

"Hold on," he said, before muting the phone. "Bauer plans to speak with an analyst who might be able to get us some deep intelligence on these colonels and their units' local activity. She wants the names of the two counterintelligence analysts Helen identified as sleepers. I say we give them to her. If the wrong person sees Audra talking to the Baltics team, we could tip our hand."

"I don't have a problem with it," said Devin.

"Does anyone have a problem with it?" said Marnie.

The group collectively shook their heads, so he unmuted the call and passed the names of the two analysts.

"Damn," she said. "One of them is pretty high up in the Counterintelligence Center Analysis Group. Fortunately, they're located on the other side of the building and several floors from the Office of Russian and European Analysis. The chances of running into either of the analysts in question is close to zero, but I'll make sure it's absolutely zero before I make my way over there."

"I guess that only leaves one question. Shall I come to you, or you to me?" said Berg.

"Are you still in the area?"

"I'm at that very rustic resort you and your husband visited right before President Crane's administration was gutted."

"Have the conditions improved out there?" she said.

"I think it's fine, but everyone else is shaking their heads," said Berg. "Don't worry, we'll tidy the place up for you."

"Sounds like this might be a good time for my husband to visit his brother in Maine, for a few weeks of flyfishing and sailing," she said. "Get him off their radar."

"Probably not a bad idea, given that I didn't have a lot of friends left at the CIA when I left," said Berg. "After Baltimore, I can't imagine they wouldn't keep an eye on you."

"I can scan for trackers and run a nice long SDR," she said. "If they're watching me, it makes more sense for me to head out early Saturday morning after my husband leaves. Make it look like I'm taking a little trip of my own. Then I can stay for the weekend and really dig into Helen Gray's files, along with the evidence you've added to it. I may stay longer. I really need to take my time with this. The Baltimore attack is an unprecedented escalation on several levels, especially considering the Russian connection to the last shootout a few weeks ago. Someone is almost psychotically desperate to deep-six Helen's work, which makes me even more curious to know why."

"We're working the problem from a few other angles. Hopefully we'll have more for you to examine when you get here. A lot can happen by then," said Berg.

"I'll call you to confirm my departure Saturday morning and then again when I'm about forty-five minutes out, to give you the opportunity to run countersurveillance on your end," she said. "Can't hurt, right?"

"We happen to have a countersurveillance expert or two handy," said Berg.

"If I have to call this off before or during the trip, I'll send you a message."

"See you Saturday," said Berg. "Stay safe."

"See you then," she said, and ended the call.

Everyone looked like they wanted to talk at once, but Berg cut them off. Bauer's upcoming visit represented a unique opportunity, but they needed to move fast to take advantage of it.

"Devin. I need you to call Brendan Shea immediately and let him know that the CIA has taken an interest in this and will be here around midday on Saturday. Ask him to pass that information along to DEVTEK and request that they send a team here to meet with the CIA. Say whatever you have to say to make this happen, even if you have to stretch the truth a little."

"Or a lot," said Marnie. "I see where Karl is going with this."

"Don't overdo it, but maybe suggest the possibility of a covert partnership to explore the intelligence implications of the honey trap operation Shea's team thwarted a number of weeks ago. Use every variation of the word *collaboration* or *alliance* possible. Remember, the rumor out there is that the CIA recently accepted DEVTEK's classified bid on what sounded like a hefty contract. They'll be eager to please Langley. It should be enough to get a team out here on short notice."

"What happens when they arrive to discover that meeting with the CIA means meeting with one CIA officer who works in an *oversight* position?" said Marnie.

"We just need to get DEVTEK and MINERVA in the same room as Bauer, and DEVTEK won't cut us out of the loop. She's never been what some might call a high-profile CIA figure, but everyone in the Beltway knows who she is—and respects her. In the ever-shifting political and fiscal sands of the Beltway, having someone like Bauer on your side is worth the hassle of keeping us involved."

"Why do I get the feeling you won't tell Audra about the visitors coming specifically to meet with her on Saturday—until she arrives on Saturday?" said Jessica.

"Because she wouldn't agree to it," said Berg.

"I love how he says that without a hint of guilt," said Melendez. "And everyone thinks the shooters are the cold and calculating ones?"

"She invited herself," said Berg. "I saw an opportunity. We don't have time to play games. Not with the stakes this high."

"I'm not saying I didn't dig it," said Melendez. "Just pointing it out."

"Devin. You make your call while I put together a quick briefing on what Audra relayed to me. Everyone meets in the conference room in an hour?" said Berg.

"Sounds like a plan," said Devin. "But I'm wondering if it might be better to have you on the call with Shea."

"Absolutely not. I guarantee Shea has some reservations about me. Unlike Audra, I come with baggage," said Berg. "He'll trust what you have to say more if I'm not part of the conversation."

"This should be a fun weekend," said Melendez.

"We'll have to do better than Ragu and spaghetti," said Berg. "Conference room in an hour."

CHAPTER 37

The encrypted satellite phone on the ground immediately in front of Richard Farrington buzzed and illuminated. That didn't take long. He'd been here less than twenty minutes, after crawling nearly two hundred yards through seemingly every variety of thorn bush in Russia to nestle into a dense thicket of high brush and young trees overlooking Kuznetzov's secure compound. Richard Farrington lowered his eyes from the binoculars to check the phone. *Berg.* He swapped the binoculars for the phone.

"Hope you have some good news," said Farrington, swatting a mosquito buzzing near his other ear. "Because we decided to take another look at the secure compound, and there's no way we're getting in there without a small army. We managed to find sort of a hilltop about a half mile away, with a clear view. It's worse than I thought."

"What about grabbing an employee?"

"That's the funny thing. We arrived in the area around four in the afternoon Moscow time, to assess the after-work traffic leaving the compound. Nothing. Nobody coming out. Nobody going in."

"They're probably on a shift schedule that switches at irregular times. Usually when there's little to no traffic," said Berg. "That's a standard practice at sensitive facilities. Makes it harder for people like yourself to blend into traffic and trail employees."

"Maybe. But from where I'm lying, covered in mosquitoes, by the way—"

"I read an article about mosquito tornadoes in Russia last year," said Berg. "Has something to do with climate change."

"One more reason never to return," said Farrington. "Anyway. The compound looks like a small military base from this slightly higher vantage point. Possibly self-contained. I'm seeing a few motel-like buildings, a small pool, a soccer field, and larger structures that might be barracks and a cafeteria. I haven't been here long, but I've seen personnel going back and forth from the larger buildings. Then there's the main building with all the antennas and comms arrays."

"If they're working in shifts, it's probably more of a two-weeks-on, two-weeks-off kind of situation," said Berg.

"We won't be able to spend that kind of time out here without giving ourselves away. I'm nervous spending part of an afternoon and evening out here. One call to the police could very easily put an end to our trip."

"Then don't waste any more time on it," said Berg. "Same with the private terminal. Audra got back to me about thirty minutes ago. She managed to identify Kuznetzov's mystery friends. A general and a colonel."

"I knew it."

"The general commands the Seventy-Sixth Guards Air Assault Division, and the colonel commands the First Helicopter Assault Brigade. Both based around Pskov, less than thirty miles from the Russian-Estonian border."

"Sounds like some of us are taking a trip," said Farrington.

"I hate to split you up, but my gut tells me that getting some eyes on the helicopter brigade is important. They're based out of Ostrov, to the south of Pskov. Audra agrees, and she's going to try and dig up some targeted intelligence from the group that analyzes the Baltics situation," said Berg.

"Having a friendly contact in the area would be helpful, too," said Farrington. "Nikolai hasn't been back to Moscow since his extraction back in 2007, but he's been instrumental in navigating the intricacies of the city. We'd be lost without him."

"I'll check if that's a possibility," said Berg. "Don't hold your breath. How do you think you'll split up the team?"

"I'll keep Nikolai and Jared in Moscow to keep an eye on Kuznetzov," said Farrington. "Jared's Russian is okay. With Nikolai's knowledge of the city and fluent Russian, the two of them should be fine. Alex and I will drive up to Ostrov."

"A motel on the outskirts will be your best option. Most of them take cash and don't require a credit card for incidentals," said Berg. "Because there are no incidentals. The place looks rustic."

"We don't mind roughing it a bit," said Farrington. "So. A full division—and a brigade in the same place? That's a lot of ground to cover."

"Yes and no. I did some quick research into the two units. The First is actually a reinforced battalion-size unit with integrated aviation support. Basically, a stand-alone Army aviation unit, unlike the Seventy-Sixth Guards, which is comprised of three air assault regiments and a separate aviation element that the commander allocates to the regiments based on need. I'm thinking that Kuznetzov has to cozy up to both of them, since they're in the same chain of command, but whatever business he has planned in the region will fall to the First Helicopter Assault Brigade. It can operate independently, and its chain of command is a straight line down from its commanding officer."

"Makes sense. A full colonel in command of a battalion-size unit is top heavy," said Farrington. "He's basically a god to them."

"That's why I'm sending you to Ostrov," said Berg. "To see what kind of trouble a god could get into on behalf of Yuri Pichugin."

CHAPTER 38

Devin knocked on Marnie's door with his free hand. The other held two ice-cold beers. When she opened the door, he offered her one of the bottles.

"What's the occasion?" she said, accepting the beer.

No makeup. Hair pulled back in a ponytail. Ripped sneakers, tan cargo pants, and a beat-up gray T-shirt from Goodwill. She looked amazing no matter what.

"A little downtime," said Devin. "I was hoping you'd be up for taking a sunset walk."

"Sunset walk?" said Marnie. "Sounds like a date. Sort of."

"Then consider it sort of a date," said Devin. "It's the best I can do, given our circumstances."

"I'll take what I can get at this point," she said, shutting the door behind her. "Where are we headed?"

"Through the woods west of the clearing," said Devin, retrieving a bottle of mosquito repellant and handing it to her. "There's a small rise about a half mile from here. The tree cover is kind of sparse there, so we should have a nice view of the sunset. Mosquitoes aren't bad up there, but they're pretty brutal on the way."

Marnie sprayed the exposed skin on her arms and neck before smearing a little on her hands to rub on her face. She handed the bottle back to Devin, and they left hand in hand, avoiding everyone as they made their way to the front door and out of the house. Halfway across a worn path through the overgrown clearing, the deep-orange sun dipped beneath the trees.

"I didn't mean for this to be a forced march," said Devin. "But we need to pick up the pace or we'll miss the sunset."

"We could have borrowed one of the ATVs," said Marnie.

"It gets a little tight in the forest," said Devin, gently pulling her along.

The mosquitoes attacked in full force when they entered the trees, each of their free hands now preoccupied with swatting the onslaught away.

"This is fun," said Marnie.

"Sorry. They were pretty bad when I scouted this during the afternoon. I should have guessed they would be way worse around dusk," said Devin, before swiping at a buzzing sound next to one of his ears. "Did you get ahold of your parents earlier?"

"I did," said Marnie. "Sounds like they might be enjoying themselves a little too much."

"Right?" said Devin. "Ocean view from the backyard. Pool. Private chef when they're not ordering takeout. My dad jokingly said there was no hurry putting this whole thing to rest. I'm not entirely sure he was joking."

"Same on my end," said Marnie. "Sounds like everyone is getting along, too, which is a bonus. I think your sister is getting a little bit antsy."

"She is," said Devin, before helping Marnie over a fallen log. "Sorry about this. It's not exactly the romantic stroll in the woods I had envisioned."

Devin cringed internally. The chemistry between them was undeniable, but under their current circumstances—on the run from Russian assassins—they'd both informally agreed to put their feelings on the back burner until things had settled. And they were far from settled now. He considered apologizing but decided against it. There was no harm in bringing up his stance on their growing relationship, if he didn't press it. Marnie swatted a mosquito on her neck.

"I'm sure the sunset will be spectacular," she said, squeezing his hand.

"I hope so. Otherwise, this will be a bust," said Devin.

"Not possible as long as we're hanging out," said Marnie. "How long do you think Kari will last at the house?"

Devin wanted to address the first part of the statement but knew it would take their conversation to the next level of awkwardness. And the last thing either of them needed was that kind of distraction.

"It depends," said Devin. "She's worked for a nonprofit that champions women's issues. Protecting reproductive health-care rights. Sheltering at-risk women. The gender-pay-gap disparities. Workplace discrimination. You name it. Coincidentally or not, the people that took them in work in the same field—though I got the impression they did private investigative work. I think there might be an opportunity for her with this firm. She mentioned something about hanging out with them for a few days—in the field. Whatever that means."

"Garza works with them," said Marnie. "I'm not sure how he got dragged into this mess, but it had something to do with Farrington's financial backer."

"Did he say anything about the kind of work they do in LA?" said Devin.

"No. He's pretty tight lipped about everything," said Marnie.

"They all are," said Devin. "It's frustrating. I hope Kari doesn't make a rash decision without the full picture of what she'd be getting into."

"What did she say?"

"I didn't talk to her," said Devin. "Let me rephrase that. She didn't want to talk to me. Kari can hold a grudge, and dragging her away from work for a few weeks didn't sit well with her."

"Sorry," said Marnie.

"Nothing to be sorry about," said Devin. "My mother created a complicated dynamic in our family. Everything has been a little strained over the years."

"A little?" she said, elbowing him.

Devin laughed. "Yeah. Just a smidge."

They picked up the pace until the trees cleared to reveal the small knoll he'd found earlier in the afternoon during a solo exploration. They climbed through the scattered brush until they reached the top—the last vestiges of the sun reappearing as they summited the modest hill.

"Just in time," said Marnie.

Devin found them a somewhat-clear spot a few feet away and invited her over, starting to sit down. He immediately got back up, muttering a few curses under his breath.

"I think we have to stand for this one," said Devin. "If we sit, the sun vanishes behind the trees."

"This is totally fine," she said, pulling him back down and nestling in next to him.

"Cheers," said Devin, clinking her bottle. "Our first sunset drink together."

"And nowhere close to our last," she said, clinking his bottle before taking a drink.

They spent the next few minutes holding hands, finishing their beers, and watching the deep-reddish-orange orb vanish from sight below the distant sea of green treetops. On cue, the mosquitoes swarmed. Devin removed the bottle of insect repellant and offered it to Marnie.

"Need a refresh?"

"And a refill," she said, tipping her empty beer bottle upside down.

"Let's get out of here," said Devin, starting to head out—but immediately stopping in his tracks. "Marnie?"

"Yeah?"

"Thank you for being here for me. I'm glad we're in this together—even though I wish I had never involved you. The thought of anything bad happening to you or your family can be overwhelming at times. Most of the time."

"I'm glad I stuck around," said Marnie. "Not that I had much choice after the Airbnb ambush."

"I'm really sorry about that," said Devin. "I shouldn't have brought you into this. I truly had no idea things would spiral out of control that night."

She shrugged. "Don't beat yourself up. Even Karl didn't anticipate the full extent of it—and he comes across as borderline prophetic most of the time."

"He does," said Devin, a long, awkward pause ensuing. "I never stopped thinking about you after college."

"I never stopped thinking about you, either."

"I really want to kiss you," he said. "But the mosquitoes and our general predicament are getting in the way."

She pulled him into a tight embrace and they kissed briefly—Devin's eyes remaining closed long after the kiss ended. Mosquitoes buzzed around both of his ears, breaking the sublime trance.

"I didn't anticipate sharing this moment with a few hundred mosquitoes," said Devin.

"It's probably a good thing that they showed up," she said.

"You're probably right." Devin's mind flashed through the possibilities as they headed back to the compound.

CHAPTER 39

Felix Orlov set his phone down on the picnic table before throwing back the half-filled plastic cup of vodka Oleg had poured him moments before the call had come through. Lashev took his cue and finished his drink.

"That bad?" said Oleg, refilling both cups.

"Actually, not that bad at all," said Orlov. "We haven't been fired."

"Are they still going to pay us?"

"Same payment amounts each of you originally agreed to," said Orlov. "But strictly paid on an individual basis. I'm no longer paying you, so the whole concept of shares is out the window. The client will pay directly when we fulfill the new contract."

"What's the new contract?" said Oleg.

"It's less of a contract than an implicit understanding that we do what we're told, when we're told to do it. Period," said Orlov. "Until Pichugin is satisfied that he's gotten his money's worth out of us."

"Wonderful," said Lashev, before taking a long drink from his cup. "I'm Pichugin's bitch until he says otherwise."

"It could have gone way worse for us," said Orlov.

Lashev finished the shot and held the cup out for a refill.

"Are we still working on the same job?" said Oleg, pouring Lashev a much smaller amount this time.

"I'm told it's related," said Orlov. "All I know is that we're headed to Miami."

"We're probably going to be dressed in uniforms and reassigned as security guards in one of the buildings he owns down there," said Lashev, downing his drink in a single gulp.

"No more for Mr. Cheery," said Orlov. "We need to get on the road in a few hours. He wants us in Miami by tomorrow night. I was very kindly informed that it was an eighteen-hour drive, and that we were to drive straight through, only stopping for gas. So we need to grab sandwiches, snacks, and drinks. Whatever it takes to last eighteen hours on the road. He was very adamant about us not stopping for anything but gas."

"Why?" said Lashev. "I don't see why they don't fly us down."

"What do you mean, why?" said Orlov. "Do I really have to explain why our accents might alarm people right now?"

"Okay. Okay. I get it. You don't need to pile it on," said Lashev.

"Maybe I do. Maybe I don't. But that's also why they don't want to fly us down, even on a private jet. All ten of us piling into a private jet, saying *da* and *spasibo* every five seconds? I don't think half of Severny's people speak any English."

"They don't," said Oleg. "And the rest can barely ask for a bathroom."

"That's why they put us in RVs right from the start. We have our own toilets. I was going to complain, but after losing twenty-six operatives and a drone team in under ten minutes—and probably drawing a lot of undue attention to Mother Russia—I graciously accepted what was offered. It didn't seem very practical, but now it makes perfect sense. They were planning ahead," said Orlov.

"One of us will have to drive with the other group," said Oleg. "In case the other RV gets pulled over by the police, or they have a problem with a gas pump. Basically, any situation that might require them to communicate in English."

"It's not going to be like that," said Orlov. "We're going to split the team evenly between the two RVs. It'll be me and whoever wins the coin toss between the two of you, plus three of Severny's people that I select. The loser gets to ride with the remaining four."

"I thought the winner got to choose," said Oleg.

"Just for that, I'm taking Lashev," said Orlov.

CHAPTER 40

Audra Bauer did not look happy. In fact, she looked extremely pissed off. And she hadn't taken her hand off the carry-on-size suitcase she'd brought with her. The hushed argument playing out on the main house's farm porch didn't look promising. DEVTEK had brought some heavy hitters, who expected to see a representative from the CIA at the table. Her absence would undoubtedly start things off on the wrong foot and potentially jeopardize Devin's proposal.

Devin opened the screen door and stepped onto the porch, accidentally letting it slam shut behind him. They turned to face him at the same time, a feigned smile on Audra's face. A combination of cringe and dread spread across Berg's.

"Ms. Bauer. I'm Devin Gray," he said, offering a hand. "It's a pleasure to meet you. Thank you for coming. Can I grab your suitcase?"

She shook his hand. "Nice to finally meet you, Devin. I'm very sorry about what happened to your mother. Not just what happened a few weeks ago, but over the years. If everything Karl tells me is true, I'll make clearing her name at the agency one of my top priorities."

He swallowed hard, still unable to predict when the mention of his mother would provoke an overwhelming emotional response. Devin took a few moments to center himself.

"Sorry if I—" she started.

"No. It's fine. It's just hard for me to think of all those years that we thought she'd lost touch with reality. Her own family didn't believe her. Thank you for the kind words and the generous offer to help clear her name."

Devin wasn't just saying this to win her over, but Berg mistook it and winked at him. Fortunately, Bauer didn't see it, or she would have walked back to her car and driven away.

"It's the least I can do," said Bauer.

"It means a lot," said Devin. "And so does the meeting Karl under-handedly shoved in your lap at the last moment."

She glanced between the two of them a few times, her glare finally settling on Berg.

"You are on the thinnest ice imaginable," said Bauer. "You're lucky Devin intervened when he did."

"I'm very sorry, Audra," said Berg.

"No. You're not," she said. "Smart of you to wait. I don't like strangers, and I don't like being used as a prop."

"That wasn't my original intention. The idea came later," said Berg.

"Devin, be honest with me. When did Karl spring the idea of putting me in the same room as DEVTEK?"

"The moment he ended your call," said Devin. "But I don't think he had it in mind when he first picked up the call. He'd never mentioned it previously."

She studied his face for a few moments before turning back to Berg.

"My conditions. You do not introduce me by name. Just as a senior CIA officer looking into connections between Yuri Pichugin and the sleeper network. You don't solicit questions from me or try to lead me into any conversations with questions. Consider me a silent attendee. I'll share my thoughts when and if I decide to. Agreed?"

"Agreed," said Devin.

"Karl?" she said.

"Absolutely."

"All right. Let's get this over with," said Bauer, handing Karl her suitcase. "Devin will show me to the meeting while you put this in the cleanest bedroom on the property."

"Karl spent a lot of time cleaning and prepping one of the rooms for you this morning," said Devin.

"Sounds like he was racked with guilt," she said.

"More like fear," said Berg.

"What are we having for dinner tonight?" said Bauer.

"Tuna steak over Mediterranean rice," said Berg. "Grilled asparagus. Salad."

"Karl drove an hour each way yesterday to do some grocery shopping," said Devin.

"Okay. Enough of your intel drops," said Berg.

"And Karl? Can you bring a Perrier and a glass full of ice to the meeting for me?"

"It's already waiting for you," he said.

She glanced at Devin. "Definitely fear."

CHAPTER 41

Karl Berg hustled into the conference room and sat at the end of a no-frills rectangular wooden table, flanked by Devin and Marnie. Gupta sat a few seats down from them, in front of two laptops arranged toward the middle of the table. DEVTEK's five attendees occupied the opposite end of the table, along with Brendan Shea, MINERVA's sole representative. Berg was a bit dismayed to find that Bauer wasn't seated at the table. She'd rolled her chair to the corner behind Devin, where she sat with a sweating glass of mineral water and ice—not exactly looking enthused to be here. *She better not torpedo this.*

"Sorry about that," said Berg. "I needed a word with the security team. Has everyone gotten somewhat acquainted, or do we need some introductions?"

The woman seated at the other end of the table answered without hesitation. "We can go through it again quickly, for those that just arrived."

It was more likely she wanted to make sure Bauer understood how seriously they were taking the meeting.

"So. I'm Jenna Paek, chief technology officer at DEVTEK," she said, before motioning toward the man seated next to her. "This is Randall Powers, head of security. All security. Seated across from him is Anna Shipley, head of cybersecurity. Then her chief security tech, Carlos Herrera. And Rafael."

Interesting that she didn't give Rafael a title or a last name. Karl stood up.

"I thought we'd start off with an overview of what Helen Gray discovered and what we've done with it so far. To get us all on the same page," said Berg. "Then talk through how we can help each other."

"Let's start with that," said Randall. "Based on Mr. Shea's briefing and the materials he provided, I feel like we're far enough along in the timeline to skip the overview. What would you do in our shoes, and how can you help us?"

Berg hadn't been prepared for them to skip to the bottom line. Audra chuckled, sensing the same. He stood there for a moment, Devin taking the cue and rescuing him from an awkward pause.

"To keep it as simple as possible for now," said Devin, "I suggest you fake Brian Chase's departure from DEVTEK. Something that gets him out of there immediately. Before knowing about the sleeper network, I would have assumed Chase was the target of a standard honeypot operation to blackmail him into stealing and passing along information. But the more we learn about the sleeper network, the more I'm inclined to think that they were looking to blackmail him into quitting. It's far less complicated and safe than a long string of risky asks, especially for an aging group of sleepers like Harvey and Jolene Rudd. The blackmail trick rarely works for long for any number of reasons. In fact, most of the time, it backfires rather quickly."

"That's true," said Randall. "So you're suggesting that Chase's departure would open his position to a sleeper?"

"Yes."

"But the hiring process could take weeks, even months, and there'd be no guarantee that their sleeper would get the job," said Randall.

"Unless the sleeper is already at DEVTEK, waiting for an opportunity to move into his position. I assume an internal candidate for a job would have preference over all external candidates?"

Randall glanced at Paek, who responded: "Yes. They would. And I'm sure we have several potential candidates who fit the initial profile Mr. Shea outlined."

"I'll order detailed background checks into any of the software and systems people that fit the initial profile. Age forty to fifty-five," said Randall, before turning back to Devin. "So you're suggesting an internal sting?"

"Correct. I don't pretend to know much about any of the magic that goes on behind the cybersecurity curtain, but Anish assured me that you'd probably have some way to let this sleeper think that they'd hit the jackpot, for lack of a better term, but compartmentalize from the real code and systems configurations—while keeping an eye on them. Something ironically known as a honeynet?"

"We do," said Anna.

"Perfect. Then you can watch the sleeper's every move within the system and figure out exactly what Pichugin wants from DEVTEK," said Devin.

"And what do we do with that information?" said Paek.

Share it with us and CIA, Berg wanted to shout.

"Protect your clients from whatever Pichugin has planned for them," said Devin.

"So why do we need you?" she said. "Sorry to be blunt."

Berg tensed, knowing that Devin could make or break the collaboration in the next several seconds.

"It's a fair question."

"And I'm not saying we aren't grateful for your suggestions and insight," said Paek. "I'm just saying that we have a very robust cybersecurity team that can handle this from here."

"Two reasons. First. We're working this investigation from the other end—its source in Russia—to identify possible targets. If Pichugin wants the operating system for one of your more widely used products, we can identify the specific target, so you can do more for your clients than just protect them in the background. Knowing that a healthy number of your clients are government agencies and sensitive industries, domestic and abroad, this provides a unique opportunity for you to tailor your services and differentiate yourself from competitors."

Jenna Paek smiled. "How many times have you rehearsed that sales pitch?"

"About thirty times over the past twenty-four hours," said Devin.

"It's good," she said.

"Thank you. Hopefully I don't fall flat on reason number two," said Devin. "Pichugin's moves can be purely selfish, but outside of the occasional personal power play against another oligarch, most of them align closely with the Russian Federation's geopolitical objectives. Putin's objectives. Narrowing down Pichugin's targets is something the CIA might be interested in."

"We are," said Bauer.

Thank you, Audra!

"That's something we'd be interested in delivering to the CIA," said Paek.

Slam dunk.

"We'll keep you posted on the sting. You'll keep us posted on your Russia investigation. And we'll both keep the CIA informed. Everybody wins," said Paek.

Berg nearly jumped out of his chair, but Devin picked up on the attempted brush-off before he exploded.

"Everybody except us," said Devin.

"I don't see how this isn't a win for you," said Paek. "Unless you're in this for less-altruistic reasons."

Berg looked to Devin, who shrugged off the not-so-subtle dig with an immediate rebuttal.

"We're in this for one reason. To protect the United States from Yuri Pichugin's sleeper network. Nobody at our end of the table, except for Anish, is paid to be here. Yes. This is all very personal for me. That's definitely what you might call a less-altruistic reason, but in the end, just like DEVTEK's self- and client-protective interests in this collaboration—regardless of our motivations—our actions ultimately serve that one reason."

"To protect the US from Pichugin's sleeper network," said Paek.

"Right. And we still haven't identified most of the network, which is all I'm asking for in exchange for our help," said Devin.

"We really don't need your help," said Randall. "This is the kind of thing we prefer to keep in-house."

"Hold on," said Paek. "Exactly what are you asking for?"

"All we want is a lead on where Pichugin's sleeper sends the information he or she steals," said Devin. "Anish walked me through the concept of zero-day exploits earlier. The dummy version."

A zero-day vulnerability is a software flaw in an operating system or application that has gone undiscovered by the native developers, and exposes the system to cyber exploitation in the form of malware or some other virus. The term *zero-day* refers to the fact that the native developers learn of the vulnerability only at the moment of the cyberattack—leaving them with zero days to develop a security patch to address the issue.

Devin continued: "In order to attack one of your clients, Pichugin would have to steal your code, identify a zero-day, and create an exploit."

"Which could take several months," said Anna. "It could take them half that time just to find a zero-day. We are constantly combing through our code for vulnerabilities."

"That's what every tech company says, but hackers still find zero-days," said Devin. "How could you speed up the process between stealing code and delivering a workable exploit?"

"Throw more people and computing power at the problem," she said. "Some hackers are way better at finding them than others, but in the end, it's a probability issue."

"Normally, zero-days are identified by individual hackers and sold to groups that specialize in creating exploits, right?"

"Yep," said Anna. "But I don't see where you're going with this."

"Pichugin isn't going to distribute the code to a hundred different hackers in a hundred different locations and trust them to not screw him over," said Devin.

"Huh," she said, like she understood where he was taking this. "The code itself would be extremely valuable, on top of any zero-days that came out of it. That's a lot of temptation for a community with very few scruples."

"How would you do it?" said Devin.

"If I were Pichugin, or whoever is pulling the strings on this, I'd consolidate everything in one secure location and pay everyone top dollar. Then I'd create a very comfortable live-at-work situation for the team, where he provides and controls everything. Secure location. No outside communications. Nobody leaves until the job is done, and they take nothing but their pay with them when they walk out the door."

Anish turned to Devin with a sly smile. "Told you."

"What did he tell you?" said Jenna Paek.

"That Pichugin is running a zero-day factory," said Anna.

"It makes perfect sense, given the hundreds of sleepers likely embedded in technology companies across the country. He's probably been churning them out for years. Look what he's done to Antheon, Boeing, Lockram Industries, and Ampere recently," said Devin. "Not only did he stain their reputations and cost them billions of dollars in contracts, but he's significantly chipped away at US credibility abroad."

Paek and Anna shared a worried look, the implications for DEVTEK finally sinking in.

"All I ask in return for our help is the location of Pichugin's zero-day factory. I've been told by my chief technology officer that even under the most encrypted data-transfer scenarios, tracing a location is possible, with the right tools and people—and a willingness to ignore a few laws."

Jenna looked at Rafael, who answered: "We can trace the sleeper's data transfers, but only after we corrupt his or her devices. It's unlikely

235

that the transfer will occur at DEVTEK, so we'll need to access all of their devices and watch them twenty-four seven."

"Brendan suggested that your team might be useful if we need to step outside of normal boundaries?" said Paek.

"That's our specialty," said Devin.

Shea leaned forward. "And you're getting a seasoned team of surveillance and countersurveillance experts. I've worked with Devin before, and he's one of the best in the business. I can put them to good use."

"Any objections? Questions? Anything? Anyone?" said Paek, her team immediately indicating that they were set. "All right. We have a tentative deal. I still need to run this by my boss. When can you fly out?"

"Anytime," said Berg, taking back the reins. "But given the circumstances of the past few weeks, I'm afraid commercial air travel is out of the question."

"Brendan explained the situation ahead of time," said Paek. "We have room on the jet to bring eight of you back this afternoon. I don't know how big of a team you intended to supply."

"Off the top of my head, I'd say Devin and Marnie," said Berg, knowing that he couldn't split them up. "Me and Anish. Definitely Jess and Daniel. I can see them coming in handy. Do we need Rico or Emily?"

Devin shook his head. "We want to keep as low a profile as possible."

"Six of us," said Berg.

"Perfect," said Randall. "And while we're talking about low profile. Pistols only, if you insist on bringing firearms. They'll have to remain stowed in the luggage hold for the duration of the flight. I normally would insist that you don't bring any on the trip, but after everything you've been through over the past few weeks, I'd probably be sleeping with one under my pillow."

"Most of us are," said Marnie.

While the two groups started to get up from their seats, Berg slid over to Bauer, who remained seated. She looked up at him, a deadpan expression on her face.

"This weekend keeps getting better," she said. "Now you're standing me up for dinner?"

"Look I'm—I don't know what to say. I didn't expect them to fly us out this afternoon," said Berg. "I feel horrible leaving you here, but I didn't feel like I could say no."

Jenna Paek appeared next to Berg. "Sorry to interrupt. It's a pleasure to meet you. Randall tells me we're in good hands if you're the kind of company Mr. Berg keeps."

"I figured someone might recognize me," said Bauer, shaking Paek's hand.

"Randall has an encyclopedic memory," said Paek. "And he spent twenty-three years at the NSA before jumping ship to work for us."

"That's very kind of him to say," said Bauer.

"And I couldn't help but overhear that Mr. Berg is somehow standing you up for dinner?"

"I kind of lured her out here with the promise of good food and good company," said Berg.

"Ms. Bauer had no idea we would be here, did she?" said Paek.

"Was it that obvious?" said Berg.

"Maybe not to the guys, but I could tell right away," said Paek. "Her eyes have been shooting daggers at you throughout the meeting. Thank you for coming, even if it was sort of against your will."

"It's fine. I'm mostly giving him shit," said Bauer. "We worked together off and on at Langley. It's hard to stay mad at him for too long."

"I'm going to push our flight back by four hours so Mr. Berg can keep his promise," said Paek.

"She just saved your hide," said Bauer.

"That'll give us time to take a look at Helen Gray's files and hear more about your other investigation," said Paek. "Shea said you had a team in Moscow running some kind of surveillance on Pichugin?"

"We do," said Berg. "And we can definitely talk about what they've found so far. Devin can walk you through his mother's files with Anish's help. Anish and Graves archived as much as they could before the apartment was attacked."

"Shea told me what happened," said Paek. "I'm very sorry. I hope we can put these people out of business for good."

"That might be a tall order," said Berg. "I'd settle for unraveling whatever endgame Pichugin recently set in motion. I get the sense from his desperate actions that it's something bigger than we suspect."

PART FOUR

CHAPTER 42

A knock at the door drew all their eyes across the hotel suite. Daniel got up and grabbed the pistol sitting on the table in front of him, tucking it into his waistband before heading to the door. Nobody was expecting trouble on the top floor of the Four Seasons Hotel, but they couldn't entirely discount it. Pichugin's people had repeatedly proved to be unusually well informed and fanatically relentless. Daniel activated the digital peephole screen next to the door.

"It's Randall Powers," said Daniel, flipping the security latch before opening the door.

Powers stepped inside and made his way through the entry foyer to the spacious living area. Devin rose with Marnie from one of the couches and invited him to join them. He picked an empty wing chair facing the floor-to-ceiling windows and made himself comfortable as the rest of the team settled into the contemporary furniture arranged around the wall-mounted TV.

"Looks like you've settled in," said Randall. "I can arrange a second room if the sleeping arrangements are a little tight. A regular guest room to use as a crash pad."

"We'll survive," said Devin. "The suite is generous enough."

"If you change your mind, let me know," said Randall. "It's probably not going to be the most exciting week."

"That's fine by us," said Devin. "Trust me. We're anxious to get rolling on this, but if it moves slowly, I don't think any of us are going to complain."

"We'll see what shakes out," said Randall. "Chase will give his notice tomorrow morning. Since we all agree he's not exactly the best under pressure, we'll perp-walk him out of the building shortly after he hands in his notice. He works on one of our more sensitive projects, so nobody will think twice about us handling him this way. We can't have him fending off questions from coworkers for two weeks. He'll screw it up."

"That's a good call," said Berg. "Colleagues will still reach out to him by phone. What's the cover story?"

"We coached him to say, *I can't discuss it right now due to a nondisclosure, but everyone will know soon enough.* That'll lead them to believe he landed a new position."

"Simple enough," said Berg. "You might want to consider getting him out of the area, so colleagues can't stop by and press him for information. It could get uncomfortable for him."

"I don't think that's a good idea," said Marnie. "If the cover story is that he got another job, he wouldn't just vanish. That might look a little odd."

"It would," said Randall. "We told him to stick around for two weeks, and if this lasts any longer than that, we'd send him on a little vacation. We're actually sending him on an extremely nice vacation later this year, accompanied by a sizable cash bonus, for agreeing to this."

"How quickly will things move once Chase leaves the building?" said Jessica.

"The position he's leaving is considered a critical fill. It's not only a sensitive project—it's considered one of the most important to DEVTEK's near future. Everyone tried to get in on it when we formed the initial team, so I'd be shocked if we didn't have a full slate of internal candidates by noon."

"Full slate?" said Devin. "So this isn't a slam dunk for the sleeper."

"Using the age range of your sleeper profile, I narrowed the possible candidates with the right skills down to nine," said Randall. "One is considerably senior to the others, so the job is essentially his if he wants it."

"Have you looked into his background?" said Berg.

"Only what we could access over the web. Nothing jumped out at me," said Randall. "I hired a private investigative group to dig deep into his past as you suggested. They fly out tomorrow to start interviewing friends and relatives in his hometown. Anyone that can shed light on his past."

"That's exactly how my mom confirmed over a hundred sleepers," said Devin. "She flew around the country for years posing as a reporter or security clearance investigator."

"Just when I thought her work couldn't get any more impressive," said Randall. "I'll keep you all updated as the day progresses. Like I said, this could be a done deal by noon, if the top candidate wants the job. They'll give him a few days to clean up whatever he's working on and move him right into Chase's workstation."

"What does the hierarchy look like below the most obvious candidate?" said Devin. "The reason I ask is that this feels too easy."

Randall laughed. "There's a definite second- and third-place winner. The rest would compete against each other."

"Don't be surprised if your number one pick declines," said Devin. "Pichugin may have gotten to him somehow. I know it sounds extreme, but don't rule it out."

"I won't," said Randall.

"What happens to the winning candidate when Chase returns? Doesn't this kind of mess things up internally?"

"Actually, it merges nicely with a planned expansion of Chase's group. We were planning on opening up another software-engineering position within the month," said Randall. "Let's meet here tomorrow evening at eight to discuss next steps. Just to be up front, I plan to use your team to access the sleeper's house or apartment, cars, gym locker, whatever and wherever—to upload our tracking software on every device in their possession."

"We can take care of that," said Jessica. "With Anish's help."

"Perfect. Shea will incorporate everyone else into the twenty-four-hour surveillance effort," said Randall. "It's very possible that our sleeper will physically hand the goods over to another sleeper or trusted contact. We have to be there when and if that happens."

"How will you trace the data transfer after it has been handed off?" said Berg. "The contact will go straight home and transfer the data."

"That's when you'll have to truly decide how far you're willing to go to find the zero-day factory," said Randall. "If you provide us with the contact's devices, we can more than likely figure out where the data was sent. I won't say any more."

He didn't need to. The implication was obvious. The only way to acquire the contact's devices would be to break in and grab them, which presented a dilemma. How do you prevent that contact from warning Pichugin? He could think of only one correct answer to the question, given his experience dealing with the sleepers.

"We're willing to go as far as it takes," said Devin.

CHAPTER 43

The encrypted phone provided by DEVTEK rang, catching the team unassembled. Marnie and Jessica had left about forty minutes earlier to go for an early afternoon run. Daniel had taken off for the hotel's gym around the same time. Anish and Berg were out hunting down tacos at one of the nearby taquerias.

Devin snatched the phone off the table in front of the couch. "Devin Gray."

"Hey. It's Randall. We've hit a bit of a snag."

"Nobody wants the job?" said Devin.

Randall laughed. "No. Quite the opposite. Everything played out exactly as we predicted. Sean Erickson submitted his name to HR and directly to the project lead by ten thirty. And on down the line, almost to the person."

"That team must be working on one hell of a project," said Devin, refraining from blurting out that he knew it was a modular communications encryption system.

"It's a game changer," said Randall. "And everyone wants in on the next shiny thing."

Game changer. That was exactly how Graves had described it. A universally interoperable, fully encrypted communications interface that would revolutionize military and government agency operations. But how did a prototype communications system only recently green-lit by the CIA for testing have anything to do with an air assault brigade poised to strike one of the Baltic states? Maybe there was no connection, and the two Army officers were being groomed for something far down the line.

"Something tells me you have bad news," said Devin.

"Depends on your perspective," said Randall. "Erickson checks out. The group I hired to dig into his background reported back to me about ten minutes ago. Sean and his wife are high school sweethearts from Duluth, Minnesota, and both sets of parents are alive and well. His parents still live just outside of Duluth in the same house they raised Sean in, with one of Sean's grandparents. His wife's parents moved to Bemidji after they retired. Her dad always loved the fishing up there. They spoke with teachers, neighbors, friends. Even drove out to Bemidji to have a chat with Jeanine's folks. Nothing but their age fits the profile you gave me."

"Well . . . shit," said Devin.

"My sentiments exactly," said Randall. "Though like I said. This is either good or bad news, depending on your perspective. Good if you think we no longer have a sleeper threat. Bad if you think that the sleeper problem isn't gone—it's just more complex than you originally expected."

"I'm leaning toward the latter," said Devin.

"Me too," said Randall.

"Any chance Erickson is compromised?" said Devin.

"Impossible to say, right?" said Randall.

"Right," said Devin. "I suppose we could treat him like he's a suspect, until proven otherwise. Upload your software to all of his devices. Put him under twenty-four hour—"

"He doesn't fit the profile, Devin. Not even close," said Randall. "I can't subject him to that without a single shred of evidence. This played out exactly as I expected, because it was the most logical outcome with Chase leaving. The investigative team will keep digging into the Ericksons, but I'd be surprised if they unearthed anything that would change my mind."

"Don't take Erickson out of the lineup, but I agree with you," said Devin. "Let me ask you this. What are the chances of you telling me, in somewhat vague terms, what Brian Chase was working on?"

"Zero," said Randall. "Sorry. I discussed it with the head shed, and they said no."

"Fair enough," said Devin. "Then let me float something by you, as food for thought."

"Sure. Fire away."

"Does Brian Chase's departure make any sense if Pichugin was plotting against one of the Baltic states' governments or militaries? He's up to something in that region. Whether it's related to DEVTEK is unknown right now," said Devin. "I'll leave that with you. Maybe it'll help make sense of what they were trying to accomplish by trying to blackmail Chase."

"We'll look at the problem through that lens and see if anything jumps out," said Randall. "Let's keep our eight o'clock meeting. We'll throw some more ideas around. My guess is we're missing something. The Russians wouldn't have put that much effort into blackmailing Chase if they didn't have a good reason."

"You can drive yourself crazy thinking about all of the possibilities," said Devin. "But that's exactly what we need to do. Because you're right. We're definitely missing something. See you at eight."

"Eight it is," said Randall, ending the call.

Devin sat back on the couch and closed his eyes. Of course it wouldn't be as easy as they'd hoped. Why would it? Back to the drawing board. A delay at best. A reset at worst. Wasted time either way. And instinct told him that time was running out.

CHAPTER 44

The knock came at precisely eight. Devin opened the door to find Randall and a woman he hadn't met before standing in the hallway.

"Follow me," said Randall.

"Just me?"

"Everyone," said Randall. "And leave all electronic devices behind. Erin is going to wand everyone as you exit the room."

"What's going on?" said Devin.

"We're taking a little trip," said Randall.

"Is this a good thing or a bad thing?" said Devin.

"Depends on your perspective."

Devin returned to the living area and explained Randall's request, leaving his phone in the newly formed pile of devices on the dining room table. They filed out of the room one at a time, each of them spending a few seconds with Erin and her metal detector. Daniel, the second to last out of the room, set off the wand's alarm. He raised his untucked shirt and turned a quarter of the way around to expose the pistol jammed into his waistband. Erin glanced at Randall.

"It's fine," said Randall.

Jessica exited last, raising her left knee tight against her chest and lifting her pant leg—removing a five-inch serrated blade from a sheath hidden in her boot.

"That's fine, too," said Randall. "Any other surprises?"

A second knife appeared in her left hand, Devin having zero idea how she produced it.

"Now you can wand me," said Jessica.

"She's clean," said Erin, spending a little extra time on her. "Where did the other knife come from?"

"Wouldn't you like to know?"

"Behave," said Daniel. "Or we won't get invited back."

They all laughed for a few seconds before Randall led them down the hallway toward the elevator lobby.

"Where are we headed?" said Marnie.

"The eighth floor," said Randall.

They passed the elevators and entered the adjacent stairwell, stopping one floor below at a locked door that Randall opened with a keycard. A quick knock on room eight zero four's door gained them entrance to a bustling suite the same size as their own.

The dining room table had been pushed against the back of the couch that faced the massive wall-mounted TV, its four available seats occupied by people typing on laptops. Three picked-over pizza boxes and several partially consumed plastic soda bottles sat on the coffee table in front of the couch. Pretty much every horizontal surface in the living area was occupied by a fast-food box or soft drink container.

"Did DEVTEK's headquarters lease expire?" said Berg.

Randall chuckled. "No. I felt that I needed to put a little distance between my investigative team and DEVTEK."

"Okay," said Devin. "This sounds interesting."

"Take a seat and I'll walk you through it," said Randall, before shooing a few of his team members from the couches.

After they were seated, Randall made room for himself at the table behind them and took over one of the laptops. After a minute or so of back-and-forth with the laptop's owner, he clicked its mouse pad, and the TV screen displayed a woman's face. Neutral smile. Dark-brown hair. Blue eyes. Middle-aged.

"Meet Sarah Ingraham. DEVTEK's human resources director. Forty-eight years old from Bozeman, Montana. Married with three children. Both parents died in a hit-and-run car crash in 2009. They were sixty-one years old. We scoured the internet for information on Ms. Ingraham's grandparents, using a background-check system created in-house. As you can imagine, it's a very robust system. We found no trace of grandparents, and no trace of her parents prior to 1972. I've diverted the private investigative team working Sean Erickson's history to Bozeman."

"What about the husband?" said Berg.

"He checks out on the internet," said Randall. "But I'm sending a team to his hometown in Indiana. Mr. Ingraham is a stay-at-home dad as far as we know."

"How long has she been with DEVTEK?"

"Eight years," said Randall. "We poached her from Cisco Systems, where she'd worked for the previous eleven years, climbing the corporate ladder to deputy HR director."

"What made you suspect her?" said Devin.

"Something we talked about this afternoon," said Randall. "You asked if Erickson's job could be the target, and I kind of made a joke about Pichugin playing 3D chess. I wrote a note reminding myself to take a look at the internal candidates interested in Erickson's position, but to be completely honest, I thought it was a stretch. I mean—how would the Russians know the intrateam hierarchies at DEVTEK? I put that note aside, intending to revisit it tonight. And then I received an email from Ms. Ingraham with a slate of three candidates for Erickson's position. She's looking to start the internal security clearance process as soon as possible. All had top-secret government clearances. All were external candidates."

"Sounds a bit rushed," said Marnie.

"Yes and no. DEVTEK keeps close track of external talent, and actively pursues people with the right skills and experience. Ms. Ingraham's team has done a stellar job bringing in the best in the industry. But this felt a little—"

"Rushed," said Marnie.

"Precisely. I called HR and asked if they had any internal candidates for me to run through our background-check system. They didn't."

"You rerun background checks on employees?" said Berg.

"Every two years," said Randall. "And whenever an employee changes teams, like Erickson—although he got the special treatment. Ninety-nine times out of a hundred, nothing new shows up on any of the background checks, but that one time here and there has saved us some trouble over the years. We discovered a key employee's recent house foreclosure, which led to the discovery of a significant gambling debt. A liability like that is something foreign agents or competitors can leverage to corrupt an employee. DUIs pop up from time to time. Mostly stuff that earns the employee some extra scrutiny and possibly a tough conversation."

"So. No internal candidates," said Devin.

"None. When I pressed HR on that, I was told that they planned to use the opportunity to bring new talent into the company, followed by 'this came straight from the top.' Honestly, if we hadn't talked earlier that afternoon, and I wasn't hunting for a sleeper, I might not have thought much of it. We typically prioritize internal candidates, but if there's a chance to bring someone special into DEVTEK, this wouldn't be the first time that internal candidates were overlooked. But your question got me thinking. And I kept returning to my own question. How would the Russians know our internal hierarchy? How would they know to target Chase?"

"A sleeper inside human resources," said Marnie.

Randall shrugged. "The answer felt almost too obvious to be true, but I decided to start running HR through the internal background-check system. I started with Ms. Ingraham. We're now checking everyone in HR."

"And everyone in the slate of candidates," said Devin.

"Of course," said Randall, the wall-mounted flat-screen changing to display three faces. "Three software engineers, all currently employed by big tech companies. All flying in tomorrow. Interviews start the day after that. One coming in from Austin. The other two flying down from Seattle."

Devin examined the faces in front of him for a few moments, coming to the same conclusion as the rest of his team.

"They're too young," said Marnie.

"Too young to be second generation," added Berg. "Too old to be part of the third."

Anish cracked his knuckles, clearly itching to get his hands on a laptop. "That doesn't matter. Any one of them, or all of them, could be under Pichugin's control right now—for any number of reasons."

"We have to operate under the assumption that all of them could be compromised in some way," said Devin. "Unless Ms. Ingraham stacked the deck."

"It appears she did," said Randall. "All of the candidates are good, but one stands out. Unless she leaps over the table and tries to strangle one of the interviewers, the job is hers."

The screen displayed a single face. A woman in her late twenties to early thirties with short blonde hair.

"Meet Alyssa Briggs," said Randall.

"Ingraham's smart," said Devin. "This essentially removes her from the hiring decision process and puts a lot of distance between herself and the new employee. It almost sounds like she hopes to stick around after the employee sabotages the company."

"Which is why we're not going to let any of that happen," said Randall. "We're going to sit on all three of them the entire time they're in Palo Alto. They'll have to surrender any devices they bring to the interviews at reception, so we'll be able to bug their first line of communications. We'll also search their rooms for spare devices and upload our software."

"Will they be staying at the Four Seasons?" said Daniel.

"Normally, yes," said Randall. "But given our outsize presence here at the moment, we've booked them junior suites at the Westin."

"If you book us two basic rooms at the Westin, we'll set up well in advance of their arrival and start looking for countersurveillance. If we're not talking about an indoctrinated sleeper, then it'll be someone the Russians are either blackmailing or paying a ton of money. Either way, they'll want to keep a close eye on their investment."

"Two rooms?" said Randall.

"So we can operate independently as complete strangers," said Daniel. "We'll check in separately and make our way down the lobby and common areas to await their arrival."

"Let me run that by Brendan Shea. He'll be here shortly with his team," said Randall. "I switched them from a rental house to a suite down the hall. It'll be easier with all of us in one place."

"Having us work the hotel will keep Shea's people entirely separate and less likely to be detected," said Jessica. "We can distract or watch the candidates while other teams access their rooms. Our primary job will be to identify any Russian assets sent to watch over them—to make Shea's job easier. We'll focus on Briggs but keep an eye on the others."

"Sounds like a plan to me," said Randall. "I'll book rooms for the two of you. Regardless of what Shea decides, I like the idea of having the two of you over there. Shea will have a team in the hotel as well."

"You probably already know this, but don't put the Petroviches or Shea's crew on the same floor as any of the candidates. The less the candidates and the surveillance teams interact outside of controlled encounters, the better," said Devin. "Ideally, you'd split up the candidates to separate floors as well."

"HR usually keeps them apart. There's not much I can do if it doesn't work out that way. Any room changes will be reported to HR, even if it's a simple room swap. Ingraham would be notified, and that could raise suspicion," said Randall. "The other problem is that the

Westin only has four floors. It has a few distinctly separate sections, so I'll see what I can do."

"Don't mess with any of the candidates' rooms," said Devin. "It's not worth the risk."

"I'll make sure everyone else is on different floors or in different sections of the hotel. I didn't think of that. Thank you."

"With any luck," said Devin, "we'll have the sleeper identified by tomorrow night. After that, it's anyone's guess how long it'll take for the sleeper to access the targeted system, steal the code, and transmit it. This could be a long haul."

"Weeks. Possibly months," said Randall. "It may take them a few weeks to leave their job. And a few more to relocate."

"I suspect it'll go quickly," said Berg. "The Russians are up to something."

"Speaking of that, Randall," said Devin. "Does a sleeper in Erickson's soon-to-be-vacated role pose any threat to one of the Baltic states?"

The torn look on Randall's face for the next several moments answered Devin's question.

"I can't really comment on any project specifics," said Randall. "But I'll bring the question to Ms. Paek."

That was a big *YES*.

CHAPTER 45

Jessica Petrovich peeked over her laptop screen, catching a glimpse of Alyssa Briggs. She had just left the reception desk with a small rolling suitcase, presumably headed for the elevators. When she passed the elevator lobby and kept going toward the hotel lounge, Jessica typed a quick message for the surveillance team.

Briggs headed to lounge.

Daniel had situated himself in the lounge, at a two-person table with a commanding view of the bar and numerous conversation nooks. The lounge was more of a Silicon Valley social hub that happened to have drink service than a traditional bar, though it still gave you the option of sitting in front of a bartender. Looked like Briggs's first order of business upon arrival was to calm her nerves.

A casual glance around the lobby didn't reveal any obvious countersurveillance. About half of the seats and tables were occupied, mostly with young faces. Jessica thought about that for a moment, wondering if she looked out of place. She'd turned fifty-one this year, even though she looked at least ten years younger—or so she told herself. Daniel acknowledged her message.

She just saddled up to the bar. Bartender just placed two tequila shots in front of her.

Briggs was on edge. Then again, she was headed into a job interview. A few minutes later, Briggs left the lounge with a bottle of beer
and pulled her suitcase into the elevator lobby. Nobody in the lobby
made a move over the next ten minutes. Jessica had expected her mind-
ers to make contact shortly after her arrival. Maybe they were doing that
right now up in her room. That was Shea's territory.

JP: Nothing going on in the lobby.

DP: Same for the lounge.

BS (Brendan Shea): She went straight to her room. No interference.
Lee Babin pulling up to hotel in five minutes.

Babin was second in line for the job, according to Randall. Babin
had sounded Russian or Jewish to her, and a quick internet search confirmed that she was right on both counts. The name could be Jewish if
they were from Belarus. Otherwise most likely Russian or Ukrainian.
Possibly Serbian. The possible Russian connection struck her as interesting, but there was nothing in his background to suggest anything
but a coincidence.

The software engineer from Austin entered the lobby and headed
directly for the reception desk. He spent less than a minute checking in
before pulling his carry-on-size suitcase to the elevator lobby.

JP: Babin headed up. When is Wu due to arrive?

BS: Not until eight thirty. His flight was delayed.

Almost two and a half hours from now. She'd move around the
lobby and lounge between now and then, scouting the crowd while
Daniel took a short break. Then it would be her turn to vanish for a
short stretch so it didn't look like they were lingering. They'd alternate
back and forth like that, returning at different times to have dinner and
possibly a drink in the lounge.

She closed her laptop and considered grabbing a mojito from the
bar. Everyone in the lobby seemed to have started happy hour without
her. Jessica had started to get up when a sharply dressed older couple,
who had been sharing a cozy couch just outside of the lounge, rose and

walked briskly to the elevator lobby, leaving partially consumed drinks behind.

She sat back down and grabbed her phone from her purse, pretending that she'd just received a call. Jessica nodded and laughed a few times, interspersed with a few words and generic phrases. She continued the nonsensical conversation with herself until the couple vanished from sight.

JP: Couple in their late fifties immediately followed Babin to the elevator. Checking it out.

BS: What do you mean? What are you doing?

Jessica took off for the elevators, laptop in one hand, phone to her ear in the other. She turned the corner just in time to see the couple step onto one of the elevators.

"Can you hold that, please?" she said, before going back to her imaginary conversation.

The elevator door started to close, its occupants clearly ignoring her. Jessica rushed forward and pressed the "Up" button several times, satisfied to see the door stop and retract. She stepped onto the elevator, only taking a break from her "call" to ask Lee Babin to press the third-floor button, which was already illuminated. Babin's room was on four.

The couple and Babin rode in silence as she rambled away with her imaginary friend. After a short ride, the door opened on the third floor, and Jessica motioned for the older couple to go first.

"Damn. I forgot to check on our reservations tonight," said the husband. "We're on the wait list at Nobu. The concierge said we had a good chance of getting in. After the tip I gave him, we better get in."

"I don't mind heading back down," said his wife. "I could use another drink."

Jessica got off the elevator and started down the hallway toward her room, continuing the fake conversation until the elevator door shut behind her. She frantically typed on the secure message app that

DEVTEK installed on her phone, which mirrored the app on her laptop.

JP: Couple's room on third floor, but they didn't get off. The couple said they're headed back to the lobby. Wife getting a drink. Husband checking on a reservation with concierge. Didn't feel right.

BS: Babin just got off elevator. Headed to his room. No sign of couple.

Jessica proceeded to her room, having just shut the door behind her when Daniel messaged.

Couple back in lobby. Wife getting drink at bar. Husband headed to reception. Can't see him from my position. Looks legit enough.

She didn't buy it. Too many coincidences for one moment. The couple ditching their drinks and abruptly following Babin to the elevator. Now the wife is getting another drink? No. Jessica had interrupted something in that elevator, and the couple had improvised, buying them some time alone with Babin.

CHAPTER 46

Richard Farrington pumped the last of his mosquito repellent into a cupped hand before smearing it all over his sweaty face and neck. He'd severely underestimated the bloodsucker problem down here. Whatever nonsense Berg had said about mosquito tornadoes must be true. He'd never experienced anything even close to this before. Hundreds of mosquitoes vied for what little skin Farrington couldn't cover. He quickly put his gloves back on before they could swarm his hands. If things didn't improve somewhat after sunset, he'd put on his balaclava and tactical goggles—a last resort in this brutal heat and humidity. To put it mildly, he was getting too old for this shit. And he still had another thirty-six hours before Alex returned to relieve him.

They'd decided on forty-eight-hour shifts to cut down on the number of times their car appeared in the vicinity of the forest bordering the western edge of the Staraya Russa Airport. The locals seemed on edge, and their Moscow plates drew attention wherever they stopped.

Two days didn't sound so bad, until Farrington had traveled about a hundred yards into the forest. The hot, stuffy air so infested with mosquitoes that he didn't dare open his mouth. Even breathing heavy through your nose carried a moderate risk of inhaling one of these persistent insects. They'd have to change to twenty-four-hour shifts and carry three times the amount of repellent.

He checked his watch. Ten o'clock. Twenty-two minutes until sunset and a possible reprieve from the mosquitoes. A bit of quick math told him it was noon in California. Farrington had seen enough at the base to warrant a call back to Berg. He removed a satellite phone from his tactical vest and hit one of the preset numbers.

"Scarface," answered Berg.

"Say hello to my little friend," he whispered.

They had about thirty of these identity checks memorized, all movie quotes.

"What time is it over there?" said Berg.

"Ten o'clock," said Farrington. "And the sun is still up. So are the mosquitoes."

"I read that this is one of the worst years for mosquitoes in that area. Record rains and unusual heat have created the perfect conditions for mosquitoes to breed."

"That would have been nice to know before we set out with one spray bottle of repellent," said Farrington. "Alex may have to drive all the way to St. Petersburg to find more. All of the stores here are sold out, unsurprisingly."

"Aside from swatting bugs, what have you been up to?" said Berg. "I was beginning to wonder if you'd been pulled over on the way up from Moscow."

"It's been a long two days," said Farrington. "The trip took forever. The Russian roads are no better here than I remember outside of Novosibirsk. I was more worried about a flat tire than the police."

"Road repair wasn't a priority outside of major cities or oblast administrative centers when I was stationed in Moscow," said Berg. "Some things never change."

"We checked into a motel about two miles from the military airfield, before scouting the area near the base for places to park the car and observe the First Helicopter Assault Brigade's movements. By noon the next day, we'd identified an unusual pattern. They've been flying helicopters northeast-ish all day, both days, with only a trickle of return flights during the day. They all returned last night. I wasn't aware of any military bases within easy helicopter range to our east, so we—"

"There's an old abandoned military airfield just north of Novgorod," said Berg. "And an active airport in Staraya Russa, about thirty miles south of Novgorod, used primarily for Russian-built commercial airliner maintenance."

"I know. I'm looking at it right now," said Farrington.

"Which one?"

"Staraya Russa. We drove northeast out of Ostrov, hoping to track the helicopter traffic. As luck would have it, most of the helicopters followed the road connecting Ostrov to Dno. A little over sixty miles. Unfortunately, the roads didn't continue northeast past Dno, but it was obvious they were headed in the general direction of Novgorod. Staraya Russa made the most sense, because it's the more isolated of the two airfields."

"You're a regular Sherlock Holmes," said Berg.

"Funny," said Farrington. "Anyway, we parked at a distance and watched the MI-8 and MI-35 helicopters land and take on fully geared troops, fly away for thirty minutes or so, then return to drop them off. Then do it again and again. This went on all day. Even saw a few of those MI-26 monsters."

"That's kind of an odd location to practice embark-and-debark drills," said Berg. "They could do that back at the Ostrov airfield."

"That's what we thought," said Farrington. "So we parked the car and hiked in to get a closer look at the drill. Everything seemed normal until the last wave of helicopters departed—and left all of their troops behind."

"That's odd," said Berg.

"Odd enough for me to hike several miles through the forest on the other side of the airport this morning and crawl within a few hundred yards of a brand-new barracks complex. About twenty buildings," said Farrington.

"That transcends odd," said Berg. "More like . . . suspicious."

"That doesn't even scratch the surface of suspicious. I've been watching these soldiers for the past several hours, and I've concluded that they're not Russian Federation soldiers. They're mercenaries. They look like soldiers, right down to the weapons, gear, and camouflage, but they wear no insignia, and they don't act like soldiers."

"What do you mean?"

"It's hard to describe, but I'm not getting the sense that there's much of a difference in rank among the soldiers. There's no saluting. I see small clusters of soldiers that carry themselves like officers or non-commissioned officers, but nobody stands at attention or really reacts at all when they approach. From what I've always understood, discipline and military decorum is strictly observed and enforced in the Russian military. With a nationwide compulsory service requirement, they don't have a choice. Most conscripts don't want to be there. I didn't see any evidence of this among these soldiers."

"It's called *dedovshchina* by the Russian military. An informal system of hazing and bullying, not unlike some of our own military's initiation practices, but far more extensive and brutal—and it doesn't stop after basic training. It usually continues throughout a soldier's initial conscription. Hundreds commit suicide every year because of it," said Berg. "Basically, the career soldiers take advantage of the conscripts and abuse them. It was a serious morale issue back in the Soviet era, and it's still a widespread problem today."

"I didn't see any evidence of anyone being bossed around or harassed," said Farrington.

"Maybe it's a Spetsnaz unit?" said Berg. "The Second Spetsnaz Brigade is based in Promezhitsy, just south of Pskov. That's only about twenty-five miles north of Ostrov."

"Possibly, but I don't think so. I estimate the total troop strength based at the airfield to be around a thousand soldiers, and that's probably a low estimate, since I can't see the entire base," said Farrington. "That's just too big for a Spetsnaz unit, unless they brought an entire brigade to Staraya Russa for drills. And why would they be training with the First Helicopter Assault Brigade?"

"They wouldn't," said Berg. "They'd use the Fifteenth Army Aviation Brigade or another Western Military District transport unit."

"There's only one mercenary outfit I can think of that could field a unit this large," said Farrington.

"The Wegner Group," said Berg.

"Pichugin's private army," said Farrington.

"I need to call Audra," said Berg. "This changes everything."

CHAPTER 47

Audra Bauer excused herself and stepped out of the conference room, having just received a troubling message on her tablet from her executive assistant. Karl Berg had called her office a few minutes ago, insisting that she call him back immediately. Really gave her assistant a hard time. Of course he hadn't identified himself as Karl Berg. He'd used a fake name and a government title she could tell had been made up. That and a reference to the Baltics convinced her to skip out of the afternoon department briefing.

Bauer wound her way through the hallways and cubicle farms to her office and shut the door. There was no way she could leave Langley right now to make a call. As much as she didn't want to use her office phone, Karl's call didn't sound like it could wait. She picked up the note left by her assistant and reached for the phone, pausing before lifting it from the receiver.

Her phone and office at the CIA had been bugged before, back in the days of the Crane administration. The information gleaned by operatives working on behalf of the White House had nearly resulted in her kidnapping, torture, and murder at the hands of the True America terrorist organization. In hindsight, she should have known they would be listening to her. Like Karl, she had possessed information they didn't want publicized, painting a target on her back. Today, she had no such enemies. Bauer picked up the phone and dialed the number left by Karl.

"Audra. I wasn't expecting you to get back to me this quickly," said Berg.

"If it's not urgent, I should get back to my meeting," said Bauer.

"No. No. It's urgent. Urgent enough," said Berg. "I just spoke with Farrington. Long story short—a regiment-size unit of mercenaries, likely the Wegner Group, has taken up residence at an airport south of Novgorod. Helicopters from the First Helicopter Assault Brigade spent most of yesterday practicing embark-and-debark drills. They're up to something big."

"Is he sure they're mercenaries and not soldiers from the First?"

"He said they wore no uniform insignia, and there was no discernible rank structure or behavior among the soldiers," said Berg. "He felt confident in his assessment."

"Abandoning insignia patches was a common practice for regular Russian Army units headed into Ukraine. Soldiers driving T-90 tanks and riding in BPM-97 armored personnel carriers into battle around the Donbass region abandoned all uniform and vehicle insignia, trying to pose as separatists."

"Didn't we determine that some of those soldiers were actually Wegner Group mercenaries?"

"I guess it doesn't matter. The bottom line here is that General Grigory Kuznetzov, who we strongly suspect of running Pichugin's sleeper network, accompanied the First Helicopter Assault Brigade's commander back to Ostrov a few days ago—and now the First is practicing large-scale pickups and drop-offs with an unidentified, regiment-size air assault unit just a few hours' flight from any of the Baltic state capitals."

"That's not all," said Berg. "The DEVTEK sting has taken a few unexpected turns. Without going into all the details, I got the distinct impression from Randall Powers at DEVTEK that the job being targeted by Pichugin's sleeper network has a direct connection to the Baltics. Devin asked him point-blank if a sleeper in that job posed a threat to any of the Baltic states, and you could read the answer on his face. I'm wondering if you might be willing to give him a call and try to pry this information out of him, or possibly contact Jenna Paek. I think they're more likely to trust you with this than me."

"I'll give her a call," said Bauer. "Damn. I wish there was a way to confirm that the soldiers are mercenaries. I'd walk this right to Manning's office and propose that we stand up a compartmented operations center to start working this problem. The sooner we start a dialogue with our Baltic state intelligence counterparts, the better."

"I think if you can confirm with Jenna Paek that the targeted position at DEVTEK poses a significant threat to one of those countries, Manning will take this seriously," said Berg. "Not that he wouldn't take you seriously, anyway. You know what I mean. The multiple connections to Pichugin can't be ignored, especially when they're pointing west, toward former Soviet satellite countries."

"I agree," said Bauer. "Let me reach out to Paek and see what I can get out of her. How is the DEVTEK sting itself going?"

"We've had a few surprises, which I can explain when you have more time. But it's winding its way down to the end," said Berg. "The first round of interviews has been completed. The three candidates are back at the hotel, waiting to hear if they've been selected to return for a second interview. They're booked at the hotel tonight, in case there's a third round of interviews. The final decision will most likely be made tomorrow morning."

"Sounds like this wasn't a simple internal shift," said Bauer.

"No. The position opened to external candidates," said Berg. "And we're ninety-nine percent sure that DEVTEK's HR director is a second-generation sleeper. She's covering her tracks pretty well, so we expect a few more surprises before it's all said and done."

"Keep me posted," said Bauer. "And I'll let you know what I hear from Paek, unless she requires me to sign some kind of nondisclosure agreement restricting the information to the CIA."

"I wouldn't be surprised if she did," said Berg. "Just sign it and get the ball rolling with Manning."

"I'll bring all of this to Manning, regardless of what she says," said Bauer.

"We make a good team," said Berg.

"You looking to come back?" said Bauer.

"Only if they give me one of those cushy oversight positions I heard about."

Bauer chuckled. "I'll be in touch shortly," she said, ending the call.

She unlocked the bottom drawer of her desk and removed a metal business card organizer, quickly locating the card Jenna Paek had handed her the other day.

"This should be fun," she muttered, before picking up the phone.

CHAPTER 48

Devin stopped in front of room eight zero four, the door opening before he could knock. Erin, the ever-present security officer, motioned for him to raise his arms. Reluctantly, he did what she asked, and was admitted to the suite after a more-thorough-than-usual pass with the metal detector wand. Marnie and Berg joined him a minute later.

"Something's up," said Marnie. "I thought Erin was going to shove that wand where the sun doesn't shine."

"Definitely a different vibe tonight," said Berg.

Randall sat next to one of the security techs at the table pushed up against the couch, engaged in a conversation. He looked up and motioned for them to take a seat on one of the couches before returning his attention to the technician's laptop screen.

"Just a touch of panic," whispered Marnie.

The three of them sat on the couch facing the TV screen and waited on Randall, who had asked them to come down to the DEVTEK suite just minutes ago. A few excruciatingly long minutes later, Randall got up from the table and dropped into one of the side chairs next to them.

"As you've probably guessed," said Randall, "we're scrambling a bit."

"What happened?" said Devin.

"Alyssa Briggs was offered the job after a second round of interviews," said Randall. "Roughly two hours ago."

"As expected," said Devin. "But what happened next?"

"Precisely," said Randall. "An hour after HR extended Briggs the offer, she declined—saying that she'd changed her mind. No reason given."

"They got to Briggs before she arrived," said Devin. "Jessica was right. Babin is their ace in the hole. Damn. Ingraham is smart. She's covered her tracks like a pro."

"Fortunately for us, and unfortunately for her—we've been watching her the whole time," said Berg.

"No decision has been made regarding Babin," said Randall, standing up.

"It'll happen tomorrow morning. You'll see," said Devin. "And he'll start right away, so he can grab that code as soon as possible. Things are moving fast in Russia."

"So I've heard," said Randall, an odd look on his face. "Anyway. I don't take any pleasure in this, but I've been instructed to escort you out of the hotel and to the airport immediately. We've chartered a private jet to fly you back to West Virginia. All of your belongings from the suite will be packed up and returned to you when you board the plane."

"What the fuck are you talking about?" said Berg.

"I've received my marching orders," said Randall.

"This doesn't make any sense," said Berg.

"Yes, it does," said Devin. "You asked Audra Bauer to call Jenna Paek this afternoon. The purpose of that call was to determine whether Erickson's position, if compromised, could pose a threat to one of the Baltic countries. We already knew the answer because, despite Randall's thirty-plus years in corporate security, his poker face sucks. So here we are, with DEVTEK thinking they don't need us anymore. That they can work directly with the CIA."

Randall started to say something but sighed instead. "I don't know what to say, other than—your transportation to the airport has arrived."

"We're not leaving town," said Devin.

"You're most definitely leaving town, and staying away from DEVTEK," said Randall. "Unless you'd prefer we call the FBI and let them referee the situation. Word on the street is they'd like a word with you and Marnie. Not sure about the rest of the group, but I'm sure we could ask."

"Randall. You know this is wrong," said Berg.

"It doesn't matter what I think or what I know," he said. "It's what's best for DEVTEK—and the United States."

A knock at the door produced Anish, who was herded into the room by Erin

"What the fuck happened?" said Anish. "Everything was cool one second; then two DEVTEK goons yanked me from Shea's room."

"What did Shea say?" said Devin.

"He wasn't too happy," said Anish. "But that Paek lady showed up while I was being escorted out."

"MINERVA can't afford to upset one of their top clients," said Randall. "Or jeopardize a potential future relationship with the CIA."

"We better let Daniel and Jessica know what's coming," said Berg. "They might not respond so passively. In fact, I know they won't."

"We're taking care of that right now," said Randall.

Anish chuckled.

"What?" said Randall.

"The second I saw your two goons, I knew DEVTEK had fucked us over—so I fucked you over," said Anish. "I warned them."

"Shit," said Randall, turning to the tech he'd been talking to at the table. "Tell the team at the Westin to back off. Don't let the Petroviches out of their sight, but don't engage."

"This should be interesting," said Berg.

The tech shook his head. "The Petroviches are gone. No sign of them in the lobby."

Berg got up, nodding at Devin and Marnie. "Time to go."

"Where are we going?" said Marnie.

"Anywhere but here," said Berg. "I don't want to get caught in the cross fire."

Randall nodded at Erin. "Lock the floor down. Nobody in. Nobody out."

"You're going to hold us here against our will?" said Devin.

"You're damn right I am," said Randall, drawing a compact pistol from a concealed holster behind his right hip. "When the Petroviches board that plane, I'll release the rest of you. Maybe you'd like to contact them and explain the situation?"

Devin glanced at Berg, who smiled and shook his head. Marnie laughed at something Anish whispered in her ear, the two of them high-fiving a moment later.

"I think we're good for now," said Devin, not entirely understanding why Berg and Anish were so confident. "We'll let you know if anything changes."

CHAPTER 49

Marnie Young caught herself nodding off on the couch. They'd been held in the suite against their will for the past three hours—and still no sign of the Petroviches, though a lot had transpired in that short period of time. The most consequential event being that Babin had disappeared from his room. The Petroviches had wasted no time once they were warned by Anish. And they'd gone right for the throat, taking Babin away from DEVTEK.

"Randall. This has gone on long enough," said Marnie. "I'm tired."

"Then go to sleep," said Randall.

"This really isn't going to go well for you," said Berg. "Seriously. Just let us go. We'll get in touch with the Petroviches and tell them it's over."

"And they'll just hand over Babin?" said Randall. "You do realize they screwed you over, too. Right? Babin is damaged goods at this point. If the sleepers watching him have noticed that he's missing—game over. No sting. Even if his absence goes unnoticed, your people probably spooked him badly enough that he'll just go back to his previous life."

"If he has that choice," said Berg. "The Russians picked him for a reason."

A knock at the door startled everyone, causing Randall to draw his pistol. Erin and two members of the security team disappeared into the foyer. The few techs still working at the dining room table sat up, tensed and ready to move.

"It's Jessica Petrovich," said Erin. "And Lee Babin."

"What happened to the security officers guarding the elevator lobby?" said Randall, headed toward the foyer.

"They're fine. Zapped, bound, and gagged," said Daniel Petrovich, appearing in the butler pantry doorway holding a keycard and a suppressed pistol. "I swiped this key a few days ago. Also noticed that you never engaged the latch on the butler's door."

He tossed the keycard on the coffee table and leveled the pistol at Randall.

"To be honest, I'd kind of forgotten about that door," said Randall.

"That's what I figured," said Daniel. "Erin?"

No response.

"Erin? I'm pointing a gun at your boss's head," said Daniel. "Can you answer me?"

Randall nodded toward the foyer.

"Yes?" she said.

"Please slide any weapons more lethal than your magic wand along the floor, into the dining room, or the cleaning bill for the room will likely cost more than the stay," said Daniel, adjusting his aim a little higher—presumably at Randall's head.

Randall glanced from Daniel's pistol to the foyer before quickly nodding his approval.

Three compact pistols and a stun gun slid across the hardwood floor and came to a stop behind Randall.

"And you can just let that pistol fall from your hand," said Daniel.

Randall released the pistol, which hit the floor with a metallic clack. The moment his pistol hit the deck, Marnie burst off the couch and bolted for the weapons, slipping past Randall to grab one of the security team's Glocks. She crouched against the wall behind him and aimed into the foyer. Erin and the two security guards stood in plain sight with their hands up.

"Take it easy," said Erin.

"Please," said Randall. "We can work all of this out. I promise."

Devin joined Marnie a few seconds later, picking up the remaining weapons from the floor. When he finished, Marnie waved Erin and her team inside the suite, arranging them along the dining room wall with Randall.

"Marnie. Can you let my wife in?" said Daniel.

Keeping her pistol pointed in the direction of Randall and his security team, Marnie backed up into the foyer until she reached the door. She checked the digital peephole to be sure Jessica and Babin hadn't been replaced by a SWAT team or gaggle of DEVTEK security officers. Babin's face dominated the screen, Jessica's barely visible in the background. Marnie opened the door and let them in.

"Everything is under control," said Marnie, moving out of their way.

"For now," said Jessica, quickly ushering Babin into the suite.

Marnie shut the door and threw the security latch before joining them in the suite's living area. Daniel kneeled next to one of the seemingly frozen security techs seated at the table pushed against the back of the couch.

"I'd like you and your friends here to join Mr. Powers and his team over in the dining room. Just take a seat on the floor," said Daniel, before pointing in the general direction of Randall. "All of you, take a seat on the floor. Devin and Anish. Would you mind rustling the rest of their team out of the bedrooms? I hate to interrupt their beauty sleep, but I'd like everyone where I can see them. My trust in DEVTEK is at rock bottom right now."

"I'm sure we can work something out," said Randall.

"Oh. We are most definitely going to work something out," said Daniel.

A few minutes later, with everyone on Randall's team assembled on the floor in the dining room, Daniel Petrovich plopped one of the dining room table seats down several feet in front of them and sat. The rest of them filled in the space behind him, Jessica pulling a second chair out and seating Lee Babin a few feet to Daniel's right. She rested a hand on one of Babin's shoulders.

"Here's the deal," said Daniel. "Mr. Babin here has a problem. His parents—"

"My father," said Babin.

"His father—and therefore his mother, and therefore Lee—owe some Russian-accented Brighton Beach heavies a lot of money. They approached Lee about a month and a half ago with a proposal that would solve the Babins' debt problem. He'd quit his current job at Cisco Systems and apply for a job at DEVTEK, when instructed, where he'd commit a one-time intellectual property theft."

"How much did your father owe the Russian mob?" said Randall.

"Three hundred and nineteen thousand dollars," said Babin. "My dad borrowed it from them to buy into a 'get rich quick' real estate scheme that turned out to be a 'get poor and in debt to the mob quick' scheme. I'm pretty sure my dad was enticed into this deal by the same people that loaned him the money—just to gain leverage over me. I'm sorry. But I had to do this. There was no other way to help them."

Randall regarded him for a few moments before responding. "So where do we go from here? Where do we go from a bunch of guns pointed at my team?"

"First. You can knock off the drama," said Devin. "You held us in this room at gunpoint for three hours."

"I never pointed a gun at you," said Randall.

"Semantics," said Devin. "You pulled a gun and told us we weren't going anywhere."

"I seem to remember it being a very direct threat," said Berg.

"You got me there. So what's the proposal? What do you want?" said Randall. "I assume you didn't bring Mr. Babin back here so he could sing me his sad story."

"Nothing changes," said Jessica.

"Please explain," said Randall.

"It's very simple. We follow the original plan," she said. "Before you screwed us over."

"How can we—"

Marnie couldn't help herself. "Jesus. It's not that hard, Randall. Lee takes the job that will certainly be offered to him tomorrow and goes through the motions with us watching over his shoulder. He does what the Russians ask and leaves DEVTEK. Everyone gets what they want."

"Leaves DEVTEK?" said Randall.

"Yeah. He walks away," said Daniel. "At present, there's only one person in this room who hasn't committed a crime. Lee Babin. He could walk away right now—if he had three hundred and nineteen thousand dollars. You, on the other hand? Breaking and entering three job candidates' rooms and uploading spyware, regardless of the context, will not play out well for DEVTEK in the court of public opinion or the actual courts."

"When you really think about it," said Marnie, "this works out better for DEVTEK."

"Really?" said Randall.

"With Lee acting in the capacity of a double agent on your behalf, you have complete control of the situation and all of its variables," said Marnie. "You can give him whatever the Russians ask for, after spiking it with your voodoo cyber magic. This is a no-brainer. Daniel and Jessica did you a favor."

"We'll smuggle him back into his room tonight," said Jessica. "With nobody the wiser."

Randall looked like he might be reluctantly coming around to the idea.

"And you think you're up for this?" said Randall.

"I don't have a choice," said Babin.

"Looks like you're not the only one," said Randall. "I obviously don't have the authority to say yes or no."

276

"Then you better call someone who does," said Daniel. "And I'm thinking Mr. Babin would like some assurances, in writing, that he's free and clear when he fulfills his part of the sting. Does that sound good to you, Lee?"

"Yes. Thank you," said Babin.

"I'd like the same for us," said Marnie. "Everything in writing."

"I'll call Ms. Paek and explain the situation—"

"On speakerphone," said Devin.

"Of course," said Randall. "I'll explain the situation, and we'll go from there. I can't guarantee anything. I had nothing to do with the decision to cut you out of the loop and send you home. Ms. Paek pulled a U-turn tonight for a reason."

"I think I know the reason," said Berg. "It's three letters long, starts with a *C*, and ends with an *A*. There might be an *I* in the middle."

"This couldn't have been Bauer's idea," said Marnie.

"No. But I think Ms. Paek may have gotten her signals crossed while talking to Bauer earlier today," said Berg. "And got a little ahead of herself."

"She nearly got people killed tonight," said Daniel. "If Anish hadn't warned us, things could've gotten ugly at the Westin. Please be sure she understands that."

"And make sure she understands that whatever arrangement she's made with Audra Bauer will dry up and blow away in the wind if we can't work this out," said Berg. "And uncancel our room. We're not going anywhere until Mr. Babin delivers the code to the Russians."

"I will," said Randall. "May I use my phone now? It's in my front pants pocket. I don't want to reach for it and get shot."

"Go ahead," said Daniel.

"That was a hint to maybe ease up on the guns pointed at us," said Randall.

"I got the hint," said Daniel, keeping the suppressed pistol pointed vaguely in their direction. "I just didn't take it."

CHAPTER 50

Audra Bauer finished her summary of the sleeper situation and slid a file across the desk to Thomas Manning, director of the Special Activities Center.

"I included copies of the files Helen Gray assembled for the two suspected sleepers in counterintelligence," said Bauer. "Along with a timeline of the events that I just discussed, and photos taken by Farrington in Staraya Russa. You really need to dig into the timeline yourself to fully appreciate the scope of what has unfolded. I don't expect you to just take my word."

"Any reason to suspect that Farrington or Berg are making stuff up to fit a narrative?" said Manning.

"No. Starting with Helen Gray's research and ending with Farrington's report, I don't detect any logic gaps or stretches of any kind," said Bauer. "And the attacks are undeniably real. Someone very badly wants to bury any evidence of the sleeper network."

"The attacks have the Beltway on edge. Every agency, politician, and think tank has floated a theory. None of them involving a late-Soviet-era sleeper network under the control of a Russian oligarch," said Manning, tapping the file in front of him. "All of the original evidence was lost in the fire on Lafayette Avenue?"

"Five files were removed from the apartment during the attack, including the two suspected sleepers in this building," said Audra. "Most of the sleepers identified by Helen have vanished, presumably recalled to Russia. The Russians probably worked backward to figure out Helen's method. Everyone she identified, outside of the two CIA officers, were public facing."

"How did she identify the two in counterintelligence?" said Manning.

"According to their files, she methodically researched every name she ever came across at Langley," said Bauer.

"Incredible," said Manning. "And she brought this to her chain of command's attention?"

"She brought her early findings to her section head," said Bauer. "But at that point she only had maybe a half dozen names and no hard evidence. It sounds like she pushed her theory a little too hard on her superiors and started to develop a bit of a reputation. Even Karl wasn't sure what to think of her theory back then."

"And now he's convinced," said Manning.

"A true believer."

"And you?"

"I don't want to believe it," she said. "But the chain of recent events and the evidence, both direct and circumstantial, supports the existence of a sleeper network. Whether Pichugin is the one pulling its strings is still up for debate, though I think the circumstantial evidence is starting to favor that conclusion. Farrington's surveillance in Russia has been eye-opening."

"How long do they plan on staying in Russia?" said Manning.

"Until this is over," said Bauer. "Whatever that means. Farrington and another operative are in the Ostrov area. They've checked into a motel with a direct line of sight to the military base. If the Russians launch a brigade-size air assault headed west, they're in the perfect position to detect and report the attack."

"I wish we could confirm that the soldiers are mercenaries," said Manning.

"Does it really matter who they are?" said Bauer. "All signs point to trouble in Estonia. DEVTEK's chief technology officer confirmed that the job targeted by the Russians at their company poses a significant risk to Estonia's technology and power infrastructure. The Estonian government hired DEVTEK to secure their critical infrastructure on the heels of the repeated Russian-attributed cyberattacks against them. The Estonians are the most outspoken critics of Russia. The job at DEVTEK is in the division that maintains, updates, and troubleshoots the cybersecurity systems protecting Estonia. Add the unusual military activity in the area to the mix, and I'd say the Russians are looking to bring that trouble to Tallinn."

"Estonia is a member of NATO," said Manning, "What the hell are the Russians thinking?"

"It all boils down to one madman with a bad idea," said Audra. "And who knows what he's thinking? We've been trying to figure that out for more than two decades."

"And how exactly does Berg stumble on this stuff? He's like a conspiracy magnet."

"Tell me about it," said Bauer. "I won't answer his calls if I'm about to go on vacation."

Manning laughed. "I don't blame you. Though we may have to put a special clause in your employment contract that requires you to remain accessible to Karl on a twenty-four-seven, three-hundred-and-sixty-five-days-a-year basis."

"Lucky me," said Bauer. "So. What are you thinking?"

"I think we need to take this seriously. It could be nothing, or it could be everything. Better safe than sorry in this business," said Manning. "I like the basic framework of the plan you've presented, and I agree that we should get started immediately, while we look into pushing this up the chain of command. Let's set up Karl, DEVTEK, and you at one of our secure, off-site suites in Tysons Corner, since we'll essentially be working this off the books. I'll get you a small team of Baltic analysts and an officer who the Estonians have worked with before—and presumably trust. This will be your show. I'd say your primary objective is to take the steps necessary to shield Estonia until I can generate enough upward momentum to bring this into the official fold."

"Can I suggest an alternate location?" said Bauer. "Somewhere I know for a fact is secure, won't require transport back and forth to hotel rooms, and will eliminate the possibility of the Russians following anyone on the team?"

"I think I know where you're going with this," said Manning. "Are you sure it'll suit your needs?"

"I'm going to need a mobile encryption-communications package capable of secure overseas video," said Bauer. "And a few techs to keep it up and running."

"How are the accommodations out there?" said Manning. "Food situation? Is it livable?"

"It's livable but rustic. Food shouldn't be an issue, as long as every-one is fine with basic meals," she said.

"I'll arrange a communications package with a support team, plus a four-person security detail," said Manning. "We have some Special Operations Group folks looking for a little R and R. This sounds about right for them."

"Perfect. I'll let Berg and DEVTEK know right away," said Bauer.

CHAPTER 51

Devin threw on the swimsuit he had purchased a few days earlier at a nearby Target and grabbed one of the Four Seasons bath towels from the bathroom before emerging from the bedroom. He needed to get out of this room. Three days had passed since DEVTEK had tried to send them home, and while an agreement had been reached that guaranteed them information regarding the suspected zero-day factory, the company had essentially cut them out of the investigative loop.

With Lee Babin cooperating as a double agent, the surveillance burden had significantly lightened, requiring less than half of Shea's people. Daniel and Jessica were removed from the detail immediately. Not surprising, given the stunt they'd pulled. Anish never returned to Shea's suite. Another nonsurprise. DEVTEK clearly wanted all of them in one place, where they couldn't cause any more trouble. Brendan Shea visited occasionally, to keep them in the loop and assure them that DEVTEK still intended to hold up their end of the bargain.

The only person who had managed to escape the monotony was Karl Berg, who had flown back to West Virginia with a DEVTEK team to stand up a CIA-supported mobile operations center that could coordinate the overall effort to thwart whatever scheme Yuri Pichugin had devised against Estonia. The assumption still being that Estonia was Pichugin's target. If it turned out to be Latvia or Lithuania, they'd have some serious explaining to do.

"Looks like someone has thrown in the towel," said Anish, taking his eyes off the TV long enough to assess Devin's situation.

"More like picked up the wrong towel," said Marnie. "Want some company?"

"Sure. Sorry," said Devin. "I kind of woke up from my nap and decided I was going for a swim, because it's not like I have anything else to do."

"I'll get changed really quick," said Marnie, hopping up from the couch. "Anish. Do you mind finishing the episode later?"

"Not at all," said Anish, pointing the remote at the TV. "I started the latest season of *Love Island UK* last night after everyone went to bed. I can't get enough of those trashy British accents. You thought I was going to say trashy British women, didn't you?"

"I quit listening after *Love Island*," said Devin.

"I'll be right back," said Marnie, before shutting the bedroom door behind her.

"Any sign of the Petroviches?" said Devin.

"They're having a late lunch somewhere fancy," said Anish. "They did not invite me."

"Maybe next time," said Devin, taking a seat on one of the side chairs.

Anish laughed.

The phone on the coffee table in front of them buzzed and started ringing.

"Bat phone," said Anish, referring to the DEVTEK-provided secure device. "You want it?"

Devin swiped the phone from the table and answered it.

"Devin. This is Randall. We have a location."

"What? Seriously?" said Devin. "That quick?"

"Mr. Babin transmitted the relevant system files from his car during lunch hour," said Randall. "The Russians bounced this stuff all over the place. It took us close to two hours to track the data packets' ultimate destination, which turned out to be a server bank geolocated at 1103 South Miami Avenue, Miami, Florida."

"What's at 1103 South Miami Avenue?" said Devin.

"A fifty-two-story, luxury-high-rise condominium building," said Randall. "Purchased five years ago by Alexei Doronin, an obscenely wealthy Russian national."

"He's one of the dozen or so sanctions-free oligarchs who have been suspected of purchasing real estate for Vladimir Putin over the years," said Devin. "It's not a stretch to think that Doronin may have extended the same straw-buyer service to Pichugin."

"Looks like you have your work cut out for you," said Randall. "Getting in and out of a high-rise won't be easy."

"Unless Pichugin buried his zero-day enterprise in the basement or stuck it on the mezzanine level," said Devin.

"Wishful thinking," said Randall. "It's going to be on one of the top floors, and you know it."

"I'm pretty much counting on it," said Devin.

"Smart man. Plan for the worst," said Randall. "So. In light of this development, DEVTEK's obligation has been met."

"And you want us out of here?" said Devin.

"No hurry. But your flight departs from San Jose International at seven," said Randall. "Which gives you about two more hours to enjoy the hotel. Pickup at five."

"I assume you're delivering us all the way to the compound in West Virginia," said Devin.

"You assumed correctly. A car will pick you up at the Four Seasons—at five."

"We'll be there," said Devin. "Thank—"

The call ended.

"Thank you for the hospitality," said Devin, before tossing the phone on the table. "DEVTEK's sending a car to pick us up at five. Flight back to West Virginia at seven."

"And?"

"Eleven oh three South Miami Avenue, Miami, Florida," said Devin. "Pichugin's zero-day factory sits somewhere in a fifty-two-story, luxury high-rise building."

Anish grabbed his laptop from the coffee table and started typing.

"Right downtown," he said. "Gonna be tricky. That's a busy area."

"But doable?" said Devin.

"If the factory is somewhere near the ground floor, it's doable," said Anish. "If it's at the top of the building, like I expect? The answer is maybe—with a helicopter."

"We do have our own helicopter pilot," said Devin.

"Which does us no good without a helicopter," said Anish. "You should bring this up with Berg the moment we get back. Maybe the CIA can arrange a helicopter."

"I don't think the CIA arranges helicopters," said Devin.

"You'd be surprised by what they can arrange, when they want to," said Anish.

"I guess it never hurts to ask," said Devin.

Marnie stepped out of the bedroom wrapped in a hotel bathrobe. "Never hurts to ask what?"

"Never hurts to ask if you'd like to fly the helicopter that drops us on top of Pichugin's Miami high-rise. DEVTEK traced Lee Babin's data transfer to a building presumably owned by Pichugin—in downtown Miami."

"Whoa. They found it! That's great news," said Marnie. "What kind of helicopter?"

"Good question. Maybe you should be the one to work with Berg on getting one," said Devin.

"If a rooftop landing or fast roping is even possible. I've seen some funky building designs in Miami," said Marnie. "Berg might want to start out by hiring a helicopter and a photographer to take pictures of the building."

"Tell Berg when we see him tomorrow," said Devin. "Until then, we have two hours until our ride to the airport arrives. Still up for the pool?"

"I think we can fit in an hour," said Marnie. "Anish? Last chance to charge drinks to DEVTEK."

"I don't drink," said Anish.

"A Sprite costs eleven dollars here," said Devin. "We can break DEVTEK's quarterly budget if we plan this right. Come on."

"No. You guys have fun. I'll order something up to the room. Turn that eleven-dollar Sprite into a fourteen-dollar Sprite with the room-delivery fee. Might order one every ten minutes until we leave," said Anish.

"That's the spirit. Think of Randall's face every time you dial room service," said Devin. "While you're up here, can you get in touch with the Petroviches? Make sure they don't miss the pickup?"

"I'll try," said Anish. "But they're slippery. For all we know, they might be headed to San Francisco International Airport right now to make their way back to wherever they came from."

"Something tells me they plan on sticking around," said Devin.

CHAPTER 52

Devin forgot how run-down the farm looked from the outside. A carefully crafted disguise. The paint-chipped, two-story red barn looked condemned, but it concealed a garage, the collapsing roof held up by a sturdy steel-beam framework. Loaded front to back, the barn could hide eight vehicles, possibly ten if nobody minded dents and scratches.

The worn-down, wooden cowshed connected to the main house by a covered breezeway hid the conference room and office they'd been using, an emptied armory and bunk space for twenty—including bathroom and shower facilities. He strongly suspected that a cache of weapons and ammunition belonging to the armory lay buried on the property—but none of Farrington's people seemed to be in a hurry to unearth it.

A small safe hidden in the kitchen provided the original security detail with ten thirty-round M4 magazines, a nine-millimeter P320 Sig Sauer compact pistol with four magazines, and several boxes of loose nine-millimeter and .45-caliber ammunition. More than enough to recharge the entire group's ammo supply. Maybe they'd break out the weapons stash for the Miami job. They were bound to need more than they'd carried back from Lafayette Avenue.

The thought of what Pichugin's mercenaries had done to his mother's building, not to mention the rest of the block, created a pit in his stomach. Devin partially blamed himself. The Russians had obviously been closing in on them, but bringing Brendan Shea to the apartment had been the final straw. What had felt like an undersize risk turned out to be anything but small. A black swan event on a smaller but no-less-consequential scale for everyone involved.

Henrietta Silver's every possession burned to ashes, along with the rest of her family's belongings. Fortunately, Devin's mother had kept the insurance on the building up to date and had paid the next three years of premiums in advance on their behalf. A copy sat in the binder his mother had assembled with all the legal paperwork transferring ownership of the building into Ms. Silver's name. He'd insisted that she bring the binder with her when she vacated the building for a few weeks. It wouldn't replace what was lost, but it would allow them to rebuild. And he'd help them pay for something temporary while they waited.

The floor creaked inside the house. He turned and looked through the screen to see Marnie in the center hallway, headed his way from the kitchen with a coffee mug clasped between her hands. She joined him on the farmer's porch and clinked his mug.

"Cheers."

"Cheers," he said, before taking a sip of the coffee they'd found vacuum-sealed in the pantry. "This is good coffee."

"Exceptionally good," said Marnie. "Even better backstory."

They'd finally heard the story about the beans. Munoz's Blend, created by Jeffrey Munoz, the owner of several coffee shops in and around the Hartford, Connecticut, area. Like Daniel Petrovich, he'd been around from the birth of the original black ops program that had eventually morphed into Richard Farrington's for-hire group. There had been some talk of trying to temporarily lure Munoz out of retirement for this job, but no apparent action—which was too bad. They would need all the help they could get in Miami.

"Any sign of Berg or the others?" said Devin.

"I saw some lights on inside the cowshed a minute ago when I grabbed the coffee," said Marnie, placing her head on his shoulder. "How long have you been up?"

"I never really went to sleep," said Devin. "I'm too wired over this Miami thing."

"Wired or worried?" said Marnie.

"I guess there really isn't a difference," he said. "I'm doing the math, and I don't think we have enough people to pull this off. Not without bringing Rich and his team back from Russia."

"It doesn't sound like they're going anywhere," said Marnie. "For now, they're the only early warning the Estonians will get if there's an attack."

"Are you really okay with flying a helicopter?" said Devin.

She lifted her head off his shoulder and took a sip of coffee before responding.

"It really depends on a number of factors," she said. "My main concern was the rooftop, but there's a pool and a decent-size pool deck, so I don't see a problem dropping you off with a short fast rope. I just don't know how I'll retrieve the team. There's too much shit on the pool deck. I highly doubt I'll be able to set the helicopter down."

"We can climb up a Jacob's ladder or a knotted rope," said Devin.

"That's a possibility, but I'm going to need a crew member to help with that," said Marnie. "Unless we insert the team with the same rope or ladder used to get you out of there."

"Good idea," said Devin. "What are your other concerns?"

"The type of helicopter always makes a difference," said Marnie. "The Bell 429 I flew back in the Ozarks would work. The controls responded beautifully. But I'm not sure that would give us enough room for passengers."

"Given the fact that we don't have many passengers, it should work. We have Rico and Miralles. The Petroviches. Me. Anish. And maybe the two mercenaries Farrington hired—Rip and Garza. We need to have a chat with them this morning. Same with the Petroviches. I get the impression that they could split at any moment," said Devin.

"I'm surprised they showed up for the flight back," said Marnie.

"I figured they would. Since they left their SUV here," said Devin. "But I don't think we can count on them if the plan sounds sketchy."

"Sketchy sounds somewhat synonymous with suicidal."

"Six shooters, including me, a computer guy, and a sniper," said Devin. "It may or may not be enough, depending on what we encounter inside the zero-day factory."

"How the hell are we going to recon that building?" said Marnie.

"I have no idea," said Devin. "We can take pictures of the outside, like you said, but if Pichugin owns it, we're going to have a hard time getting any kind of picture of the inside. We may not even be able to determine the location of the zero-day factory before we hit the building. Everyone seems to think it'll be on the top floors, but who the hell knows."

"I'm sure Anish can figure that out during our reconnaissance," said Marnie.

"That's the other problem," said Devin. "I don't know my ass from a motherboard. We're going to need Anish to enter the building with us. Normally, he works from the sidelines, casting his magic computer spells and monitoring external threats."

"Maybe one of the people from DEVTEK will be willing to do it," said Marnie.

"Don't count on it," said Devin. "They're only interested in the CIA side of things at this point."

"Yeah. DEVTEK isn't going to stick their neck out any farther," said Karl Berg, pushing the screen door open. "What time did you guys get in?"

"Around four," said Marnie.

Berg checked his watch. "That's two hours ago. Shouldn't you two be passed out upstairs?"

"Can't sleep," said Devin. "I'm worried about the size of our team. I don't think it'll be enough to breach a heavily defended high-rise."

"You'd be surprised," said Berg. "This is a resourceful group."

"I'll feel better once we get a solid commitment from Ripley and Garza. Same with the Petroviches."

"Rip and Garza are in. Don't worry about them," said Berg. "Daniel and Jessica are a different story. I don't see them fast roping from a helicopter, but they'll be there for us. They're—"

"Slippery?" said Devin. "That's how Anish described them."

"Slippery sounds about right," said Berg. "But they're reliable."

"And they're still on board?" said Marnie. "They seemed pretty aloof on the flight over."

"They're always aloof," said Berg. "It's a long story with those two. Like Munoz. They've paid their dues, and then some."

"Speaking of aloof. What about the CIA? What are they focused on?" said Devin. "They've been silent since they arrived."

"The same," said Berg. "But they also have an interest in shutting down Pichugin's zero-day factory and swiping information from those servers. So you can count on logistical support. But I don't see the CIA authorizing personnel to accompany you into the high-rise."

"What about a copilot? Or a crew chief for the helicopter," said Marnie. "If I can't land on the rooftop, I'm going to need help raising and lowering ladders or lines. Whatever we decide on for the extraction."

"That's a definite possibility," said Berg. "I might even be able to convince one or more of our CIA-provided security officers to take a trip to Miami. They're here on loan from the Special Operations Group. All former tier-one military special operators."

"Let's work on getting them interested," said Devin. "How is the back-and-forth with the Estonians going?"

"Slow. We started with a very small group of trusted intelligence officers at Estonia's Ministry of Defense, their Foreign Intelligence Service, and the Internal Security Service," said Berg. "They're cautiously reaching out to members of the military. DEVTEK's team already had a very solid working relationship with Estonia's infrastructure cybersecurity team. If the whole thing went down right now, Estonia's power grid and communications infrastructure would be fine, but the military would probably fail to stop whatever Pichugin has in mind for Tallinn. It's going to take a little more time to get the right people working on the problem, without tipping off Moscow."

"Sounds like things are going well," said Marnie.

"They are. Surprisingly," said Berg. "Then again, maybe not so surprisingly. Having Audra Bauer on your side tends to make a difference. She single-handedly convinced her boss, the head of the CIA's Special Activities Center, to stand up this remote operations center and fully staff it."

"I can't wait to see how you've redecorated the place," said Marnie.

Berg laughed. "About that. Things are a little different in the conference room area now."

Devin finished his coffee and placed his mug on the wide porch railing.

"Why does this sound like it's going to rub me the wrong way?" said Devin.

"Because it is," said Berg. "The conference room is fair game, unless our CIA friends are giving a classified briefing. They'll post signs on the door to the room if that's the case. The office is off-limits to anyone outside of the CIA-DEVTEK team. They're using that space to work with Estonian officials. That's considered beyond your pay grade. Sorry."

"I'm fine with that," said Devin. "As long as we get the support we need to take down Pichugin's Miami operation."

"I don't see a problem with that," said Berg. "The CIA is very excited about the prospect of getting a look at Pichugin's digital treasure trove. They're hoping the servers in Miami contain the zero-days and exploits he's produced over the past few years."

"That would be a dream come true," said Devin. "But I strongly suspect he keeps those in Moscow."

"Don't be so sure," said Berg. "There's a theory going back and forth on the team. It all centers on why Pichugin picked Miami in the first place. He could have just as easily set up the factory at the secure compound on the outskirts of Moscow. Security would sure be easier. They think he'll launch the cyberattack from the Miami tower, once the zero-day exploit has been delivered, so the attack will be traced back to the United States."

"Traced back to his own building?" said Marnie.

"That's what I keep saying," said Berg. "But I'm told that it doesn't matter, because the Russian misinformation machine will focus on one thing: the fact that the attack originated in the US, and we'll never be able to spin it any other way without looking guilty."

"It makes sense in the context of what Pichugin's doing with his sleepers over the years. Eroding the world's trust and confidence in the United States," said Devin.

"All the more reason to burn down his operation in Miami," said Marnie.

"But no actual burning," said Berg. "We can't be starting high-rise fires in downtown Miami, or anywhere."

"I meant that as a figure of speech," said Marnie.

"I'm not worried about you," said Berg.

"Thanks," said Marnie, nudging Devin's arm.

"I promise I won't burn down the building," said Devin. "Unless I'm given no choice."

CHAPTER 53

Devin and Marnie picked up the pace for the last stretch of their run. For the past five mornings, they'd hit the dirt road that delivered them here right after watching the sun rise. The road wound through the woods for about two miles before reaching the narrow turnoff along the paved local road, where they'd turned around and head back. Four rutted and uneven miles on what basically amounted to an improvised Jeep trail had been far enough for the first few days, but this morning they felt like pushing it a little farther. Maybe a little too far.

They'd purposefully taken one of the wrong turns on the way back, hoping to add another mile or so onto the run, but they'd somehow missed the main dirt road after turning around. An hour and ten minutes after initially setting off, they emerged from the forest, sprinting past the CIA officer hidden in the trees next to the road.

Halfway to the barn, a few paces behind Marnie, Devin noticed Karl Berg headed in their direction from the porch steps. Something must be up. They both slowed to a jog and turned toward the house.

"You still won," Devin said, breathing heavily.

"Was there any question?" she said.

"Not really," said Devin, before coming to a stop in front of an agitated Karl Berg.

"What happened? Did you get lost?" said Berg. "Everyone's waiting for the two of you in the conference room."

"We went for a longer run," said Devin, before checking his watch. "Did I miss something? I didn't realize we had a meeting right now."

"Sorry. I called a meeting shortly after you left, thinking you'd be back long before seven," said Berg. "The zero-day exploit showed up in the Estonian infrastructure network about an hour ago."

"That was fast," said Devin.

"Five days to find a vulnerability and create an exploit?" said Marnie. "Pichugin must have hundreds of people working at his little factory."

"That's what DEVTEK thinks," said Berg. "You're going to have your work cut out for you down there. Why don't the two of you clean up and meet us in the conference room in ten minutes? I'll have hot coffee waiting for you."

"I don't need to clean up," said Marnie.

"Same," said Devin. "But I will grab some coffee on the way over."

"Me too," said Marnie. "And some water."

Five minutes later, still sweaty from their run, Devin and Marnie stepped into the conference room with steaming cups of coffee—all eyes turning to greet them. He was surprised to see everyone present, including two of the CIA's SOG officers. If Devin had to guess, he'd say they were headed to Miami shortly. As in by the end of the day. Karl Berg got up from the far end of the table as soon as they dropped into the only two remaining seats—folding chairs behind the table, next to the CIA officers.

"All right. We'll kick this off with a quick rundown of the situation from DEVTEK," said Berg.

Seated at the other end of the table, Rafael, the mystery man from their first meeting in this conference room, close to a week and a half ago, shut his laptop and addressed the group.

"Approximately an hour and a half ago, foreign code entered Estonia's secure infrastructure network. The code was immediately identified by the network and shunted to a honeynet, where it immediately went to work installing an exploit and opening a back door into the system. We know for a fact that the exploit originated from the zero-day factory in Miami, because it contained several signature strings of code embedded by our team back in Palo Alto. We basically stamped the code in as many places as possible before handing it to Mr. Babin. There's no doubt that the exploit came from the code Mr. Babin transferred to Miami."

"How did it get into the system?" said Anish, seated near Berg.

"Presumably, it was hand delivered, since no network security attacks were detected," said Rafael. "And nobody has managed to hack into Estonia's infrastructure network since we started handling their cybersecurity."

"And thanks to everyone here," said Berg, "DEVTEK's impressive cybersecurity record continues unblemished."

"Look," said Rafael. "I don't know what went on back at the Four Seasons, and frankly I don't care. Neither does anyone on my team. This is all a job very well done—for now."

"For now?" said Devin.

"Exactly. Here's the rub," said Rafael. "We're watching the fake network from Palo Alto and the room next to us for any signs of activity, so we can mimic any test actions initiated by whoever thinks they've successfully infiltrated the real infrastructure network. They might momentarily overload one of the microgrids, where they have a spy working in the control room who could verify the spike. Or they might shut down the internet to a neighborhood in Tallinn for a few seconds, once again verified by someone watching their router internet signal. Small stuff that won't draw any attention from the Estonians but will confirm that the exploit works."

"Wouldn't you normally catch these anomalies?" said Anish.

"We would, but that's a well-preserved secret," said Rafael. "And the nondisclosure agreements everyone signed at one point or another, either here or back in Palo Alto, will continue to preserve it. We prefer to keep our cyber adversaries guessing about our capabilities."

"Makes sense," said Anish.

"Anyway. Back to the rub I mentioned. Since the back door is open, they're watching the network, too. Eventually, they're going to discover that the network they're observing is bullshit," said Rafael.

"How long do you think we have?" said Devin.

"I'd say we're looking at days," said Rafael. "Especially if they keep studying the network for additional exploit opportunities."

"Don't sugarcoat it," said Berg. "Could be hours, if one of the hackers analyzing the code gets lucky. Which is why we think Devin's team should hit the Miami tower as soon as possible. To force Pichugin's hand before he figures out that we're playing him. If he discovers what we've done, he'll take everything off-line long enough for the trail to go completely cold. And he'll make damn sure we don't see the next attack coming."

Rafael nodded in agreement. "Not to diminish what we've accomplished, because we've moved mountains, so to speak, but a lot of what it took to get to this exact moment was the result of a string of unrepeatable events. Call it luck. Call it fortuitous timing. Call it whatever you want. But the bottom line is that I don't see us replicating this opportunity. We need to convince Pichugin that he's the one running out of time, and if we also manage to get a look at what he's storing on those servers—all the better."

"The CIA and their Estonian counterparts concur," said Berg.

"Has any thought been given to a diplomatic solution? Like maybe tell Russia through back channels to knock it off?" said Marnie. "I'm just asking."

"The Estonians would prefer to kick Putin's teeth out now, regardless of the mess it will cause, rather than let him regroup and try again a year or two from now," said Berg. "The stakes are too high for them."

"Then I guess we better not let them down," said Devin. "Where do we stand on implementing the plan?"

"We've secured a short-term apartment lease in the building catty-corner to Pichugin's building," said Berg. "It's on the fifty-third floor, facing the target."

"That'll come in handy," said Melendez.

"I had you in mind when we secured it," said Berg. "It's slightly elevated above the rooftop pool deck yet should still provide you with lines of fire into the top five floors. The distance between the apartment and Pichugin's building is less than two hundred feet."

"Damn. That's like shooting fish in a barrel," said Melendez.

"On top of that, it'll give the team an unparalleled surveillance opportunity," said Berg.

"Have you thought about trying to rent an apartment inside Pichugin's building?" said Daniel Petrovich. "Jess and I could pose as wealthy jet-setters and feed the team inside information. Then meet up with the team after they land."

"I can't believe I didn't think of that," said Berg. "We'll look into that right away."

"Speaking of landing the team," said Marnie. "Have you made any progress toward acquiring a helicopter?"

"We've tentatively arranged a Sikorsky S-76," said Berg.

"Tentatively?" said Marnie.

"The whole deal is conditional on a test flight," said Berg. "Which I'm sure you'll pass with flying colors."

"Obviously, they have no idea that I'm going to try to land their helicopter on the roof of a high-rise. Right?"

"Correct," said Berg. "All they know is that someone paid a shitload of money to rent their helicopter for two hours. You'll lift off with Devin and maybe a few other team members, all dressed for success, like you're going on some kind of big-shot aerial tour—then you'll divert to a second location to pick up the rest of the team and the gear. We're still working out the second location."

Anish raised his hand, getting a nod from Berg.

"Do we have any information on the building itself?" he said. "Like schematics?"

"We're in the process of acquiring a set of schematics," said Berg. "Whether they reveal the location of the zero-day factory is anyone's guess."

"Even if it's right where we expect it, I'm going to need the team to buy me enough time to figure out the server setup and instruct it to transfer its data," said Anish. "I've done most of my work remotely, so we might be looking at a little bit of a learning curve once we get into the server room."

"I don't think we're going to have time for learning curves," said Devin.

Rafael leaned forward in his seat. "This won't be a problem for you. We're going to provide Mr. Gupta with a customized digital terminal that you will connect directly to one of the server interface's ethernet ports. It's literally a plug-and-play device. It'll initiate the process of transferring the network's data to one of our server networks. They would literally have to cut power to the entire building to stop the transfer once it's initiated—unless they have a kill switch in the server room."

"We can leave behind some nasty surprises to keep them out of the server room for a while," said Miralles, sounding gleeful about the opportunity to use her explosives again.

"It almost sounds like you don't need me at all," said Anish. "I mean—anyone can connect an ethernet cable."

"It won't be that easy. It never is," said Devin. "You're still coming with us."

"I had to try," said Anish.

"And it is absolutely imperative that you return the device," said Rafael. "In the wrong hands, it could do some serious damage."

"I'll stuff it down my pants," said Anish.

"Please don't," said Rafael. "It comes with a custom carrying case. Just use that."

"Fair enough," said Anish.

Devin leaned forward and made eye contact with one of the CIA officers.

"Matt. Am I correct to assume that you'll be accompanying us in some capacity?" said Devin.

"In a very limited capacity," he replied. "And I'm Steve."

"I'm Matt," said the SOG operative sitting next to Steve.

"Sorry for the missed introduction, Devin," said Berg. "Steve and Matt will accompany you in the helicopter. They will be armed, but they're not to be considered shooters for mission-planning purposes. They'll spot targets for the team and assist Marnie in your recovery."

"That's plenty. Welcome aboard," said Devin.

Steve and Matt nodded.

"All righty then," said Berg. "Rico will bring everyone to the bunker, where you can put together an appropriate gear-and-weapons package. I'd like to get you on the road by ten. Eleven at the latest. You have a solid seventeen-hour drive ahead of you."

"No Gulfstream with drink service?" said Jessica Petrovich. "You're not exactly putting me in the jet-setter frame of mind."

"We're already way over budget with the helicopter and twenty-seven-thousand-dollar, three-month lease that we're only going to need for a day," said Berg. "That and the small issue of hauling tactical gear and weapons for eleven people."

"Nothing better than a road trip," said Devin half-heartedly.

"A private jet would be better," said Anish.

"Pretty much anything would be better," said Marnie, nudging Devin.

He was already lost in thought, once again trying to reconcile wishful thinking with reality. As much as he wanted to believe he could pull this off with the ragtag group sitting around the table, he wasn't entirely convinced it would be enough.

PART FIVE

CHAPTER 54

Marnie stared through the balcony slider at the rooftop deck roughly two hundred feet away. From her slightly elevated vantage point, it almost looked like you could jump from the balcony into the pool. A trick of the mind at seven hundred feet above the ground, the human brain losing much of its capacity to accurately judge distances, both horizontal and vertical. As a helicopter pilot, she'd been taught how to compensate for these innate flaws, mostly by relying heavily on instrumentation.

The numbers never lied, even when your brain didn't agree with them. Right now, the numbers were telling her that if she jumped for the pool, she'd be lucky to hit the street fifteen feet away from the base of the building she jumped from. She glanced over her shoulder at Devin, who held a pair of binoculars to his eyes. Beyond Devin, Melendez sat on the couch, looking through a handheld spotting scope. The rest of the team hung out in the dining room, which didn't directly face Pichugin's building.

She raised her binoculars for another look, spotting Daniel and Jessica Petrovich on lounge chairs next to the pool. Berg had managed to score them a month-long rental on one of the lower floors of the building. They checked in late this morning and scouted the general layout on the way to the pool, their reconnaissance proving invaluable.

One of their first observations removed any doubt about the general location of the zero-day factory. The elevators in the lobby didn't serve the top twenty-five floors, except for the pool deck. The buttons for those floors had been removed entirely, replaced by a touchpad they guessed could access those floors with a code. The assumption was important, because they discovered a second set of elevators located on the other side of the ground floor, which were totally inaccessible without a keycard.

They reasonably presumed that these elevators directly served floors twenty-eight through fifty-two. Interestingly, they didn't appear to reach the pool deck. The Petroviches had checked out the entire rooftop deck and hadn't seen another set of elevators. Apparently, Pichugin didn't want his hackers mingling with the lower floors' legitimate tenants. He'd set aside close to half of a one-hundred-and-fifty-million-dollar building to house his zero-day project. A secret he undoubtedly wanted to preserve for as long as possible.

The five floors immediately below the pool deck featured no balconies, only heavily tinted glass windows that gave up nothing. There was little doubt on the team that the server room sat on one of those floors. Marnie hoped the windows were permanently tinted and not some kind of smart-glass product.

Regular tinting would work against the building's occupants at night, dimming their view while exposing them to the outside. Melendez would be able to give them some idea of what they were up against inside, and he'd be able to even the odds with his rifle, if necessary. If the windows were adjustable smart glass, they would be going in blind.

"What do you think?" said Devin.

"I wish I could look as relaxed as the Petroviches," said Marnie. "Look at them."

"They're something else, that's for sure," said Devin. "What do you think about the rooftop as a landing pad?"

"I can't land on the way in," said Marnie. "Not with the lounge chairs, sun umbrellas, and tables cluttering the pool deck."

"The Petroviches could clean it up before we arrive," said Devin. "Throw it all in the pool so it doesn't blow around."

"We have to assume they have cameras on the pool deck, piped right into their security hub," said Marnie. "We'd give up whatever surprise we managed to achieve with the helicopter insertion. Plus, they'll have their hands full taking care of the rooftop security at the last possible moment."

She took another look at the two men the Petroviches had identified as likely mercenaries. It was hard to tell from here, since they weren't openly carrying weapons, but they certainly didn't look like tenants enjoying a sunny afternoon at the pool. The long pants, black T-shirts, and sports jackets gave them away.

"And we have to consider the likelihood that the lobby elevators connect to the zero-day factory—and the rooftop pool deck," said Melendez. "We could be looking at a quicker-than-expected response to our unexpected appearance."

"Fast roping would get everyone down quickly," said Marnie.

"Roping down is going to be dicey without an attachment point above the door," said Devin. "Steve and Matt said they would have to tie the line to something immovable inside the cabin and help each person out. It sounded time intensive. We might be better off having the Petroviches clear the deck."

"I could hover about ten feet over the pool—and everyone could jump. At that height, the water would totally cushion your fall," said Marnie. "We could offload in a matter of seconds. A near simultaneous drop."

"I like that idea," said Melendez.

"But you won't even be there," said Devin.

"I like the idea of watching all of you jump into a pool and waddle off soaking wet," said Melendez.

"Aside from the entertainment value, what do you think?" said Marnie.

"It's definitely your quickest and least-dicey option," said Melendez, before lowering his voice to a whisper. "Anish is going to be a problem if you rope the team in. Trust me on that. But he'll jump into the pool—because it's fucking cool."

"Are you sure he'll jump?" said Marnie.

"Hold on," said Melendez, turning his head toward the dining room. "Hey, Anish! Would you jump from the helicopter into that pool, if it was the only way to get you into that server room?"

"Hell yeah! I'd do it even if there *was* another way to get me in there!" said Anish. "Wait. How far of a jump?"

Marnie raised an eyebrow.

"Ten feet," said Melendez. "Give or take a few."

"Not just hell yeah—but fuck yeah!" said Anish. "Hey. Is there any way you could get that on video?"

"No!" said Melendez.

"Come on, dude!" said Anish, heading over from the other side of the apartment. "I finally get to do something cool, and you can't even press a button on a video camera. This is something I could break out to show the grandkids one day. Shock everyone at the Thanksgiving Day table. That kind of a moment."

"What are you even talking about?" said Melendez.

"I don't know," said Anish. "I just want a video of me jumping into that pool."

"If you go away and never talk about your imaginary grandchildren again in my presence, I'll press the record button on whatever camera you set up," said Melendez.

"Sweet! I'll set it up now," said Anish, before taking off for one of the bedrooms.

Marnie turned to Melendez.

"You're not actually going to record us committing a crime that would land us in a federal penitentiary for the rest of our lives, are you?"

"Not a chance," said Melendez.

"Good. Just wanted to make sure we're on the same wavelength," said Marnie.

CHAPTER 55

Marnie hugged the coastline, keeping the Sikorsky S-76 around two hundred feet above sea level, Miami's downtown night skyline growing in the distance. A quick look at the navigation screen told her they were seven minutes and twenty-two seconds away from reaching Pichugin's building, and that she'd nearly reached her first waypoint. In twenty-two seconds she'd bank right and pass south of Key Biscayne, before turning north again. She triggered the internal communications net.

"I'm about to start our dogleg pattern into the Port of Miami," said Marnie. "ETA seven minutes once I turn seaward."

"Copy that," said Devin. "Let me know if the ETA changes by more than fifteen seconds in either direction. I need to keep the Petroviches apprised."

"If we lose any time, it'll be during the final downtown approach. I've never landed on a high-rise before. Spacious amphibious assault ship deck? Yes. Postage stamp–size pool deck? No," she said. "I'll keep you posted."

"You'll do great," said Devin. "Nobody back here is worried."

"I'm worried," said Anish. "About what kind of splash I'm going to make when I hit that pool! Jackknife or cannonball. Which one?"

"Swan dive," said Miralles.

"Whatever you do, just get the fuck out of the way so the rest of us don't land on your head," said Ripley.

"Tough crowd here," said Anish.

"Go with the cannonball," said Marnie, seeing that she'd reached the first waypoint.

"Cannonball it is!" said Anish.

She eased the helicopter into a starboard turn for a few seconds before straightening out on a nearly due-east course. The helicopter was a dream to fly compared to the Sikorsky CH-53 Super Stallion she'd flown as a Marine pilot. Same aircraft manufacturer, but Sikorsky had obviously smoothed out nearly every aspect of the experience for their bestselling commercial helicopter.

Marnie could have put the aircraft on autopilot after lifting off from Homestead Air Reserve Base and hung out in the passenger cabin until they entered the Port of Miami. The helicopter was equipped with a four-axis autopilot system, which could control the roll, pitch, and yaw of the aircraft, in addition to the fourth axis—automatic hover.

She was tempted to engage the system once she was in position over the pool. The automatic-hover experiments she'd conducted against a stiff ocean breeze during the test flight convinced her it would hold the helicopter in place. The perfectionist pilot in her shunned the idea. Given that she shouldn't be hovering for more than a minute, she was more inclined to retain the controls than turn them over to a computer. That said, the wind conditions fifty-two stories above downtown Miami would ultimately decide. Her one-hour of experience flying the S-76 was no match for the helicopter's computer if the winds started giving her trouble.

Two minutes later, they reached the next waypoint, and she turned north to fly along Key Biscayne's eastern shore.

"Five minutes," she said over the internal communications line, before switching to the tactical control network. "Overwatch. This is Boss Bitch. We're five minutes out. How are things looking at the target building?"

Boss Bitch hadn't been her idea for a call sign. Unfortunately, both Ripley and Garza were all too familiar with the fact that pilots did not get to choose their call signs. They were picked by fellow pilots, or, in this case, a bunch of miscreant mercenaries.

"This is Overwatch," said Melendez. "Still no sign of the security team."

The two overdressed gentlemen who had staked out the rooftop had taken the stairwell down around midnight, depriving them of the keycard they had hoped might facilitate their entry into the zero-day factory.

"Copy," said Marnie, switching over to the internal net. "Devin. Why don't you have Daniel and Jessica head up now and pretend like they're going for a swim. Maybe that'll draw the security guys back up to the roof."

"It's worth a shot," said Devin, switching nets. "DJ. This is Devin. Are you up on the net?"

"Affirmative," said Daniel.

"Grab some towels and head up to the pool deck," said Devin. "We need to lure at least one of those security guards back up so we can grab their keycard."

"Yep. We're on our way," said Daniel.

"Coordinate directly with Overwatch for sniper coverage," said Devin. "Overwatch. How are things looking inside the building?"

The windows had mercifully turned out to be commercially tinted. Once the sun went down, Melendez had a fishbowl view inside the top two floors. He could see about half of the third floor from the top and maybe a quarter of the floor below it. The lowest level of the zero-day factory remained mostly concealed, only a thin strip of workstations visible to him from his balcony perch.

"Same. Not very busy," said Melendez. "I'm seeing maybe twenty people typing away at their workstations. No obvious security staff from what I can tell."

"Keep an eye out for the Petroviches," said Devin. "They should be topside in a few minutes."

"Copy," said Melendez.

Roughly two minutes later, they hit the last waypoint. Marnie banked hard left and aligned them with the final point in the system. Pichugin's building. Downtown Miami filled her cockpit view, its dozens of tightly packed high-rises and skyscrapers glimmering with color. She pulled up on the collective while keeping the cyclic pushed forward to start gaining altitude for the final approach.

Marnie had decided to climb to one thousand feet before reaching the downtown area to avoid the tallest buildings entirely before dropping down onto Pichugin's head. She'd make more noise this way, potentially alerting the building's security detail, but she'd definitely avoid drawing immediate law enforcement attention to their gambit. Flying between high-rises at one in the morning was guaranteed to light up the nearest 911 call center.

"Three minutes out," she reported.

"All units. D and J have arrived at the pool deck," said Daniel. "We're going to sit poolside and see if we can give Rico some business."

"I'll take what I can get," said Melendez.

She checked the altimeter. Four hundred feet and rising. Distance to target: three miles. At one mile, she pulled the collective a little higher to make sure she cleared the waterfront buildings by a few hundred feet.

"Feet dry. One minute out," said Marnie, letting everyone know that they had just entered downtown Miami.

"Breach team is switching exclusively to the tactical net," said Devin.

She glanced over her shoulder for a moment to see the team remove their internally wired aviation headsets. All communications with Devin's team from this point forward would flow through their encrypted Motorolas, which were attached to throat microphones—freeing their hands for other work.

Marnie moved the collective into a neutral position at one thousand feet, while simultaneously easing the cyclic back to decrease speed.

The combined input put them into a steady thirty-mile-per-hour drift toward the target building.

"This is Overwatch. I can hear you," said Melendez.

"This is JP. I can see you," said Jessica Petrovich. "Still no security on the pool deck."

"Looks like they didn't take the bait," said Devin. "I'm sure they'll head up the moment they see a helicopter dropping people into the pool."

"We can deal with them when they arrive," said Jessica.

"This is Overwatch. If you need my help, drop flat, and I'll take care of business."

"Copy that," said Jessica. "We'll see how it plays out."

Marnie checked the navigation screen.

"We're less than a minute out," said Marnie.

"Pull your mask over your face if you haven't already," said Devin.

Marnie had adjusted her balaclava before taking off from the airfield. The chance of a security camera catching a glimpse of her through the reflective cockpit window was minuscule, but it existed—and she'd rather not make it easy for police to identify her. She already had enough explaining to do when all of this was finished.

"About to start my descent," she said.

Marnie lowered the collective a little too quickly, dropping them precipitously enough to generate a chorus of complaints from the passenger compartment.

"Sorry about that," she said. "Thirty seconds."

"You're doing great," said Devin. "Open the starboard-side doors."

Since Marnie was seated on the starboard side of the helicopter, she'd decided that they'd jump from the same side so she'd have the same view as the jumpers while she kept the helicopter in a hover over the pool. The moment of truth came rushing at her a little faster than she'd anticipated. She cut the collective and centered the cyclic, bringing the seven-ton composite-metal-alloy contraption to a hover about fifty feet above the rooftop.

Marnie glanced through the cockpit window beneath her feet at the bright-blue pool juxtaposed against the darkened deck. The helicopter's rotor wash rippled the water and slid the lounge chairs away from the pool.

"Steve. Lower the rope," she said.

She'd instructed the CIA guys to mark off twenty feet, in five-foot intervals, on one of the ropes and use it to measure her height above the deck.

A few seconds passed before he responded. "Just tossed it over the side."

Marnie made a few quick adjustments to her position over the pool and lowered the collective gently until she estimated the helicopter was roughly ten feet above the deck.

"How am I looking?" she said.

"You need to come down about another five feet," said Steve. "And slide about ten feet to port."

She took a few seconds to make the adjustment.

"How about now?"

"Perfect. Hold her steady!" said Steve.

Marnie stared straight ahead, locking several points of reference into place at once with her forward and peripheral vision. For the next minute, her only job was to work the controls so those points of reference didn't drift.

"We're steady. Time for Anish's cannonball," said Marnie.

CHAPTER 56

Anish hesitated at the door, his hands gripping the sides of the fuselage. Devin nestled in right behind him.

"Time to make that video for your grandkids," said Devin, before sticking his head out of the door. "We're right above the pool. Cannonball time. On three. Two. One. Go."

When he didn't move, Devin nodded at Steve, and they simultaneously peeled Anish's hands free from the side of the door and shoved him out. Anish briefly flailed in the air before tucking his knees into his chest and grabbing his shins. He hit the water a moment later, the splash rising as high as the door. A perfect cannonball.

Devin didn't wait for Anish to get out of the way; he took a few steps back and bolted through the door, dropping into the warm pool a few feet beyond him. He immediately grabbed Anish and pulled him to the closest ladder while the rest of the team splashed down in the hurricane-like conditions created by the helicopter's rotor wash.

By the time the Petroviches had helped everyone out of the pool, the helicopter had risen a hundred feet overhead.

"Thanks for the lift," said Devin, waving at the helicopter. "Don't stray too far."

"I'll be no more than two minutes away," she said. "Make sure you clear the pool deck before I return. Good luck."

Devin was about to respond when Melendez transmitted.

"Two targets exiting the stairwell door."

Every weapon in the group rose simultaneously, leveled at the brightly lit, glass-enclosed elevator lobby next to the pool. Two men barreled out of the door next to the elevators, holding compact rifles. The air cracked overhead, and the plate-glass window in front of the two men fell to the tiled pool deck and scattered in every direction, one of the Russians dropping to his knees. Devin pressed his trigger at the same time as everyone else, the two security guards convulsing from the bullets before toppling over.

"I couldn't resist," said Melendez.

"Nobody's complaining," said Devin. "Nice shot."

Soaked from top to bottom, Devin kneeled to unzip one of the waterproof bags thrown from the helicopter, removing a loaded MP7 submachine gun.

"Jessica! Catch!" he said, tossing the weapon the moment she turned around.

She snatched it out of the air and immediately passed it to Daniel, ready to catch the next one before he'd even freed it from the bag. Devin sent the second MP7 Jessica's way a few seconds later, then slid the bag along the pool deck toward her.

"Spare magazines and flash bangs inside," he said, taking off for the elevator lobby.

Miralles, Ripley, and Garza had already reached the two dead Russians by the time Devin stepped through the missing glass pane. Ripley held up a keycard, which Devin pocketed before moving to the blood-splattered stairwell door. He peeked through the horizontal window above the door handle, finding the stairs clear.

"Ready to move to sub-one," said Devin, keeping an eye on the stairwell. "Overwatch. How are things looking below?"

They'd labeled the five floors below them sub-one through sub-five, sub-one being the closest to the pool deck.

"The helicopter drew a few lookie-loos to the windows on sub-one and sub-two," said Melendez. "But I don't see any unusual movement yet."

"Copy. Call out anything you see the moment you see it," said Devin, turning to Miralles. "Stairs are clear. Lead the way."

She opened the door and stepped inside the landing, just as two men in suits rounded the switchback at the bottom of the first flight of stairs. Miralles drilled a single bullet through each of their surprised faces. Neither of them had managed to lift their submachine guns more than an inch before their brains hit the wall behind them. Less than two minutes in, and they'd already killed four guards. Something told him this wasn't going to be the simple in and out that he'd hoped for.

"This is Overwatch. I have some movement on sub-two. A half dozen or so guards with weapons just poured out of a door in the center of the floor. I'm seeing a mix of rifles and SMGs," said Melendez. "Nothing headed in the direction of the stairwell from what I can tell— but you definitely have their attention."

Any hope of a simple in and out vanished with Melendez's report.

"Keep going," he said to Miralles, and followed her down the stairs.

CHAPTER 57

They reached the door for sub-one, which didn't contain a window. Devin held the keycard a few inches from the card reader next to the door.

"Overwatch. What are you seeing on sub-one?" he said.

"We're wasting time," said Miralles, putting a hand on the door handle.

"People are starting to leave their workstations," said Melendez. "I don't see any security yet. The group on sub-two is gathered in front of a suite of offices in the middle of the floor."

"Copy," said Devin, pressing the keycard against the reader.

The door clicked a moment later, Miralles, Ripley, and Garza slipping into sub-one with their compact rifles leading the way. Devin glanced over his shoulder at Daniel and Jessica, who stood halfway up the flight of stairs, Anish sandwiched between them. He turned his attention back to sub-one and stepped through the doorway. The other three operatives had already taken covered positions on the periphery of the elevator lobby.

A quick look down the hallway leading into sub-one didn't reveal any immediate threats. Voices echoed down the hallway, but they didn't sound frantic. He motioned for the Petroviches to bring Anish out of the stairwell.

"Hallway out of elevator lobby looks clear," said Devin. "Let's grab one of the hackers before they evacuate the floor. They should be able to identify the location of the server room. Grab two just to be sure."

"Snatch and grab. Got it. Let's go," said Miralles, leading Ripley and Garza down the hallway.

Devin moved up to one of the hallway corners, while Jessica Petrovich settled into a crouch opposite him on the other side of the opening. Anish joined her a moment later, while Daniel remained just inside the stairwell, a spare MP7 magazine propping the door open a foot or so—just in case security decided to send anyone up from one of the lower floors.

"This is Overwatch. Four security officers just emerged from the offices in the middle of sub-one and are headed to the elevators. Request permission to engage."

"This is Devin. Overwatch is cleared to engage any armed hostiles," he said, earning a nod from Jessica.

The team in the hallway disappeared into sub-one, followed immediately by automatic gunfire.

"Taking fire from center of sub-one," said Miralles. "Feels like more than four guns shooting at us."

"I have a few blind spots," said Melendez. "One hostile down. Miralles. Fan out directly toward the windows from your current position. I see three hackers hiding under their workstations at the end of the row."

"We're on it," said Miralles.

A fierce gun battle erupted a few seconds after she responded, causing everyone in the elevator lobby to shift into shooting stances. Devin leveled his rifle at the end of the hallway, finger off the trigger so he wouldn't make a split-second mistake and fire on any friendlies retreating to the elevator lobby.

Two men dressed in suits rushed into the hallway and took positions next to the door used by Miralles less than thirty seconds ago, their rifles shouldered and ready for action. Devin sighted in on the closest of the two oblivious security guards and pressed his trigger twice, spraying the second man with dark-red gore. Jessica's MP7 barked twice in rapid succession. The second guard's head snapped sideways before he had a chance to react to his colleague's unceremonious death. The man slid in place to the marble floor, leaving a soccer ball–size red splotch on the wall next to the doorway.

"Two hostiles neutralized in the elevator lobby hallway," said Devin over the relentless gunfire echoing through the corridor.

"This is Miralles. We're on our way back with three—"

The gunfire intensified to a new level inside sub-one, a deafening discordance of automatic and semiautomatic fire booming through the hallway and elevator lobby.

"Scratch that. Two hackers," said Miralles. "Hold your fire—we're headed back into the hallway."

"Watch the doorway on the opposite side of the hallway," said Devin.

Miralles popped into view, her rifle pointed at the open doorway he'd just highlighted. She moved into the middle of the hallway to make room for the rest of the team to escape the gunfire inside of sub-one. Ripley appeared next, pushing two stooped-over hackers in Devin's direction—a young woman dressed in baggy basketball shorts and a purple LA Lakers tank top jersey, followed by a middle-age man wearing khaki pants and a light-blue, short-sleeved button-up shirt.

Garza trailed closely behind Ripley, firing short bursts through the doorway into sub-one. He tapped Miralles on the shoulder as he passed her. She backed up slowly, covering both doorways as Ripley and Garza hustled the two hackers into the elevator lobby. Devin grabbed the young woman by the wrist and swung her out of the hallway, going to work on her immediately.

"We're looking for the server room," said Devin.

"I can't . . . I really don't know where it is," she said.

He glanced at Jessica, who had a gun to khaki guy's head. She shook her head. "I think he's more afraid of the Russians than us."

Devin placed the barrel of his rifle against the woman's forehead. He hated doing this, and had no intention of shooting her, but they didn't have the time or firepower to search the entire five-story complex.

"I'm going to count to three. There won't be a four. Where is the server room?"

Bullets stitched through the air a few feet to his right, sparking off the stainless steel elevator door behind him. Miralles, Ripley, and Garza unleashed a long volley of automatic fire down the hallway, their fusillade yielding a brief, high-pitched scream.

"One," said Devin.

"Can I just shoot this one?" said Jessica.

"Give me a few seconds," said Devin, pushing the barrel into the woman's cheek. "Two."

"They're gonna kill both of us if I tell you," she said.

"I think I have a way to prevent that," said Devin.

"They're just going to kill us, Desi," said the man.

"I promise we won't kill you," said Devin. "Three!"

"Okay! Okay! The server room is two floors down from this level," she said. "In the middle of the floor."

"You're not fucking with me, right?" said Devin.

"No," she said. "Just let us go. Like you promised."

Devin removed the rifle from her face and activated his radio.

"Server room is on sub-three," said Devin. "Overwatch. I'm sending two neutrals up to the pool deck. They're going to clear the landing zone, then hide from the Russians. If they try to pick up any of the security guards' weapons, consider them hostile and engage to kill."

"Copy that," said Melendez. "You better get moving down to sub-three. They're assembling a small army on sub-two."

"We're on the move," said Daniel, before turning to the young woman. "Desi. You heard what I just said, correct?"

She nodded.

"Get up to the pool deck and throw all of the lounge chairs, tables, umbrellas—anything that's not bolted to the deck—into the pool. Don't ask why, just do it," he said. "Can you do that?"

"Yes. Everything in the pool," she said.

"The police will be all over this place before the Russians find you. There are plenty of places to hide up there. After you clear the pool deck. And don't touch any of the weapons up there. My sniper will not hesitate to end you. Got it?"

"I got it," she said.

"Then get going!" said Devin, before tapping Miralles's shoulder.

Desi took off, grabbing her hacker colleague on the way to the stairwell door, where Daniel opened the door far enough for them to get through.

"Go. Get the fuck out of here!" said Daniel, his MP7 pointed up the stairs.

Devin crouched next to Miralles. "Slag the stairwell door with one of the thermite sticks. I don't want anyone getting behind us. We'll do the same on the sub-two level."

Farrington's team had dragged a bag full of tricks out of the bunker on the edge of the West Virginia compound's clearing. One of those novelties was a three-inch thermite stick, which when ignited would burn at four thousand degrees Fahrenheit for a dozen seconds—enough to create a small river of slag that should freeze the door-locking mechanism in place.

"Easy enough," said Miralles, ducking behind the corner to dig through the overstuffed bag slung around her shoulder.

A whisper came across the tactical net.

"This is Daniel. We have company coming up the stairs."

Miralles removed a fragmentation grenade from her bag and held it up in front of Devin. He nodded in agreement, and she slid it across the polished marble floor. The grenade hit the MP7 magazine propping the door open, and bounced over it into the stairwell.

"That'll work," said Daniel.

"You're welcome," said Miralles.

"Pass him a few more," said Devin. "Just to be sure."

CHAPTER 58

Felix Orlov crouched inside his office, next to the open door, still unsure what was happening in the building. Reports had been sporadic and frantic. Something about a helicopter landing on the pool deck and dropping off a team of shooters—which sounded completely asinine. The gunfire was real. That much he could confirm with his own ears. Someone was shooting up the floor directly above them, but who? The sad assortment of Russian mobsters that Pichugin had assembled to guard this place?

Pichugin had a lot of firepower in the building, but the quality of personnel left a lot to be desired. Mostly wannabe Russian *mafiya* heavies looking to make enough of a name to pick up regular work for Pichugin. Orlov's reassignment to Miami had made sense the moment he arrived. The oligarch needed someone competent to run security. At least that was what he told himself, knowing full well that the job was essentially a punishment for the fiasco in Baltimore—and the Ozarks.

Oleg burst into the office. "I just confirmed the helicopter landing. One of the security officers on the floor above saw it on the closed-circuit feed. They sent two groups up. None of them are responding to calls over the security net. There's a ton of—"

The muted crunch of an explosion shook the office. Lashev slipped through the door a moment later and crouched next to Orlov, a dire look on his face.

"This is more than we bargained for," said Lashev.

"Do you want to call Pichugin and tell him that?" said Orlov. "We need to get up there now. Split the team and use both stairwells. Grab all of the security officers you can find."

Oleg stepped into the doorway and raised his radio, the doorframe next to his head exploding in a barrage of splinters a moment later. He stood there for a few seconds, his scratched and bloodied face not fully registering what had just happened. Lashev reached up to pull him down, but Oleg's head exploded before Lashev's hands could grasp anything. Oleg stumbled forward, his shattered head spraying the office walls with bright-red blood.

"Sniper!" said Lashev, before scrambling behind Orlov's desk.

One of Severny's mercenaries appeared in the doorway, yelling in Russian.

"We have a sniper in one of the—"

His left collarbone shattered, spinning him one hundred and eighty degrees to face the cubicle farm just outside of the office. Orlov lurched for the mercenary, hoping to save him from Oleg's fate, but Lashev grabbed Orlov's belt and held him in place—well clear of the doorway. A second bullet punched straight through the man's upper torso, penetrating his bulletproof vest and striking the back wall.

Orlov scooted back and bumped into Lashev, who was focused on the hole in the drywall.

"Heavy caliber, but not a fifty. Three-three-eight Lapua Magnum or something similar. Coming from one of the buildings north to northeast of us. Could punch right through these walls," said Lashev, patting the drywall above Orlov's head.

He dropped prone on the carpeted floor, heeding Lashev's warning.

"Grab your sniper rifle and follow me," he said.

Orlov snagged his compact M4 from behind the desk and crawled out of the office, staying flat against the floor. Several security guards crouched between the workstations, popping up every few seconds to fire at a sniper they almost certainly hadn't spotted. Their panicked gunfire was essentially punching holes in random condominium windows, each bullet another 911 call. He crawled next to one of the guards and tapped his shoulder.

"What are you shooting at?" said Orlov.

The man ducked below the desktop. "There's a sniper in one of the buildings out there."

"And you're just shooting at all of the buildings?" said Orlov.

"We're suppressing the sniper," said the guard.

One of the curved wide-screen monitors a foot above the guard's head burst into several pieces of loosely connected plastic.

"You're not suppressing shit. It's the other way around!" said Orlov. "Tell your people to knock it off! They're shooting into condominiums—almost guaranteeing that we'll get a visit from Miami PD's SWAT unit."

The man spoke into his radio, and the gunfire slowed to a few single random shots.

"Okay. Now start requesting contact reports from each of the floors, starting with the one above us," said Orlov. "A helicopter dropped off some kind of team. We need to know where they are right now and where they're headed."

The guard handed him the radio. "Sounds like you know what you're doing."

"We'll see about that," said Orlov, reluctantly accepting the Motorola.

CHAPTER 59

Melendez sat on the edge of one of the lounge chairs, the RPA Rangemaster sniper rifle's handguard resting on the balcony's top rail. Without taking his eye out of the Schmidt & Bender variable power scope, Melendez pulled the rifle's bolt to the rear, ejecting the spent .338 Lapua Magnum shell casing before removing the empty magazine and stuffing it into the duffel bag next to him. He inserted a fresh ten-round magazine and sighted in on a guard occasionally peeking out of one of the office doors on sub-two.

Melendez centered the crosshairs on a point along the wall about six inches from the doorframe, at the same height as the guard's head. On a long exhale, he pressed the trigger, punching a small hole through the building's exterior window and knocking the man backward into the office, the interior drywall no match for a heavy-caliber bullet traveling three thousand feet per second.

He scanned for more targets on sub-two, finding none. They'd finally wised up, after losing half of their number. A quick look at sub-one yielded a similar result. The entire security team had quit shooting at nothing and taken real cover. Someone was coordinating their response.

"This is Overwatch," said Melendez. "Looks like security has gotten their shit together. I get the sense they're acting as a unit now. Watch yourself."

Melendez shifted the scope's view to sub-three, anticipating Devin's response.

"Copy. We're on sub-three, making our way down the hallway from the elevator lobby. Any movement on sub-three?"

"Negative," said Melendez. "But I know you have at least five hostiles on sub-three. They're very wisely keeping a low profile."

"Well. We're about to flush a few of them out," said Devin. "You should be able to see us in the doorway facing the northeast side of the floor."

He eased the rifle right until the doorway appeared in his scope's field of view. Miralles leaned out of the doorway, her rifle directed toward the rows of workstations standing between her and the server room in the center of sub-three.

"I see Emily," said Melendez, moving the scope's field of view back to the cubicle farm. "You're clear to proceed, but keep in mind that I can only see half of sub-three."

"Moving out," she said.

Miralles and the rest of the team made it halfway to the presumed server room before the first security guard broke cover to engage them. Melendez caught the man's movement in the gap between two monitors and immediately centered the scope's crosshairs on his last detected position. He pressed his trigger just as the man rose to fire at the team, the bullet striking him in the chest and knocking the guard backward over the workstation behind him.

A second security guard popped up, appearing unsure where to aim. Miralles and the team flattened him with a quick volley of gunfire before he figured it out. Two figures burst into view in front of the server room, headed in the team's direction.

"Two shooters inbound from server room," said Melendez, quickly lining up a center mass shot at the first guard.

He pressed the trigger, the RPA Rangemaster biting into his shoulder, as the two guards raised their rifles to fire on the team. The bullet spun the first man ninety degrees to the left, his rifle muzzle flashing on fully automatic. The team rushed forward in a wedge formation, their rifles and submachine guns tearing through the two men as they advanced on the server room.

With the team in his line of fire on sub-three, Melendez shifted his aim back to sub-two, gauging their response to the gunfire one floor below. Someone was crawling for the door that exited into the elevator lobby. He centered the crosshairs on the prone guard's torso and pressed the trigger, giving the security team one more reason to stay put.

CHAPTER 60

Orlov remained perfectly still. He sincerely hadn't thought that the Russian he'd just sent to his death would become visible to the sniper at any point along the short journey to the elevator lobby hallway. They needed to get off the workstation floor and into real cover. It was only a matter of time before the sniper started randomly firing low into the workstations, which would offer little protection from the high-power bullets.

"Lashev. Where's the sniper? What's your best guess?" said Orlov.

"Guess? I don't guess," said Lashev. "There's a science to this."

"Then break out the science and tell me how to get the fuck out of here," said Orlov. "I'm afraid to wipe my nose at this point."

"Based on the angle of the entry wounds, I'd say the sniper is situated somewhere to our northeast. The Flatiron Building, most likely," said Lashev.

"Fuck. We're basically trapped here," said Orlov. "Aren't we?"

"Given the sniper's presumed field of view? Yes," said Lashev.

His radio crackled. "This is security on the forty-ninth floor. The server room has been breached. We can't get anywhere near it without taking heavy fire or getting popped by that sniper. There's only three of us left down here."

They're after information? What exactly was Pichugin running from this building? In the end it didn't matter. Pichugin had gone through a lot of trouble to stick a computer farm at the top of a Miami high-rise—along with a large security detail. And someone else had gone out of their way to land a helicopter on the roof to steal whatever Pichugin valued so dearly. His only mission from this point forward was to protect Pichugin's investment. Anything less would result in his termination.

"How big is the hostile team?" said Orlov.

"At least five," said the security guard. "We couldn't stick our heads out long enough to tell."

"Can you pin them in the server room?"

"I don't see how with just the three of us," he said. "We can barely get a shot off before all hell breaks loose, and we can't move anyone to the east side of the floor to catch them in a cross fire. The sniper has that side of the building locked down hard."

"We're all dealing with that problem," said Orlov. "Okay. Here's what we're going to do. I need to get people down to forty-nine so we can trap them in the server room, but my entire group is pinned down by the sniper. I need you to send one of your people through the elevator lobby hallway to fire at the server room from the door on the other side."

"You want one of us to commit suicide?" said the guard.

"No. Here's what you do," said Orlov. "Enter the hallway from the west side, where the sniper can't see you. Pop into the doorway on the east side and fire a few bursts at the server room, then get out of sight immediately. And get low, as in flat on your stomach. The sniper can shoot through walls."

"This still sounds like a suicide mission."

"I just need that sniper distracted for a few seconds, to get my people out of the shooting gallery," said Orlov. "If you fire two quick bursts and duck back into the hallway, the sniper won't have time to line up a shot. You'll be fine."

"We'll see about that," he said. "I'm on my way."

"Let me know when you're in position, and I'll give the go-ahead to start shooting. Make sure you stay out of the sniper's line of sight when you approach the doorway. We suspect the sniper is in the closest building to the northeast. If the sniper detects any movement in that doorway or hallway, you're a dead man."

"I don't see how this is worth the money I'm being paid," he said.

"It's not about the money. It's about who hired you," said Orlov. "If we don't stop these people, our employer will not be pleased. And I take it you understand who you're working for?"

"I do," said the guard.

"Then get moving," said Orlov.

Lashev crawled next to him. "There's a good chance that he won't make it."

"Keep that to yourself," said Orlov, lowering his voice to a whisper. "There's also a good chance the sniper won't fall for our little trick—and not all of us are getting out of here alive."

"None of us are getting out of this alive," said Lashev.

"Don't say that."

CHAPTER 61

Devin crouched next to Anish, trying not to crowd him.

"How are we doing?" said Devin.

"I would be doing better if you weren't sweating me," said Anish, running his hands along the ethernet wire that connected DEVTEK's "device" to an interface in the server rack. "I think I have this right. It's been a while since I messed with servers in person."

"Take your time, but hurry the fuck up," said Daniel Petrovich from the end of the server-stack aisle.

"Thanks. That's really helpful," said Anish. "You want to come over here and figure this shit out?"

"You want to come over here and make sure nobody kills you?" said Daniel.

"He has a point," said Devin.

"He always does," said Anish, tapping a button named "Run interface" on the tablet's screen. "We'll know if this is going to work in— never mind, it looks like it's working."

Anish showed Devin the screen, which indicated that the device and the server were communicating.

"How long?" said Devin, starting the stopwatch function on his wristwatch.

"Rafael said it could take a few minutes to hijack the server," said Anish. "And that we needed to make sure the connection remained intact until the tablet tells me I can disconnect. Be nice if this had a countdown timer or something."

Devin hit his radio transmit button. "Anish is connected to the server, but we need to hold this position for three to five minutes until DEVTEK's device finishes working its magic."

Gunfire erupted before anyone could respond, two short bursts presumably aimed at the door on the other side of the server cabinet aisle. A few bullets ricocheted into the drop-ceiling tiles just inside the door. The team responded, two firing from inside the server room and two from positions just outside the room.

"This is Overwatch. The gunfire on sub-three was a distraction. Five guards on sub-two just entered the elevator lobby."

"Sub-two stairwell door is slagged," said Devin. "We shouldn't have a problem."

"What about the elevators?" said Melendez.

"They'd be crazy to use the elevators," said Devin.

The team had agreed to avoid the elevators for two reasons. First and foremost, there was absolutely no way to know what awaited them on the other side—and there was no escaping once the door opened. Second, they had no idea if the security team guarding the zero-day factory had control over the elevators. Their raid would end rather unceremoniously if security shut down the elevator while they switched floors.

"They might not be crazy, but I get the sense they're desperate," said Melendez.

A scary thought hit Devin.

"They could take the elevator down to sub-four and access the stairwell. Hit us from below," he said. "Miralles. Rip. Garza. I need you in the elevator lobby now. Watch the stairwell—and the elevators."

"On our way," said Miralles, gunfire exploding a moment later.

"Daniel and Jessica. You have the server room door," said Devin.

Daniel took off, disappearing around the end of the server-stack aisle. The gunfire outside the server room intensified a few moments later, followed by an explosion that shook the floor.

"Miralles. What's going on?" said Devin.

"I fragged the elevator lobby," said Miralles. "One of the guards had taken a position inside. It's all clear now."

"Okay. Just hold down the fort. Watch the stairwell and the elevators. We'll be on the way shortly," said Devin, turning to Anish. "Any update on the time?"

Anish shook his head. "I know it's communicating with the server, but the device isn't giving me any indication of how much time remains. Rafael insisted it wouldn't take any longer than five minutes."

"And you're sure everything is hooked up right?" said Devin.

"One hundred percent," said Anish. "I went over this with Rafael a dozen times."

Devin took a seat on the floor next to him. "How long do you think we should give it?"

"Rafael said five minutes," said Anish. "I say we give it a few more than that."

Devin checked his watch. "It's been two minutes. Five more and we're out of here."

His earpiece crackled. "This is Overwatch. Police frequencies are going crazy. I'm starting to hear sirens."

"Copy. Any movement on any of the floors?" said Devin.

"Negative."

"How is the pool deck looking? Did the two hackers I sent up do what they were told?"

"The pool deck is almost clear," said Melendez. "They're working pretty hard to get it done."

"Good."

"Devin. This is Miralles. You were right," she whispered. "We've got movement in the stairwell below us."

"Do whatever you have to do to keep the stairwell clear. Unless you want to ride the elevator up," said Devin.

"No thanks," she said. "We'll hold the stairwell."

He turned to Anish. "This is going to be a long five minutes."

"Or not," said Anish, who held up the tablet, which read PROCESS COMPLETE. UNPLUG DEVICE.

"Beautiful. Pull the plug and don't leave any trace of what we've done. And don't forget the device," said Devin. "We'll be waiting for you at the door."

"I'll be there in thirty seconds," said Anish, disconnecting the device.

Devin snaked his way through the aisles of server racks to reach the room's exit. Jessica kneeled in the doorway, her MP7 pointed in the direction of the guards on the west side of sub-three. Daniel crouched on the other side of the door, covering the rest of the cubicle farm, just in case.

"Anish is packing up. Looks like DEVTEK's little trick worked," said Devin. "Jessica. What are you seeing?"

"Nothing. But they're still there," said Jessica.

"How many?"

"Used to be three, but it sounds like Miralles fragged one of them," said Jessica.

Devin reached into one of his cargo pockets and removed two round, olive drab fragmentation grenades, handing them to Daniel.

"No point in bringing these back," said Devin. "Frag the other two on the way out."

"Sounds like someone is done fucking around," said Daniel.

"What can I say? You guys are starting to rub off on me," said Devin, before triggering his radio. "Marnie. This is Devin. Start your run for the pool deck. We should be on deck in a minute."

"I'm . . . ninety-three seconds out," she said.

Anish appeared at the end of the aisle, carrying his backpack over one shoulder. The moment he reached the door, Devin contacted the team in the elevator lobby.

"Miralles. We're on our way," said Devin. "All hell is about to break loose over here."

"Same here," said Miralles. "So hurry the fuck up."

Devin patted Daniel's shoulder. "Let's go."

Daniel pulled the pin on one of the grenades and released the safety lever, which sprang off the grenade and clanked along the tile floor. He counted to two under his breath before leaning out of the door and sidearming the grenade in the direction of the two remaining guards. Jessica fired a quick burst before backing into the room. A deafening crunch hit them a moment later, the wall next to Devin shuddering.

Jessica was out the door, firing her MP7 in the blink of an eye. Daniel pulled the pin on the second grenade and followed her out.

"Stay on my right side," said Devin, pulling Anish into position next to him. "Ready?"

"Ready," said Anish.

They piled out of the server room just as Daniel underhanded the second grenade into the twisted, smoking wreckage of the first. All three of them scrambled toward the elevator lobby, just clearing the corner when the grenade exploded. Daniel followed Jessica through the hallway door. They positioned themselves at the door on the other side of the corridor, firing several bursts into the western half of sub-three.

Devin ushered Anish past the Petroviches and into the elevator lobby, where Garza waited for them.

"Shit's about to go down in the stairwell," he said, nodding at the closed, windowless door.

Devin hit his transmit button while approaching the door. "Emily. What are we looking at?"

Two closely timed explosions rattled the lobby, dropping Devin and Anish to a crouch next to the stairwell entrance.

"We just fragged sub-four," said Miralles. "Bring everyone through."

He pushed the crash bar with his elbow and entered the smoke-filled landing, pinning the fully opened door against the interior wall. Devin kept his rifle aimed down the stairwell while Anish, Garza, and the Petroviches mounted the stairs. Miralles pulled the pin on a smoke grenade and tossed it into the darkness.

"Let's go," she said.

Devin caught up to Anish and the others on the sub-one landing, Miralles and Ripley following closely behind. One flight up from the landing, Miralles tossed a second smoke grenade over her shoulder. The metal cylinder bounced out of sight down the stairs. If anyone tried to follow them up after the fragmentation grenades, they wouldn't be able to see more than a foot in front of them until they reached the rooftop.

A deep thumping sound filled the stairwell when they opened the door to the pool deck, the Sikorsky S-76's rotor blades thrashing the air nearby.

"Marnie. This is Devin. We're on the pool deck. Sounds like you're close."

"I'm on final approach. Stay inside the stairwell until I land. I still see a few loose items around the landing zone," said Marnie.

Miralles and Ripley headed back down to the next landing to watch the flight of stairs on the other side of the switchback. Devin kept the stairwell door open a crack to watch for the helicopter. A few seconds later, the wind instantly picked up on the pool deck, rippling the pool surface and knocking over a table and chair that the two hackers had missed. The artificial squall intensified for several seconds while Marnie brought the helicopter to a seemingly effortless landing next to the pool.

"Contact! Elevators!" said Marnie.

Devin pushed the door open in time to see four armed guards pour into the elevator lobby and start to fire at the helicopter. He raised his rifle and sighted in on the nearest shooter as automatic gunfire erupted from the helicopter door. Devin pressed his trigger repeatedly, switching from target to target until all the security guards had toppled to the lobby's white tile floor, either dead or bleeding out from the cross fire.

"You're clear! The elevator is empty," said Marnie.

He rushed into the lobby and checked out the elevator—just in case. Finding it empty, he signaled Daniel to get everyone moving toward the helicopter. Devin kept an eye on the dead or dying Russians as the team sprinted across the pool deck, leaving only when the last member of the group started to climb aboard.

The helicopter lifted off the moment Steve pulled him inside, Marnie wasting no time getting them clear of this mess. Devin watched the pool deck shrink beneath them until the helicopter's nose dipped, and the building drifted away. They had pulled off the impossible.

CHAPTER 62

Orlov coughed hard as he limped up the stairs. He slid his hands along the railing, barely able to see his feet through the insufferably thick smoke. Not much farther to go. The helicopter's engines whined over the thumping of the rotor blades. One more flight of stairs. That was all he asked of his legs. He wouldn't get another chance if the helicopter escaped. He might not get one anyway. God knew what they had been up to in the server room.

"Orlov, you're bleeding all over the stairs," said Lashev from just behind him. "We need to get you out of here."

The grenades tossed down the stairwell had caught him off guard, Orlov barely managing to dive for cover before they exploded. Unfortunately, not all of him had escaped the grenades' fragmentation, his left leg taking shrapnel just below the knee and above the ankle. His left shoe squished every time he took a step, leaving a bloody shoe print behind for Lashev to slip on.

"And go where?" said Orlov, adjusting the rifle sling on his shoulder. "This ends here."

He pushed onward, stepping over a pair of dead guards on the next landing before reaching the top of the stairs. Orlov started to open the door, but the wind created by the helicopter pushed it shut. He glanced through the vertical window above the doorknob to see a dark shape lifting away from the pool deck. This was his last chance.

"Help me open this!" he said, pulling Lashev up the last few stairs.

They both pushed against the rotor wash until the door swung wide open. The helicopter was gone.

"No!" said Orlov, unslinging his rifle.

He limped through the lobby and across the pool deck as fast as he could, just barely catching sight of the helicopter's white taillight beyond the west side of the building before it vanished. Orlov unleashed a string of obscenities into the night sky before throwing his rifle to the tiled deck. He screamed a few more times before turning toward the elevators. Smoke poured out of the stairwell into the elevator lobby, partially obscuring Lashev.

"We need to get down to the ground—"

Lashev's head disintegrated, a sharp crack passing overhead at nearly the same time. How stupid. They'd forgotten about the sniper. Orlov turned and sprinted for the pool, diving into the aluminum tangle of lounge chairs and tables just as a bullet passed within inches of his head. He landed hard, smashing his hands, arms, and face, before finally slipping under the water. Once safely below the surface, Orlov squirmed through the gauntlet of deck furniture to reach the northern edge of the pool, where he should be safe from the sniper. His lungs burning, Orlov slowly rose to take a breath, allowing only his mouth to break the surface.

He drank in the air for a few seconds before breaking into a violent cough. A bullet exploded the tile a foot to the left of his head, forcing him back down. Sitting underwater, coughing uncontrollably, he decided he'd had enough. What was the point of trying to survive this? He could either die right here, right now, or wait for Pichugin's thugs to pull him off the street and torture him to death.

Orlov decided to die on his own terms. He pushed off the bottom with his good leg and stood up in the pool, his torso and head exposed to the condominium tower to the northeast. Still coughing, he stood upright and waited. And waited. The bullet he so desperately wanted never arrived.

CHAPTER 63

A warm ocean breeze drifted across the tarmac, gently blowing Marnie's hair. She stared at the dark shape of a helicopter on the other side of the airfield, wondering where the CIA pilots who delivered it would fly it next. Somewhere far from here, for sure. For a while anyway. The Sikorsky S-76 was a distinctly recognizable helicopter. It wouldn't be long before the police and feds reviewed the building's security feeds and identified the aircraft model. Then the hunt would be on. Or maybe not.

Maybe the CIA could make the investigation into the S-76 go away, just like it could somehow arrange for the use of Homestead Air Reserve's tarmac for the covert launch and recovery of a helicopter at one in the morning. She suspected the investigation into the helicopter would hit a dead end before it built any momentum. Marnie wandered back to Anish's Suburban and leaned against the hood next to Devin.

Two SUVs sat in a line behind the Suburban, their occupants taking advantage of the downtime. Everyone was waiting for Melendez to drive down from Miami before heading out. He'd managed to pack up and slip out of downtown Miami before every police unit in the city arrived at Pichugin's building. The car Melendez drove had been provided by the same group that had arranged the helicopter. They'd been instructed to leave it in the easternmost hangar, where the convoy had been parked.

The Petroviches had driven away moments after they landed, with-out saying a word to anyone—their contract, or whatever had bound them to this mission, fulfilled. The couple remained a mystery that nobody in the group cared to shed any light on.

"Are your hands shaking?" said Devin, holding both of his hands in front of him.

She took one of his visibly trembling hands and held it tight.

"You all right?" she said.

"Yeah. I think it's adrenaline withdrawal," he said. "Either that, or the insanity of what we just pulled off finally caught up with me. Could be both. How are you holding up?"

"I feel fine, but I honestly have no idea how I'll be later," she said. "All I do know is that I need a few weeks at an all-inclusive resort. Doing absolutely nothing."

"That sounds perfect," said Devin. "Mind if I join you?"

"Shouldn't we go on a proper date or something first," she said, "before we spend two weeks together at a resort?"

He squeezed her hand. "I wasn't suggesting we stay in the same room, but since you brought it up—just one date?"

She shook her head and laughed. "I guess we could skip the date. It's not like we haven't spent nearly every minute together for the past three weeks."

"When this business is finished, I'll take you on a real date," said Devin. "We'll see if we can stand each other when we're not being hunted by Russian mercenaries."

"Count me in," she said.

Anish hopped down from the Suburban. "Rico is ten minutes out. He thinks he nailed the guy that shot Graves and Daly. Right after the helicopter flew away, two guys busted out of the stairwell. One of them carried the same kind of sniper rifle we saw outside your mother's apartment. He took the guy out before he had to scoot."

"I'm really sorry you lost a good friend," said Marnie.

"We drove each other crazy, but in a good way," said Anish. "I'm going to miss him."

"Sounds like the two of you had been through a lot together," said Marnie. "You'll always have that—"

Anish's satellite phone rang, and he answered in the middle of her sentence.

"What's the good word?" he said, listening for a few seconds before passing on the news. "Karl says DEVTEK is copying all of the data in Pichugin's servers, and that the Russians would have to kill power to the entire building to stop the data transfer."

"How long will it take to copy the server data?" said Devin.

"Several hours," said Anish.

Devin grumbled about the length of time.

"It'll be fine," said Marnie. "They won't be able to cut the power with Miami PD on the scene, and I don't see the police leaving them alone for quite some time."

"You're right," said Devin. "And they'll probably evacuate the entire building for a few days while they study the crime scene and sweep for evidence."

"Karl wants to know when we can get back to the compound," said Anish.

"We just landed forty minutes ago," said Devin. "We're still waiting on Rico."

Anish relayed the information. "He says we should get on the road as soon as Rico arrives."

"Are we allowed to stop for coffee and breakfast on the way back?" said Devin. "Don't ask him that. Tell him we'll get moving as soon as Rico shows up."

While Anish passed along his response, Marnie leaned her head against Devin's shoulder.

"I need some sleep," said Marnie. "And not a car nap."

"Don't worry," said Devin. "We'll put some distance between ourselves and South Florida—then crash at a motel for most of the day.

If they want to rush back to West Virginia, there's plenty of room in Anish's Suburban."

"And a Denny's. We need to hit a Denny's," said Marnie.

"We'll have to run that by Karl," said Devin, the two of them breaking out in laughter.

"Karl says he totally expects you to ignore him," said Anish. "But that you need to at least get out of Florida before you stop for any length of time. He says it's about seven and a half hours to Savannah."

"That's like seven and a half cups of coffee," said Marnie.

"Tell Berg that'll work for us," said Devin, before whispering to Marnie, "Don't worry, we're still getting breakfast."

"That doesn't count for our date," said Marnie. "Just in case you're wondering."

"Nothing counts until we've put this ordeal behind us. How does that sound?"

"Deal."

PART SIX

CHAPTER 64

Yuri Pichugin listened impatiently to Kuznetzov's report, until he finally sensed that the blowhard had run out of new information to pass along.

"Grigory. I need to interrupt you," said Pichugin. "When will we be able to get our people back into the building? Specifically, when will our IT and cybersecurity team be able to get inside? We need to know what that team was doing in the server room."

"Nobody's getting into that building for a while," said Kuznetzov. "The police have it completely locked down."

"You mean to tell me if I flew down there myself, I couldn't get into my own fucking building?" said Pichugin.

"Not after they found a few dozen shot-up bodies and recovered a small arsenal of unlicensed automatic weapons on the upper floors," said Kuznetzov. "And that's not even considering the potential fallout we face when the police start examining the top five floors—and questioning the building's supposed residents. I suspect that the building will go radioactive within twenty-four hours."

"Do we know for sure who hit the building?" said Pichugin. "I mean real evidence. We all can guess that Devin Gray and Karl Berg's people are behind it."

"Nothing so far. They used a helicopter to drop the team onto the pool deck," said Kuznetzov. "They also had a sniper in one of the nearby buildings, who wreaked havoc on the top three floors and rooftop. The police are all over that as well."

"Can we hack back into our own server and regain control?"

"We're working on this from a few remote sites," said Kuznetzov. "But I'm afraid that the damage is already done. They've most likely copied the server data by now."

"How the hell did they find the Miami site?" said Pichugin.

"We may never know," said Kuznetzov. "Whoever is behind this will likely wipe the entire server database when they're finished. It might already be erased."

"This smells like the CIA," said Pichugin. "Farrington's people may have shot up the place, but they're not sophisticated enough to hijack a server and copy the data."

"We have to consider every possibility," said Kuznetzov. "The server intrusion certainly suggests a state sponsor or savvy partner."

"Then we need to bump up the BLACKOUT timeline," said Pichugin, "before they can make sense of the zero-day exploits."

"I'll fly down and talk with Colonel Petrushev about accelerating the timeline," said Kuznetzov. "Shall we say T-minus five days until BLACKOUT?"

Pichugin checked his watch. "More like T-minus twelve hours."

"There's no way they can launch tonight," said Kuznetzov. "And I need time to notify and assemble the new government and military commanders."

"Make it T-minus thirty-six hours," said Pichugin. "BLACKOUT launches tomorrow night."

"Thirty-six hours is pushing it."

"Then fucking push it," said Pichugin. "I don't need to remind you who will be the most disappointed if BLACKOUT has to be canceled."

A long pause ensued, Kuznetzov hopefully coming to his senses. BLACKOUT was the cornerstone of the president's strategy to re-create eastern Europe's Soviet Bloc. Failure to successfully execute BLACKOUT would set the entire effort back by however long it took to organize another coup in Tallinn. Likely years. It was now or never.

"Tomorrow night then," said Kuznetzov.

"Keep me posted every step of the way today and tomorrow," said Pichugin. "And do not hesitate to ask for my help with any obstacles or delays. BLACKOUT is my only priority right now."

CHAPTER 65

Karl Berg ended the call with Jared Hoffman and turned to Audra Bauer.

"Kuznetzov just boarded a Sukhoi Superjet 100 at Sheremetyevo International Airport with sixty-two of his best friends."

The CIA contingent and the DEVTEK cybersecurity team stopped what they were doing and glanced in his direction.

"Sixty-two of his best friends?" said Bauer.

"Dressed in suits or full-dress military uniforms," said Berg.

"Sounds like a replacement government," said one of the CIA officers.

"Looks like one, too. According to my team on the ground. They'll forward pictures shortly, so we can try to identify some of these VIPs," said Berg. "Tonight could be the night."

"Fingers crossed," said Bauer. "Rafael. Does anything on your end suggest that tonight is the night?"

"They ran a few more tests on the infrastructure system about an hour ago. Small stuff we wouldn't notice if we didn't know what to look for," said Rafael. "They haven't tested it in a few days, so it could be an indication that they're verifying control of the system."

"We should put the Estonians on alert," said Berg. "It's an hour-and-a-half flight to Staraya Russa Airport from Moscow. That puts them on the ground around ten thirty p.m. local time. My guess is they'll arrive before the helicopters, because they'll need the entire runway to land the brigade simultaneously. An hour to load a regiment of mercenaries and conduct final pre-assault checks. Ninety minutes to reach Tallinn. One in the morning arrival time. Give or take thirty minutes."

"Perfect time for a soft coup," said Bauer.

"Nothing soft about it," said Berg, turning to the CIA side of the office. "You have to make it crystal clear to your Estonian counterparts that they cannot rely on any of their integrated air defense systems. They need to assume the Medium Extended Air Defense System protecting Estonia will not work as designed. This isn't just a function of the electrical grid going down. We have no idea how many other zero-day exploits are at play in Estonia, but if the Russians are sending helicopters, we can assume that they've neutralized their ability to shoot down helicopters."

"They've quietly moved several hundred shoulder-launched surface-to-air missiles and the teams to fire them to dozens of locations around the city and airport. High-rises. Old city walls. Hilltops. Commercial buildings. They'll have clear lines of sight to the inbound helicopters," said one of the CIA officers. "And within an hour's notice, they can deploy hundreds of self-propelled antiaircraft gun vehicles and troop-loaded armored personnel carriers to every conceivable landing zone within a mile of the government buildings, the airport, the president's residence, and all of the major media broadcast outlets."

"Sounds to me like they have this covered," said Bauer.

"They're not fucking around. That's for sure," said Berg.

CHAPTER 66

General Grigory Kuznetzov fought the same urge to vomit that had already consumed half of the New Estonia government. The low-level approach to Tallinn had been rougher than advertised. Hugging the terrain to stay off radar until the last possible moment required the pilots to maintain a constant altitude. They dodged power lines and banked hard around hilltops. Dropped into valleys and just as quickly rose out of them. All to stay under two hundred feet, well below the altitude limits programmed by their sleeper into the Estonian Air Defense network's EPAC-3 missiles.

A series of red lights started flashing in the cockpit, immediately followed by a panicked voice in his headset.

"Fire-control radars have locked on to our helicopter!" said one of the pilots. "This better work."

The moment of truth.

"Hold your altitude at two hundred feet," said Kuznetzov. "They can't touch us. I promise you."

He peered through the dark cockpit window, completely unable to determine what he was looking at. The night was pitch black except for the stars and the occasional streetlight below. The southeastern approach to Tallinn was mostly farmland, forests, and rural villages. Few signs of life at one in the morning.

"Missiles inbound! Coming from everywhere," said the pilot.

"We'll be fine," said Kuznetzov, searching the darkness for any sign of the missiles.

A few seconds later, he caught a brief glimpse of something ahead—a flash directly above them. A second flash passed overhead before he could trigger his radio, two successive sonic booms rocking the behemoth Mi-26 transport helicopter. Kuznetzov poked his head between the two pilots and scanned the sky to the left and right of them, seeing no explosions. It worked!

"See? I told you there was nothing to worry about," said Kuznetzov over the internal communications net. "How far until we can see Tallinn?"

"We should be able to see the city lights by now."

Kuznetzov saw nothing but darkness through the cockpit windshield, which was exactly what he'd hoped to see.

"I can see the city skyline with night vision. Looks like a total blackout," said the copilot.

"What's our ETA at Linnahall?" said Kuznetzov.

The Soviet-era Olympics amphitheater sat just a few blocks from the Estonian Government Office and several other key government locations—including the Parliament building. Several Mi-8 helicopters carrying Wegner Group shock troops would land just ahead of them, in the vast open spaces around the amphitheater, to secure the routes to the buildings, where the New Estonia government would declare itself in charge of the country.

At the same time, several small helicopter groups would land across Tallin to take control of the airport, key police stations, and major media outlets. Two larger flights would seize the Ministry of Defense building and the Presidential Palace. Roughly twelve hundred of the Wegner Group's most elite mercenaries would descend on a city crippled by a sudden power-and-communications blackout. When the Estonian people woke up tomorrow, they would once again be part of Russia—and there was nothing NATO or the European Union could do to stop it.

An explosion lit up the sky near the city, followed immediately by another.

"What's happening?" said Kuznetzov, a third explosion illuminating Lake Ülemiste, just south of the city.

"The lead wave is taking surface-to-air missile fire," said the copilot. "Possibly handheld launchers."

Two more helicopters burst into flames above the lake, instantly dropping into the water and disappearing.

"Nothing to worry about!" said Kuznetzov, as a sixth helicopter exploded in midair, its wreckage slamming into the lake's northern shoreline.

The red warning lights flashed briefly.

"Someone is trying to get a lock on us," said the pilot. "We can hold here until the attack helicopters clear the approach route."

"No. This'll be over in thirty seconds," said Kuznetzov. "They must have a few missile teams with portable launchers at the airport. The attack helicopters will clear them out."

From left to right, neighborhood by neighborhood, Tallinn's electrical power swiftly came back online, until the entire city skyline blazed brightly in front of them.

"Something isn't right," said Kuznetzov.

A thick wall of bright-red tracers rose from the southern edge of the city, crisscrossed by heavy gunfire from the airport, as dozens of antiaircraft gun systems simultaneously fired at the inbound assault wave. Several helicopters plummeted, some spinning wildly out of control on the way down. Most just fell like rocks, exploding in rapid succession when they slammed into the ground, the rest swallowed unceremoniously by the lake.

A long burst of antiaircraft fire passed down their port side, momentarily casting a deep-red glow throughout the helicopter's interior—a ZU-23-2 antiaircraft gun system based on the volume of fire spit at them. A system the Soviets exported by the thousands to its former satellite states. The irony of possibly being shot down by a Soviet mass-produced weapon system was not lost on him.

"We're out of here!" said the pilot, putting the helicopter into a steep turn to port.

Behind Kuznetzov, the New Estonia government had started to panic, barking questions. All he knew for sure was that something had gone terribly wrong.

And that was all he'd ever know.

A long, bright-red stream of tracers erupted from the center of the bridge ahead, stitching dozens of high-explosive twenty-three-millimeter shells through the starboard side of the helicopter—instantly killing Kuznetzov and most of the New Estonia government.

Anyone who survived the onslaught perished moments later when the thirty-ton helicopter slammed into the forest below.

CHAPTER 67

Devin sat up to the sound of cheering in the adjacent office. He checked his watch: 7:12 p.m. One twelve a.m. Tallinn time. General Grigory Kuznetzov should be getting the surprise of a lifetime right about now.

"Sounds like something went right," said Marnie.

"Maybe they're watching the Orioles game," said Devin. "Or god forbid—the Nationals."

"Isn't that a Canadian team?" said Marnie.

"Good one," said Devin, high-fiving her.

He hoped the cheers from the office meant that their war with Pichugin was over. Devin had sworn to stay in the fight until it was finished, but it had become clear that the longer the war lasted, the less chance *they* had of surviving it. *They* mostly meaning Marnie. She was loyal to a fault, which was going to get her killed, and he couldn't allow that.

If they didn't strike a mortal blow to Pichugin's operation tonight, he'd have to find some way to get Marnie out of harm's way. Like he did with his sister and their parents. He couldn't stand the thought of anything happening to her. This wasn't her fight—and maybe it wasn't his any longer. Perhaps he'd taken his mother's cause as far as he could, personally, and it was time to let the CIA-DEVTEK partnership take over. He didn't see a future role in this war, but he could see a future with Marnie.

He took Marnie's hand. "No matter what Berg says, I think we should—"

The office door opened to reveal Karl Berg and Audra Bauer—both of them smiling.

"We did it," said Berg. "Every helicopter was shot down. Every single helicopter. It's over."

Everyone jumped up and cheered before turning to the person next to them for a high-five or a hug. Devin went for the hug, stealing a quick kiss while disentangling himself. Marnie looked pleasantly surprised, which told Devin that he was on the right path. They had a future together.

"And we've just learned that a remotely controlled truck bomb was driven into the heart of Pichugin's command-and-control compound a few minutes ago, lighting up the sky west of Moscow for everyone to see."

"Remote control, huh?" said Devin. "That's an interesting detail that I wouldn't expect you to know that quickly."

"The explosion was reported by our Moscow team," said Berg. "The remote-control aspect may have been provided by an outside source."

"That source wouldn't happen to be Israeli?" said Devin.

"I couldn't say," said Berg, smiling slyly.

"Nobody here heard anybody mention anything about the Israelis," said Bauer, turning to Berg. "Especially you."

"Can I tell them the rest?" said Berg.

"As long as the word *Israeli* doesn't find its way back into the discussion," said Bauer.

"I can work with that," said Berg. "DEVTEK and the CIA have been scouring the data recovered from the Miami server farm. The tower must have served as a communications routing center, because they identified a list of nearly six hundred phone numbers, some of which have already been matched to confirmed sleepers. We think this could be a comprehensive list."

"That's incredible news," said Devin. "It shouldn't take long to identify all of them."

"No. It shouldn't," said Berg. "My guess is that most of them have been recalled, or they will be very shortly, so this is our top priority. We need to grab a few of them for safekeeping, right?"

"As long as *safekeeping* means safely locked away," said Marnie. "Forever."

"We might have to trade them at some point," said Berg. "But I guarantee they'll fetch a good price on the prisoner swap market during the next round of US-Russia political negotiations."

"I wouldn't be surprised if Russia pretended they didn't exist," said Devin.

"There's always that chance, but the Russians are pretty loyal to their people," said Berg. "They'll most likely negotiate a silent trade that none of us will ever hear about. That's assuming they haven't already fled the country. Pichugin probably has other ways of contacting them."

"What about the two CIA counterintelligence officers?" said Marnie. "Have they fled the country?"

"What CIA officers?" said Bauer.

"I'm not sure where she got that from," said Berg.

"You know. The ones that—" she started, before chuckling to herself. "Never mind."

Berg winked at her. "And that shall remain our little secret, meaning nobody in this room will ever mention them again."

"CIA who?" said Anish.

"Exactly," said Berg. "Last thing. We grabbed hundreds of files from the server, containing millions of lines of code. Our assumption being that this is the source code for a bunch of different systems. We didn't find any obvious marked *zero-days* or *zero-day exploits*, but we've only just started to unravel the data find. It's going to take a while to match the code to specific company products, but eventually we'll get there. You all made it possible to start repairing the decades' worth of damage done by this sleeper network. Cheers."

"Hold on a minute," said Melendez, heaving a sizable cooler onto the table from the floor and opening it. "There are no cheers without beers."

While Melendez and Miralles handed out ice-cold bottles to the team, Marnie turned to Devin.

"What were you about to say before Berg opened the door?"

He thought about what he'd originally planned to say but decided to up the ante. They'd just saved Estonia, and possibly the rest of the Baltic states, from Russian occupation and unraveled what had to be the most consequential espionage attack against the United States or any country—ever. They'd earned the right to jump the line.

"I was going to say that we should skip the date and take that vacation . . . together."

She raised an eyebrow. "I'll have to think about it."

"No pressure," he said, starting to feel like he may have overstepped a boundary. "A formal date works just as well."

"Well. I gave it some thought," said Marnie. "And my only condition is that we go to an all-inclusive place in Mexico. But not Cancún. I have bad memories of Cancún."

"You can pick the resort," said Devin, kissing her to rowdy applause.

"About time," said Berg, accepting a beer handed to him by Anish. "How about a toast?"

Devin and Marnie twisted the tops off their bottles and turned to face Berg.

"To those that gave their lives," said Berg, raising his bottle. "So the rest of us could go on. Never forget."

"Never forget," said Devin. "Hear! Hear!"

CHAPTER 68

Yuri Pichugin was a dead man, and he knew it. The devastating car bomb attack that had leveled the FIREBIRD compound and killed close to two hundred of his people was just the beginning. He assumed the Israelis were responsible for that one. Undoubtedly, retribution for the Iron Dome disaster he had ordered, but certainly not the last he'd hear from them. They'd come for him next—but they'd have to get in line behind Putin and the Americans.

Putin especially. The BLACKOUT debacle had sealed Pichugin's fate. No amount of money or future schemes could make up for the fact that he'd not only failed Putin miserably but also undermined the president's personal mission to expand Russia's influence westward into Europe. Russia's grand revival had come to a flaming halt less than a mile south of Tallinn's city center.

The political and economic fallout would be colossal, the wreckage of nearly fifty Russian Federation Army helicopters and the corpses of a thousand Wegner Group mercenaries providing the West all the leverage it needed to sanction Russia and bolster NATO's force posture in central and eastern Europe. A decade of military, political, and economic maneuvering by Putin—wiped out in the blink of an eye. An unforgivable setback.

Which was why he sat in morning rush-hour traffic south of Saint Petersburg, a few miles from Pulkovo International Airport, where his Hawker 4000 jet waited to fly him as far away from Russia as possible. He'd fly due west over the Baltic Sea and refuel in Oslo before turning south for Africa. Pichugin had several armed compounds in equatorial Africa, having provided nearly all the region's dictators and despots with mercenaries, heavy weapons, and ground-attack aircraft over the past two decades.

He glanced through the window to his right. Four rough-looking, Middle Eastern men in a beat-up sedan stared mindlessly forward, probably on their way to a minimum-wage construction site in the New Port area, where dozens of luxury high-rise condominiums had sprung up over the past few years. Pichugin was intimately familiar with the particulars of this project, since he owned four of the buildings.

Not that any of that mattered now. Putin would freeze his Russian assets and seize his projects, leaving him to survive on the two-point-three billion dollars he'd spread around the world. He'd survive—if he didn't get sloppy.

The men in the car next to him opened their doors. For a moment, he thought they might run to the side of the road to urinate. He'd seen that before during traffic jams around Saint Petersburg. The traffic could be brutal, taking an hour or more to travel a few miles.

Instead, the four men surrounded Pichugin's SUV. The mercenary in the front passenger seat reacted prematurely and opened his door, taking two rapid gunshots to the head. The driver instantly reached across the dead man's lap and shut the door before the shooter could do any more damage. Quick thinking that would earn him a spot promotion if they survived the attack.

The mercenary seated next to Pichugin started barking orders over his radio to the teams in the four additional armored SUVs that formed Pichugin's convoy. Nineteen mercenaries, minus the one bleeding out in the front seat, should be more than enough to counter any conventional attack thrown against him on the highway.

A quick look through the blood-splattered windshield and over his shoulder indicated that the attack was anything but conventional.

Men and women with submachine guns and pistols had swarmed the vehicles in his convoy.

"Get us the fuck out of here!" said Pichugin.

Before the driver could react, one of the men from the adjacent car slapped a soda can–size cylinder down on the hood of the SUV and pulled an oversize tab off the top. The device exploded, warping the armored hood and killing the engine. Smoke poured through the vents as a dozen or more detonations rocked the rest of the convoy. Smoke and fire poured out of the windows of the other SUVs.

The man standing next to his window held up a black device the size of a square tissue box and attached it to the door. He pressed a blue-and-white flag of Israel against the window for a few moments, before giving Pichugin the middle finger—which he used to pull the safety pin on the device.

Pichugin had unbuckled his seat belt and lurched halfway through the gap between the front seats when an insanely hot sensation consumed his waist and legs. He glanced back to see a horizontal fountain of white-hot molten steel spraying through the rear passenger-side door—lighting everything on fire. His pants burst into flames at the same time as the leather seats and the mercenary seated next to him. Consumed by flames and screaming wildly, the mercenary desperately tried to open his door, but the men outside held it shut. Same with the driver, who threw his shoulder into the driver's door but couldn't budge it an inch. The Israelis intended to burn him alive and watch.

"I go out on my terms," muttered Pichugin. "Not yours."

He yanked the PP-2000 submachine gun out of the front passenger's lap and put the barrel in his mouth. He pressed the trigger. Nothing happened. His fingers scrambled for the safety. Before Pichugin could flip the selector switch, something hard slammed against the right side of his head, knocking him temporarily senseless. In the time it took him to regain focus, the PP-2000 was yanked from his hands. Two gunshots erupted moments later, a single bullet each into the heads of the driver and the flame-engulfed mercenary in the back seat, before the front passenger door slammed shut.

They were hell-bent on burning him alive—and there was nothing he could do about it. His thoughts shifted to the driver, who carried a pistol. He had started to frantically search the dead man for the weapon when a rapid series of detonations shook the SUV, his view beyond all the windows instantly obscured by wide splashes of dark-red blood and thick smoke—on the outside. The deep booming continued for a few more seconds, followed by several bursts of automatic gunfire, before everything went quiet—except for the crackle of flames that engulfed the back seat and his legs.

All four doors opened simultaneously, followed by the billowing swoosh of fire extinguishers, which instantly doused the flames but did nothing to alleviate the excruciating burns that consumed his legs. A pair of hands dragged him over the dead mercenary in the front seat, dropping him on the road next to the SUV. A quick glance around revealed that his would-be murderers had been slaughtered by a heavy-caliber weapon—their bodies torn in half or missing limbs. The deep sound of nearby helicopter rotors suggested they'd been targeted from the air by attack helicopters.

Pichugin started to speak, but a masked Russian Federation soldier in full body armor jammed a hood over his head, turning day into night. Zip ties followed, pulling his wrists tightly together and eliminating all doubt that he would have been better off burning alive inside the SUV.

Putin had no intention of letting him off the hook that easy.

CHAPTER 69

Devin and Marnie barely stirred in their seats when the conference room door finally opened. They'd been waiting for close to forty-five minutes since Audra Bauer had dropped them off in the room with Karl Berg—after spending nearly thirty minutes navigating the mazelike series of hallways and lobbies of the George Bush Center for Intelligence. Audra Bauer entered the room, followed by a man Devin presumed to be Thomas Manning, director of the Special Activities Center.

The two of them moved to the right of the doorway to make way for a woman Devin recognized. Theresa Gardner. Director of the Central Intelligence Agency. When Berg shot up out of his seat, Marnie gave Devin a quizzical look. He mouthed the word *director* and pushed his chair back to stand. Marnie did the same, as Thomas Manning took a few steps forward.

"The director wanted to say a few words before we get started," he said.

"I'd ask you all to remain seated, but I'd really like to shake your hands," said the director. "I can't thank all of you enough for what you've done on behalf of the United States."

She made her way over to Karl first, shaking her head before clasping his hand.

"We can't seem to get rid of you. Can we?" she said.

"I've been told that I stick to people like napalm," said Berg. "And burn like it, too."

The director laughed. "Well. A burn or two now and then is a small price to pay for your contributions to national security. Thank you. I hear that the Special Activities Center is looking for part-time consultants—particularly well-rounded, highly accomplished agency retirees. Something to think about."

"Can I give you my answer now?" said Berg, looking both surprised and pleased at the same time.

"Take it up with Thomas after I leave," she said, patting him on the shoulder. "Welcome back."

The director took the long way around the conference table, which put Marnie next in line. Devin touched her hand briefly.

"Ms. Young. We owe you a debt of gratitude that can't easily be repaid," said the director, shaking her hand.

"Oh. There's no need. I'd gladly do it all over again," said Marnie.

"Careful what you ask for," said the director. "I hear you're interested in a job on the Hill?"

"Primarily," said Marnie. "But I'm not picky."

"I may be overestimating my general clout within the Beltway, but I can't imagine a direct call from the director of the CIA to the office or offices of your choosing would hurt your job search."

"Quite the contrary," said Marnie, chuckling. "Thank you so much. This means a lot to me."

"It's the least I can do. And if it doesn't work out, I'm sure we can find something equally worthy and interesting around here. Maybe not as interesting as your work with Karl and Mr. Gray over the past month, but good work, nonetheless," said the director, handing her a card. "Let me know who to call, when you're ready. Send an email or leave a voice mail."

Incredible. The director of the CIA just gave Marnie a direct line to contact her.

"And now for Mr. Devin Gray," said the director, offering him her hand.

He shook it vigorously, the two of them examining each other's faces for several seconds before releasing hands.

"The Agency owes your mother and her family an apology," she said. "More than an apology, to be frank. Her steadfast devotion to duty, against all odds, to include the shameful wall of doubt built around her by the agency, has saved the country from whatever nightmare the Russians had planned for us. If the events that transpired in Estonia are any indication, I can guarantee it would have been catastrophic. Thank you for carrying on her legacy, which shall go down in CIA history as nothing short of legendary."

Devin had prepared a speech—more like a short diatribe—for this moment, but the director's heartfelt words, and her teary eyes, entirely disarmed him. He dug deep to keep from breaking down.

"Thank you," he said, swallowing hard. "I had more to say than that, but it's all gone. Sorry."

"I'm sure you had a few choice words to say," she said, putting a hand on his shoulder. "Please. Accept my apology on behalf of the agency. I can't rewind time, but I'm willing to do whatever I can to make things right for you and your family. Unfortunately, I don't have too many tricks up my sleeve other than offering you a job or reaching out to MINERVA on your behalf. Or whoever. You name it. Ms. Young has my card."

Devin nodded. "I accept your apology. Thank you."

The director spent a few more moments with him before turning to Thomas Manning.

"Ten minutes?" she said.

Manning nodded, and the director departed—after shaking each of their hands one more time. As soon as the door shut behind her, Manning asked them to take their seats and passed a file to each of them.

"We're on a bit of a tight timeline. Ten minutes to be precise," said Manning. "The files in front of you contain secrecy agreements. A few steps above a nondisclosure agreement. Bottom line? Everything related to the Russian sleeper network has been classified Top Secret Sensitive Compartmented Information. If there was a higher security classification, we'd slap it on this. But there isn't. So what these agreements basically say is that none of this ever happened. Even though it did. I need you to sign these before I proceed."

"Proceed with what?" said Marnie.

"A very brief debrief," said Manning. "Which you'll want to hear."

"So. If we don't want the debrief, we don't have to sign these?" said Devin.

"The last thing I want to do is twist any of your arms," said Manning. "But I need you to sign these. It's more of a formality, since I have zero doubts about your loyalty to the United States."

"But you need us to sign these," said Berg. "Even me."

"Even you," said Manning. "Please."

"Can we read through them?" said Devin.

"Of course," said Manning.

"It's only a page long," said Marnie.

"I fought the agency's red-tape Mafia—a.k.a. the lawyers—to keep this as simple and painless as possible," said Manning. "CYA at the CIA."

Devin read the document, which effectively reiterated what Manning had stated earlier. The CIA didn't want any of them talking about anything that had transpired related to the sleeper network—in the interest of national security. The penalty for breaching the agreement was so severe it wasn't worth dwelling over. The CIA wanted to close the book on this, and for good reason. The entire situation was nothing short of an abysmally embarrassing stain on the agency's reputation. Devin signed and dated the agreement. Berg and Marnie did the same, all of them pushing their files toward Manning, who briefly examined the agreements before handing them to Bauer.

"Did everyone sign one of these?" said Devin. "Farrington? Gupta? The rest?"

"Yes," said Manning. "Same with Brendan Shea and anyone he showed the files to at MINERVA. Same with DEVTEK."

"Why aren't they here?" said Devin.

"Two reasons," said Manning. "First. We'd like to share some information with you that we don't plan on sharing with the rest of the group. You've more than earned the right to know what has come of your efforts. Audra?"

Bauer nodded and joined Manning at the head of the table.

"We're a bit short on time," he said, before fading into the background.

Why were they in such a rush? Devin and Marnie had spent the better part of the afternoon making their way to this conference room—only to be shuffled out in ten minutes?

"Right," said Audra, before checking her watch. "Here's the short version. I'll make time later for questions."

So there would be a later. Good.

"Yuri Pichugin's convoy was attacked the morning after the attempted coup, on the way to Pulkovo International Airport. It's assumed that he was trying to flee Russia," said Bauer.

"For good reason," said Berg. "Russia is in the hot seat right now."

"Putin is in the hot seat," said Bauer. "Protests have erupted throughout Russia and across eastern Europe over the Estonia incursion. It's bad enough to annex a pro-Russian region of Ukraine, but entirely another thing to fly over a thousand heavily armed mercenaries in fifty-one Russian Federation Army helicopters across the Russian-Estonian border to seize Estonia's capital in the middle of the night. It's also quite impossible to erase the evidence of fifty-one downed Russian Army helicopters—particularly when they crashed on Tallinn's doorstep."

"What happened to Pichugin?" said Berg.

"Good question," said Bauer. "Unfortunately, nobody seems to know the answer. What we do know is that the Israelis don't have him. They've confirmed as much."

"And you believe them?" said Berg.

"Yes. They lost over a dozen operatives in the attack," said Bauer.

"The Israelis attacked Pichugin?" said Devin. "Never mind. I guess that makes sense. So how did he survive?"

"We don't know that he did, but four Army attack helicopters swooped in at the last moment and wiped out the Israeli ground team," said Bauer. "Whether the Russians got to him in time is unknown."

"God knows Putin would have liked a word or two with him," said Berg. "Before slowly lowering him into an acid bath."

"While lowering him," said Manning.

"We can only hope," said Marnie.

"As far as the sleeper network goes, the list of phone numbers retrieved from Pichugin's Miami servers has led to the identification of five hundred and eighty-two sleepers. Five hundred and seventy-three have either fled the country or been killed by your team. The remaining nine are in custody, including the two CIA officers. One of the nine apprehended turned out to be the saboteur behind the EPAC-3 missile glitch we predicted. George McDonald, a senior principal software engineer at Lockram, inserted code into the seeker-sensor software, which prevented Tallinn's primary antiair defense system from engaging targets flying below three hundred feet."

"He hadn't left the country?" said Berg.

"He flew from here to Amsterdam, where Dutch intelligence alerted us to his presence," said Bauer. "One of our teams yanked him out of an Airbnb room in De Wallen, the city's red-light district."

"A costly detour," said Marnie.

"Indeed," said Bauer.

"Are the sleepers in FBI custody?" said Devin.

Bauer glanced over her shoulder at Manning, who subtly shook his head.

"They're in custody. Let's leave it at that," said Bauer.

"Fair enough," said Devin. "And the kids? The third generation? Did we manage to grab any of them?"

"No. We suspect they were flown directly to Russia after the Ozarks raid," said Bauer.

"How extensive was the network's penetration of our companies and infrastructure?" said Devin.

"Frighteningly extensive. Sleepers like George McDonald were just the tip of the iceberg," said Bauer. "They had sleepers anywhere and everywhere that mattered. The non-public-facing side of the network was undoubtedly the most dangerous to the United States and the West."

Manning checked his watch. "Audra. We have to get moving."

"Why the rush?" said Devin.

"Because of the real reason you're here today," said Manning.

"Why does this sound like a bad thing?" said Marnie.

"Because you're sitting in a conference room deep inside of CIA headquarters?" said Devin.

Berg got up from his chair. "Trust me. It's not a bad thing."

"Quite the opposite," said Bauer.

They followed Manning and Bauer through several hallways and cubicle farms until they finally emptied into the Old Headquarters Building lobby, which they'd passed through earlier in the afternoon. A dozen or so people stood in a semicircle facing the Memorial Wall, where CIA employees who died in the line of duty were memorialized by a star carved into the white marble wall. One hundred and thirty-seven stars—he'd been told by Karl Berg. Thirty-seven unnamed due to the secretive nature of their missions at the time of their deaths.

He was about to suggest they take a different route, so they didn't disturb the group's private memorial service, when he recognized his sister and father—standing next to the director of the CIA. The two of them glanced in his direction and nodded, solemn-but-heartening smiles on their faces. It was only then that he realized the lobby was mostly empty except for the small group huddled next to the Memorial Wall and a few security guards watching over the security turnstiles.

Now he understood the tight timeline. The lobby had been packed with CIA employees passing through the turnstiles, headed in both directions. Shutting down back-and-forth traffic between the new and old buildings represented a significant disruption at Langley.

"I was mistaken earlier," said Karl Berg, who stood a few feet in front of Devin.

"What do you mean?" said Devin.

"I was off by one," said Berg. "There are one hundred and thirty-eight stars on that wall."

"How many unnamed?" said Devin, not expecting his mother's name to be included in the book beneath the carved stars.

"Still thirty-seven," said Berg, turning to face him. "Your mother earned a place in that book."

"The board in charge of approving the stars voted unanimously to include her name," said Manning. "Shall we?"

Devin took Marnie's hand, tears streaming down his face, as they joined his family in front of the Memorial Wall, which read:

IN HONOR OF THOSE MEMBERS

OF THE CENTRAL INTELLIGENCE AGENCY

WHO GAVE THEIR LIVES IN THE SERVICE OF THEIR COUNTRY

ABOUT THE AUTHOR

Steven Konkoly is a *Wall Street Journal* and *USA Today* bestselling author, a graduate of the US Naval Academy, and a veteran of several regular and elite US Navy and Marine Corps units. He has brought his in-depth military experience to bear in his fiction, which includes *Coming Dawn* and *Deep Sleep* in the Devin Gray series; *The Rescue, The Raid, The Mountain,* and *Skystorm* in the Ryan Decker series; the speculative postapocalyptic thrillers *The Jakarta Pandemic* and *The Perseid Collapse*; the Fractured State series; the Black Flagged series; and the Zulu Virus Chronicles. Konkoly lives in central Indiana with his family. For more information, visit www.stevenkonkoly.com.